The Zephyrus

Book one of The Skyknight Skypirate trilogy

J H FOSTER

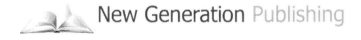

New Generation Publishing

For my family,
who always believe,
even when I don't.

Chapter 1

Asher awoke with the rain hitting his cheek, and he knew that this was a sign of how bad the day was going to be. As an orphan to grow up in the lower city of Actalia, which was the largest and capital city of the Kingdom of Angard, meant that most days were not going to be good.

This was due to the awful conditions the working class found themselves subject to, the honest men worked fourteen hour shifts in the mines or down on the docks for barely more than a copper, whilst the women of the lower city were lucky to find any work at all which didn't involve whoring themselves out.

Asher pulled himself up from the rags he had been using as a bed and looked up at the grey sky through the opening in the roof of the run down shanty he had been using for the last few weeks as a place to sleep and stay out of the elements, he knew that he would have to find another shelter soon, as other squatters would find this place and the idea of waking one night to find a shiv at his throat held by one of the numerous junkies that his home had to offer wasn't one he wished to live.

As Asher made his way out of the shanty he caught a glimpse of himself in the remnants of a shattered mirror that hung on the wall, his reflection stared back at him with hollow eyes.

Asher raised his hands to his face and traced the lines of his sunken cheeks and over pronounced jaw, he noted how both features made him look more like a walking corpse than a living person, not that there was much he could do about that, what with the general lack of food his surroundings provided.

At the mere thought of food Asher felt his stomach tighten, he immediately dropped his hands to his stomach and applied a little pressure, which allowed him to ride the hunger-spasm out.

Once the spasm had passed Asher ran his hands up the ragged under-shirt he wore, his fingers tracing the unmistakable lines of his exposed ribs.

Coming back to stare at himself once again, Asher ran his hands through the mess of dirty brown locks he called his hair before he tied it with a length of string into a rough tail, where it sat at the nape of his neck. With his lice ridden hair now tied back Asher was met with the sight of his small rounded ears, the left of which had a bite-mark scar on it where he had gotten into a brawl with another desperate orphan over a crust of stale bread.

If the circumstances of his upbringing had been different then Asher liked to think that he would have been described as handsome, what with his strong jawline, bow shaped lips, and small nose which was not bent in the slightest despite the many beatings he had taken throughout his young life, but he knew that his most distinguishable feature were his piercing blue eyes, which always gained him attention wanted or not.

From the look of him you would have guessed that he was about fifteen summers old, although growing up on the streets forced him to grow up a lot quicker than most, as making a mistake down in the lower city either meant death or resulted in a beating so bad that death seemed like a mercy.

Asher had been on the receiving end of one such beating, it had been just after the Rats were disbanded and Asher alone and desperate had just walked straight up to a stall and sunken his teeth into the nearest piece of fruit. The owner outraged at such a blatant act of thievery hadn't pulled any punches, even though Asher couldn't have been any older than six at the time. The beating left Asher in such a bad state that he hadn't been able to move for a week.

The memory made him shudder.

"I guess we'll see if today is any better than yesterday."

As Asher emerged from the shanty into the morning light, he was immediately met with the chaotic atmosphere that filled just about every street in the lower city.

The local 'merchants' stood at their stalls hollering about their wares which included everything from battered clothing to mold covered cutlery. One such merchant, a man of middling years with teeth as black as coal was claiming to have discovered how to make a potion that would cure any illness.

What a load of bull.

Tucked in between the merchants at varying intervals were the food stalls, each owner claimed that the charred husks that they served were the finest meats available in all the lower city, Asher thought it a lot more likely however that they had just hunted down a plague of rats and skewered them, not that he could fault them for that, it wasn't like they were in the upper city where the citizens dined on succulent pheasants or tender cuts of beef until they were fat and could barely move.

How can they be so ignorant?

After these somewhat legitimate stalls came the swarm of men and women offering whichever service they could, whether that be selling knock-off jewellery, liquor or narcotics as well as offering special services to anyone desperate enough to get a leg over with an emaciated whore or rent boy, faced with these sights every morning Asher felt anger and shame wash over him.

"There has to be something better than this out there," said Asher to the grey lifeless sky before making his way through the crowded street towards The Bleeding Lizard pub to try and find something to eat and get work from old One Eye.

Breaking off the main street Asher headed down one of the numerous back alleys that made up the majority of the lower city, the smell of piss and vomit permeated the air assaulting Asher's nose in sickening waves, you would think that after having spent his entire life living here the smell would be nothing more than a mild inconvenience but unlike many of his fellow denizens Asher had never developed the ability to deal with the smell then again he wasn't shoving copious amounts of Faerie Dust up his nose every day.

Rounding the corner of the alley Asher was met with a meaty fist to the jaw which sent him crashing to the urine covered cobbles in a heap.

"What's up squirt?"

Asher looked up to find Rollo standing over him, the sight of the fat boy sent a wave of fear and anger through Asher, for as long as he could remember Rollo had been the bane of his life, taking every opportunity to fuck with him and ever since Rollo had begun working for the Smiler's it had only gotten worse.

"You off to see One Eye?"

"And what if I am?"

"Well, you see One Eye's been cutting into our business and Smiling Jack isn't happy."

"Am I supposed to give a fuck."

Faster than Asher thought possible Rollo lashed out with a sharp kick that caught him straight in the stomach and launched him a few paces through the air before he once again hit the cobbles.

"If your boss keeps cutting into our business then I'm going to take it out on you... you got that."

Asher knew he should just nod and hope that the beating would end but something inside him had had enough of this shit, "You know what, Rollo. Why don't you just go back to Smiling Jack and suck his cock, like a good little boy."

Rollo's face turned red with anger, "I'm gonna kill you, you little shit."

Asher readied himself for the beating but before Rollo could attack another voice cut through the alley.

"I wouldn't do that if I were you."

Both Rollo and Asher looked to where the voice had come from and standing before them was Kat, the runner for Mother Genevieve was only a year older than Asher but already she had made a name for herself as someone not to be messed with, plus when you had the protection of the most powerful criminal guild in the lower city not many people would dare mess with you in the first place.

"This don't concern you," spat Rollo, the veins in his neck bulging.

"Actually it does," said Kat walking forward. "You see Asher's my friend so if you pick a fight with him you pick a fight with me as well."

Rollo's face twisted with anger but even he was smart enough to know when he was beat, "You got lucky this time squirt."

With that Rollo skulked back down the alley towards the main road, leaving Asher alone with Kat.

"Seriously, Ash, you need to learn to look after yourself."

"I can look after myself just fine," said Asher getting to his feet.

"Looks like it." Kat looked Asher up and down in appraisal. "You know if you worked for Mother than you wouldn't have to worry about people like Rollo messing with you."

"Yeah but where would the fun be in that."

Kat's brows furrowed as they always did when she was frustrated but she had known Asher long enough to know that there was no way to convince him, after all she had been trying to recruit him to the Roses ever since she joined herself, "Well just be careful, okay."

"You know me," replied Asher with a smile.

"Yeah that's why I'm telling you to be careful, anyway I gotta get going Mother won't be happy if I'm late."

"See you later, Kat."

"Yeah catch you later, Ash."

After Kat left Asher continued on his way down the winding maze that was the back alleys until finally he came out onto Shadow street and came face to face with The Bleeding Lizard pub.

The Bleeding Lizard wasn't much more than the shanty Asher used for shelter, the pub was two stories of rotting wood with windows made from a single pane of glass, which barely held in place if a strong wind ran through the street whilst the chimney was little more than a hole in the roof which expelled a thick fog into the air around it like an old man who had over stuffed his pipe and the then there was the sign. At one point, it had been the most luxurious thing Asher had seen but now it had become worn and barely showed the skewered lizard that gave the pub its name.

As Asher walked into the Lizard, he was immediately greeted with a cloud of acrid tobacco smoke and the smell of cheap ale, both of which formed a fog that scratched at Asher's throat and eyes. Asher peered through the miasma and just managed to spot the stocky frame of One Eye standing at the back of the room by a small alcove.

Asher made his way through the smoke and One Eye's features slowly came into focus. Skin nearly as dark as midnight identified the old thief as Onmori, his kinky black hair was beginning to bald and a jagged scar ran from the top of his forehead down through his left eye giving him the literal nickname. One Eye was talking with his two most trusted henchmen. Jared stood a head above One Eye, his pale skin and blonde hair were the complete opposite of his boss and Asher couldn't help but shiver when he caught sight of the makeshift necklace that hung around the big man's neck, which consisted of the teeth of over a dozen men tied around a thin piece of cord, but the giant's cruelty was nothing compared to the other man who was talking with One Eye. Snake was well known for his love of rape especially when it came to young boys and as if he could feel Asher watching him the small pock faced man turned and offered a smile that made Asher shudder, it was obvious that the greasy haired fuck wanted him for his sick vice but thankfully One Eye had said that Asher was off limits.

"Nice to see our most trusted delivery boy," said Snake in his usual mocking tone as Asher came to stand amongst the men.

"Your words warm my heart," replied Asher sarcastically.

"Now now boys lets not have any hostilities between members of my organisation," interjected One Eye.

"You got any work for me?"

"Indeed I do, Asher, it's a very special job, one that will make you well off for a good few months, if not longer."

Asher didn't like the sound of this, in all his years working for One Eye, he had never heard the man proclaim that a job was special. "And what is this special job."

"Well I need your particular set of skills as well as your agile frame to sneak onto a Skyship by the name of the *Zephyrus* and steal an important package."

Asher felt a cold wave wash over him this was far worse than he had expected, sneaking onto a Skyship would be unlike anything he had done before and if he was caught, well he was as good as dead and yet he couldn't stop himself from asking, "How much would I be paid?"

"One gold and 5 coppers," replied One Eye.

Asher's heart did a somersault, One Eye was right that amount of money would keep Asher fed for well over a month and could even buy him a room in an inn for a couple of days, at least it would if he didn't get robbed the moment the money was in his hands.

"Well don't leave me hanging by my balls, lad."

Asher's mind was still racing; it was a massive risk to take but with that amount of money on the line he couldn't refuse.

"Fine, I'll do it."

"That's a good lad," said One Eye smiling from ear to ear.

"So what am I stealing from this Skyship?"

"You're going to steal a book titled The Fundamentals of Skycore Technology."

Immediately, Asher wanted to ask One Eye why he was interested in such a strange thing but he knew the old Onmori wouldn't answer him at least not truthfully, "And how the hell am I supposed to find something like that I can't even read."

One Eye drew a small slip of paper from his pocket and handed it to Asher, "The title will look like this."

Asher looked at the strange lines that marked the paper and found himself getting angry, even the simple ability to be able to read was denied him, tucking the paper into his breeches where it could mock him no longer Asher asked, "Wouldn't something like that be heavily guarded?"

"Normally yes, but today is the King's Nameday which means that every Skyknight and Royal guard in the city will either be attending the party or guarding the palace which leaves only the city guards to watch over the ship and its contents."

The news that no Skyknights would be patrolling the Skyship made Asher feel slightly better, hundreds of stories revolved around the Angardian's premier military force and even if only half of them were true it would still mean Asher's end should he meet one.

"Where's the ship docked?"

"The Skyship's docked in the upper city in the eastern Skydock."

"I'm off then," Asher turned for the door, but before he could take a step one of One Eye's meaty hands grasped hold of his shoulder.

"Don't fuck this up, lad, cause if you do then the guards will be the least of your worries, ain't that right, Snake."

"Oh yes."

As soon as One Eye released his grasp, Asher ran out of the Bleeding Lizard as fast as his legs would carry him.

Running back through the lower city market Asher did his best not to think about what would happen to him if he failed, but One Eye's threat kept playing over in his mind, if the guards didn't kill him then his employer would and that probably meant Snake having his way with him beforehand.

No don't think like that you've got this.

Focused Asher made it through the market and turned down onto Wilkerton's Way, the battered and run down homes of local workers streamed past in a myriad of dilapidation as he sprinted by.

Down at the Blackwater canal, Asher had to slow his sprint to a walk as a crowd of over a dozen men stood about the canals walkway silently. Asher knew that the men were waiting for the gates to the warehouses to open and the arrival of the foremen who would pick a handful of them to work at their respective sights for the day whilst the others were sent packing. As he made his way through the crowd Asher took the opportunity to pick a few of the men's pockets. The first pocket Asher slipped his hand into lay empty, as did the second and third, the fourth however produced a half-copper and the fifth and final pocket a grime covered ring.

Emerging on the other side of the crowd Asher heard the unmistakable whine of the warehouses iron gates as they opened but he didn't turn to look and once again set off at a run.

A little further down the walkway Asher passed by a few of the local working girls, their offers of companionship went in one ear and out the other, but the flesh they revealed caught Asher's attention long enough for him to only just see the dog that came bounding out of the nearby alley, with all of the strength he possessed Asher leapt into the air, the mutts face twisted with surprise but it didn't slow and a few seconds later Asher knew why, as a group of children carrying stones and sticks emerged from the same alley. Asher felt sorry for the poor creature but he had no time to waste and he continued on.

Drenched in sweat and breathing heavily Asher finally made it to one of the sewer tunnels that ran down from the upper city to the lower city canal and then out into the Dremeli sea.

"Time for the fun part," said Asher to himself as he climbed into the tunnel.

The putrid smell of human waste filled the air of the sewer. Asher immediately retched, no matter how many time he used these tunnels he never could get used to the sickening stench but it was the quickest and easiest way to get around the city, well only if you knew your way around.

Over the years Asher had found dozens of bloated corpses strewn throughout the tunnels and it was easy to see how people got lost down here, after all there was barely a flicker of light and to the untrained eye everything looked the same, but Asher knew these tunnels like the back of his own hand.

After a couple of candlemarks of moving through the twisting passages and trudging through a mile or more of shit Asher made it to the ladder that would take him up to the eastern Skydock.

"Right... lets get this over with."

Chapter 2

Asher emerged from the sewer and was meet with a downpour. The grey clouds from earlier had now become great black monsters that stole the light away, and left the dockyard shrouded in darkness.

A few moments later lightning flashed across the sky illuminating the dockyard and that's when Asher saw the Skyship that he was supposed to sneak onto.

The ship's hull looked more like the body of the legendary leviathan that so many of the drunks told stories of, the hatches that lined the ship's hull only added to the image as they shimmered in the light. But they were quickly forgotten about when Asher caught sight of the figurehead that sat at the ship's prow.

The enormous ornament was carved into that of a winged man who was looking up into the sky, and was so lifelike that for one moment Asher thought he was looking upon an Angel.

The approach of lamplight however forced Asher from his musings.

Shit.

Looking around quickly for somewhere to hide Asher spotted a stack of storage barrels.

That will do.

With impressive speed Asher dove behind the barrels and waited. His heart pounded in his chest as the light moved closer to his hiding spot. Sinking lower to the ground Asher held his breathe and waited. As the orange glow of the lamps swept over him, Asher heard the voice of a guard

"Why do we always get the shite guard duty, Gus?" From the sound of the voice the guard couldn't have been that much older than Asher.

"Because you always end up running your mouth off to the Captain," replied a husky voice. "Can't believe I'm stuck babysitting your idiotic ass anyway."

"Babysitting!" The younger man's voice went high with surprise. "You make it sound like I can't handle myself, you old bastard."

The older guard sighed to himself before replying, "Look, let's get our patrol over with so that I can go home, god-damn skies look like they're about to open." With that the two guards passed by and walked off towards the warehouses at the other side of the dockyard taking the light with them.

That was close.

With silent grace Asher moved through the dockyard using one hiding spot after the other until finally he was standing next to his target.

Looking up at the monstrously majestic vessel Asher felt a hot hatred begin bubbling in his gut, how could so many people be starving and homeless when it was possible for ships like this to exist. Shaking the thoughts away Asher started to climb up one of the support ropes that held the Skyship firmly in place.

After about ten minutes Asher pulled himself up over the Skyship's bulwark and sprawled out on the deck looking up into the black clouds, his hands were on fire from the climb and when he lifted them to his face he saw an angry red line running down either palm.

"How can things get any worse?" said Asher to the darkness.

In response, a deep rumble broke out from within the clouds and the heavens opened in a torrent of rain, each droplet felt like a tiny needle as it hit Asher's skin, unfortunately he had to bare the rainfall as his muscles felt lifeless from the climb and he didn't trust them to keep him upright.

Several minutes passed with Asher taking deep breaths. Slowly life began to return to his tired and aching limbs and the pain in his hands began to fade to a dull ache. Using this slither of strength, he pushed himself up into a sitting position and that's when the true magnificence of the ship dawned on him.

Thirty of the Bleeding Lizard's common room could have fit onto the deck if not more, whilst each of the ships three masts stood easily twice that of the Lizard's two storeys.

Once a little more strength had returned to his limbs Asher pushed himself up to his feet and began walking along the deck, the wood beneath his feet was freezing from the rain.

Forget the cold you've got a job to do.

It occurred to Asher then, that One Eye hadn't given him a precise location on the whereabouts of the Skyship's document.

The most likely place for that sort of information would be in the Captain's quarters.

Looking around Asher spotted a door at the back of the ship right below the helm. As he came to stand before the door Asher became aware of just how large it was, the massive oak slab easily stood the height of Jared and the ring handle was twice the size of Asher's hands put together.

Asher suddenly had the feeling that this was all too easy, there was no lock on the door and he had already snuck past the guards, surely the fabled Skyknights would have better defences than this, but as Asher placed his hand on the handle a line of intricately shaped symbols flared to life. Asher tried to pull his hand away from the cold metal but found that he couldn't and then out of nowhere the world around him grew dark and he passed out.

Asher awoke sometime later to the greetings of the worst headache he had ever felt and the rain hadn't eased up whilst he had been unconscious and he was now soaked from head to toe. With all the strength, he could muster Asher pulled himself up to a sitting position, the world around him swayed and danced as he did and it took all his will not to throw up all over himself and the deck.

After a few minutes of just sitting and breathing Asher felt slightly better and he pushed himself back up to his feet and once again he was faced with the door to the Captain's quarters.

Reaching his hand back out towards the handle Asher felt his heart start to race, clearly his body remembered the effects that the symbols had caused, but nevertheless he forced his quivering hand forwards until finally he grabbed a hold of the metal again.

After a few moments Asher realised he had been holding his breath and expecting the same events to occur but this time no symbols appeared on the handle and he found that he could easily open the door to the Captain's quarters.

The quarters of the Skyship's Captain were nothing like Asher had imagined.

The walls weren't adorned with rich fabrics or beautiful paintings like he had thought they would be, in their place were lamps and maps of faraway lands, all of which were worn from use. The back wall however was another matter; the entire surface was made from glass. Asher imagined that the glass provided quite the view but with the storm blocking out the sun all that he saw was a shroud of darkness. A desk and chair stood in front of the window-wall, both of which were sturdy pieces of carpentry but nothing more.

Turning his attention to the left-hand wall Asher was met with a giant bookshelf, dozens of books filled its shelves, their titles nothing but gibberish to Asher.

Now to find my book.

Asher took out the slip of paper One Eye had given him and began looking through the bookcase for the tome.

After what felt like hours of searching Asher still couldn't find the book he was looking for but then he spotted a large book on the top of the bookcase the title that marked its spine matched perfectly with the note Asher held.

Moving the chair over to the bookcase Asher stood on top of it and grasped hold of the book but found that he couldn't move it, the tome was heavier then Asher had expected, using all his strength Asher managed to pull the book off the shelf but as he did he lost his balance on the chair and fell, the book landing right on top of him as he hit the hard-wooden floor knocking the wind from his lungs.

"Spending most of this job on the floor," said Asher as he heaved the heavy book off himself.

Getting back to his feet Asher picked the book up, the wiry muscles in his arms bulged with the effort.

"This is gonna be one hell of a trek back to the lizard."

Asher was just about to leave the Captain's quarters when he froze, was that footsteps he heard, pushing his ear up against the door Asher's fear was confirmed, coming from out on the deck were a group of muffled voices, Asher's heart jumped into his throat. If they caught him now, he was as sure as dead.

Calm down, let's just have a look at the situation and go from there.

With extreme care Asher opened the door of the Captain's quarters just enough so he could look out onto the deck, in front of him illuminated by lantern light stood two women and two men. The two men looked identical, their lithe bodies were tanned and both had deep green eyes, the only thing that told them apart was their hair, one had his long sandy hair tied back into a ponytail, while the other had his cut short and slicked it back.

Standing next to them was an Onmori woman, she was at least a head smaller than the two men, unlike One Eye whose skin was nearly black this woman's drawn face was grey like that of a statue and the way her features stayed completely still only added to the image, a pair of black sandals were all that protected her feet from the hard ground whilst the rest of her body was covered in thick black robes that hung loosely off her figure and at the head of the group stood a tall powerful looking women who was by far the most pale person Asher had ever seen, but the thing that caught his attention the most was the sword that sat at her hip.

How the fuck am I supposed to get past them.

Asher was forced from his thoughts of escape when he heard the accented Angardian of the pale woman. "Wraith, can you please explain why you dragged us here?"

"I felt a shift in one of my hexes," responded the Onmori woman known as Wraith in a monotonic accent.

"Are you sure?"

"Give me a moment."

Asher heard a strange murmuring and the small robed woman walk off into the darkness, a moment later he heard her monotonic voice dully ring out. "A hex is gone."

"Is it possible the hex is faulty? Maybe one of the city guards set it off."

"It's possible."

"Or we're dealing with a thief," said the man with long hair.

"That too, is a possibility," added the short haired man.

The pale women pinched her nose in annoyance, "Okay, Vida, Runa, you start a sweep of the ship, but I don't suspect we'll find anything even if there was an intruder he's probably long gone."

Asher had to stifle a laugh.

If only you knew.

As the two men began walking about the deck of the ship, a strong wind swept over the ship causing the door to the Captain's quarters to swing open and then slam shut just in front of Asher's face.

Asher heard the surprised voice of one of the men, "The Captain's door just shut."

"But with Wraith's hex on it, it shouldn't move," said the other man.

A cold gripping sensation crept up Asher's spine.

"Wraith, is that Hex gone, as well."

Silence.

"Yes, the hex is gone but I can feel some residual energy."

"Where?"

"Coming from inside the Captain's quarters."

The pale women took a couple of steps forward, "This is Commander Vaeliria Wintergrave of the Skyknights, come out with your hands raised and no harm will come to you."

"I don't think that's gonna happen!" shouted Asher as he opened the door of the Captains quarters an inch. "You see I ain't so stupid as too believe that you ain't gonna kill me. I know what happens to people like me who have no one waiting for them to come home, if I disappear nobody will be the wiser I'll just be another victim of the lower city."

"You know nothing of us or the nature of our Order, but you have my word as a member of the Skyknights that no harm shall come to you if you are civil and surrender immediately," replied the Commander.

There was something in the woman's voice that made Asher believe that what she said was true but then the part of him born through experiences of betrayal to him not to listen to a word this woman said.

"Like I said I ain't stupid, so I'm gonna have to turn down your most gracious offer."

The commander sighed, "Fine, but don't say I didn't offer you a better option." The woman turned to the two men in her company, "Capture, the intruder alive, we'll need to find out who hired him or if he's working alone."

With that the two men broke out into a sprint straight towards Asher, with only moments to think of a way to escape Asher took a few steps back from the door and waited, "I hope this works."

As the two men burst through the door Asher raised the heavy tome above his head and using all the strength he possessed he let the book fly.

The monstrous tome seemed to sail through the air in slow motion but despite that it still managed to clip the two men in their shins, which sent both crashing to the floor in hollers of pain.

Knowing that he only had moments before the two men picked themselves up Asher ran from the Captain's quarters and out onto the deck, where he was immediately met by the pale woman.

"I'll give you one last chance to come peacefully," offered the Commander as she took up a more offensive posture.

"No can do I'm afraid," said Asher as he turned to run up towards the helm.

"Do it Wraith!"

With a flash of light another hex appeared beneath Asher's feet.

Asher immediately felt a shudder run up his spine at the thought of going through the effects of one of these symbols again, but as the hex died, he realised he felt completely normal.

"Seems your tricks are failing," mocked Asher.

"I wouldn't be so sure of that," replied the Commander confidently.

Asher tried to move, but found that his body would not react to his commands, he was paralysed from head to toe.

"Now that you can't escape, how about you tell us why you're trying to steal classified information," said the Commander stepping up to Asher.

Asher looked at the robed women quizzically.

"You still have the ability of speech," explained the one known as Wraith.

"I was doing it so I wouldn't starve for a couple of months okay, but then you wouldn't know what that feels like."

"Like I said before you know nothing of me nor my men," retorted the Commander evenly. "Now I'll ask again, who hired you to sneak on board an Imperial Skyship and try to steal classified information?"

"You know, I would prefer my interrogation take place in a nice warm cell instead of out here in this wind and rain, I'm freezing my arse off."

Oh, good one Asher antagonize the women who holds your life in her hands, that'll get you far.

"You're foolish to think that this is an 'interrogation', all I've done so far is ask you simple questions but if you insist, I'm quite willing to use force to get the answers from you, but I had hoped I wouldn't have to harm someone so young as yourself," was there a hint of disappointment in her voice.

"We'll continue this interrogation at headquarters, Vida, you head over there and let them know we'll have a suspect to interrogate."

"Will do, Commander," replied the long-haired man before he left running.

"Runa, you head to the Captain's estate, he should be back from the party by now, inform him of the situation."

"On it," said the short haired man before he too disappeared.

"Wraith, you're with me."

"Yes, Commander, should I release the hex?"

"Just make sure he can walk."

"As you command."

"What the hell have you done to me!"

Neither of the two women replied and Asher was lead from the Skyship to the dockyard below.

Great gusts of wind and rain swept over the dockyard slowing Asher down but Vaeliria didn't seem affected, the muscular women kept her pace and pulled even harder on Asher's arms.

"Would you slow the hell down ain't like I'm going anywhere!" shouted Asher over the wind.

"Oh I'm sorry I thought you wanted to get out of this."

The trio continued to walk against the onslaught. The icy wind cut into Asher's face leaving it numb, and his wet hair felt frozen to his scalp, mercifully Vaeliria turned down between two warehouse's and Asher was protected from the elements for a few brief moments before they emerged and stood at the front of the dockyard. A small guardhouse made from quarried stone sat next to a large wooden gate. Vaeliria strode purposefully towards the guardhouse dragging Asher along as she did and knocked heavily on the door of the guardhouse, the sound of the wind and rain was the only thing that answered Vaeliria so again she pounded on the door, this time the door practically rippled with each hammer of her fist and a moment later the door of the guardhouse opened and a stocky barrel-chested man appeared, he looked at them with the bleary eyes of someone who's just been woken up from a peaceful dream, "You don't have to try breaking the damn door down, I heard you the first time."

"Is that anyway to greet your superior," replied Vaeliria curtly.

The guard just stood there, confusion twisting his face into a sneer.

"Guess he hasn't got his wits yet," said Asher.

"I'm Commander Vaeliria of the Skyknights, what's your name soldier?"

The guard finally seemed to come to his senses, "Clyde, Ma'am."

"Listen carefully, Clyde, I want your guard rota on my desk by the end of the night, is that clear." The sharpness in Vaeliria's voice could've rivalled any blades.

"Yes, Ma'am," said the stocky guard standing at attention.

"Good now off with you."

The door of the guardhouse slammed shut as the guard rushed to look for the rota.

"That sure showed him."

A heavy blow connected to the side of Asher's face, knocking the sense out of him.

"Anything else to say?" said Vaeliria into Asher's ear.

Asher couldn't reply, stars danced before him and his head was a jumble.

"I thought not."

As Asher tried to recover his senses, Vaeliria dragged him past the guardhouse and out into the street beyond.

The surroundings past him in a daze, he was still reeling from the blow, it had felt as hard as iron. Sucking in a short breath Asher looked around, he was in the Randolph's way, no that couldn't be right, after a few more blocks had passed by Asher's senses came back to him in a nauseous wave.

"That was one hell of a punch," said Asher gingerly.

Vaeliria didn't reply.

Row upon row of terraced houses passed by as Asher was led through the upper city, dark timber walls were visible in the pale light of street lanterns. Lush green lawns stood in front of the houses surrounded by small brick walls, bright yellow daffodils, bold marigolds, deeply coloured violets and strikingly red roses were scattered throughout the gardens creating a mosaic of colour. On the other side of the street lay a multitude of business's, beautifully crafted vases of all shapes and sizes sat in the window of one store, thick leather bound books, engraved with intricately designed patterns sat in the window of another, a tailors shop displayed the elegant high-necked dresses and fine suits that were in fashion and on the corner of the street sat a wine merchants shop which was in the middle of being redecorated into an apothecary, suddenly it hit Asher he had been here before.

A couple of years back One Eye had given Asher the task of sending a message to the merchant who had owned this store, after he had refused to sell a large shipment of Dalinthini wine to One Eye.

Asher had snuck into the store in the dead of night and opened every bottle of wine in the place, which had effectively ruined the man. However, as Asher had been pouring the last of a sweet red wine onto the cold floor of the stores cellar the merchant's Castian wolfhound, awoken from its slumber by the overpowering scent of the spilled wines attacked Asher. This had resulted in both

Asher and the hound falling to the ground in a shower of glass and wine, and before Asher could do anything to defend himself the hound sunk its teeth into the flesh of his left arm.

Even now Asher could remember the sheer agony that the beasts bite had caused him and he immediately had the urge to rub the rough puncture wounds that lay around his forearm.

I still can't believe I made it out of there alive.

Before Asher could contemplate his miraculous escape from that night Vaeliria spoke and he was brought back to the present.

"We're here," said the Skyknight coldly.

Without realising it Asher had continued to walk along behind Vaeliria, not that he had much choice.

Standing in front of him was a large square building made of stone and glass. The grey walls shone menacingly in the moonlight. On the roof of the building stood twelve statues, from this distance Asher couldn't make out the features of the statures but he presumed they were legendary knights whose great deeds had seen them forever immortalised. Hundreds of windows ran along the face of the building, faint lights penetrated the darkness from the top tier of windows. To either side of the square building stood two circular towers made from the same grey stone as the central building, heavy wooden doors sat at the base of the towers. Looking up at the towers Asher saw that there were no windows lining their faces instead sat murder holes, the tiny slits allowed defenders to rain death down on their enemies whilst not having to worry about enemy fire themselves.

Coming to the massive wooden doors of the central building Asher had a sense of foreboding, for all he knew he was never going to come back out.

Vaeliria pushed one of the giant doors open and motioned for him to follow. Asher walked into the building and was instantly grateful to be out of the elements so much so that it took a moment for the world around him to come into focus. A large well lit room stood before him, the wooden floor of which felt like a lush carpet compared to the cold cobbles of the street he had just traversed, walking along behind Vaeliria. Asher was led passed a line of wooden benches, hanging above the benches were portraits and tapestries depicting noble men and women as well as great deeds, the open show of wealth sickened Asher and he turned to face the end of the room and that's when he saw there were two doors sat into the back wall of the room, one was solid and made of wood while the other was barred and made of iron.

"You got night duty again, Waylon?"

Asher pulled his attention away from the foreboding iron door to find a lanky man sat behind a curved desk, he smiled wearily at Vaeliria, "Aye, watch master Stallton's really got it in for me this week."

"Knowing you, you did something to annoy the old goat."

Waylon stifled a laugh: "That sounds about right, so what yah need, Commander."

"I've got a suspect who needs a cell."

"Oh yeah. Vida said I should be expecting you." Waylon walked over to a set of large books that sat on a table behind his desk. "Ahh he we are, seems the closest cell available is thirty-seven."

Waylon produced a set of keys, which jingled as he handed them to Vaeliria.

"Thanks Waylon, oh and do try to keep yourself out of trouble."

"I make no promises."

Vaeliria unlocked the barred iron door and lead Asher and Wraith through.

"Watch your step," said Vaeliria.

"Why?" replied Asher.

"Because the stairs to the holding cell are quite steep."

Asher followed Vaeliria down the dark staircase, the light from the lanterns she and Wraith brought with them from the top of the stairs did nothing against the sea of darkness that lay around them and then Asher misjudged the length of a step and twisted his ankle, "Argh damn it," said Asher sucking in a breath.

"I believe I told you to mind your step," replied Vaeliria in an amused tone.

"I can barely see," replied Asher in defence.

"Fine. I'll lead you down the steps is that better," said Vaeliria still amused.

"Oh, much better," said Asher sarcastically.

Asher was lead down the last few steps into the holding cell area without any more mishaps. The stone floor was far colder down here and the insane ramblings of other prisoners filled the air, from the sounds of it they had spent too much time down here locked away, Asher had a sense that the darkness must be used as an intimidation method, most prisoners probably spilled their guts after spending a couple of days down in this never-ending night, but Asher wasn't so weak willed, if these Knights wanted any information from him they were going to have to try a lot harder than that.

"Right here we are," said Vaeliria as she came to stand before a door of solid iron.

The sound of metal screeching on stone filled the air as Vaeliria opened the cell door, Asher shuddered at the sound.

"In you go."

Asher walked into his pitch-black cell, "You think I'm gonna crack from sitting in the dark?"

"Time will tell," replied Vaeliria. "Wraith you can dispel the hex now, our young guest won't be going anywhere."

Asher heard the same strange chanting coming from Wraith as he had back on the Skyship and the he felt a twinge in his arm and the numbness began to fade, but joy at being able to feel his arms again was quickly cast aside as the door to his cell was closed and locked leaving him in utter darkness.

"Well I best get comfortable."

Chapter 3

After exploring blindly for who knows how long, Asher realised the cell he occupied was a tiny room even by prison cell standards, using the iron door as his centre he found that a stone slab sat up against the left-hand side of the wall, on top of the slab crumpled into a tight ball was a thin sheet, that was more holes than fabric. In the corner of the right-hand wall was a tiny hole set into the ground, the smell of piss and shit seeped from the hole in a nauseating fog that had Asher gagging every few minutes.

"I think even the shanty beats this shithole."

Hours passed and the only thing Asher had to do to pass the time was lie on the stone slab and replay the events that had led him to this point in his mind. He tried to come up with a way he could have escaped the four Skyknights repeatedly but each scenario ended with him in custody or dead.

"Guess I'll have to try and talk my way out of this."

Yeah that'll be the day, said a voice inside Asher's head.

"Shut up!" spat Asher to the darkness.

There was no reply and Asher couldn't help but wonder if he was already going insane.

Asher awoke sometime later to the jarring sound of metal scrapping alone stone.

Rolling to his left Asher fell face first off the stone slab and onto the cold stone floor, with the fog of sleep thick in his mind it took Asher a few moments to remember where he was and why, but then in one jarring moment it all came flooding back to him and he shot up into a sitting position where he was met with the lantern-lit form of Vaeliria.

Gone were the casual clothes that she had worn last night and in their place, was the official uniform of a Skyknight. Asher had only seen the uniform from afar but there was no denying the sword and wing-tipped shield insignia that sat over Vaeliria left breast.

"I hope you had a good night's sleep?" said Vaeliria.

"I've slept better," replied Asher as he got to his feet and stretched.

"Is this your first time in a cell?"

"Nah, been locked up in Penance House before."

"Then you should be used to this, now if you'll come with me I have a few questions that need answering."

"I'm guessing this is the part where you rough me up."

"How this proceeds is entirely up to you."

"So you expect me to pour my heart out and tell you everything, well I'm afraid that's not going to happen." As soon as the words left his mouth Asher knew he should have just kept his mouth shut, this woman was his one chance to get out of this alive and so far, all he had done was antagonize her when he should be trying to play the helpless orphan and get her on his side.

"Okay then, I guess we're doing this the hard way." Vaeliria produced a set of hand shackles.

Asher let Vaeliria bind his hands without any struggle, "Now follow me."

Again, the corridor was shrouded in shadow, but having spent a night in complete darkness Asher found himself being able to see, every twenty metres or so he would pass another iron door, the doors looked impenetrable, heavy bolts sat deeply into the tunnels face and the doors looked to be at least three inches thick. Asher continued to follow Vaeliria in silence through the various tunnels, his mind ablaze with thoughts of how he was going to get himself out of this dungeon alive and free, but nothing came to him and before he knew it he was standing in front of another iron door which he could only assume was the entrance to the interrogation room.

"Time for answers," said Vaeliria as she opened the door of the interrogation room.

"I guess I ain't got much choice in the matter."

The interrogation room wasn't what Asher had expected, it was carved entirely of stone like his cell, but unlike his cell furniture filled the room, a heavy metal table was fixed into the centre of the stone floor and was accompanied by two wooden chairs that sat on either side of its body.

"Please take a seat," asked Vaeliria softly.

Asher did as he was told and took up the chair closest to the back wall, Vaeliria hung the lantern up on a hook that protruded from the wall before taking up the chair opposite, reaching across she unlocked one of Asher's shackles and he thought she meant to free him but instead she looped it through a metal ring that sat in the tabletop and quickly refastened it to his wrist.

"We'll start with some simple questions, what's your name?"

"Thaddeus Darkstrider," replied Asher.

With snake like quickness Vaeliria struck Asher across the face, the blow rocked Asher, stars danced before his eyes, if it wasn't for the shackles holding him firmly in place he would have sprawled out of his chair.

"Now I'll ask you again, what's your name?"

"How do you know my name's not Thaddeus Darkstrider?" asked Asher blinking.

"You're the famous thief responsible for robbing Pope Benedict's sceptre fifty years ago."

"What can I say, I age slow."

Again, Vaeliria struck out, this time she hit Asher across the other side of his face.

"So, are we still Thaddeus or am I going to get the truth."

Asher popped his jaw from side to side before replying: "Names Asher."

"Okay Asher, who hired you to trespass onto a Skyship and try to steal classified information?" Vaeliria's voice was as hard as iron.

"You think I'm going to tell you just like that," replied Asher. "I know what happens when you've gotten what you want."

"And what exactly is that?"

"I get strung up in Penance Square, for all to see."

"If you cooperate, I'll work a deal out with the court so that you only serve a prison sentence," replied Vaeliria

"I don't think that's gonna happen, way I see it I give you the brains of the operation and you let me walk free simple as that."

"You can't honestly believe that you're going to walk away from this," said Vaeliria incredulously.

Silence filled the room, Asher knew there was no way he was just going to walk free but he wasn't about to let himself be thrown into prison and then an idea struck him, "Okay how bout a compromise?"

"I don't think you're in any position to be making requests."

"Just hear me out," snapped Asher. Vaeliria was about to say something but Asher cut her off, "Look you don't have to accept it, but just hear me out."

Vaeliria shrugged, "Fine I'll hear what you have to say."

"I don't want to be stuck in the lower city for the rest of my life, I've seen what that does to people, I want something better for myself and the way I see it you can give that to me."

"How might I do that?"

"I serve my sentence but I do it working on your ship," said Asher, his heart in his throat.

A look of utter surprise shot over Vaeliria's face, clearly she hadn't been expecting this and Asher couldn't blame her it was a long shot but it was the only idea he had that didn't end up with him being inside the King's dungeon or swinging from a noose.

After recovering from the surprise Vaeliria spoke: "You would need the approval of the Council for that and only Captains and the Admirals can address them directly."

"Okay, so go talk to your Captain."

Vaeliria's expression turned hard, "Do you have any idea what you're asking, you want me to ask my Captain, a man I have the utmost respect for, to take on a prisoner as a deck hand."

"Just talk to him, that's all I'm asking."

Vaeliria was silent, her brow furrowed in deep thought, finally she spoke, "Okay I will do what I can, but let me make this absolutely clear, you tell me everything, otherwise I will see you sent to the darkest depths of the Pit."

A cold wave washed through Asher, Vaeliria wouldn't just send him to prison, no she'd send him to a living hell if he wasn't honest with her and from what he had heard he knew that the Pit wasn't a place you left alive, hell as the stories went anyone who was sent there would mine in the cold dark depths of the earth until they could no longer lift their pick and then their bodies would be left down there to rot.

"Fine, I'll tell you everything."

"That's what I wanted to hear, now start from the beginning."

Asher told Vaeliria everything, how he had gone looking for work from One Eye, the details of the job given to him, the amount One Eye had been willing to pay him for the job and finally how he had snuck on board the Skyship, throughout the entire tale Vaeliria just sat and listened quietly as if she was determining for herself whether what he was saying was the truth or not.

"And that's everything right up to the point where you and your crew showed up and caught me," finished Asher.

"Okay," said Vaeliria standing. "You're going back to your cell, until I can verify what you have said is the truth, once that's done I will speak with my Captain about your proposal and we'll go from there."

"You still think I'm lying?"

"Would you trust the word of a thief?"

Asher couldn't help but chuckle: "Guess you're right."

"Good now let's get you back to your cell."

Chapter 4

Asher stood before a group of hooded spectres, he was trying to convince the group that he was worth placing in the custody of one of their Captains, however the specters didn't say anything in reply and Asher felt the icy cold tendrils of fear wash over him.

Without warning the shadowy chamber disappeared and he found himself standing in Penance Square amongst a press of bodies, pushing through the crowd Asher made it to the front of the gallows, looking up he was shocked to find his own lifeless body swinging from a noose, his skin had taken on the grey hue of the long time dead, the horror of the sight paralysed Asher and despite his best efforts he couldn't stop starring at his dead self. A spasm shot through the lifeless body jerking it into life and then another and before Asher knew what was happening he was suddenly face to face with his own cold corpse, dead grey eyes looked at him mockingly.

"You seriously think you're going to live?" said the corpse smiling.

Asher tried to speak but the fear and horror of the site before him muted any words that came to him.

"What Deadman got your tongue?" laughed the corpse. "Oh come on, where's that sharp wit of yours?"

It took Asher a few moments to calm himself enough to reply and even then, his voice was weak and shaky, "This isn't real, I'm not dead."

"Not yet," said the corpse as he began dancing around Asher, "but I wouldn't hold out too much hope, if this council doesn't agree to your little gamble, you'll be swinging from a noose faster than you can pray to the Firstborn."

I need to wake up.

The corpse stopped dancing: "Well why don't you wake up then?"

Asher was dumbfounded by the corpse's apparent ability to read his thoughts.

"Oh don't look so surprised I'm you after all, I know the way yah think." The corpse poke Asher's temple three times.

Asher swatted the hand away.

"Well, aren't we touchy," said the corpse stepping back. "Here let me help you."

"And how are you going to help me?"

In a blur of motion the Deadman slapped Asher across the face.

Asher awoke aching and confused, his head was pounding and his jaw felt twice its normal size, as if on cue the door to the cell opened and once again Vaeliria appeared in the doorway.

"It appears you were telling the truth Asher," Vaeliria's tone made it clear she was surprised.

In his dazed and aching state, it took Asher a moment to gather his wits.

"Told yah I was."

Vaeliria shrugged, "You can't blame me for not trusting your word, thieves generally tend to be liars as well."

"I happily admit I'm a thief and I will lie if it benefits me, but if you grew up in the lower city then you'd do the same."

Vaeliria seemed to ignore what Asher had just said and changed the subject, "My Captain has agreed to take your case to the council."

Asher couldn't believe it; he knew he shouldn't get his hopes up but somewhere deep inside him a small flicker began to burn.

"Come on, we need to arrive at the council chamber early so you can meet the Captain."

Asher sprang to his feet, "Lets go then."

"First things first," said Vaeliria holding out the hand shackles.

Again, Asher allowed himself to be shackled, "Okay now can we go?"

Vaeliria pulled on Asher's shackles in reply.

The walk through the dungeon felt like it was taking forever, every corridor looked the same as the last and from what Asher could tell they snaked back and forth like a labyrinth.

After turning down what felt like the hundredth corridor Asher was finally greeted with a different sight, carved into the wall face were a set of narrow stairs, as he stood looking at the steps Asher realised he hadn't asked what had happened when Vaeliria had gone after One Eye.

"So what happened with One Eye?"

"We found the pub you described."

"And, you arrested them?"

Vaeliria shook her head, "As soon as we arrived it became clear that your former employer and his goons had no intentions of coming quietly."

"So you killed them?"

"Yes," replied Vaeliria matter-of-factly.

Surprisingly Asher felt a pang of grief at the news that One Eye was dead but rather than voice that he found himself asking, "How many men did you have with you?"

"Just Vida and Runa."

"You're messing with me, you only had those two with you and you took on Jared, Snake and One Eye."

Vaeliria let out a short bark of a laugh: "HA! It would take a hell of a lot more than that band of street thugs to cause us any problems."

Asher was stunned into silence but he didn't have time to think about what he had just been told as Vaeliria gave his shackles a pull and they began their way up the stairs.

After the gruelling climb up the mountain of stairs Asher was soaked in sweat and his legs ached terribly, he bent over sucking in deep gulps of air, looking over to his side he saw Vaeliria standing tall, no hint of exertion in her.

"How longs... it gonna take... to get to this meeting," said Asher in between breaths.

"The council chamber is located on the highest floor, so about another ten minutes," responded Vaeliria evenly.

Asher let out a groan, "Argh, how big is this place anyway."

"The Skyknight Headquarters is second only to the Church of the Firstborn, have you ever seen the church?"

Asher had only seen the Church of the Firstborn once, it had been the most sickening thing he had ever seen, the church was made of the same grey stone as the Skyknights Headquarters but inlaid into the stone were veins of gold and silver, the decadence didn't stop there though. Lining either side of the church's giant hall were a set of twelve stained glass windows, everything colour imaginable was used in the designs and it was said that when the light hit those glass murals at the right angle colour streamed into the world and it's great spire reached up into the air as if trying to grasp the heavens themselves and at the top of the spire stood a statue of the Firstborn, his arms spread wide inviting all to his house, except his home wasn't open to everyone as corruption has made it so only the Royal family, the Pope and the High-Cardinals were allowed to step foot in there regularly.

"Yeah I've seen it."

If Vaeliria noticed the venom in Asher's voice as he spoke about the church then she didn't show it, "Well unlike the Faith who allow all to see the glory of their Holy house, we Skyknights choose to hide the true majesty of our Headquarters."

"By building underground," finished Asher.

Vaeliria nodded before heading off down the passageway with Asher in tow.

"What I don't understand is why'd you need to build underground in the first place?" said Asher breaking the silence that had once again stretched out between him and Vaeliria.

Vaeliria looked over her shoulder, "Are you sure this history lesson won't bore you?"

"Might as well hear it, as you can see I ain't going anywhere."

"Alright then, five hundred years ago the first knights of the land came together with King Edward II and together they decided that the newly formed knights needed to be able to hold high value prisoners in secrecy and act outside the authority of the King's court."

"Why would they need to do that?" interrupted Asher.

"I was just getting to that," snapped Vaeliria annoyed at being interrupted. "The Knights and King Edward were aware that members within the court were corrupt, so a series of underground levels were built alongside the construction of the original Headquarters, thus eliminating the possibility that a corrupt member of the court could assist a prisoner in escaping or help them to commit suicide before the Knights had a chance to question them."

"So the result is a giant maze of corridors and stairs."

"This 'maze' has held some of the most dangerous people this Kingdom has ever seen."

"I'm sure it has," said Asher in a tone that showed he didn't believe it. "How much further we got to go anyway, my legs are burning more than a man's dick after a night with a two-copper whore."

"This way," answered Vaeliria turning down another corridor with a hint of annoyance in her voice at Asher's use of such a derogatory term.

Asher turned down the corridor and was meet with a horrid sight, standing in front of him was another set of stairs.

"We've got to go up again?" asked Asher in despair.

"Yes," replied Vaeliria smiling.

"Bloody wonderful, I don't understand what is it about people in power that makes them think they have to elevate themselves above the rest of us."

Vaeliria didn't reply to the comment she merely turned to look at Asher and shook her head as if she was wondering whether he was worth trying to save, surprisingly the look cut Asher before he could say anything Vaeliria had turned back around and began leading him up the stairs.

Reaching the top of the stairs and the final level of the Skyknight Headquarters, Asher found himself in a richly decorated corridor. The floor of the passageway was covered in a rich scarlet carpet; the smooth fabric was the softest thing Asher had ever felt against his bare feet it but the wonders didn't stop there.

A series of beautifully woven tapestries hung from the corridors walls, each depicted act of valour from knights long passed.

Asher guessed then that this level was used for more political matters and the only people who saw this level on a regular basis were the Skyknights, high ranking nobility and other government officials, he was most likely the only person from the lower city to ever set foot here, but before he had time to consider whether that was a good thing or not Vaeliria gave his shackles a tug and dragged him off down the passageway.

As he stepped out of the corridor and into a wide atrium Asher found himself faced with yet another wondrous sight. Lining the rounded walls of the atrium were a series of eight paintings, each scene was unlike anything Asher had ever seen before and then it dawned on him, the paintings were depicting the life of a single man.

The first scene depicted a beautiful dark haired woman holding a young green eyed babe.

The second scene showed the boy as a child of about eight or nine, running through a field of flowers, his face a picture of happiness.

The next painting however was one of death and destruction, a burning village surrounded the boy, who was now an adolescence as he cradled his mother's lifeless body, the grief and anger were clear in his face.

The fourth and fifth scenes showed the boy leaving his village behind and travelling to far off-lands.

Next came a scene which showed the boy as a young man, leading a small group of soldiers into battle against a horde of enemies, his face a roar of defiance as he charged forward.

The seventh scene showed the man battling against a dark armoured warrior alone on top of a mountain, both warriors had dealt killing blows to one another. The hero's golden blade had pierced the dark warrior's chest, whilst the vicious broadsword of the dark warrior had cut a deep gash into the hero's side.

The eighth and final scene showed the hero laying lifelessly on a marble slab whilst a golden light shone down upon him.

"Who's the man in these paintings?" said Asher in awe.

"His name has been lost to history, but we knights call him Artorius," said Vaeliria, respect clear in her voice.

"Artorius," mouthed Asher tasting the name. "How long ago did he live?"

"I have no idea," shrugged Vaeliria. "You'd have to ask one of the scribes and even then, they'd only be able to give you an estimate."

"So why's there paintings of his life here?"

"Now that I can answer, he is known throughout your Kingdom as a hero and is considered the first true knight of the lands."

It's all Faerie tales though, you know that.

Vaeliria pulled Asher away from the paintings and across the atrium towards a set of tall oak doors, strange markings ran along the frame of the doors, before opening the doors Vaeliria turned to Asher and said, "Once the trial starts don't speak unless your addressed directly, do you understand?"

"Got it keep my mouth shut unless I'm spoken to."

"Good."

Vaeliria opened the door to the council chamber and a bright light hit Asher's eyes blinding him, after blinking for a few moments his vision started to return to normal and the room came into focus. The council chamber was a large rectangular room with a high vaulted ceiling, the floor was made of the same cold white marble as the atrium, taking up a large portion of the room were rows of cushioned benches but Asher barely had time to register their existence as he stood transfixed at the sight that lay to his left, the entire wall was made out of glass, walking over to the glass wall Asher looked out to the city before him, the afternoon sun created a kaleidoscope of colours as it began to dip below the skyline. Far off in the streets below Asher could see a colony of activity, hundreds of indistinguishable figures walked about going to and fro, tearing himself away from the scene Asher saw that a large raised platform sat at the end of the council chamber, five seats were set into the platform, just in front of this raised platform was a smaller square podium which Asher assumed was used to allow a speaker to address the council. Walking to the front row of the benches Vaeliria sat down and motioned for Asher to do the same.

"We here early or something?" said Asher as he dropped down beside Vaeliria.

"My Captain wishes to meet with you before the hearing begins," replied Vaeliria stretching her legs out.

"And why's that?"

"So he can talk with you openly and not be bound by protocol, plus it saves you having to walk through a crowd of gossiping nobles."

Asher couldn't believe what he heard, "There's going to be a crowd?"

"Unfortunately, this is an open hearing."

"Great," said Asher sarcastically, "a bunch of pompous peacocks looking down at me, what could be better."

Vaeliria let out a short laugh, but didn't reply to the comment and the two of them sat in silence awaiting the arrival of the Captain.

Asher felt as if he had been sitting in silence for an eternity, he had tried to ask Vaeliria questions about her Captain but she just cut him off telling him that now was not the time for discussion and that was the end of that and now his mind began to wonder, what was the Captain like, would he be like Vaeliria and try to help him or would the Captain condemn him to death for his crimes but before Asher could think any more on the matter the sound of the council chambers doors opening filled the air.

Vaeliria leaned over and whispered into Asher's ear, "Don't be scared of my Captain, Asher."

"Why would I be scared?"

"Most people feel a little intimidated when they first meet him."

"Well I ain't most people," said Asher defiantly.

Vaeliria shrugged slightly in response.

As the footsteps grew closer, a deep booming voice rang throughout the room, "I know you said you'd get him here early Vaeliria but don't you think this is a bit much, the poor lad must be worried senseless."

Vaeliria stood and turned towards her Captain: "It's good to see you as well Captain."

"It's just like you to make someone sweat," replied the Captain playfully as he walked to stand in front of Asher. "It's nice to finally meet you, Asher. I'm Abraham Brightfellow."

Looking up at the Captain, Asher was immediately intimidated by the man he saw before him.

Abraham Brightfellow was more of a mountain than a man, his wide muscular frame could easily have filled the frame of a door, but despite that his eyes were soft and when he smiled Asher immediately felt himself calm.

"I've heard some impressive things about you from both Vaeliria and the Twins," said Brightfellow still smiling.

"You can't seriously be praising me," said Asher, "I broke onto your ship and tried to steal information that was worth more than most will ever see in a lifetime and you praise me for it, you gotta be the weirdest knight in the history of the world."

Captain Brightfellow let out a booming laugh, "HAHA! You're not the first to tell me that."

Before another word could be said, a door opened behind the council platform and a single man emerged, the man was a head shorter than the Captain and where Brightfellow was thick with muscle this man was slim, he had a pale complexion and his long red hair was tied into a complex braid. Asher didn't like the look of this man, his sea coloured eyes seemed to be observing every little detail like he was looking for a weakness and the fact that he wore leather armour and had a long slender blade sat at his hip didn't help, as he approached the man flashed a wolfish smile.

"How is it that you seem to be in this council chamber more than any other member of the Skyknights, Abraham." The man offered his hand to the Captain.

"You know how it is, Delander, I just wanted to come see an old friend while I'm back in the Capital," answered Brightfellow grasping Delander's outstretched hand.

"It's good to see you as well, Vaeliria," said Delander breaking his handshake with the Captain.

"Seneschal," replied Vaeliria with a nod.

"And this must be the one who's caused all the commotion." the Seneschal directed his attention on Asher.

"Name's Asher."

"Well, Asher, you've caused quite a bit of trouble here in the upper city, nobles are gossiping and the higher-ups are trying to save face all because of you, now that's something that I thought only Abraham here could do." Delander smiled at the Captain.

This brought a smile to Brightfellow's face as well. "As I remember, you were standing right beside me on several occasions."

"Misadventures of my youth," said Delander still smiling, but then his smile faded. "I'm afraid I must cut our reminiscing short Abraham, the council shall be here any moment, I just wanted to let you know that you're going to have a hard time convincing the council to agree to this alternative sentence."

"Why is that Seneschal?" asked Vaeliria abruptly.

"Because Councillor Abaro is determined to see the boy hang," said Delander matter-of-factly.

This made Asher's heart sink, the small flicker of hope that was in him was being snuffed out. The voice inside his head rang out mockingly. *"It's your own fault you stupid boy, how could you ever think that you were going to walk out of here, haven't you learnt by now that the world doesn't care about you and what you want."*

"I must be going, it was good to see you again, Abraham. Goodbye, Vaeliria, Asher," and with that Delander left through another hidden door.

The doors to the council chamber opened shortly after Delander's exit and the nobles of the upper city started flooding in, casual chatter filled the air as they did, Asher turned to look at the nobles, each looked like they were trying to out do the other, lavish suits and dresses cast a sea of wealth and decadence, many of the ladies wore gemmed necklaces, earrings and rings whilst the men walked along with canes of ivory and polished oak. As they took their seats Asher could feel all their eyes on him, were these people's lives so boring that they had nothing better to do than come here and ogle at him. The overpowering smell of a dozen different perfumes assaulted Asher's nose making him grimace, he couldn't understand why nobles tried so hard to cover up the fact that they are people who sweat and smell. The nobles began to whisper amongst themselves which made Asher feel about the size of a half cooper piece but he wasn't about to let that show, a few of the more 'gracious' nobles spoke low enough that he couldn't hear what they were saying but others who lacked the same level of dignity were openly calling him a feral child, a lost cause from the lower city or evil and that the best cure for him would be to hang from the gallows with the rest of the lower city scum. Asher turned to Vaeliria, her jaw was clenched shut and her hands were balled into fists, it looked like she wanted to wade into the group of nobles and teach them some common decency, even Captain Brightfellow's demeanour had shifted slightly, he stood there arms crossed against his thick chest with a look on his face that could've curdled milk, when it became clear the nobles showed no signs of stopping their barrage of insults, Brightfellow turned around to face the crowd and spoke loudly, "It would seem you forget yourselves."

To Asher's amazement the entire crowd fell silent, satisfied the Captain turned his back on the crowd and a moment later the door that Delander had come through earlier opened and so emerged the first of the Councillors.

The first member of the council to emerge was an old frail woman who leaned heavily on a cane, despite that her bluish grey eyes observed the crowd with an intensity and clarity Asher hadn't thought possible for someone so old.

"Who's that?" whispered Asher to Vaeliria, as the woman was helped to her seat.

"That is Lady Elizabeth Grey the oldest member of the Council," replied Vaeliria.

Before Asher could ask any more questions, a tall tanned man who looked no older than thirty summers old emerged through the entrance, Asher quickly noted how well the man was dressed, a set of black silk trousers trimmed with silver sat over a pair of leather boots and a black tunic which was adorned with the same silver thread as the trousers covered the man's torso. From the reaction of the noble women in attendance Asher could tell this man was something of an idol, he smiled as he took the seat furthest from Lady Grey.

"And who's this guy?" asked Asher still whispering.

"That man is Lord Peter Silvermane, owner of the Silvermane mines and one of the richest men in the Kingdom."

"I know that name, most of the people in the lower city work in his mines."

"I'd be surprised if you didn't."

"Why is he on the council?"

"Because his money is used by the crown."

"So he bought his way onto the council?"

"In a manner of speaking."

The third member of the council was a tall man; his pale skin was flawless and not in the artificial way that many of the nobility achieved but more enthralling were his eyes which were golden in colour and shone like miniature suns. The man effortlessly made his way up the stairs of the council platform and took the seat next to the elderly woman.

Before Asher could ask, Vaeliria spoke, "That's Lord Caewyn Lightfoot of the Enshyi and High Speaker of the Forest."

"Enshyi?" asked Asher in bewilderment.

"The Enshyi are from a Kingdom far to the east and have just been offered a seat on the council," replied Vaeliria.

"What's a High Speaker of the Forest?"

"A Title from the Enshyi Kingdom."

Asher had a dozen other questions that he wanted to ask but he knew he didn't have time as another member of the council emerged. The fourth member of the council was a middle-aged woman who had pale skin, her eyes were an icy blue like that of frost while her hair was a scarlet red. She wore a black dress which was similar to the one worn by Lady Grey but where Lady Grey's dress was elegant this dress was audacious, the neck line was cut low revealing more flesh than Asher would have thought possible, as she got closer Asher could see that her complexion was near perfect, the only signs that gave away her age were the beginning of wrinkles around her eyes. Asher could see that this woman worked very hard on her appearance and from the reaction of some of the noble men in the room it appeared that it was paying off, as she sat down next to the young man she looked over at the crowd and gave a smile.

"Lady Sara Thorne," said Vaeliria again before Asher could ask.

"And how is she on this Council."

"The Thorne's are distant relatives of the royals."

"You gotta be kidding, how the heck am I supposed to get her on my side?"

"You're not, Asher."

"What in the seven hells is that supposed to mean?"

"The council works as a democracy no one member of the council can determine your fate, once they have heard your plea, they will vote on the sentence so we need at least three of them to vote in favour of the alternative sentence."

"I don't like those odds," replied Asher nervously.

"Try to relax, Asher. The Captain can be very persuasive when he wants to be."

Before Asher could reply the last member of the council emerged from the hidden door.

The last member of the council to emerge was a man who looked a couple of years older than Captain Brightfellow but where the Captain was solid with muscle this man was thin like a rake and he was quite small although anyone looked small when compared to the massive bulk of the Captain but even compared to the other two men on the council he stood a head smaller. His salt and pepper hair had receded into a peak and a pair of lavishly designed optics sat across his face magnifying the deep brown eyes that lay behind them. He wore the same black tunic and black trousers as the younger men on the council albeit a couple sizes smaller. As the man got to his seat he flashed a look at Captain Brightfellow that could've killed, clearly there was no love lost between this man and the Captain. A moment after the Councillor took his seat a herald emerged and announced that the hearing had begun.

"Who's that?" asked Asher quickly.

"Thomas Abaro, now be quiet."

43

To Asher's surprise Captain Brightfellow walked up onto the smaller platform and began talking, "My Lords and Ladies, it is most gracious of you to hear our proposal."

The man known as Thomas Abaro replied, his voice low and hoarse, "I hope you have a good reason for bringing this case to the council, Captain."

"I do, my Lord, I wish for an alternative sentence for the young boy known as Asher," replied the Captain.

The Crowd reacted to the Captains words with gasps and low chatter.

Lady Elizabeth Grey was the next member of the council to speak, her voice was level and cool, "And why would you do this, Captain? the boy was found on your ship trying to steal classified information."

"My Lady, Asher here was doing what he had to so that he wouldn't end up dying on the streets of the lower city, I have no ill tidings for him."

"You may have no ill tidings towards him, Captain," interjected Lady Thorne, "but he still committed a crime and must be punished for it, you can't expect us to let him loose."

The Captain turned his attention towards the Councillor, "You misunderstand me, my Lady. I'm not suggesting a pardon for the crime, I'm asking for an alternative sentence in which Asher will serve on my ship as a deck hand for the entirety of his sentence."

That gained even more gasps and whispers from the crowd.

"This is most interesting, Captain," said Lord Lightfoot in a thick accent.

Lady Thorne cut into the conversation. "Interesting! is that what you think, Caewyn, the Captain is asking us to place a thief onto one of the finest ships in the Angardian fleet, how can we allow that?"

"I can see the High Speakers point," said Lord Silvermane, his voice smooth like honey.

"Can you now, Peter and might you enlighten the rest of us to yours and the High Speakers thoughts?" asked Lord Abaro clearly unhappy.

"Well the idea of providing this boy with an alternative sentence shows that we nobles understand the plight of the common folk, which means that they will see us in a different light," replied Lord Silvermane nonchalantly.

"It also shows that we are weak, how can the Skyknights and the city guard allow a mere boy to sneak onto a class one Galleon and not punish him for it," replied Lady Thorne, her voice growing a few octaves with anger.

"You should ask him?" said Captain Brightfellow pointing towards Asher.

"I agree," said Lord Caewyn clearly interested in the story.

"Are you serious?" said Lady Thorne seething.

Vaeliria leaned over and whispered to Asher, "Go on, this is your chance."

Asher stood, his heart began pounding in his chest, this was it, he had to convince at least three of these councillors otherwise it was the end for him. Lord Abaro and Lady Thorne seemed like lost votes, so he that left him with Lady Grey, Lord Lightfoot and Lord Silvermane. Asher walked up onto the platform and stood beside Captain Brightfellow.

"Could you tell me how you got onto the *Zephyrus*?" said Lord Lightfoot smiling warmly.

When Asher spoke, his voice sounded far away and foreign, "I snuck into the dockyard through the sewers." Asher coughed to clear his throat. "I then snuck past a patrol and scaled up the side of the ship using the support ropes."

Members of the crowd openly scoffed at the idea.

"What did you do then?" said Lord Lightfoot.

"Once I was on the ship I found the Captains quarters and was about to make my way in when a strange symbol flashed in front of me, I think I passed out because of it."

Lady Thorne laughed at Asher's words, "This boy sure has an imagination."

Asher was about to retort but managed to hold his tongue and continued with his story, "Anyway, I made my way inside and found what I was looking for, on the way back out I ran into the Commander," Asher motioned towards Vaeliria, "and three other members of the Captain's crew, I put up a fight but they quickly caught me and here I am."

"And are you repentant for your crimes?" said Lord Lightfoot leaning forward in his chair.

Before Asher could reply Lady Thorne cut into the conversation, "What does it matter if he's repentant, he still committed a crime and as such needs to be punished."

Lord Lightfoot ignored Lady Thorne's outburst and once again addressed Asher, "Are you sorry for what you've done."

"Yes," said Asher doing his best to sound genuinely sorry, not that he was, he had only done what he needed to but saying that was as good as tying the noose around his own neck.

"Very well, I have no further questions."

"Then I believe we've heard enough," said Lord Abaro, "Lady Thorne, what is your verdict."

Lady Thorne's was as cold as ice as she said, "The boy should hang."

Asher hadn't expected anything less, it was obvious from the start that Lady Thorne was against him.

"Lord Caewyn?"

Asher turned his attention towards the dark haired Enshyi, "I can't willingly put one so young to death, I vote for the alternative sentence."

"Your decision, Lord Silvermane?"

Lord Silvermane was quiet for a while, his hands laced together in thought, Asher couldn't bare this, so far he was one for and one, he needed Silvermane's vote, "Both parties can benefit if the boy is spared," said Silvermane finally, "alternative sentence."

Several people in the crowd were stunned into silence.

Asher scanned the faces of the council, Lady Thorne's face had twisted into an angry sneer, Lord Caewyn was smiling openly and both Lady Grey and Lord Abaro were looking on passively.

"What on earth are you thinking, Peter," said Lady Thorne angrily, "he's a low-born and a thief, how can you suggest that he be allowed to serve aboard a Skyship?"

"I'm making an investment," replied Silvermane calmly.

"Enough!" shouted Lord Abaro, "Lady Grey your decision."

The older Councillor sat silent for what felt like an eternity, but then she spoke "We cannot afford to look weak. I'm sorry, Captain, but he must hang."

Asher felt numb, the small flicker of hope that he had been holding onto had all but been extinguished, he looked at Lord Abaro, the man's expression was a mask but Asher had seen that look from enough nobles to realise he was laughing on the inside.

"I agree with Lady Grey for the good of the Kingdom, the boy must hang, guards take him away."

The crowd cheered in approval of the verdict.

Vaeliria stormed passed Asher and Captain Brightfellow towards the council her face a mask of cold fury, "Is this what you call justice!" shouted Vaeliria above the noise.

Lord Abaro looked down at Vaeliria contempt clear on his face, "Hold your tongue, Commander, otherwise you will find yourself in a cell."

Vaeliria was about to say something but a look from the Captain stopped her.

"Wise decision. Guards, take the boy to a cell, he'll be hung at first light tomorrow."

Asher felt completely numb, he couldn't believe it his gamble had failed and now he was going to die. As he was led away by the two guards he looked over at Vaeliria and smiled sadly.

Chapter 5

Adessa was sat in the garden of summer with her mother, listening for the spirits of the garden.

At sixteen summers old Adessa was the oldest member of her generation to still not have passed her trial of apprenticeship for the Forest Speakers. The prevailing theory and rumor was that because her father hadn't been a member of the Enshyi, Adessa herself hadn't inherited the ability of a Speaker, but if that were true than Adessa wouldn't have been able to speak with any spirit, but as it was the only spirits that remained silent to her were those of the trees, unfortunately the requirement for one to become an apprentice Forest Speaker was for them to show the ability to speak with a single tree.

With a deep breath Adessa focused and let herself slip onto the spirit plane. The first spirits that she found were the spirits of a group of lilies, their cheerful auras danced around Adessa lifting her mood, next came the fiery spirits of some amaryllis, their warmth washed through Adessa leaving her skin tingling, lastly Adessa heard the quiet spirits of dying orchids, turning her own spirit towards the orchids Adessa began the words of passing, the orchids offered their thanks before falling silent.

After she finished the words of passing Adessa brought herself back from the spirit plane and looked over at her mother.

Sakala Shinepacer was one of the most powerful and beautiful Speakers of her generation, her flawless skin and auburn hair were the envy of just about every other woman in Alfheim.

Adessa hated the fact that she looked so different from her mother. Where her mother's skin was pale and white like that of a pearl Adessa's was almond in colour and freckled in the sun, but that was just the first way in which the two differed. Adessa had curves where her mother was lean and whilst her mother's auburn hair was fair Adessa's hair was raven in colour and so thick that it was a challenge to brush it every morning.

When she looked hard however Adessa could see a couple of similarities between herself and her mother, both had the same button nose and their lips curved into the exact same bow shape, but the similarity that made Adessa feel better about herself was that she had the same golden irises as her mother.

"Adessa, don't let your mind wander."

Heeding her mother's advice Adessa cleared her mind and once again dove onto the spirit plane.

The spirits of the lilies and amaryllis greeted Adessa again followed shortly by the spirit of a young elk and a old fox. Adessa continued to listen, hoping against hope she found the spirit of a tree.

Minutes passed and still the trees remained silent.

Shame and anger washed over Adessa, she had failed her initiation and would never be considered a Speaker.

Releasing herself from the Voice, Adessa once again turned to her mother.

"Do the tree's talk to you, my child?"

Tears began streaking down Adessa's cheeks and when she spoke her voice was quiet and weak, "No, mother, the trees remain silent. I'm sorry I've failed you."

Sakala enveloped her daughter, "You could never fail me."

Once Adessa had regained her composure, her mother released her, "Adessa, try again, remember to clear your mind of any distractions and open your spirit to them, the trees have the oldest souls and will only speak to one who truly walks the path of a Forest Speaker."

"I shall try," replied Adessa feeling worried.

Adessa took a deep breath and calmed herself, before she dove into the sea of spirits that was the garden of summer. Again, the spirits of the plants, flowers and animals greeted her but the trees remained silent.

Panic began to fill Adessa's mind.

Mother told me to clear my mind of all distractions and open myself up to the trees, okay open yourself up, let the trees see the whole you and let's see if they judge me like everyone else.

Adessa calmed her racing mind and offered all of herself to the trees, but only silence greeted her and she began to believe she had truly failed when a single voice rang in her mind, the voice was old but felt powerful.

"It has been quite some time since I've spoken with someone new, it's a pleasure to meet you, Adessa Shinepacer," said the mysterious voice.

"How do you know my name?" replied Adessa stunned.

"You offered your soul to me, Adessa."

"Offered my soul?" said Adessa confused.

"As you know, your spirit or Voice as you know it is your connection to the world around you, when a Speaker wishes to communicate with the world around them they use their Voice, you offered yours and I deemed you worthy to hear mine."

"Wait you've always been able to hear me?"

"Yes, but you weren't ready to hear me."

"And I'm ready now?" said Adessa in disbelief.

"You are, because in the moment when you offered your spirit, you accepted who you are."

Suddenly it hit Adessa that she didn't know which tree she was talking with. "My apologies," she said bowing. "I have forgotten to ask your name and where I may find you in the garden."

"The Enshyi call me the GrandOak, I am the oldest being in the garden of summer."

Instantly Adessa knew where she could find the GrandOak, he was the largest tree in the garden and stood alone on an island in the middle of the Lake of Life which ran through the centre of the great forest of Alfheim.

"How can I be speaking with you; it is said that there can only be one Speaker who talks with you and that is the High Speaker?"

50

"Yes he was the last to hear my voice but that was before he was High Speaker and you are just as worthy as he," replied the GrandOak.

Doubt crept back into Adessa's mind. *How can this be, the other Speakers say that only a pure blooded Enshyi can communicate with the GrandOak.*

Adessa felt the GrandOak's spirit flash with power before becoming the same sea of calm, "Your brothers and sisters fear change, too long bound in their fears and traditions. Thus, they will do anything to hinder progress."

"What do you mean?"

"Speakers are capable of wondrous things, but we will talk more on this matter when you come to me. I believe your initiation is complete and it would seem your mother has something to discuss with you."

The voice of the GrandOak fell silent returning Adessa to the physical world, turning to her mother Adessa noticed she was holding something.

"You heard the voice of a tree?" asked Sakala holding the object tightly.

"Yes, mother, I heard a tree," replied Adessa joyously. "I'm a true Enshyi."

"You always have been," replied Sakala embracing her daughter. "Which tree did you hear?"

"I heard the voice of the GrandOak."

Sakala's body tensed at Adessa's words, "Are you sure, my child?"

"Yes, he announced himself to me."

Sakala was quiet for a few moments as she digested the information, coming out of her thoughts she spoke, "I will let the High Speaker's know, but before that, I must give you this." Sakala released her hold of Adessa and produced a small acorn necklace from within the folds of her robes.

Adessa was overcome with joy, the acorn necklace was the sign of an apprentice Speaker.

Now no one can deny that I'm Enshyi.

Sakala approached and tied the necklace around Adessa's neck, Adessa could feel a pulse of energy coming from the acorn, it was a warm sensation like that of a summers breeze, stepping back Sakala looked at her daughter approvingly, she raised her hands and began speaking, "By the light of the Sun, I Sakala of the Forest Speaker's hereby recognise that Adessa of clan Shinepacer has passed her initiation, starting today she shall begin her training so that one day she may serve as a bridge between Alfheim and the Enshyi." Sakala took a breath before continuing, "Adessa will you except this honour and swear by the Forest that you will always act in the best interest of Alfheim and your fellow Enshyi?"

Not trusting herself to speak Adessa nodded to her mother.

"Very well." Sakala stood still for a moment, Adessa could feel the power radiating throughout her mother, then the forest around them began to pulse with energy and a faint rumble came from within the ground, the rumble grew louder and louder, until finally an enormous vine shot up out of the ground into the air cresting the tree line. Adessa nearly fell over in surprise. Peaking the vine slowly began to descend.

As the vine came level with Adessa it stopped, and Adessa found herself looking upon the tome of Enelya.

"Adessa, place your hand upon the tome and swear before the forest that you shall not break your vow."

Adessa placed her hand upon the tome, "I Adessa of clan Shinepacer swear to act in the best interests of Alfheim and to help my fellow Enshyi, and by the honour of the Forest Speakers, I shall not break my vows."

Sakala walked forward and placed her hand over Adessa's, "I Sakala of the Forest Speakers have witnessed this child's vow, from this day forth she is a Speaker bound to the work of Alfheim."

The garden fell completely silent and for a few precious moment Adessa felt at peace with herself.

"What happens now Mother?"

"Now you're an Apprentice, you shall begin to learn what being a Speaker really means."

Being addressed as an Apprentice Speaker filled Adessa with pride, this was all she had wanted for so long, that now it was here she couldn't believe it.

Blinking back tears Adessa asked, "When do we start?"

"Your training shall begin as soon as I have talked to the High Speakers."

Adessa could only nod in response, so much had changed in the last few hours, she had completed her initiation and in doing so had found the voice of the GrandOak, the oldest and wisest being in the great forest of Alfheim, the only other Enshyi who spoke with the GrandOak was Caewyn the High Speaker of the Forest,

"Now go home, Adessa. I'll inform the High Speakers of your success."

"As you wish mother."

Despite what her mother had told her Adessa hadn't gone straight home like she had been told, instead she found herself wandering through the Garden of Summer.

The sea of flowers that stood to either side of the path seemed brighter than they had been when Adessa had walked this path earlier. Adessa continued to follow the path and eventually passed by the line of gnarled willows that marked the edge of the garden and stepped out into the true majesty that was the great forest of Alfheim.

The hooting of old owls rang high in the branches above. Adessa looked up into the darkening maze of branches hoping to catch a glimpse of the owners of the hoots but before she could a Nighthawk came swooping past, a giant moth hung lifelessly from its hooked beak, it quickly flew off and was lost amongst the other trees. Adessa made the sign of passing for the Moth's spirit.

The last rays of sunlight faded from the sky as Adessa made it to a ring of Roses, their petals the colour of blood. Walking into the centre of the ring Adessa sat down and entered the spirit world, the sweet childlike spirits of the

Blood Roses swirled around Adessa, "I did it, my friends. I've become an apprentice Forest Speaker."

The spirits of the Roses blossomed warmly, telling Adessa they knew she would do it.

"You guys always know how to make me feel better."

The Roses whipped around Adessa and passed through her, through the Voice the spirits managed to whisper to Adessa, *"We'll always be here."*

Adessa felt tears begin to form in her eyes, she knew that when she began her studies she wouldn't be able to come and visit her friends as much as she would be too busy.

Then enjoy their company while you can.

Adessa cleared her mind of the sad thoughts and allowed herself the simple pleasure of her friends' company.

Adessa awoke hours later to the voice of the GrandOak ringing in her mind, "Adessa, I wish to speak with you please come to the Lake of Life, as soon as you are able."

Adessa hadn't meant to fall asleep but the events of the last day had drained her both emotionally and physically, but as she pulled herself up from the ground Adessa saw the full moon looming high in the sky, that was good she hadn't been asleep for too long.

"I have to leave now my friends, the GrandOak wishes to speak with me. May the sun shine on you," said Adessa straightening her robe.

The Roses leaned towards Adessa and she could feel the warmth of their spirits wash over her.

The warm wind swept over Adessa as she cleared the cover of the trees and came to stand before the Lake of Life.

The massive body of water shimmered in the moonlight and at its centre stood the GrandOak and his island, even from this distance it was easy to see that he was easily twice the height and width of a normal oak.

Peering out through the darkness Adessa thought she could see a small figure standing on the island next to GrandOak but that couldn't be, only the High Speaker was allowed to step foot on the island and he was in the Kingdom of Angard.

Following the curve of the lake Adessa ended up on a jagged peninsula, the rushing water whipped past in a torrent of noise, Adessa stood at the edge of the water wondering how she was supposed to get to the GrandOak when a bridge of vines began to form at her feet, shocked Adessa just stood there looking at the vines but then the GrandOak's voice filled her head, "The bridge will hold."

Adessa began walking along the vines tentatively.

As she got closer it became clear to Adessa that there really was another person on the island but more surprising was that the person was High Speaker Caewyn and he was made entirely out of wood. Adessa knew the High Speaker was powerful in the ways of the Voice but what stood before her was something that she had never believed possible.

Stepping off the bridge and onto the island Adessa was able to take in the true majesty of the GrandOak, he was unlike anything she could have imagined his bark was a richer brown than any other tree in the forest and his leaves were all a vibrant green that could have rivalled even the most precious of gems. The bark of the GrandOak twisted and a gnarled elderly face formed.

"You're beautiful," said Adessa in awe.

"No more than you, my dear," replied the GrandOak smiling.

This felt like a dream to Adessa, how could she be here on this sacred ground talking with the GrandOak and standing beside the High Speaker.

Sensing her thoughts once again the GrandOak spoke, "You are worthy of being here remember that."

"This just doesn't seem real."

"I thought the exact same thing when I first came here," said the High Speaker.

This awoke Adessa from her reverie, and she instantly dropped to her knees and placed her head to the ground, "High Speaker, it is an honour to be in your presence."

"Please stand, Lady Shinepacer, I have enough people who bow to me."

Adessa stood before the High Speaker feeling awkward, she was trying not to look at him because she believed he would take her quizzical gaze as an insult.

"I bet your wondering what this is," said the High Speaker indicating himself.

Adessa nodded in agreement.

"The link you and I share with the GrandOak is strong but being as far away from the forest as I am makes the link weak, making it near impossible to communicate through the spirit world, thus I created this vessel."

"But how does it work surely it would be easier to use the voice then to create this vessel?"

"You would think so but here in my apartments in the Angardian Kingdom I have another vessel which is linked with the one here in the garden allowing me to communicate with the GrandOak and you."

"That's amazing."

"Adessa we have a matter most important to discuss, you can talk with Caewyn at another time."

"My apologies," said Adessa bowing to the GrandOak, "what is this matter you wish to discuss?"

"You are to become mine and Caewyn's apprentice."

Adessa stood dumbfounded, surely she had misheard "I'm sorry did you say I'm going to become yours and the High Speaker's apprentice."

"That's correct," smiled the High Speaker.

Adessa bowed before the GrandOak and High Speaker, "I'm honoured, and by the honour of the Enshyi I will not fail you I swear it."

The GrandOak smiled, "I know you won't. You should be on your way home now, Adessa, the High Speaker and I have other matters to discuss and you need to rest as your training begins tomorrow."

Adessa bowed again, "May the sun shine on you both."

"May the sun shine on you also," responded the GrandOak and High Speaker in unison.

Adessa quickly made her way home all the while contemplating the changes that were going to occur in her life.

Chapter 6

Asher hadn't been able to sleep, how could he when he was about to be put to death not to mention the fact that he was chained up by his wrists to a wall and even if they hadn't his mind was filled with the events of the last few days. He shouldn't have accepted the job in the first place, sure he may have gotten a beating from Snake and Jared as a warning but at least he would be alive but no he had been swayed by the money and now he was going to hang for it.

"See this is what happens when you trust somebody other than yourself," said a voice in the darkness.

"Shut it I ain't in the mood for you."

"Oh come now, you've only got yourself to blame I've tried telling you countless times that you can't trust anyone but do you listen".

"I said Shut up!"

"Fine," said the voice in surrender, "it ain't like we're going to be alive much longer anyway."

"Death don't look so bad from where I'm sitting," said Asher as he rustled the chains against the wall.

Only silence greeted Asher in reply. "Think I'm going cracked in the head." With nothing but the silence around him Asher's thoughts once again turned to his impending death.

The sound of footsteps awoke Asher from his dark reverie sometime later.

As the footsteps got closer Asher could hear a muffled voice, "This is the one."

I guess this is the end.

The lock turned and the door of Asher's cell opened flooding the room with light which blinded him.

"Sonovabitch."

"Is that anyway to greet us Asher?"

"Who's there?" replied Asher blinking.

"Surely you know my voice by now."

"Vaeliria is that you?" said Asher as the spots before his eyes disappeared.

"Yes, now we don't have much time."

"What do you mean, we don't have much time?"

"No time for answers, just hold still for a moment."

"You're getting me out of here, aren't you?"

Vaeliria smiled at Asher but said nothing as she began unlocking his shackles. As the last shackle was unlocked Asher noticed that Wraith was standing in the doorway of his cell and he felt his gut tense.

"What's going on?"

Vaeliria ignored him and instead addressed Wraith "Wraith are you ready?"

"Yes," replied Wraith in her usual monotone.

Vaeliria turned back to Asher, "Okay let's do this."

As Wraith walked over to Asher, the voice inside his head started speaking again, "This don't look like a rescue."

"What in the seven hell's is going on?" said Asher as Wraith approached him.

"Just trust me."

"Commander you'll need to hold him still."

"What the fuck for?"

"I'll explain later," said Vaeliria as she grabbed a hold of Asher. "Now hold still."

Wraith approached slowly, again she was murmuring in her lifeless tone, Asher felt his already tensed stomach cramp in fear, there could only be one reason for her chanting, Wraith was about to cast a hex on him. Asher struggled against Vaeliria but her hold was as hard as iron.

As she continued chanting Wraith slowly began tracing her finger along Asher's neck. Asher felt an icy cold sensation seeped into his flesh at the touch and he readied himself for whatever was to come.

A few moments later Wraith, satisfied with her work took a step back and clasped her hands together. Asher let out a sigh of relief.

Maybe this Hex isn't like the others.

Not a moment after Asher had the thought a hot searing pain shot across his neck. Instinctively he tried to fight his way free from Vaeliria's grasp, but it was useless as the Skyknight's hold remained fast.

After another few minutes of struggling against Vaeliria, Asher finally felt the pain begin to subsided and as he relaxed Vaeliria released her hold of him.

"What... the fu... fuck was that about?" said Asher as he lay on the floor of his cell.

"I'm saving your life now shut up and let me put these on." Vaeliria placed a shackle over Asher's neck and re-shackled his hands before she pulled him to his feet, "Can you find your way back Wraith?"

"Yes, Commander."

With that Asher was dragged from his cell.

As he traversed the dizzying maze of corridors Asher found himself thinking about the crappy little shanty again and how grand it seemed compared to the claustrophobic atmosphere of the cells and tunnels he had found himself in of late.

Eventually the maze gave way to a large domed chamber, a dozen different passages broke off from the room in every direction, each shrouded in darkness. Vaeliria's footsteps echoed throughout the room as she led the way across the chamber towards one of the passages, as Asher grew closer he saw that the passage consisted of yet another long staircase.

"This place is ridiculous; all I've seen since being here is corridor after corridor and more fucking stairs then one man should see in a lifetime and now you expect me to climb these."

"Yes, do you have a problem with that."

"Your bloody right I have a problem with it, I ain't going to climb to my own death."

"I'm afraid you don't have a choice in the matter," said Vaeliria as she once again tugged the shackles around Asher's wrists. "Now move."

An iron portcullis stood at the top of the staircase, rays of light filtered through the thick bars outlining the two guards who were standing watch in an eerie light, both guards were covered in the grey leather and iron caps of the city guard along with the tipped pikes that were the standard. As Vaeliria and Asher approached both guards saluted.

"If you would be so kind as to open the gate, gentlemen." The guards looked at each other than the shorter of the two yelled an order for the gate to be opened and it began to rise.

"Thank you," said Vaeliria as she led Asher through the archway and out into the morning sun.

Asher was blinded for a few moments, but once his eyes adjusted to the light he saw that he was outside the city on a nearby hill, in the near distance stood Actalia. The lower city was barely visible, a few of the taller buildings just managed to poke their broken heads over the city walls, looking like the broken teeth in the head of a junkie whilst the large decadent apartments of the upper city stood oppressively over the lower city, their clean white walls a vast contrast against the grey and decrepit environment Asher knew.

Returning his gaze to the upper city Asher spotted a dozen or more manors dotted amongst the urban sprawl, most were made from wood, others brown brick and mortar.

Asher turned his sight from the oppressive city and his gaze fell upon a set of gallows, the worn rickety frame was struck deep into the wet swollen earth, obviously, this had been erected some time ago, a single noose hung from the gallows, Asher swallowed nervously.

I can't believe this is the end.

Walking up the steps of the gallows Asher suddenly realised there was no crowd, this surprised him a great deal as every hanging that took place in the lower city was treated as a spectacle.

The local merchants would set up their stalls around the edge of Penance Square, whilst the general populace, eager to see something that helped distract them from their own miserable existence packed in as close as possible to the gallows.

"Where's the crowd?" said Asher voicing his thought.

"The Captain managed to convince the council that hanging you in public would cause tensions between the lower city citizens and the guard to boil over, so only those who need to witness this are present," replied Vaeliria.

"And who needs to witness this?"

"Two members of the council will be witness to your execution; they will officiate your death and make sure that justice has been served."

As Vaeliria finished speaking, Asher saw four figures ascending the hill towards the gallows. "I thought you said there would only be two?"

"There is," replied Vaeliria curtly. "Lord Caewyn and Lord Abaro are the witnesses from the council; the other two witnesses are Captain Brightfellow and Seneschal Delander."

"Why does the Seneschal need to be here?"

"Because he is in charge of protecting the Councillors."

As Vaeliria removed the shackle from around Asher's neck and placed the noose over his head, Asher felt despair sink into every fibre of his being, this was the end.

The noose was rough and solid against his neck. Once Vaeliria had the noose in place the witnesses to the execution had made their way to the base of the gallows and were looking up at Asher. Asher scanned the faces of everyone there, Captain Brightfellow had a grim mask upon his face, deep thought lines ran across his forehead and his eyes were cold with sadness, Seneschal Delander's expression was one of reluctant duty, Lord Caewyn looked utterly mortified and Lord Abaro was smiling triumphantly.

"Do you have any last words?" asked Vaeliria softly.

"Yeah I do in fact," said Asher addressing everyone. "You call this justice, this isn't justice, everyone in the lower city does what they have to in order to survive me included, just because you nobles can eat every day and have a nice warm home to shelter you, you think that we poor folk are all criminals when actually you're the criminals for letting the lower city become what it is."

"Pull the lever Commander," said Lord Abaro.

Before she pulled the lever Vaeliria whispered into Asher's ear, "I'm sorry," and then the floor beneath Asher's feet fell away and the noose jerked into place, instantly the air was forced from his lungs in a painful wrench, he managed to struggle for only a few moments before the world went dark and the last thing he heard was the voice inside his head mocking how foolish he had been to trust these people.

Chapter 7

"This isn't working," said Adessa as another of the wooden sword the GrandOak had made for her splintered on the stone she had been striking for the past three days.

"And why do you think that is, Lady Shinepacer?" asked the High Speaker.

"I don't know, maybe you could just tell me rather than always asking me what I think the reason is," replied Adessa sharply.

If the High Speaker had noticed the edge in her voice he did not show it, and when he finally spoke his voice was completely calm, "Do you really want to know why I ask you what you think the reasons are for me teaching you these techniques are and why you seemingly can't learn it?"

"Yes," replied Adessa, her voice still sharp.

"I ask you so that you think for yourself Adessa, what good will come of me telling you what to think or how to act, you are the GrandOak's apprentice as well as mine, you are not a simpleton who needs to be told what to do." At the High Speaker's words, all the fire left Adessa and she felt ashamed of herself.

"I'll ask again, what do you think the reason for me teaching you this technique is?" said the High Speaker as he sat down on a nearby rock.

Adessa started to think, what could the reason be?

"I'm waiting?"

Adessa had an epiphany, in all the tales and legends of the great Speakers, conflict of one sort or another was always present. "You are teaching me, so that I can protect the Enshyi."

The High Speaker smiled at her words, "That is correct, it is a sad fact of life but peace only lasts so long."

A cold chill took hold of Adessa, "High Speaker, do you really believe that we are heading for conflict, I mean who would want to attack us, our people have lived peacefully for over a hundred years now."

"I know, child, but not everyone is as pure hearted as yourself, there are several people even here within Alfheim who would result to violence if it meant personal gain and my time here in the Angardian capital has only reaffirmed my opinion, that we must be ready to protect ourselves if we are to rejoin the world beyond our forest." Adessa could tell from the High Speaker's words that something must have happened in the Angardian Kingdom but she dared not pry.

The High Speaker seemed to shake himself free of his reverie "Forgive me, child, it has been a most troubling time of late, we shall leave it there for today unless you wish to try again?"

Adessa felt a fire light within herself, if the High Speaker was working so hard to protect Alfheim and his fellows why shouldn't she, that was what the GrandOak and High Speaker were training her for after all. "I shall try again."

"Please proceed, Lady Shinepacer." The High Speaker tossed another wooden sword towards Adessa.

As the sword flew through the air Adessa could tell it hadn't been made by the GrandOak, the other wooden swords she had been using where the same rich brown as the GrandOak's bark and had a hint of his power whereas this sword was pitch black and as she caught the sword she was surprised to find that it was cold to the touch and a foreign power ran through it, inspecting the wooden blade she noted how there was no guard or pommel to speak of and the length of the blade curved rising to a point.

"Where did this sword come from?" said Adessa more to herself then the High Speaker.

"I found it in High Speaker Zanbuhh's quarters after he passed onto the undying lands, when I left for the Angardian capital I asked the GrandOak to keep it safe."

Adessa cleared her mind using the mental technique the GrandOak had taught her and entered her Voice, the soul of the sword came to life as she offered her own soul to it.

"What do you command of me my Speaker?" said the sword in an ethereal voice.

"I wish to protect my people and I call on you to help me," replied Adessa.

"I am yours to command from this day forth until my last."

Adessa raised the sword high above her head with both hands. Taking a deep breath, she focused all her will into the blade and then using every ounce of power she possessed she slammed the sword down onto the stone where it sang a high-pitched note.

"Well done Adessa you have succeeded," said the High Speaker as he stood. "What is the name of your sword?"

Adessa felt the swords spirit reach out to her "You're my Speaker, so you may name me."

"His name is OathKeeper."

"OathKeeper, that's a fine name," replied the High Speaker nodding. "Our lesson is finished for today."

"Thank you for believing in me, High Speaker."

"No need for thanks, Lady Shinepacer, I'm just doing what every teacher should do, now I believe you have a lesson with the GrandOak."

"May the sun shine on you, High Speaker."

"And you, Lady Shinepacer," said the High Speaker before his vessel became inanimate.

After a few minutes of quiet contemplation, the GrandOak's face twisted into life, "Caewyn was never good at knowing his own limits."

"Does he truly believe we are in danger?"

"The Enshyi have been locked away in this forest for far too long, Caewyn's departure to the Kingdom of Angard is the first step in trying to rejoin the outside world but with that comes a number of risks which is why he is trying to teach you as much as possible so that if the need ever arises you will be able to protect yourself."

"Protect myself," said Adessa incredulously, "what would I have to protect myself from."

"As Caewyn said not everyone is as pure hearted as you and for all we know the alliance with the Angardian's could fail, which is why Caewyn insisted that he travel alone to their Kingdom because if the worst should come to pass then only he will be at immediate risk, but that's not to say that you shouldn't be wary of your fellow Enshyi either, many of your peers will not agree with you being taught by the High Speaker or myself and Caewyn has many enemies of his own."

"So he's pushing himself for my sake," replied Adessa feeling guilty.

Sensing her guilt through the bond they shared the GrandOak gave her some reassuring words, "Do not worry, Adessa, Caewyn can look after himself after all he is the High Speaker of the Forest."

"You're right, if the High Speaker can believe in me then I should believe in him as well, may we begin today's lesson."

"Well said."

Adessa began her lesson with the GrandOak by practicing the Tree in the Wind. Already Adessa was beginning to see why this was a good technique to have, it allowed her to keep her mind quiet and focused despite all the spirits around her.

"Can you see the spirits Adessa?"

"Yes, there's so many of them," replied Adessa in awe.

"Now I want you to focus and find the voices of the Blood Roses."

"But there's so many spirits how can I possibly find them?"

"Come now, Adessa, the Blood Roses were the first spirits that you found, you have a special connection with them, focus and you'll find them," said the GrandOak reassuringly.

Adessa looked at the spirits around her but the Blood Roses were nowhere to be found, and more voices were becoming visible, the painful pressure behind Adessa's eyes began building, slowly she began to feel her mind slip from the calm island that was the Tree in the Wind and into the chaotic sea of spirits around her.

"There's too many," gasped Adessa.

"Focus."

The pressure continued to build blinding Adessa, dropping to her knees she cried out in pain.

"Come on, Adessa, focus."

"It hurts."

The pressure continued to grow despite Adessa's best efforts to quieten her mind but then she caught a glimpse of a familiar spirit in the distance. Taking as deep a breath as she could Adessa focused her will and began following the weak trail that stood before her.

The spirits of the forest swirled around Adessa in a chaotic cyclone. Adessa had never known the spirits to be so violent but she managed to keep them at bay by continuing to focus on the warmth of the familiar spirit.

Several minutes passed and Adessa felt her mind begin to tire, but nevertheless she carried on until finally the chaos around her disappeared and the spirits of the Blood Roses came into full focus.

Adessa took a deep breath as she let the warm comforting aura of her friends enveloped her.

"You gave me strength, my friends."

"No, Adessa, they didn't give you the strength, you found it in yourself," said the GrandOak his voice filling her mind again.

The Blood Roses spirits shifted indicating that they shared this thought.

"But I felt you calling to me."

"You found them, Adessa, all you had to do was focus," answered the GrandOak. "This is what I was trying to teach you, you have the power inside yourself, you have to realise that."

"I understand."

"Our lesson is finished for today; I shall leave you to think on what I have said."

The GrandOak's voice faded and Adessa was left alone with the Blood Roses.

The Roses, twirled around Adessa, brushing against her to see if she was okay.

"I'm fine," lied Adessa as she broke her connection to the spirit world and began walking home.

Chapter 8

Asher sat in an all-encompassing darkness, he didn't know how long he had been here or even what this place was, how could anyone have, it was like the sun had been stolen. The last thing he remembered before he woke up in this place were Vaeliria's words, he then remembered that she had pulled the lever which opened the trapdoor of the gallows and then there was the intense burning sensation as the noose dug into his neck, he rubbed his neck but he didn't feel anything.

I'm dead.

As he scanned the darkness a small flicker of light twinkled, hardly believing the sight before him Asher sat there in bewilderment, how could he have missed this, finding his feet Asher slowly began to walk in the direction of the light. Every step felt like he was wading through mud, his legs were growing heavier with each step and his mind was becoming clouded, moments later a series of symbols flashed before his eyes, all were indescribable to his foggy mind. Wading on Asher was met with the corpse of One Eye, the old thief's face had been cleaved in two, which revealed a mass of blood and bone. Asher tried to turn away from the corpse but he found his gaze wouldn't leave the body.

"You did this boy."

With all the strength in his legs Asher pushed past One Eye and carried on towards the light. A few steps later he found the body of Snake slumped against an invisible wall, his neck had been slit open from ear to ear, a torrent of blood flowed out of the wound covering his entire body in scarlet red, Asher spat on the corpse and was off.

Suddenly the slither of light disappeared and Asher found the human mountain that was Jared standing in front of him, for a moment he thought the giant man was alive, but then he saw the massive gash running across Jared's torso, entrails were beginning to fall out of the wound and the smell of shit and blood quickly followed. Gagging Asher walked around Jared's corpse and continued on his way towards the small beacon.

Asher felt like he had been walking for miles and the spark of light had only grown to the size of a watermelon. Asher stopped, his muscles were quivering in exhaustion, taking a deep breath he slumped to the ground, "Giving up are we." said Vaeliria as she formed before Asher.

"Just taking... a br... break," replied Asher breathlessly.

"Well it's time to get up," said Vaeliria offering her hand.

Asher grasped the offered hand and pulled himself to his feet, once he was on his feet Vaeliria walked off ahead, "Come on." Asher had to will his legs to move, slowly one foot moved in front of the other and he began making his way towards Vaeliria and the growing light.

"You know, I should be angry at you for hanging me," said Asher as he caught up with Vaeliria.

Vaeliria said nothing in reply and the two continued on towards the light.

Before long Asher found himself stood before a door of pure light. Asher turned to Vaeliria but the Skyknight was nowhere to be seen.

Well if I am dead at least it looks like I'm going to paradise.

Asher stepped into the light and was immediately blinded, he blinked several times but still his sight wouldn't return and then moments later the same intense pain he had felt when Wraith had cast her Hex upon him lanced across his neck.

Asher screamed out in pain as everything went dark.

Asher opened his eyes and shot up out of bed, his vision was hazy but he managed to make out the blurred face of a young girl.

"Doctor Estrada, he's awake, Doctor Estrada!" said the young girl as she ran from the room.

Asher slumped back down into the bed, he lay there for a moment waiting for his vision to return to normal.

Once his vision had returned to him, he sat up and looked around the room he was in. The walls and floor were made from a richly coloured wood. A long table sat at the base of his bed, a variety of medical supplies sat atop it. A large wardrobe and tall mirror lined the back wall and another smaller table lie in the corner opposite with two chairs accompanying it, Asher pushed off the covers and sat on the side of the bed, looking down he found that he wasn't wearing his ruined under-shirt and trousers but was dressed in a white gown that ran to his knees. Asher placed his head in his hands and took a few deep breaths before trying to stand but as he did the room swayed from side to side and he found himself falling straight back onto the bed. After a few minutes of silence the door to his room opened and a woman who Asher had never seen came walking into the room followed by the young girl he had seen when he first woke up. The woman was tall and slender like a swan, she looked to be no older than forty summers old, her hair was a rich brown and was tied up in a high ponytail, her eyes were a sea foam green and had a warm look to them but Asher immediately forgot all of that as he laid eyes on the blood-stained apron that sat over the green overalls the women wore.

"I told you he was awake."

Asher turned his attention towards the young girl, she looked very similar to women she was stood next to, they both had the same soft eyes and rounded ears.

"How do you feel?" said the woman as she crouched down and took a hold of Asher's head and looked in his eyes, if he had had the strength Asher would've tried to fight her off but as it was he could barely hold himself up.

"Where am I?" asked Asher, his voice weak and hoarse.

"You are on the *Zephyrus,*" replied the woman, turning his head to the left.

"What?" Surely he had misheard.

"Captain Brightfellow and Commander Wintergrave brought you here," answered the young girl.

"How long have I been asleep?"

"Six days," replied the woman matter-of-factly, turning his head to the right.

"Can I speak with Vaeliria?"

"I'm afraid that won't be possible," the woman lifted Asher's head towards the ceiling, "she and the Captain are currently at Headquarters and they won't be returning until it's time for us to depart also they have given strict instructions that you aren't to leave this room until they return." The woman slowly released her hold of Asher's head and nodded to herself before she stood, "Now try to get some rest, come Lucianna, let's leave Asher to rest."

"It was nice meeting you," said Lucianna smiling as she left.

Asher couldn't make sense of what was going on, one moment he was hanging from the gallows the next he was on board the ship which had gotten him into this mess in the first place, and then there was the woman he had just spoken with and the young girl called Lucianna.

Asher lay back down on the bed and was overcome by a wave of fatigue.

When Asher awoke the following day, he was once again met by the face of Lucianna looking over him.

"Morning," said Lucianna smiling.

"Lucianna right?" replied Asher his voice was still hoarse but now at least there was a hint of strength behind it.

"That's right, would you like something to drink?" said Lucianna walking over to the table at the corner of the room.

"Now that you mention it," said Asher but to his surprise Lucianna was already bringing over a steaming cup.

"What's this?"

"This is a herbal tea, it will help with your recovery," said Lucianna handing the cup to Asher.

Asher looked down at the strange concoction in front of him.

The tea looked rather conspicuous, what with its green colour and floral scent but as he took a small sip Asher was pleasantly surprised by the sweet taste that filled his mouth.

"Could I have another?" said Asher as he drained the last of the tea.

"Of course," smiled Lucianna as she took the cup from Asher and proceeded to refill it.

Asher watched Lucianna as she walked across the room, she couldn't have been older than seventeen, but she was the most beautiful girl Asher had ever seen, it wasn't like this was his first time seeing a member of the opposite sex, but where the 'working girls' of the lower city wore all manner of perfumes and make-ups to attract customers, Lucianna had a beauty so natural that Asher couldn't help but think that she resembled an angel from the stories of the Firstborn.

"Here you go," said Lucianna holding the steaming cup out for Asher.

Swallowing his sudden awkwardness Asher took the cup from Lucianna, "Thank you."

"That's alright, it's my job to look after you."

Asher nearly spilled his tea, "You're looking after me, where's the woman from before?"

"Doctor Estrada's busy with other business, so she placed me in charge of you, said it would be good for me, now you stay put and I'll go get you something to eat." With that Lucianna left and Asher was alone once again.

So Vaeliria saved me.

Asher was about to get out of bed and have a look around when Lucianna returned carrying in a tray full of food, she walked over to the nearby table that had the chairs and placed the tray down. Asher was suddenly aware how hungry he was, after all he had been unconscious for six days.

"Is all of that for me?"

"Of course it is you need to eat to get stronger," replied Lucianna cheerfully as she took a seat at the table.

Asher pulled back the covers and sat on the edge of the bed again, remembering what happened the last time he tried standing Asher got to his feet slowly.

After a couple of seconds Asher found that he was fine the room wasn't spinning in front of him like it had been the last time, gaining confidence that he wouldn't fall and make an arse of himself Asher crossed the room to the table and took the seat opposite Lucianna. Asher couldn't help but eye up all the food that was in front of him, there was a steaming bowl of stew, full of carrot, potato, onion and beef, next to the stew was half a loaf of bread freshly baked and there was a tall glass of milk to wash it all down with.

"Eat up," said Lucianna.

"I can't believe this is all for me."

"Well it is, so eat."

Asher tackled the food with an animalistic intensity, he finished the stew and bread in a matter of minutes and drained the glass of milk in three deep gulps before wiping his mouth dry with the back of his arm and sighed in satisfaction. As Asher sat there he realised that Lucianna was looking at him with quizzical eyes.

"Is there something on my face?" said Asher drawing his arm over his mouth again.

This seemed to embarrass Lucianna as her face turned slightly red, "No there's nothing on your face."

"Are Vaeliria and the Captain back yet?" said Asher changing the subject.

"I don't think so, but I could go ask if you like."

"That would be great, I'll come with you I'd like to have a look around."

"I'm afraid that's not possible we were given strict orders that you had to stay here until the Commander comes to get you."

"Why do I have to stay here?"

"I don't know, I'm just following orders," replied Lucianna softly.

"So what you're saying is that I'm stuck here till Valeria gets back."

"I'm afraid so," said Lucianna as she cleared the tray off the table and left the room.

Asher sat in silence recalling the events of the past week when the door to his room opened and in stepped Vaeliria holding a pair of boots and some folded clothes.

Asher felt a confusing mixture of anger and relief wash over him at the sight of the Skyknight.

"I'm glad you're awake," said Vaeliria.

"Are you?" replied Asher venomously.

Vaeliria didn't reply to the jab and just stood quietly waiting for Asher to calm, as the silence stretch on Lucianna walked back into the room, "Oh, Commander, I didn't know you were back."

"Only got back a few minutes ago," replied Vaeliria. "I take it you two have met."

"Yeah she's been taking care of me, since I woke up," said Asher from his seat.

"Good work, Luci, your mother would be proud of your progress as a Medic."

"Thank you, Commander," said Lucianna bowing slightly.

"Now these are for you," said Vaeliria holding out the clothes and boots. "We'll leave you to get changed, once you're done come meet me and Lucianna in the corridor its time you spoke with the Captain."

Vaeliria placed the clothes and boots in front of Asher on the table, then she and Lucianna left the room leaving Asher alone.

Looking at the clothes Asher realised they were of a similar design to the Skyknight uniform worn by Vaeliria but these clothes were charcoal black.

After a few minutes of struggling and cursing Asher stood fully dressed and was looking at himself in the tall mirror. He was shocked with what he saw, his hair which had been a dirty brown mess was now as white as freshly fallen snow and had been cut into a short militaristic style. He felt like he was looking at the face of someone else and the uniform he now wore only added to that feeling. For as long as he could remember the only pieces of clothing he had ever worn were torn, uncomfortable and never fit him properly, whereas the clothes that covered him now felt like they had been made just for him to wear.

Nodding to himself Asher headed for the door.

Asher emerged from his room to find Lucianna waiting for him, her face once again being the first thing he saw, as she caught sight of him, her face developed a look of pure surprise.

"What?"

"The uniform suits you," said Lucianna a smile tugging at her lips.

"Where's Vaeliria?" asked Asher looking up and down the corridor.

"She had to speak with Thomas."

"Who's Thomas?"

"He's the head engineer here on the *Zephyrus*," replied Vaeliria as she appeared from within another room.

"What's an engineer?"

"He makes sure that everything on the *Zephyrus* is in working condition, but that's a conversation for another time, let's have a look at your uniform then?" Vaeliria indicated that she wanted Asher to turn around on the spot. Asher did as he was told and turned in a slow circle, when he faced Vaeliria again she was smiling.

"Well?"

"You look like a cadet straight out of the academy," said Vaeliria continuing to smile, "now let's go see the Captain, he wanted to be here but his duties wouldn't allow it."

With that Vaeliria began walking off down the corridor, Asher and Lucianna quickly fell in line behind her.

Coming to the end of the passageway Asher caught sight of a strange door, dozens of crisscrossing metal arms linked together to form the door and just from looking at it Asher guessed that it had to be at least three inches thick, this led him to wonder as to the purpose of such a door and how it was supposed to open, but his answers came quickly enough as Vaeliria grasp the door and began to push, as she did the metal arms shortened and the door slid to one side, revealing a depression that had been cut into the bottom and top of the doors frame.

"Shall we?" said Vaeliria entering the room behind the metal door.

Asher followed Lucianna into the room masking his growing apprehension.

"What is this?" whispered Asher to Lucianna as they turned around and Vaeliria closed the metal door.

"This is a lift," replied Lucianna.

"And what does it do?" asked Asher feeling stupid.

"It allows for crew members to travel between the different levels of the *Zephyrus*."

As Asher stood there trying to wrap his mind around what he had been told, Vaeliria turned a series of dials that sat in the room's wall before pushing a button which jolted the lift into life and with his gut in his chest the lift began to ascend.

As the lift continued its ascension Asher could hear the grinding of metal wheels all around him and he felt his stomach tighten, what was stopping the room from falling and killing them all.

Finally, the lift reached its destination and came to a stop, Asher immediately felt himself relax. Vaeliria slid the metal door open and they disembarked from the lift and onto the deck of the *Zephyrus*.

Asher was stunned at the activity going on around him, everywhere he looked he saw people going about their tasks with practiced efficiency, dozens of men and women carried heavy looking barrels filled with unknown contents to and fro, others were tying ropes down and up in the rigging Asher saw Vida and Runa working with other members of the crew to secure the sails. With all the activity going on around him Asher didn't realise where Vaeliria was leading him until he stood outside the door to the Captain's quarters, the sight of the massive wooden door sent a chill through Asher, even now his body still remembered the effects of that Hex. Vaeliria opened the door and Asher quickly followed her inside.

As soon as Asher entered the room he couldn't help but feel that something was different about it, like it was warmer somehow, but looking around everything was exactly the same from the maps adorning the walls to the giant bookcase that sat up against the wall, the only thing that was different was Captain Brightfellow himself. The huge man sat behind his desk dressed in the formal uniform of a Skyknight Captain.

"How do you feel?" asked the Captain.

"Like I've just been hung," replied Asher running a hand across his neck.

Captain Brightfellow lifted himself out of his chair, as he did a low groan escaped from the wooden frame like it was pleased to be rid of its burden, in a few of his giant strides the Captain walked around his desk to stand in front of Asher.

"I feel as though I owe you an apology, I wasn't able to convince the council and for that you very nearly died." Sincerity was clear in the Captain's voice.

"Look, Captain, your apology isn't needed, after all you're not the one who put me there. I mean you and Vaeliria are the first people I've meet that actually care enough to try and help me, which is a damn lot more than those nobles on the council did for me."

"You're right in some ways but wrong in others, as I remember two of the council's members voted in your favour," said Vaeliria entering the conversation for the first time.

Asher found himself lost for words, in his anger at being hung he had forgot about Councillor Lightfoot and Councillor Silvermane voting in his favour. There were a few moments of silence until Lucianna's voice filled the room.

"Captain, I don't wish to rush you but Caleb still needs some time to recover from his wounds."

Asher was confused, why was she calling him Caleb, he turned to look at Vaeliria, who gave him a look that told him to be quiet.

"Forgive me, Lucianna, I won't keep Caleb for long I just wanted to explain a few things to him now that he's awake, would you mind leaving us, Vaeliria will take him back to his room." Lucianna nodded her agreement before leaving the room.

Turning his attention back on Asher, Captain Brightfellow began talking, "You already know we are leaving the Angardian Kingdom," Asher nodded in reply. "Well, we are travelling to the land of Onmoria far to the south, the reason for us being deployed there is that we are to begin talks with the Sultan to open trade routes with our Kingdom."

"What's this got to do with me?".

"I'm glad you asked," replied Captain Brightfellow smiling. "Me and Vaeliria have agreed that you are to begin training as a initiate of the Skyknights, but this won't be possible as long as you are, Asher."

"So that's why you were calling me Caleb, you want me to change my name?" replied Asher still slightly confused.

Vaeliria answered Asher's question, "There's more to it than that, we need you to become a completely different person, Asher died at the gallows six days ago."

"So how am I supposed to become a completely different person?"

"You are to become Caleb Wintergrave, a Skelwori nomad like myself," replied Vaeliria.

"I have absolutely no idea what you're talking about."

"Don't worry," said Vaeliria with a smile, "I will be teaching you everything there is about the Skelwori and the Wintergraves."

"Okay that solves one problem but if all Skelwori are as pale as you how am I going to pass as one?"

"That won't be a problem," said Captain Brightfellow entering the conversation, "Vaeliria and I have witnessed Skelworians who are roughly the same complexion as you."

"Not to mention the few Wintergraves I've known who are nearly as tanned as you," said Vaeliria to the Captain.

Asher let out a long sigh: "So when do we start with this transformation?"

"It starts today, from here on you are Caleb," said Captain Brightfellow.

"That's gonna take some getting used to."

Thus, it was that the boy known as Asher died at the gallows on Hangman's Hill in the cold and rain and Caleb Wintergrave was born on the deck of the *Zephyrus* in the light of the sun and the freedom of the air.

Chapter 9

As Caleb stepped out onto the deck of the *Zephyrus*, he was overcome with the sense that he must be dreaming, but not even in his wildest dreams would he have imagined that he would be joining the ranks of the famous Skyknights.

"Go and get some rest, Caleb," said Captain Brightfellow. "Tomorrow we set sail for Indaea and that is when your training begins."

"I'm guessing that's the Onmori capital?" replied Caleb still half in thought.

"That's right."

"How long's it gonna take us to reach this Indaea?"

"About ten days maybe two weeks depending upon the wind."

Caleb was shocked he had heard that Skyships were fast but surely it would take longer than that to reach the Onmori Kingdom and its capital, "And how far is it to Indaea?".

"The Onmori capital is about seven thousand miles away," answered Vaeliria.

Caleb had no idea what or how far a mile was let alone seven thousand, so maybe it was possible for the *Zephyrus* to make the journey in only a week and a half.

"C'mon, Caleb. I'll show you back to your room," said Vaeliria breaking Caleb from his reverie.

As Caleb followed Vaeliria back across the deck of the *Zephyrus* he looked around at all of the Skyknight's that were going about their work. Dozens of men and women sat about tying the bases of the rigging in complicated knots, whilst overhead Vida and Runa effortlessly climbed up towards the crows-nest.

The possibility that he would learn to replicate the skills of these men and women filled Caleb an excitement had never felt before, but then he thought of the tactics that would be taught to him and how he would learn to fight like a Skyknight and he felt positively giddy. No longer would he wake in the middle of the night heart racing, feeling scared and helpless whilst scanning his surroundings for intruders, like he had done on many a night, now he was going to become someone who could defend himself and act against the injustices that had befallen him.

Once back inside his room Caleb felt physically drained and he dropped straight onto his bed.

"I'll leave you to rest," said Vaeliria as she left the room.

Caleb lay still for a few moments enjoying the quiet and peace before the voice of Lucianna brought him back into the world, "Would you like something to eat?"

Caleb shot upright, the prospect of more of the delicious food he had tasted before made him forget his tiredness, "That would be great."

"I'll be back shortly."

When Lucianna returned, she did so holding a tray laden with plates, there was a small loaf of oven backed bread dripping with butter on one plate, thin cuts of pork were stacked high on another and in three different bowls were pieces of orange, apple slices and a bunch of grapes.

"Okay, this isn't all for me, is it?" asked Caleb salivating.

"I thought you might like some company while you eat."

Caleb smiled, "I'd like that."

"Wonderful," replied Lucianna as she began laying the plates out on the table.

Caleb made his way over to the table and sat down, up close the food smelt and looked even better than it had when Lucianna had first brought it in and once it was all laid out he tore into the food as if he were a beast and this his first meal in a week. As he was chewing a mouthful of pork Caleb saw that Lucianna was using a knife and fork to eat her food where as he was using his hands.

I guess I better start practicing manners.

Caleb mimicked Lucianna and took the knife in his right hand and the fork in his left and resumed eating, you could say he got it about half right as he was using the knife and fork but he still ate with the intensity of an animal.

Once they had both finished eating Caleb began asking Lucianna questions about herself.

"You been on this ship long?"

"My entire life, my mother's the head medical officer on the *Zephyrus*." Pride was clear in Lucianna's voice.

"Your mother's Doctor Estrada?"

Lucianna nodded, "Mother's the best there is and one day I'll be just as good as her if not better."

"I'm sure you will."

Lucianna smiled, "Well it's about time I left, mother will want to go over the medical charts with me and you need to rest." Luci stood, "I'll see you tomorrow."

"Ain't going nowhere."

Lucianna cleared the plates up and began leaving when she said, "Night."

"See you later," replied Caleb who was already undressing.

The door closed and Caleb dove into bed, he lay there a while just enjoying the feeling of the feathered mattress, but before he knew it he was asleep, dreaming of the possibilities that awaited him out in the world.

The next morning Caleb found himself being dragged out of bed by Vaeliria, she didn't say anything as Caleb got dressed nor when she marched him through the *Zephyrus*'s depths and out onto the deck. It was dawn and the first rays of light were marking the sky in magnificent reds, oranges and purples, a cold morning wind swept through the dock and Caleb shivered. The crew of the *Zephyrus* were out in full force, dozens of men and women stood shoulder to shoulder covering the deck of the mighty Skyship from bow to stern in a sea of bodies. Caleb was about to ask what was going on when, Captain Brightfellow appeared up at the helm and began speaking, "My friends, we sail for Onmoria, for some of you this will be you're first assignment," a few people nodded their heads at this, "for others this will be another time you follow me into a less than ideal situation"

"We'd follow you into hell, Cap!" shouted someone amongst the crowd. A cheer went up at that but the Captain waved it off.

"Allow me this moment to thank you for trusting me and I wish for you to look at the men and women around you, from now on this is your family, I don't care where you've come from or what you did before now, all that matters is that you trust one another and you know that the man or woman next to you will lay down their life for yours." The Captain's words struck Caleb, it was as if he were talking only to him, a cheer went up that sounded like nothing Caleb had ever heard before, he could feel the sound vibrating within him, it was like the roar of a legendary beast.

"Now let's get this ship in the air!" boomed Captain Brightfellow

"The Captain sure knows how to get everyone excited," said Vaeliria as the cheer dissipated.

"So we're finally leaving this place behind?" said Caleb more to himself than Vaeliria.

"Yes, now we begin our assignment."

"When do I begin my training?"

"As soon as we're in the air, you'll be joining me in the training room."

"Finally."

"Now I suggest you hold on to something."

Before Caleb could find something to hold onto a great shock rippled through the *Zephyrus* knocking him flat on his arse, regaining his feet Caleb saw that the ship was beginning to rise into the air, a great humming sound accompanied the ascension.

"Hugo, release the anchors," said Captain Brightfellow above the hum.

"On it, Cap," replied a short, hard looking man as he raced over to the side of the ship.

A chinking sound came from where Hugo was standing and then the Ship pulled higher than Caleb would have thought possible but that thought was quickly lost as he looked out over the side of the *Zephyrus*'s hull. The entire lower city lay before like a map, he immediately caught sight of Main Street, filled with its hundreds of bodies, that from this height looked like a colony of ants, his attention then turned to the web of back alleys that made the lower city a maze for anyone who didn't know them and he couldn't help but think they looked like the drawing of some mad man.

"Full speed ahead!" shouted the Captain.

With that the *Zephyrus* shot forward and the city of Actalia was quickly left behind, only to be replaced moments later with lush green fields that stretched for as far as Caleb could see.

"Are you ready?" said Vaeliria, awakening Caleb from his reverie.

Caleb nodded.

"Then follow me."

Before Caleb went below deck he allowed himself one last look back at the city he had called 'Home' and he felt a great release wash over him, like he had been a caged bird and now he was free to fly.

Walking into the training room Caleb was immediately taken aback, all manner of weapons and armour filled the room, he recognised some of the weapons like the long sword, spear and short-bow that any of the city guard were equipped with but some looked like other worldly items, there was a sword that was easily as tall as Caleb that looked like it was designed for a giant to wield. A spiked

ball the size of a small melon sat on top of an iron pole
that was easily the size of Caleb's forearm. Up on the
second level of the training room, Caleb saw a skinny man
practicing with a hand slingshot that didn't seem to have
any conventional ammunition of its own but rather it fired
whatever you could find around you whether that be a
stone or a nail. Further in Caleb saw two women sparring,
the weapons they were using were made of two wooden
handles that had a chain linking them, the attacks they
were throwing were too fast for Caleb to see but neither
combatant seemed worried by the speed, gracefully
countering and pirouetting around one another as if they
were dancing. Coming to the back of the massive armoury
Vaeliria led Caleb through an archway and into another
room that was far smaller and had no weapons or armour
in it.

"This is where you shall be training," said Vaeliria
sweeping her hand over the room.

"Why am I training in here and not out there with
everyone else?"

"Because this is where I train."

"You train on your own?"

"There are no other Skelwori on the *Zephyrus* thus I
have had to train on my own until now."

"But I still don't understand why you have to train on
your own."

"Because I practice the Shakan."

"The Shakan?"

"It is the fighting style of the Skelwori, passed down
from one generation to another."

"Aren't you going against your culture by teaching
me?"

"Of course not," replied Vaeliria leaving no room for
argument. "Now let's see what you're made of." Vaeliria
threw off her overcoat and rolled up her sleeves, a
multitude of scars ran across her arms, but Caleb didn't
have time to wonder about their origin as Vaeliria dropped
into a fighting stance

Caleb took up the stance he had taught himself through his years of fighting on the streets and Vaeliria slowly began to circle him.

From the way, she moved Caleb could see that Vaeliria was someone who knew how to inflict pain, but before he could admire his teacher anymore, Vaeliria darted forward and drove a fist straight into the bridge of his nose. Pain exploded through the entirety of Caleb's face but he quickly shook the pain aside and charged towards Vaeliria.

For one moment Caleb believed that he would get the drop on Vaeliria, but that quickly changed when Vaeliria effortlessly knocked his strikes aside and retaliated with a sharp hook of her own. As the blow crashed into his ribs, Caleb felt the air forced from his lungs and he immediately doubled over in pain.

"Is that all you've got?"

Caleb looked up to find Vaeliria regarding him with a look that said she was rather disappointed.

"You're joking right," said Caleb pushing himself upright. "I'm just getting warmed up."

Vaeliria nodded approvingly and the two went back to their spar.

With his side still radiating pain Caleb advanced slowly towards Vaeliria. Once he was in range Caleb began throwing a series of sharp jabs that he hoped would keep Vaeliria on the defensive but his hopes were immediately dashed as Vaeliria stepping in under one of his punches and grabbed a hold of his arm. Caleb instinctively went to deliver another strike from his free hand but before he could Vaeliria flipped him straight onto his back but rather than letting go of his limb she dropped down on his arm and locked her legs across his chest.

"Do you give?"

"Yes," said Caleb through gritted teeth.

His arm was released and Vaeliria sat beside him, as Caleb sat up his ribs ached in protest and he instinctively held them. "Could'a gone easy on me."

"Every Skelwori must be initiated into the Shakan," said Vaeliria matter-of-factly.

"So that was only the initiation, argh." Pain shot through Caleb's body, "Can't wait for the real lessons to start."

"Come on, let's get you looked at."

"Was it really necessary, for you to break his nose," said Doctor Estrada as she looked at Caleb's wounds, the Doctor's hands were light as she inspected Caleb's swollen nose.

"He'll be fine," replied Vaeliria casually.

"That's not the point, how do you expect to train someone who's sprained two ribs and has a broken nose."

"We Skelwori train as if we are in real combat, I for one wound up bedridden for a week after my initiation."

"Is such brutality really needed?"

"I'm fine, ain't nothing I can't handle," said Caleb hiding the pain he truly felt.

"Hmm, I can see there's no way to convince either of you but I insist that Lucianna be present to provide first aid to you both."

"That's a fair compromise, it will be good training for them both."

"At least we agree there, now hold still Caleb, I'm going to apply a bandage to your ribs, that should keep you from re-injuring them, if you take it easy."

As Doctor Estrada applied the bandage, pain streaked through Caleb's side, but he dealt with it by gritting his teeth and clenching his fists, once she was finished Doctor Estrada looked at Caleb with knowing eyes.

"You'll rest for the remainder of the day, then you can resume training tomorrow."

"Thanks, Doc," said Caleb slipping his shirt back on.

"Just doing my duty," said Doctor Estrada standing.

"I'll be taking my leave as well," said Vaeliria, "make sure you're up early tomorrow."

Caleb nodded and Vaeliria and Doctor Estrada left the room leaving him alone with only his bruises for company.

Chapter 10

Adessa found herself in the Chamber of Elements sitting before all the High Speakers, the reason for her audience with the four most powerful Enshyi in all of Alfheim was that several reports had come in from concern citizens of a high pitch metallic sound coming from the GrandOak's island and that coupled with the knowledge that Adessa had found the GrandOak's voice is what led the High Speakers to summon her.

Despite her current situation Adessa couldn't help but marvel at the chamber around her. The giant domed hall was divided into four equal parts one for each of the four elements and their Speakers, each section was covered in hundreds of brightly coloured tiles which ended up forming almost lifelike mosaics.

The Forest Speakers were represented through a mosaic made up of forest green and earthy brown tiles which depicted the GrandOak and sat at the table in the high-backed oaken chair of the Forest Speakers was High Speaker Caewyn's vessel. Sat to Caewyn's left in the pure white chair of the Wind Speakers was High Speaker Rasesso, who was the youngest of the High Speakers and the first woman to become High Speaker of the Wind. Compared to her fellow Enshyi High Speaker Rasesso smiled and laughed a lot especially at the expense of her fellow High Speakers. Behind her lay the mosaic of the Wind Speakers which depicted Oscara. The giant eagle soared high in his domain. Adessa couldn't help but feel that the light blues used to depict the sky around Oscara looked rather anemic when compared to the royal blue sea that surrounded the Water Speakers portrayal of Lynna, which was one of the most beautiful things Adessa had ever laid eyes on and sat at the head of the mosaic in the icy blue chair of the Water Speaker's was High Speaker Zydar. The High Speaker of Water looked like any other

Enshyi, his features all angular and his wispy white-blonde hair was cut into the popular swept back style whilst his face was completely free of hair but despite his rather average appearance Adessa couldn't help but think there was more to him then met the eye. Finally, there was the Fire Speakers mosaic which represented Ohen in all his fiery glory, molten rock fell from within the giant serpent's mouth and its eyes were ablaze with the flames of a thousand fires and sitting at the table in the chair of obsidian was High Speaker Roujin. After having just seen his ninety seventh summer High Speaker Roujin was the oldest of the High Speakers but where you would expect to find a frail, old looking man you found the exact opposite. High Speaker Roujin stood taller than just about every other Enshyi and was easily twice as broad. His eyes were still bright and full of intensity and although his face was full of lines and creases he had no white in his big black beard or shoulder length hair which flowed down behind his ears, the left of which was nothing more than a lobe. Adessa knew the story of how he had battled with his brother for the title of High Speaker of the Flame, hell everyone within the great forest of Alfheim did, it was said that the battle had lasted for three days and that great funnels of flame had danced across the sky until finally Roujin emerged victorious but at the cost of his brother's life.

"What are you up to, Caewyn?" said High Speaker Roujin awakening Adessa from her reverie.

"I'm merely training my apprentice here with the assistance of the GrandOak," replied Caewyn calmly through his vessel.

"What sort of training might that be?" said High Speaker Zydar in a cool tone.

"I am preparing Adessa for her role as a Speaker."

"So it is true that she has heard the GrandOak's voice," interjected High Speaker Rasesso smiling.

"Yes she has heard his voice which means that Adessa has the right to learn from him."

"Do you really think that is wise?" said High Speaker Roujin shaking his head.

"Why is that a problem?"

"You're damn well right it's a problem she's just a babe." High Speaker Roujin looked at Adessa, "How many summers have you seen?"

Scared at being in the presence of the four most powerful people in the Enshyi Kingdom Adessa stuttered "I've seen six... sixteen summers High Speaker."

"By the Flame-mother, she's far too young to be learning Speaking techniques I mean she's only just started her Apprenticeship."

"She's only just started her Apprenticeship but I'm the High Speaker of the Forest and I believe that I have every right to teach her."

"That you do, Caewyn," said High Speaker Zydar trying to diffuse the tension, "but don't you think it would be better to wait till she has at least finished her normal schooling."

"No I believe Adessa is better off learning from myself and the GrandOak then sitting in a classroom for hours merely reading from old tomes."

"My dear girl, could you perhaps show us what you have learnt so far?" asked High Speaker Rasesso.

"What would you like to see?" asked Adessa in reply.

"How about the sword you've been given," said High Speaker Zydar.

Adessa stood dumbfounded.

How does he know about OathKeeper?

"Here you are, Adessa."

Adessa awoke from her thoughts to find High Speaker Caewyn produce OathKeeper from within the depths of his Vessels body.

As Adessa took hold of OathKeeper his ethereal voice filled her mind, "My Speaker."

"I'll see what this so-called 'sword' can do," said High Speaker Roujin standing from his chair of obsidian.

"You can't be serious, Roujin. You are the last Enshyi to be given the title of Swordmaster, how can you fight this poor young girl."

"This way," said High Speaker Roujin ignoring High Speaker Rasesso's plea, the massive Enshyi walked away from the stone table and stood just inside the Fire Speaker's mosaic.

High Speaker Caewyn stood and he spoke into Adessa's ear, "Remember what we've been practicing and you'll be fine."

"How can I fight him? Just look at the difference between us he's a giant compared to me, plus he doesn't even have a weapon."

"You'll be fine," said the High Speaker ignoring the last part of what Adessa had said.

As she walked to meet High Speaker Roujin the fear Adessa felt was now becoming absolute terror but she steadied herself using the GrandOak's technique and once she stood before High Speaker Roujin she drew OathKeeper and focused her will into the blade.

"Let's see if your worthy of that blade."

The High Speaker threw off his robes to reveal a body covered in crimson armour and a sword at his hip. As his blade was freed from its sheath Adessa could've sworn she saw flames dancing across the length of the obsidian.

For a moment, there was utter silence in the Chamber of Elements as the two combatants stood facing one another with their weapons drawn but then the silence was broken and the battle began but the first to strike was not the High Speaker but Adessa.

Adessa lunged at High Speaker Roujin deciding that the element of surprise was the best course of action against such an experienced opponent, but much as she had expected the High Speaker was ready and he effortlessly knocked OathKeeper aside and countered with an overhead strike of his own, Adessa managed to get OathKeeper up just in time to block the strike but the power in the blow knocked her down onto her back, there was no time for rest as the High Speaker began raining strikes down at Adessa but again OathKeeper was there to defend the blows. As the High Speaker continued his assault the muscles in Adessa arms were burning and felt utterly weak.

I can't deal with this for much longer.

"Then strike back," said OathKeeper through the link they shared.

Adessa kicked out with her foot at the High Speaker, while he already knew it was coming the only course of action was for him to take a step back, this gave Adessa her opportunity, she sprang to her feet and slashed at the High Speaker this time he was forced to defend the attack rather than just parry it away but Adessa's advantage lasted less than a second as the High Speaker parried another of Adessa's blows and kicked her straight in the stomach knocking the air out of her and propelling her across the chamber to land in a tangled mass.

"That's enough, Roujin!" commanded High Speaker Caewyn.

"I say when it's enough!" replied High Speaker Roujin menacingly, "Get to your feet."

The pain in Adessa's stomach was on fire and she was sure she had broken a few ribs and her head was ringing from hitting the mosaic floor but she answered the High Speaker's demand and drag herself to her feet.

"That's good, no Enshyi should accept defeat," said High Speaker Roujin as he took a defensive pose. "Now let's see how much more you can endure."

Adessa took up her offensive pose and started to circle her target, this wasn't so she could find an opening in his defence but rather she just wanted a chance to regain her senses.

Once her head felt relatively clear Adessa began testing the High Speaker's guard, the attacks were easily defended but Adessa noticed that the High Speaker kept letting his blade fall slightly too early after parrying her attacks.

It could be a trap.

"Battle is not a time for second guessing, you must decide and act," said OathKeeper.

"You're right."

Adessa attacked again but as the High Speaker lowered his blade she drove a second strike towards his armoured ribs, but to her amazement OathKeeper's tip merely scratched off the side of his armour.

"If your opponent gives you an opening make sure you don't waste it."

So, it was a trap, the High Speaker had wanted to see if she could inflict any damage on him and she had failed but there was no time to berate herself as the High Speaker quickly began pressing Adessa, he wielded his sword with practiced mastery, no movement was wasted and every strike was fast and strong, it was clear that the High Speaker had been going soft on her and was only just starting to show a glimpse of his true power. Adessa couldn't believe how stupid she had been of course there was no way she could win against one of the High Speakers.

I should just yield.

"Forget about the pain and focus on the battle," sounded OathKeeper's voice.

"Easy for you to say," replied Adessa as she kept retreating on her tired legs.

"I am your sword, I feel what you feel, open yourself to me and I'll show you what we can do together."

"Fine."

Adessa dove deeper than she ever had into her Voice and suddenly OathKeeper was there, his spirit was rich with strength and wisdom.

"Do you see now, my Speaker, if we are one our power grows."

The blade of the High Speaker met OathKeeper but this time the blades were more equal and Adessa wasn't pushed back as far as before, than another strike landed and again Adessa moved back even less than the last, finally another strike hit OathKeeper and Adessa didn't move at all and then both blades became locked in a tight struggle.

"Well I'll be damned, it seems you've got some talent after all," said High Speaker Roujin, a smile creeping into his hard eyes.

Adessa tried to continue pushing forward but suddenly her whole body felt heavy and she found herself falling to the ground.

Adessa awoke in the ring of Blood Roses, but something wasn't right the world around her was missing something.

Looking around Adessa realised that everything was grey, the Roses should have been a rich red and the grass a sea of bright green, instead they were a lifeless grey, Adessa looked down at her arms and found that they too were grey.

Where am I?

In response to Adessa's thought the voice of High Speaker Caewyn shook through the world of grey, "Can you hear me, Adessa?"

"Yes, but where are you?"

"I'm talking to you through the Voice."

"What!"

"Adessa, you've gone too far into the spirit world and are currently in a catatonic state, you have to let go and come back to us."

"But I can feel the power, I mean I was fighting on par with High Speaker Roujin."

"That you were, my dear, but you need to learn to control your Voice, all of the High Speaker's including myself could feel the power within you but it was erratic and there is nothing worse than a Speaker who cannot control themselves."

"You think I can't control myself?" replied Adessa venomously.

"I think that's evident with the current situation, now release your Voice and come back."

Adessa took a deep breath and begrudgingly began to release her hold on the spirit world, she could feel the power around her dispersing and in the blink of an eye she was back in the Chamber of Elements, looking up at the ceiling.

"Nice of you to join us again," said High Speaker Rasesso smiling.

"That was quite the performance, wouldn't you agree Roujin," added High Speaker Zydar.

"Humph, she's got some talent I'll give her that but as far as her swordsmanship goes she's barely qualified to hold that sword."

"Adessa's barely been training a month, imagine what she'll be able to do with more time," said Caewyn as he helped Adessa to a sitting position.

"He does have a point after all I've never seen one so young as Adessa show such potential," said High Speaker Zydar.

"I agree," said High Speaker Rasesso.

"There's no convincing you three is there, fine you continue training her in the ways of Forest Speaking Caewyn, but she'll learn her sword-play from me."

"That's fine with me as long as Adessa doesn't mind."

Suddenly all eyes were on Adessa, she didn't want to be taught by High Speaker Roujin but she couldn't turn him down, it would be a grave insult to refuse training from a High Speaker let alone one as skilled in the ways of the sword as High Speaker Roujin.

"I would be honoured for you to teach me High Speaker."

"Let's see if you think that after a week of training."

"That can wait, right now Adessa needs some time to rest, I mean I can tell just from looking at her that some of her ribs are broken and we'll have to deal with them before they become an issue." Concern was clear in Caewyn's voice, "I'm going to wrap you in a cocoon which will aid with the healing you'll find yourself feeling tired but don't fight it just relax and let yourself fall asleep."

"Thank you, High Speaker."

High Speaker Caewyn tore off part of his vessel and began working it within his hands. Every part of Adessa ached, her face and hands were covered in cuts and scrapes, searing pain penetrated her ribs and her head was ringing uncontrollably.

"Now relax, Adessa, and let the cocoon do its job," said High Speaker Caewyn as he placed the small part of his vessel on Adessa.

The cocoon quickly began growing over Adessa and before she knew it she was looking at the inside of the cocoon, almost immediately she felt drowsy, her eyes growing heavier with every second.

"I'll take you home," said Caewyn before Adessa finally gave into the cocoon's effects.

Chapter 11

"Again!"

As Vaeliria's punch came at him, Caleb threw his own arm down into Vaeliria's knocking the punch aside, before quickly countering with a punch of his own to his tutor's ribs. Vaeliria moved away with the punch dispersing most of the damage that would have been inflicted, but rather than press the attack Caleb stood where he was, after all the purpose of the drill was to practice his guard and counter-attacking ability.

"You're getting better," said Vaeliria as she dropped back into her fighting stance. "But let's see how you deal with this."

Before Caleb knew what was going on Vaeliria lunged forward and threw a sharp jab straight towards his face. Instinct was the only thing that allowed Caleb to block the blow before it came crashing into his already swollen face.

"You've left your body wide open."

Before Caleb could react Vaeliria delivered two swift hooks to his ribs, the blows were just as hard as usual and Caleb immediately dropped his hands to his sides.

"Never drop your hands!"

"Why's that?" said Caleb through gritted teeth.

"Because now I can do this." Vaeliria delivered a heavy reverse hand punch to Caleb's solar-plexus.

The air was immediately forced from Caleb's lungs in a guttural jerk, but before he could collapse to the floor Vaeliria delivered a quick jab to his chin which she quickly followed up with a powerful hook that knocked what little sense was left in his head onto the floor of the training room.

Caleb opened his eyes sometime later to find that he was flat on his back. Vaeliria stood over him looking on impassively whilst Lucianna was knelt beside him inspecting his wounds.

"Are you alright?" asked Lucianna as she cupped his head in her hands.

"Yeah just great, I mean it's only the fifth time this morning, I find myself looking at the ceiling," replied Caleb sarcastically.

With the help of Lucianna Caleb sat up, pain laced through his arms as he used them for support.

Not sure I can take much more of this.

"That's it for this morning," said Vaeliria as if reading his thought. "Go freshen up and get something to eat."

Caleb nodded gingerly in response.

With that Vaeliria walked out of the training room leaving Caleb and Lucianna alone.

Again, with the help of Lucianna Caleb managed to get to his feet but as he stood, and looked down at the hard-wooden floor, he found himself thinking that it looked quite comfortable.

Maybe I'll just stay here.

Shaking the thought from his mind Caleb willed his legs forward, he managed a few steps before he stumbled. Surprisingly his face didn't meet the floor as Lucianna caught him and draped his arm over her shoulder.

The walk back to his room felt like a trial sent from the Firstborn, each step Caleb took sent a wave of pain through his entire body but he made it back to his room nonetheless, although the only reason he did was because Lucianna was practically carrying him.

Dropping onto his bed Caleb didn't feel like moving for the rest of his life. The feathered mattress felt like the caress of an angel. His body began to sink into the embrace but then Lucianna's voice brought him back to the present.

"Do you need any assistance in getting changed?"

"Nah I'll manage," replied Caleb smiling half-heartedly.

"Okay, be sure to put the poultice on and I'll meet you in the canteen, I think it's porridge today," said Lucianna walking out of the room.

Caleb sighed, he hated putting the healing poultice on, the soft green mass smelt terrible and stung like crazy, which left him itchy and smelling like a rubbish heap for the rest of the day.

C'mon get up.

Dragging himself up out of bed Caleb stripped off his sweat covered sparring tunic and his equally soiled shorts and picked up the small clay jar that sat on the bedside table.

As Caleb opened the jars lid an acrid smell leapt out to assault his nose and claw at his throat.

Shit smells nearly as bad as the lower city.

Doing his best not to gag Caleb took a large handful of the green pulp that sat within the jar and tentatively began to apply it to his numerous wounds. As the poultice touched the deep bruises that lined his jaw and body Caleb felt a wave of pain radiate from the wounds but within a matter of seconds the pain subsided and then disappeared completely.

Once he had finally finished applying the poultice Caleb threw on his uniform and made his way to the canteen in search of his first meal of the day.

The canteen of the *Zephyrus* was absolutely massive in scale. The ceiling rose high overhead, the intricate multi-armed lanterns that hung from the ceiling's body filled the hall with a bright light whilst row upon row of long tables and benches lined the floor in tight lines. At the far end of the canteen were the kitchens and another long row of tables where all the food was laid out when it was ready to be served.

As soon as he stepped off the lift Caleb felt completely overwhelmed by the wave of activity that swept over him. The noise and commotion was unlike anything he had experienced in such tight quarters. He was used to eating alone in a secluded spot whereas the best he had managed here was to sit in the far corner where he at least had a couple seats worth of space and could eat in relative peace.

Taking a deep breath Caleb made his way through the press of bodies and over to the serving line and grabbed a tray where he waited behind a short stocky fellow who he thought was called Edward or was it Lincoln he wasn't sure, there were too many faces and names to remember everyone, but the thought was quickly lost as his stomach rumbled in hunger. Thankfully the line moved quickly enough and after a few short minutes Caleb found himself face to face with Evelyn. The head cook of the *Zephyrus* was taller than Caleb by a few inches and at least three times as wide even though he now weighed more than he had in his entire life. Her body and face were both round like an apple but she didn't have the folds of fat like many other people her size, instead she was just a large mass of a woman, her arms were almost as big as the Captain's and from the way they bulged Caleb could tell they weren't all fat.

"Morn'n, dearie," smiled Evelyn.

Taking a moment to look at her Caleb realised he had no idea how old Evelyn was, her brown hair had patches of blonde and white in it, which gave Caleb the impression that she was at least the Captain's age, but unlike the Captain she had no wrinkles around her green eyes or across her forehead which made him question his assumption.

"Morning," replied Caleb flexing his tight jaw.

"Looks like the Wolf's done some damage," said Evelyn indicating the bruises that marked Caleb's face.

"Yeah she ain't been going easy on me." Caleb rubbed a hand over his jaw, "What have we got this morning?"

"My home-made porridge, it's a family recipe don't you know," said Evelyn as she piled a scoop of the thick porridge onto Caleb's tray.

"I'm sure it is, see you at lunch and thank you," said Caleb as he walked off into the chaos of the canteen.

"It's salted beef," shouted Evelyn over Caleb's shoulder.

Dodging left and right Caleb made his way over to his usual spot, where he expected to find Lucianna waiting for him, but Luci was nowhere in sight and in her place sat Vaeliria and next to her was an old fatherly looking man, whose face was a mix of bushy beard, wrinkles and creases.

Caleb sat opposite the two.

"Caleb, I'd like you to meet Thomas."

Caleb looked at the elderly man, his eyes were still bright blue despite how old he looked.

"Nice to meet you, Thomas."

"And you, Caleb. Vaeliria here was just telling me about your training," replied Thomas with a smile. "How's it going by the way?"

Caleb pointed at his face, "As you can see, I'm taking a beating."

Thomas laughed sharply, "Ha ha, count yourself lucky."

"And whys that?" replied Caleb before taking a big mouthful of porridge.

"Because I've seen her take down four armed men with nothing but her bare hands."

"Fair enough," said Caleb around his breakfast.

"Well it was nice meeting you," said Thomas a moment later as he stood. "Vaeliria, always a pleasure, tell the Captain I'll be ready by tomorrow."

"He's the head engineer," said Caleb in disbelief as the elderly man shuffled off.

"Yes but he is a lot more than just the head engineer he's also the man that designed the *Zephyrus*."

"He designed this?" replied Caleb in even greater disbelief.

"There's much you'll learn from him."

"Wait what?"

"The Captain has requested that Thomas take you on as a student."

"But I'm your student."

"Yes but he'll be able to teach you things I never could."

"Like?"

"Understanding the structural integrity of a Skyship, how to clean a cannon so it doesn't back fire or the inner workings of a Skycore."

"Seems like I'm going be learning a lot."

Vaeliria stood, "Remember we have our language lesson at five."

"See you then."

Once breakfast was finished Caleb decided to go look for Lucianna, she had said she'd meet him for breakfast but had never showed and although he had only meet her a few weeks ago Caleb felt that was strange for her, not to mention she was the only other person on this ship who was around his age.

Walking back towards the lift Caleb passed a group of three men, two of the men were ribbing their friend as he clutched a bucket. Lucianna had told Caleb about air sickness. Apparently, the sickness was caused by the body struggling to deal with the swaying of the ship and the lower amounts of air up here in the sky, but so far Caleb hadn't shown any signs of the sickness which Luci had said was strange as it was the unofficial rite of passage for a Cadet.

Continuing on his way Caleb came to stand before the entrance to the lift.

Damn.

He hadn't learnt how to operate the lift's counterweight system yet. Vaeliria always moved the dials faster than he could comprehend and Luci had tried teaching him but so far it had been futile.

Caleb stood there for a while wondering what he was going to do when he heard the grinding and hissing of the lift. The sounds grew closer until finally the lift fell into place and the iron linked door opened revealing a short tautly built woman.

"Getting on?" asked the woman, her voice soft.

Caleb walked into the lift.

"What floor?" said the woman as she pulled the lifts door back into place.

"Medical bay."

"Going down," the woman quickly adjusted the dials of the lift's counterweight system and just like that the lift sprung into life and began its descent.

As Caleb stood waiting for the lift to reach its destination, he took glancing looks at the lifts operator. Her hair was a mixture of light and darker brown and surprisingly it was cut short.

Where have I seen her before?

And then it hit Caleb, he had seen this woman in the training room practicing with a staff.

"I've seen you training," said Caleb voicing his thought.

The woman looked genuinely surprised, "I always thought I was the first to get there."

"I train in the back with the Commander."

The woman spun around to face Caleb, "Wait what's your name?"

"Caleb."

"So the rumours are true."

"What rumours?"

"That the Captain has brought another Skelwori onto the *Zephyrus*."

"Is that a problem?"

"No," said the woman with a smile. "It's just a surprise is all."

Caleb wanted to ask more but before he could the lift arrived on the medical bay's level. A host of people all of whom looked tired and hungry stood on the other side of the lift's door and rather than keep them from Evelyn's amazing cooking with his questions, Caleb stepped out of the lift and continued his search for Luci.

Caleb hadn't found Lucianna in the main ward of the medical bay, so he went to look for her in her room, walking towards her door Caleb could hear Lucianna humming a gentle tune to herself, he stood behind the door and listened, it was a carefree sound and it stirred emotions he had thought long dead, after several minutes of joyously listening he finally knocked on the door.

"Come in."

Caleb entered to find Luci's room filled with mountains of parchment and tomes, some of which were nearly as tall as he was.

"Mother, is that you?" said Luci from behind a stack of especially heavy looking tomes.

"I'm afraid not just me."

"Caleb," Luci's face appeared from behind the stack of tomes, "I'm so sorry about not meeting you for breakfast, Vaeliria said she wanted to speak to you so I took the time to come and study."

"That's alright you'll just have to make it up to me," said Caleb as he made his way across the room.

Treading as lightly and carefully as possible Caleb danced around the towers of leather and parchment until finally he reached the stack where Luci hid.

Lucianna sat on the floor with a tome atop her crossed legs. Looking at the tome Caleb could see several diagrams showing different parts of the body and injuries they had sustained, a broken forearm was on one page, a fractured skull lay on the other page, accompanying the diagrams were a series of tightly written words, each completely beyond Caleb.

"So what are we reading?" said Caleb as he sat down beside Luci.

Luci looked up from the diagram she was studying, "You want to read this?"

"Way I see it I need to learn how to read your language," lied Caleb, "might as well start somewhere and who better to teach me than you."

Luci smiled and Caleb found himself thankful that his new identity allowed him the chance to learn to read.

"Well," said Luci bringing Caleb out of his thoughts, "I'm currently reading up on the different types of breaks that can occur within the skeletal system and the complications that can follow if they are left unattended."

"Sounds complicated."

"It's not as bad as it looks, once you understand the language," replied Luci mocking Caleb good naturedly.

"You best get to teaching me then."

Minutes turned to hours and before he knew it Caleb was having to run back through the decks of the *Zephyrus* with Lucianna to make it to his lesson with Vaeliria. They quickly made it back to the lift and luckily it hadn't left yet, picking up his pace Caleb ran into the lift before it could close shocking the occupant in the process, Luci quickly followed.

"Sor... sorry about that," said Caleb in between breaths.

"That's quite alright, my dear fellow, you and your young lady friend here seem in quite the rush, which floor will you be needing," replied the tall well-groomed man who Caleb had shocked.

"We need to get to the training room," replied Luci.

"Very well."

After a quick ride Caleb and Luci hopped out of the lift and began running off towards the training room, shouting their thanks over their shoulders to the man.

Bursting through the doors of the training room Caleb zigzagged around the other members of the crew who were training and headed into the back room. Vaeliria was already there sat down on the floor in mediation.

"You're late," said Vaeliria standing.

"Sorry, Commander. I was reading with Luci and I lost track of time."

"For your lateness, you shall perform a hundred push-ups tomorrow morning." Vaeliria then turned her attention towards Luci.

Luci took a step towards Vaeliria and bowed her head, "I must apologise as well you see I'm partly to blame for

Caleb's lateness, I wouldn't let him leave until he finished the page we were on."

A hint of a smile marked Vaeliria's lips, "If that's the case then you can join Caleb in his punishment, let's say twenty push-ups for you."

Luci bowed low in response.

"You're relieved of duty now medical officer Estrada." said Vaeliria dismissing Luci.

Caleb smiled at Luci as she left and she returned the smile.

"Stand at attention, Cadet!" shouted Vaeliria in Skelworian as soon as Luci had left.

Caleb stood as straight as a board.

Vaeliria began walking around him, her eyes looking for the slightest sign of slack in his stance, "What is your duty?"

"To protect and serve the people of Angard," responded Caleb in his best Skelworian.

"Good," said Vaeliria dropping back into the Angardian tongue. "Now read this to me."

Vaeliria handed Caleb a piece of parchment. Written in a tight script were a series of Skelworian words. After looking at the words for a few moments Caleb realised he knew how to read them, he found it funny that although he was Angardian he actually read Skelwori better but he thought that was a good thing as it would help authenticate his false beginnings.

Caleb began reading aloud, "By the light of Oludin, I Koldar of Clan Frostfinger declare that from this day forth I will serve and protect the people of Skelwor as their king until the day I die. If I" Caleb found himself stumped by the next word.

"Falter," said Vaeliria from over his shoulder.

Caleb started the second part of the passage again, "If I 'Faaullteer'," Caleb inwardly cursed at how stupid he sounded mouthing the word like some simpleton but left the word behind and carried on reading, "in my duty, may my soul be torn asunder in the fires of Aludin's abyss by the Betrayer himself and may I never see the glory of Oludin's hall nor the joy of fighting with my brothers at the End of Days."

Taking a deep breath Caleb turned to Vaeliria to await her critique.

"Very good," said Vaeliria with a slight nod, "both your pace and pronunciation are better, but try to relax, your words sound brittle where they should sound strong and don't over extend the vowels, they need to be short and sharp, got it."

"Is there anything else?" said Caleb sarcastically.

"Yes actually," said Vaeliria walking over to a case that lay a few feet away.

The case was a made of dark rosewood that had been polished to a mirror shine.

Vaeliria held the case out in front of Caleb, "I'd like you to have these."

The locks of the case made a satisfying snap as Caleb flipped them open. Inside the case lying on a bed of red velvet were a pair of deadly elegant dirk's. The handles were ebony wrapped in leather, which had metal studs dotted along its face whilst the sheaths of either blade were made of a patterned iron. Caleb lifted one of the dirks free and drew it from its sheath, twelve inches of polished iron made up the blade, both sides of which were edged to a razor sharpness.

"Why daggers?" asked Caleb inspecting the blade further.

"Because your greatest asset is your speed, also these will allow you to stay armed even in tight quarters, go on see how they feel."

Caleb drew the other dirk from its sheath, he stood there for a moment just feeling the weight of the dirks in his hands, the blades didn't feel that heavy, but when he began swinging them back and forth he noticed just how much strength and dexterity someone would need to have to wield these weapons effectively. Sheathing the dirks Caleb put them back in their case.

"How do they feel?"

"I can see why you chose them but it still feels awkward."

"That's to be expected, from now on you when you come for your language lessons you shall also be practicing armed combat."

"You trying to bury me in the ground?"

All Caleb got in reply was a wolfish smile.

Caleb carried the wooden case back to his room with expert care, these blades were now his most prized possessions and he wasn't about to go and damage them outside of battle. Hiding the case under his bed Caleb quickly got changed before heading back to the canteen for dinner.

Dinner was just what Evelyn said it would be, salted beef cooked in a viscous gravy with fresh carrots and potato. Some of the other crew members were complaining about the dish but Caleb couldn't understand why they would be moaning, after all having a warm meal was the best part of his day, it helped him forget about his training and subsequent injuries for a few moments and just enjoy the warm satisfied sensation of the meal.

Caleb made it to his usual table, Lucianna was already there eating her meal with her usual gracefulness. Plonking himself down into the seat opposite Luci, Caleb began tucking into his own meal, despite its appearance the meal tasted fantastic, the salty beef was the perfect complement to the freshness of the carrot and the earthy texture of the potato, the enjoyment of the meal was interrupted however by the insults of two men who sat across from Luci and Caleb. Acne marked the face of one of the men giving his face an angry red complexion, the other was a fat faced man with tiny eyes.

"Why don't you fuck off back to your frozen waste sheep-fucker," said the acne riddled man.

"Yeah we don't need another savage aboard this ship," added fat face.

Caleb ignored the two men. After all he had experienced far worse than name calling down in the lower city, but his calm was quickly broken as the two men began taunting Luci for sitting with him.

"Oi, love, what the hell you doing sitting with that pasty bastard?" said acne.

"Maybe she's standing in for the sheep," said fat face.

Both burst out into raucous laughter. Caleb noted how Luci was beginning to slump in her seat clearly the insults were affecting her.

"Do you have a problem with me and my friend?" asked Caleb in Skelworian.

The two men's laughter died.

"We don't understand barbarian you halfwit," replied fat face.

"Oh I'm sorry," replied Caleb switching to Angardian "I thought two Skyknights would at least be able to understand simple Skelworian, my mistake, let me repeat myself, do you have a problem with me and my friend?" Caleb stretched the syllables of every word as if he was talking to morons.

"Yeah we've got a problem with you, you pale bastard, what the feck you doing on our ship?" said acne, spittle flying from his mouth.

"Your ship?" Caleb looked around the room mocking confusion. "If I'm correct this ship's captained by Abraham Brightfellow not an acne riddled gopher and a fat midget."

The two men shot up from their seats and scrambled over their table at Caleb, grabbing his fork Caleb sprung over his own table and jammed it down into the hand of acne, the high-pitched scream he let out got the attention of other nearby men and women. Now that one of his attackers was preoccupied Caleb turned his attention towards fat face, the man swung a meaty fist at Caleb, from his time training with Vaeliria, Caleb was used to her speed and compared this man's fist seemed to be floating through the air at a snail's pace, ducking past the punch

Caleb threw a heavy hook to the man's ribs and he went down like a lead weight.

"I think I broke this guy's ribs," said Caleb turning to Luci.

Lucianna was there in an instant, she bent down and told the man to calm down, but he didn't listen so Caleb bent down and slapped him in the face.

"Listen to her she's a medical officer."

The man calmed down at that and his breathing became easier as he did.

"Good now come with me and we'll get you and your friend patched up," said Lucianna as she helped the man to his feet.

Caleb walked over to the other man who still had the fork in his hand, "Come on you better get that treated." The man looked up at Caleb with utter hatred in his eyes but he did as he was told.

"First your master sends you to me, then you go and bring these two in here," said Doctor Estrada bandaging fat face's ribs.

"They needed to learn some manners," replied Caleb matter-of-factly.

"Well maybe you could teach them without breaking their bones or stabbing them."

Doctor Estrada finished her work, told the man not to move about too much and sent him to lie down in a nearby bed.

It looked like Doctor Estrada was going to say something to Caleb but she decided against it and sent him on his way.

Caleb wanted to check in on Lucianna but he knew better than to press the issue against Doctor Estrada, so he turned and left.

The following morning Caleb was back in the training room with Vaeliria and Luci. He was in the process of finishing his punishment, pain radiated throughout his entire upper body, Luci had finished her punishment and was cheering him on which he appreciated.

"Ninety-seven," said Vaeliria.

The pain was nearly unbearable but Caleb wasn't about to give up, he continued on through the pain.

"Ninety-eight."

You can do it, ignore the pain, its nothing, you're stronger than it.

"Ninety-nine."

"Come on, Caleb," said Luci cheering.

Caleb pushed himself back up.

"One hundred."

Caleb immediately fell flat on his face, now that he had finished he could feel just how tired and worn his muscles were, everywhere ached and it felt like fire was rushing through his veins, how Vaeliria thought he would be able to spar now he didn't know.

"Here drink," said Luci bringing over a cup of water.

Using all his remaining strength Caleb pushed himself up to a sitting position and took the cup from Luci before draining it in three deep gulps, "Cheers."

"On your feet cadet."

Caleb pushed himself to his feet, the muscles in his chest cried out as he did. Vaeliria stood opposite him in her fighting pose, Caleb took up his own and they began.

It was a horrible session. Caleb was too tired to properly fight and he found himself hitting the floor more than usual, after the twelfth time of which Vaeliria called it a day and told him to get ready, because today was his first day with Thomas.

The ride down to the Skycore was made in silence, Caleb had wanted to ask Vaeliria what he should expect down here in the depths of the *Zephyrus*, but with his chest and arms still burning plus the throbbing he felt in his jaw Caleb kept quiet and did his best to forget his many injuries.

Eventually the lift slowed before stopping all together.

The scene before Caleb astonished him, the room housing the Skycore was by far the largest room in the *Zephyrus*, Caleb guessed it was double the size of the canteen which could seat every member of the crew.

Vaeliria pulled the lifts door open and Caleb followed her out into the chaotic room, dozens of people were down here, some sat at workbenches working on various contraptions, some of which looked ridiculous while others seemed to come from a completely alien place. Several robed individuals sat at other tables reading from heavy tomes and writing notes down, the hammering of metal turned Caleb's attention away from the scribes. Sat at an anvil pounding a red-hot piece of metal into shape was Riktor, the smith's muscular arms rippled with every blow of his mighty hammer, a heavily muscled woman was doing the same on the anvil next to him and in the middle of all the chaotic activity stood the Skycore.

The giant crystal stood nearly as tall as the room and was housed inside a massive glass enclosure which had dozens of pipes running off it in every direction. An eerie blue light radiated from the crystal in waves bathing the room in colour. Standing next to the gigantic crystal was Thomas.

The old man seemed to be in his element down here, he stood a little taller and moved easier than he had when Caleb had first met him, turning he caught sight of Vaeliria and Caleb and smiled, the wrinkles and creases in his skin deepened as he did, making him look even older than he already did, despite that his eyes looked young and clear, shooing off other members of his staff Thomas came over towards Caleb.

"Nice and early I see," said Thomas grasping Vaeliria's hand.

"Good to see you've got everything in order down here," replied Vaeliria.

"I can handle these youngens."

"I'm sure you can, but can you handle this one," said Vaeliria nodding at Caleb.

"Ah you've caused quite the commotion, all of my staff are talking about your little demonstration in the canteen yesterday."

"It needed to be done," shrugged Caleb.

"Yes I'm sure it did, but you haven't come down here to talk gossip, no you've come down here to learn the arts of an Engineer and I made a promise to the Captain that I would teach you all I can." Thomas began walking off towards the Skycore, "Well are you coming or not?"

Caleb walked after the master engineer, when he looked back for Vaeliria she was already gone, lost amongst the crowd.

Caleb followed behind Thomas in silence, they walked around the core in silence, the ethereal light made Caleb's hairs stand on end, "Do you know anything about engineering?" asked Thomas finally.

"No, sir, haven't the faintest idea," replied Caleb honestly.

Thomas stroked his long beard as he thought about this reply, Caleb felt awkward in the old man's gaze, normally Caleb would stare right back but there was something there that made him look away.

"Are you being serious?"

"Yes, sir, ain't many engineers in the wastes of Skelwor and I didn't learn anything while in Actalia."

"Then you're just the student I want," said Thomas smiling.

Caleb was surprised he thought the old man would be annoyed by this, most of the professionals he had seen in the upper city wouldn't take someone on unless they had come out of their crafts respective college.

"And why am I the student you want?"

"Those arses in Actalia don't know anything, they all sit around getting fat and letting their minds rot and do you know why they do this."

Caleb guessed he was supposed to ask why so he did, "Why's that?"

"Because they've lost what it means to be an engineer, there's always more to learn and nothing is perfect, I had to sweat and bleed for this," Thomas swept a hand around the room, "to be what it is and still I'm not happy with it, but my 'colleagues' would rather sit on their laurels than keep working."

"You know I like the way you think."

Now it was Thomas' turn to be caught off guard, "Please go on."

Caleb remembered what Vaeliria had told him about the creed that Skelwori Nomads live by, "It's like we Nomads say you've always got to keep moving, you stay still, you die."

"It seems you and I aren't so different in our ideals, now come along I need to go get your studying material."

Caleb fell in beside the engineer.

"And enough with the sir crap, you'll make me feel old, call me Thom."

"Sure thing, Thom."

Thom's quarters were just as chaotic as the Skycore, dozens of books lay around the room in tight heaps. Lining every inch of the walls were hundreds of designs, each one looked even more alien than the contraptions Caleb had seen some of the other engineers wielding. Thom made his way across the room quickly grabbing a couple of books off shelves as he did, he then grabbed another three off his desk before turning back to Caleb.

"Don't worry these aren't for you," said Thom with a smile. "Gustav needs these volumes for his study." Thom moved the books into a neat pile on his desk. "No, this one is for you."

Thom walked over to one of his two bookshelves and pulled out a thick leather bound book, he crossed back across the room and handed it to Caleb, "This is Fundaments of Skycore Technology by Androssa Guilarmo and Stephen Del Fra, you'll read the first chapter by next week, then I'll test you to see if you remember any of it, that's all for now."

Caleb stood there dumbfounded, he had tried to steal this very tome not more than a month ago and now he was being given it to study for himself.

I must be dreaming.

"Is everything okay?"

Caleb looked up from the tome to find Thom looking at him with a quizzical gaze, "One chapter shouldn't be a problem."

"The first chapters the worst part," replied Thom. "Now you're free to make a start on it here or you can go back to your quarters and read it there."

"I'd rather go back to my quarters the heat doesn't really agree with me just yet," replied Caleb lying, the real reason he wanted to go back to his room was so he could get Luci to help him with the reading of this tome.

"That's fine just make sure you've read the first chapter by next week."

"Will do."

"Okay then off with yah, I've got to get these books over to Gustav."

"Aye see you next week."

Chapter 12

Wind howled through the great forest of Alfheim, whipping up leaves and twigs into cyclones of debris, every tree apart from the GrandOak bent in the wake of the gale. The creatures of the forest were nowhere to be seen, the foxes and wolves had returned to their dens, while the rabbits, badgers and otters took shelter in their burrows, even the Enshyi who called the forest home had hidden away in their treetop city, but one man found himself out in the gale.

Darrius crept tentatively through a line of Maples, as the first outsider to step foot inside the great forest of Alfheim in over a hundred years he knew that danger was only a hairsbreadth away at any moment but then again when hadn't it been. Over the course of his fifty summers Darrius had travelled to nearly every corner of the Five Kingdoms in her Holiness's service and throughout it all danger had been the only constant, but at least this time around his task wasn't to kill someone. No, this time around all he had to do was deliver a message to a Speaker by the name of Sakala Shinepacer.

Peeking out into the next clearing Darrius stood listening, if anyone found him here he was as good as dead, he shook the thought away.

No, no one will find you, you're too skilled and too careful to get caught.

With feet, as soft as a feathers touch Darrius swiftly made his way across the clearing and ducked down behind the new tree line and not a moment too soon, as two Enshyi emerged from behind a thicket and walked mere inches from where Darrius stood. Darrius pressed himself lower to the ground and stayed there for a few minutes whilst he stretched his hearing to its limit.

Nothing.

Picking himself back up Darrius moved silently and quickly from one hiding spot to another, until finally he came to the hardest part of his journey.

Separating him from the tree topped city in which his target lay was seventy feet of oak.

With a deep inhale Darrius moved his right hand to the choker that lined his throat and the flawless crystal known as the Eye that sat there and quickly chanted the incantation he needed. Exhaling Darrius slowly pressed himself up against the tree.

I hate this part.

Slowly Darrius's hands and feet sunk into the bark of the tree, the feeling that he was losing his sense of self began to creep into his mind but Darrius shrugged the feeling off and began his climb to the city above.

As soon as his shrouded feet hit the wooden walkway Darrius looked around, there was no one in sight but the light that escaped from the homes that surrounded him told him that he still needed to be careful as one wrong move could result in him being surrounded and imprisoned.

Darrius turned away from the mass of warm lights, from the Oracle's note he needed to head to the farthest corner of the city's western side.

As he moved through the city with the ease of a man who had lived there his entire life Darrius found his thoughts turning to that of the Oracle and whether or not she still looked as he remembered, after all it had been four years since he had last seen her Holiness.

I guess you'll just have to wait and see.

Coming back to the present, Darrius looked around, it didn't look like anyone would be leaving their homes tonight, he couldn't blame them what with the wind as wild as it was and the heavy rain that accompanied it.

Darrius continued along the wooden walkways of the Enshyi's city and a few minutes later he stood soaked in front of the Speaker's home. It was just as the Oracle said it would be, a small humble abode made from the upper section of one of the oaks.

I best find this Speaker.

With that Darrius climbed up to the second-floor window, but what he saw shocked him, inside sat a young girl. Darrius immediately noted just how different the girl look when compared to the two Enshyi he had seen earlier, where their skin had been a pale white this girls was tanned like an almond, and she was a lot smaller than he would have thought possible for an Enshyi, maybe he had gotten the wrong house. No this was the right house he was sure of it, but who was this girl?

The sound of soft footsteps intermingled amongst the downpour broke Darrius from his reverie and he scrambled up into the high branches of the oak cursing his foolishness.

Adessa could have sworn someone was looking at her, but when she turned to look out the window of her room all she saw was the dark night sky, the wind had picked up and thick clouds blotted out the moonlight leaving the night darker than usual. Adessa hated nights like this, it reminded her just how much power the elements commanded. Why couldn't the Wind Speakers control the wind better or the Water Speakers the rain. Adessa shook the thought away, it was wrong for her to think like that.

Moving back over to her bed Adessa picked up the book she had been reading. The tale of Daeron the Silent was one of her favourites, the story spoke to her, Daeron was an outcast in his time much like Adessa herself, she read the last part of the chapter she was on, this was her favourite part of the story where Daeron finally found his Voice.

At the heading of the next chapter, Adessa put the book back in the case under her bed, as she did she heard her mother call to her from downstairs despite the racket caused by the wind. Adessa quickly ran out of her room and towards the stairs where she was met with her mother stood at the bottom with a smile on her face.

"What is it, mother?" said Adessa as she began

descending the stairs.

"Nothing important, my dear. I just wanted to have supper with you," replied Sakala walking off into the pantry.

Adessa followed her mother into their small pantry, three cupboards lined the walls each was filled with fruits, berries, nuts and vegetables from the forest. Sakala grabbed an apple, a handful of blackberries and some pine nuts before walking into the den, Adessa followed suit, pinching a handful of cranberries off one shelf, followed by a couple of plump tomatoes and then a handful of cashews. The den of Adessa's home was a quaint little room, a long wooden couch sat at the back of the room, stuffed cushions made the couch more comfortable, an old rocking chair that had belonged to Adessa's grandmother still took up the corner of the room, the sight of that chair always brought back memories of staying up late reading stories. Sakala took a seat on the couch and Adessa joined her.

Sakala let out a sigh, "It's been a long day."

"How are the other apprentices doing?" asked Adessa, placing a cranberry in her mouth.

"Radagael and Helanroes are showing real promise but their progress has stunted in recent weeks, both are too proud to listen to what me and the other Speakers are telling them, how's your training going?"

"My training with the GrandOak and High Speaker Caewyn is fine but I hate training with High Speaker Roujin he barely says anything and he doesn't hold back, I feel like he's trying to kill me."

"That's Roujin, he teaches through actions not words, next time you train with him look for the subtle tells he gives."

"I'll try but most of the time I find myself on the floor."

"But you get up and that shows you have more heart than most of my apprentices."

Adessa and her mother enjoyed the rest of their supper in silence, once she was finished Adessa said goodnight to her mother and went back to her room and jumped into bed, where she quickly fell asleep from fatigue.

"I am your sword, I am your shield, I am your Sentinel standing watch in the night, no matter the cost I shall do what is required of me for the good of the Five Kingdoms."

Finishing his oath to the Oracle, Darrius peered down from his perch and caught sight of the Speaker he was supposed to talk with looking out of the window of her home's den and into the wildness of the night, it had been her footsteps that he had heard, but that didn't excuse him for making such a basic mistake.

You'll have time to berate yourself once you're done with your mission.

Shaking himself free of his thoughts Darrius climbed around the trunk of the tree to the other side of the house and snuck in through the window. The Speaker's room was homely much like the house itself. A warm looking bed took up most of the room. A small table stood opposite the bed, an array of books lined the table's surface and in the corner of the room stood a majestic wardrobe. Darrius could hear the Speaker moving through the house towards him but he stayed calm, experience had taught him that if he showed any sign of agitation then that would only cause his target to panic and make his job ten times harder.

The door to the room opened and in stepped the Speaker, her face turned from an image of contentment to an aspect of anger and fear as she caught sight of Darrius.

"Who are you to disturb the home of a Speaker?" said the Speaker in the Enshyi tongue.

Darrius could feel the crackle of magic in the air.

"My apologies for the intrusion, Lady Shinepacer but I bring a message of the utmost importance," replied Darrius slowly in the same tongue.

The Speaker seemed to relax slightly at hearing her native tongue and Darrius took a moment to silently thank the Oracle for forcing him to master the complex language.

"You're not Enshyi," said the Speaker bringing Darrius back to the moment.

"No milady, I'm just a simple man come to deliver a message," replied Darrius pulling down his thief's kerchief.

The Speaker did well to hide her shock, but her pupils dilated ever so slightly giving her true feelings away. If he was anyone else Darrius would have missed the cue but to his well-trained eyes this was as obvious as if she had openly gasped.

"You are Sakala Shinepacer Speaker of the Forest?" said Darrius taking a step forward.

The Speaker nodded but took a step back and the magic in the air thickened.

It was obvious she was afraid of him, he couldn't blame her she probably had never seen a man before, let alone one as scarred and beaten as Darrius himself.

"I mean you and your kind no harm, my name is Darrius and I have been asked to bring you a message."

The Speaker said nothing, so Darrius took that as his cue to continue.

"A great darkness is coming; you have to tell the High Speakers to be prepared."

Again, Sakala was quiet, Darrius knew she didn't believe him, but then the Oracle had said as much.

Darrius pulled a piece of sealed parchment from his pack, "This is a letter from my master explaining everything in detail." Darrius held the parchment out to Sakala, who took it in a shaky hand.

"May the sun shine on you, Lady Shinepacer."

With that Darrius sprang back out of the room and disappeared off into the night.

Adessa awoke the following morning feeling clear headed and happy, spending a little bit of time with her mother always cheered her up.

Jumping out of bed Adessa stretched before going to freshen herself up. As she walked through her house towards the washroom Adessa called out to her mother but there was no reply.

Mother must have left for her morning class already.

After having finished washing and toweling herself down Adessa went back to her room and threw on her apprentice robes, before she sat down on the stool by her vanity and began brushing her hair.

Half a candlemark later Adessa finally had all the knots out of her hair and she carefully tied it up into a tail.

Feeling good about the day to come Adessa made her way downstairs and into the pantry. Grabbing a few berries and nuts from the cupboards that lined the pantry Adessa made her way into the den, where she ate her breakfast quickly and was just about to leave for the GrandOak's island when she heard her mother come back.

"Adessa, are you here?"

"Yes, mother," replied Adessa walking through the pantry. "I was just about to leave for the GrandOak's island, is something the matter?".

"You know High Speaker Caewyn sits on the Angardian counsel?" said Sakala ignoring Adessa's question.

Adessa instantly knew something was wrong, "What's going on?"

"In return for allowing an Enshyi to sit on their counsel the Angardians have requested that a Speaker becomes a Skyknight."

Adessa's heart stopped at her mother's words, she knew exactly what she was going to say next.

"The High Speakers have agreed to this and have chosen you to be the Speaker who goes to the Angardian Kingdom."

Adessa stood silent, she didn't know what to say, the High Speakers wanted her to leave everything behind and travel to a Kingdom she knew nothing about, how could

125

they do this to her, she had been progressing and finally felt some sense of self and it was all for nothing.

"They want me to leave Alfheim?" said Adessa still dumbfounded.

"Adessa, this is for the good of Alfheim."

All the pent-up anger that had been inside of Adessa burst forth, "For the good of Alfheim! What about my feelings?"

"Adessa you have to understand."

"Oh I understand all right, ship the half breed off to the distant Kingdom, that will make everyone happy."

Surprised by Adessa's outburst Sakala was silent for a few moments, but when she spoke her voice was cold and full of authority, "You swore on the tome of Enelya that you would act in the best interests of Alfheim."

Adessa couldn't take this anymore, she ran past her mother and out into town.

The homes of the other Enshyi passed by in a haze as Adessa ran along the walkways of Alfheim's treetop city. Adessa could also feel everyone judging her and it made her want to scream.

Why does everyone look at me like I'm some kind of animal.

A little while later Adessa arrived at the lift, the guard on duty said nothing as Adessa stepped inside the lift, he barely even looked at her, it was as if he thought merely looking at her would affect him somehow.

After an agonisingly slow descent the lift finally touched down on the forest floor and Adessa bolted like a hare being chased. The trees and shrubs of the forest pressed in on Adessa from all sides and it felt like she was going to be swallowed at any moment.

Breaking through the oppressive tree line Adessa ran straight at the lake of life and summoned a bridge of vines thus allowing herself passage to the GrandOak's island.

Making it to the island Adessa dropped to the ground breathless.

"Are you alright?" said the GrandOak.

"I have something to ask of you?" said Adessa once she had caught her breath.

"Ask away."

"I want you to tell me about my father."

Chapter 13

"You've learnt quite a lot over the past week," said Thom as he sat at his desk.

Caleb had just finished reciting the first chapter of Fundaments of Skycore technology, it had taken all his concentration to learn how to read, but he was committed and Luci turned out to be a great teacher, plus there wasn't much else for him to do when he wasn't training with Vaeliria.

A couple of days ago Caleb had taken the lift up to the deck and had been met with an amazing sight. Overhead the sky had been a painting of blue and white whilst below the vast body of the Dultasar Sea had shimmered a thousand different shades of blue and in the distance stood high peaked mountains, but the sight hadn't lasted long as Vaeliria had come straight over and dragged him back to the entrance of the lift, where she told him that he would only get in the way if he stayed on the deck as everyone needed to be able to adjust to the wind and weather at a moment's notice and no one would have the time to babysit a Skelwori Nomad who didn't know a bowline from a stopper knot.

Thom's voice brought Caleb back to the present, "One last question, my boy, if you saw a Skycore glow red instead of blue what would you do?"

"I would activate the drop mechanism set into the bottom of the ship."

"Good, but what if it jammed?"

"Then I'd have to find the jam and manually drop the Core."

"You'd risk your life to drop the Core?"

"Yes I would... the needs of the many come before the needs of one."

"Alright, I can safely say that you've learnt all you can from that chapter, now I want you to read the next chapter of Fundaments as well as the first chapter of Applications of Crystal Fraction and the Superconductivity of Vallharian steel."

Before Caleb could answer an all mighty crash rocked through the *Zephyrus*'s hull and Caleb had to drop to all fours to steady himself, surprisingly Thom managed to keep his feet under him and he quickly made his way out of his office. Caleb scrambled back to his feet and followed.

Out in the Skycore bay Caleb was met with the head of a massive javelin protruding through the hull. The sight of the gargantuan projectile had caused the engineers and workers to either flee to the safety of a higher level or scramble around trying to gather their equipment and creations, least they lose all their work. However, Caleb did spot a small handful of men and women make their way over to Thom.

As he rushed towards the group Caleb recognised Riktor and Allie, the two smiths were stood with hammers in hand. Standing closer to Thom was Gustav, the young engineer's lanky frame made him stand out amongst the bulk of his companions, the others in the group however were unknown to Caleb.

"What's the plan ere?" shouted Riktor over the panic.

"We have to get that javelin out as quickly as possible, chances are whoever's attacking us will likely be reading more," said Thom his face a grim mask of concentration. "Riktor, you and Allie smash the prongs inwards that should get it loose. Gustav, I need you to stay here with me and make sure that the Core doesn't become unstable. Giselle, take Pip and Sam up to the cannons, tell the Cannoneers to aim for the chains of the javelins, we need to get away from the enemy before they turn their attention towards the ship itself, otherwise we'll both be going down together." Thom then whirled around to look at Caleb. "Caleb, I need you to get up on deck and inform the Captain and Commander of the situation down here, everyone understand?"

Everyone acknowledged that they understood, "Good then get going."

Caleb sprinted to one of the lifts at the end of the bay, jumping in he spun the dials to move the lift to the deck, he said a quick thanks to Oludin the Allfather that Luci had finally managed to teach him how the dials worked.

As he began to ascend another javelin head burst through the hull, dozens of the crew were sent flying along with a shower of wood, most didn't get up again.

The sounds of cannon fire, splintering wood and the screams of men filled the air as Caleb slowly ascended, the lift was taking far too long, one of the counterweights must have been damaged. After the gruelingly slow ride the lift finally made it to the deck and Caleb was met with the horrific scenes of battle. The riflemen of the *Zephyrus* were taking aim at the enemy, their flintlock rifles fired in a coordinated assault, behind the riflemen were dozens of bodies strewn across the deck, some looked like they were just sleeping whereas others were torn completely apart, blood was everywhere and Caleb retched before finally he spewed his guts up all over the deck.

C'mon get it together.

Wiping the last of the vomit from his chin Caleb began making his way across the deck.

The rocking of the *Zephyrus* combined with that of the blood-soaked deck resulted in Caleb having to take small controlled steps least he lose his footing, but it was all for naught as the *Zephyrus* was suddenly jerked downwards and Caleb was thrown onto his back.

Caleb immediately tried to scramble back to his feet but the blood made it impossible and before he knew it he was sliding across the deck.

For one terrifying moment Caleb thought he was going to slide straight overboard but then he slammed straight into the main mast, gritting his teeth against the pain that lanced through his back Caleb grabbed a hold of some of the rigging and pulled himself back to his feet, where he was met with the sight of the enemy ship.

The enemy vessel was smaller than the *Zephyrus* by a dozen floors or more but it was much wider, its hull gleamed a fiery red in the afternoon sun and flying from the ships three masts were black flags, a giant skull with bloodied eyes sat in the centre of each flag and for a moment Caleb felt as if the eyes were really watching him but the illusion was quickly broken by the sound of firing cannons, instinctively Caleb tightened his grip on the rigging and it was a good thing he did as two of the javelins that were in the side of the *Zephyrus* were blown free and the Skyship rocked uncontrollably from side to side.

Once the *Zephyrus* had levelled back out, Caleb released his hold of the rigging and turned his attention back towards looking for the Captain and Vaeliria, it only took him a moment to find the two senior Skyknights. Captain Brightfellow stood at the helm, his giant arms were locked in a brutal struggle with the *Zephyrus*'s massive wheel whilst Vaeliria stood nearby shouting orders to the men and women beside her. Caleb scrambled across the deck towards the stairs but his path was blocked by a body. As he heaved the body aside Caleb recognised the man's face, it was fat face, looking at the man's cold dead features Caleb felt ashamed.

Crewmen shouldn't fight they should help one another.

Another round of cannon fire brought Caleb back to himself, he gently placed the corpse to one side and pulled himself up the stairs.

"What are you doing up here?" shouted Vaeliria over the cannon fire.

"Thom wanted me to let you and the Captain know that the enemies Javelins have pierced into the Skycore bay."

"Shit, Captain, you hear that."

"Yeah," said the Captain as he struggled against the helm, "we need to get those last two javelins free, then I'll try and get some distance between us and the enemy that way our Cannoneers can do some real damage."

"Thom sent some of his people to tell the cannons to fire at the chains of the javelins rather than the ship."

"Good, if that ship went down with us still attached."

Before Captain Brightfellow could finish his sentence the enemy's cannons fired again and blasted into the *Zephyrus*, Caleb barely stayed on his feet whilst the Captain and Vaeliria barely moved.

"Caleb, you need to get off the deck, it's too dangerous here," said Vaeliria as the *Zephyrus* retaliate with a barrage of its own.

"You expect me to go and hide, no way, a Skyknight never runs away."

"This isn't the time for heroics," said Vaeliria but it was too late, Caleb was already back down onto the deck looking to help his injured comrades, it was too late for many of his fellow knights but Caleb wasn't going to give up he had to help. Hearing a cry of pain Caleb turned to see a young woman no older than twenty lying on her back holding her stomach, he rushed over dodging the fire of enemy riflemen as he went.

Reaching the woman Caleb instantly applied pressure to the wound, he could tell the wound wasn't life threatening but a shot to the stomach could turn nasty if left unattended.

"We've got to get you down to the medical bay," said Caleb looking at the young woman.

The young woman couldn't say anything in reply, but her eyes showed understanding.

"Can you move?"

The woman shook her head in reply.

"Okay I'm going to have to carry you, keep one hand on the wound."

Caleb hooked the woman's free arm around his neck, lifting her he was surprised at how light she felt but the fire of rifles forced this musing from his mind and he made his way down to the medical bay as fast as he possibly could.

The medical bay was just as chaotic as the battle outside. Bed after bed was filled with injured men and woman. Medical officers were rushing around, their arms filled with bandages both clean and bloody, one officer, an old frail looking woman came over to Caleb took one look at the woman in his arms and lead them to a free bed, Caleb gently placed the woman down.

"Tha... thank you," said the woman through gritted teeth.

"No problem," replied Caleb before disappearing back into the mass of bodies.

Caleb spotted Luci and Doctor Estrada over at the other end of the medical bay, from the amount of blood that stained their aprons it was obvious they were performing an emergency operation on someone. Luci looked to be in her element, despite the rocking and shacking of the ship, she was quickly passing instruments to her mother and taking others without so much as a word.

Caleb left the medical bay and proceeded back down to the Skycore.

Opening the lift door Caleb rushed out to find Thom, Gustav and Riktor all standing around the Core, which was shaking uncontrollably

"The Core can't take much more of this!" shouted Gustav from the opposite side of the massive crystal.

"I know, lad, we need to land and soon," replied Thom flipping through a book. "Riktor I need you to compress the posterior cluster... that should give us a few more minutes of stable flight."

"Just show me where to hit."

"Gus."

"On it." Gustav opened the bottom section of the crystals housing unit.

"Hold on." Riktor slammed his giant hammer into the crystal, the dark blue light of the crystal changed a fiery orange, it appeared that nothing was going to happen when suddenly the crystal jolted to a stop and once again became its usual pale blue.

"That was a close one," said Gustav wiping his brow.

"We aren't out of the woods yet, the hull's taken major damage and the enemy don't appear to be backing off any time soon."

"Doesn't look like they have any more javelins left."

As if on cue another javelin pierced through the hull, unlike those that came before this javelin had barbs running along its face.

For a moment, it looked like the javelin would fail to find purchase but then it locked itself into the hull and the ship was pulled sideways.

Grabbing a hold of a nearby workbench Caleb managed to stop himself from being pulled off his feet, his companions however weren't so lucky. Allie and Riktor fell awkwardly onto their sides whilst Thom and Gustav were thrown through the air.

A few moments later the *Zephyrus* straightened and Caleb released his hold of the bench and was about to help his fellows back to their feet when he saw that it wasn't necessary. Allie and Riktor were already back on their feet and heading towards the javelin whilst Gustav stood helping Thom back to his feet.

Dodging around the mess that lined the Core's floor Caleb made his way back to Thom's side.

"What we gonna do about that javelin?" said Gustav rubbing his neck.

"There's no way those two will be able to pry it off that javelin," said Thom staring at Riktor and Allie, "and the Cannoneers won't be able to break the tether either the entire thing's made from Bujecian steel, only way to get it off is blow what it's holding onto."

Gustav's face drained of colour, "Is that really the only way?"

"I'm afraid so," replied Thom his voice grim. "There's some gunpowder charges in my office, we'll need all three to blow that sucker off."

Before anyone could protest Caleb ran off towards Thom's office, he knew where to find the charges, they should be in a crate by the back bookshelf.

The office was a complete mess. Everything from the books on the shelves to Thom's numerous experiments had been thrown around creating a mass of chaos.

This is going to make my job a lot harder.

Again, the *Zephyrus* rocked as it was pulled in the direction of the enemy ship. A barrage of books pummeled Caleb from head to toe but he managed to keep his feet under him. Compensating for the slant Caleb began sifting through the mess of parchment and leather. It didn't take him long to find one of the charges, the thick black charge was scratched but its activation mechanism was still intact, Caleb held the charge tight against his chest as he looked for the other two, suddenly the *Zephyrus* jolted away from the enemy, again books and debris went flying, Caleb ducked into a ball to protect the charge from being damaged. Once the ship steadied itself Caleb saw the second charge, it had been hidden under a device Thom had been working on, he called it a purifier. Caleb picked up the second charge but it was cracked through.

Shit.

Caleb threw the charge away and continued his search for the third and last one. Somehow the third charge had wedged itself in under Thom's desk, placing the charge he held down on the floor Caleb lifted the desk the few inches needed to slip the last charge out, pushing the charge with his foot he could feel that it was still intact. Caleb dropped the desk more than put it down before making his way back to Thom and the others.

Back out in the bay Thom and Gustav had joined Allie and Riktor by the Javelin, Caleb ran over with the two charges.

"You got the charges?" said Thom as Caleb ran over to join them.

"I could only get two of the charges, the other had cracked."

"By the Firstborn," cursed Gustav.

"No time for cursing, we still have two of the charges all it means is that we have to plant the charges on the outer portion of the hull."

"And how do you suppose we do that? Allie and Rik are way too big to get through, and you and I are no way strong enough to hold on."

"I'll do it."

All eyes turned to Caleb, "Look I can fit through the gap and plant the charges, no problem."

"You sure?" said Thom.

"You can't be serious he's just an apprentice there's no way he knows how to detonate the charges correctly," said Gustav.

"The front panel of the charge directs the blast in a forward motion, so all I have to do is place the front of the charge as close to the ship's hull as possible that way the main force will go into the hull destroying the javelin's hold on the *Zephyrus*." Everyone apart from Thom looked surprised by Caleb's knowledge of gunpowder charges.

Caleb walked over to the breach, Gustav began to say something but Caleb cut him off, "No time for debate, I'm the only one who can do this and we've lost enough of our own, I ain't going to let this ship go down."

"Alright, lad, but you're wearing this," said Thom holding out a rope tether.

Caleb put the tether on without a word and immediately made his way through the breach.

The wind battered Caleb's face as he climbed around the javelin. Looking around he saw that the *Zephyrus* had lost a lot of altitude as had the enemy ship, actually it looked like the enemy was intentionally heading for the ground.

Are they insane?

Shaking the useless thought away Caleb climbed over to the left-hand side of the javelin and placed the first charge in place.

Turning the activation mechanism into the firing position Caleb quickly made his way over to the javelins right side, but as he did the first charge blew and the left side of the javelin swung free. The force of the javelin coming free on one side forced Caleb to have to hold onto the blades barbed face least he slip and fall.

Eventually the javelin stopped swinging and Caleb released his tight hold of the javelin's face, a trail of blood ran from either of his palms but he ignored the pain as he knew he still had to complete his job.

Placing the second charge up against the *Zephyrus*'s hull Caleb turned the activation mechanism to the right a little bit more than he had with the first one, he hoped that would give him enough time to get back inside, but as he pushed the mechanism into place and took a step back the charge prematurely detonated and Caleb was sent flying off into the air.

With his thoughts scrambled Caleb didn't know what was going on until the tether became taut and he lurched to a painful stop. As the tension in the rope continued to grow Caleb felt the tether cut deeply into his hip and he cried out in pain.

I can't stay here.

With that Caleb reached into his belt and drew one of his dirks free and in a few quick stokes the tether was cut and Caleb found himself falling, he just hoped it wasn't to his death.

Chapter 14

The GrandOak's face shifted, "Are you sure about this?"

"Yes," replied Adessa, she had never been more sure of anything in her life, it was time she knew the truth about her father and why her mother had kept it a secret from her. Adessa knew now that High Speaker Caewyn had his own secrets and agendas, after all he had kept the fact that she was having to go to the Angardian Kingdom a secret from her and allowed Adessa's mother to tell her so the GrandOak was the only one she trusted wouldn't lie to her about this.

"Once you learn the truth nothing can be the same again."

"Please, I need to know."

"Okay, my child. I will tell you everything, your father came to this land many years ago, he was found walking the forest by the rangers, I can still remember the uproar that came from him being here."

"But who was he?"

"My apologies, your father's name was Estrial."

Adessa was confused the only Estrial she knew of was the one from the tales used to scare little boys and girls into being good. In the stories Estrial was known as the harbinger of madness and the bringer of death, he had only been stopped when his brother Dalanas did battle with him, both had perished in the clash.

Sensing her thought the GrandOak spoke, "Oh no, don't worry, my child, the name was given to him because he couldn't remember who he was himself."

"So they gave him a name meaning calamity."

"People fear what they do not understand and no one was willing to try and understand him... that was until your mother came along, she quickly befriended him and she pleaded for the High Speakers to let him stay."

"They listened?"

"For a time which caused no end of tension, but the High Speakers at the time thought that it was best for the Enshyi to start thinking about the world beyond Alfheim."

"So what happened?"

"A young Enshyi by the name of Ailmer who was in love with your mother didn't like how close your father was becoming with her, he thought it was some sort of magic that had ensnared her so he along with a few of his closest allies decided to kill your father."

"What!" cried Adessa, "Why? He hadn't done anything wrong."

"Fear can bring out the best and the worst in people."

"So you're telling me he died because people were scared?"

"I'm afraid so," said the GrandOak solemnly.

"It all makes sense," said Adessa more to herself than the GrandOak. "The other Enshyi hate and loathe me because they fear me."

"Are you okay?"

Adessa didn't know how to answer that question she had just found out that her father had been killed for no other reason than because her people were afraid of him, so why had she been allowed to live.

"Adessa," the sound of the GrandOak's voice brought Adessa out of her quickly darkening thoughts.

"Thank you for telling me."

"Would you like to skip your lessons for today?"

"No, I can't afford to lose time," said Adessa jumping to her feet. "Mother just told me that the High Speakers have decided that I have to go to the Angardian Kingdom."

"Yes, Caewyn had told me about that."

"They're asking me to leave my home behind."

"But still, you'll go."

"I don't have much choice in the matter, the High Speakers have already made their decision."

"Do you know why you were chosen?"

Adessa spun around, the sight of High Speaker Caewyn's vessel walking towards her filled her with anger, he had agreed with the other High Speakers and was shipping her off to the Angardian Kingdom, that's what hurt the most, Adessa had believed him to be a friend but it was clear he wasn't.

"I have a few ideas," spat Adessa.

"Let me guess, you think the reason you were chosen is because of your birth, or do you think that I'm bitter about being here in the Angardian Kingdom on my own."

The High Speaker's words had taken all the wind from Adessa's sails, she had been thinking those exact thoughts.

"From your silence I'm guessing I'm on the right path," said Caewyn as he sat down on his usual rock. "You may not believe what I'm about to say but frankly I don't care you need to grow up and quickly because it won't be long until the Skyship from Actalia is dispatched."

Adessa felt like she had just been slapped in the face, tears began to form in her eyes, why was the High Speaker being like this, couldn't anyone see how she felt. If High Speaker Caewyn noticed her tears he paid them no mind, "I'm the one who suggested that you be the Speaker sent here to join me."

This was the last nail in Adessa's heart, she couldn't hold the tears back anymore. High Speaker Caewyn had been the sole perpetrator responsible for her having to leave her home.

"Why?" asked Adessa feeling broken.

"Because you're the only one I trust and I know you will do what is right."

High Speaker Caewyn was right Adessa didn't believe him, "You're saying that I'm the only one you can trust... there are dozens of other Speakers who are skilled enough to fulfil the role of a Skyknight, what about Gahrric or Iloan."

Caewyn shook his head at Adessa's words, "You're right they are skilled enough but I don't trust either of them."

"But you trust me?"

"Yes, since I began teaching you I've seen that you are

willing to do anything to protect your home."

Adessa hated the fact that High Speaker Caewyn knew exactly how she was feeling, how could he know so much about her after such a short time.

"Why didn't you tell me yourself?"

"I called your mother to the Hall of Elements early this morning but she knew what I was going to tell her and she told me right then and there that she had to be the one to tell you, I respected her wishes as your mother."

"She knew that I would hate the decision," said Adessa to herself. "High Speaker, I cannot apologise for the way I feel, I don't wish to leave but I will, if it is best for Alfheim."

"Very well, I will see you later for your training." The High Speaker picked himself up from his seat and bowed, "Adessa, GrandOak, may the sun shine on you both."

"And you," replied the GrandOak, Adessa bowed but didn't say anything.

With that the High Speaker's vessel resorted to its lifeless form and Adessa began her lesson with the GrandOak.

"Clear your mind," said the GrandOak, his voice filled with understanding.

Adessa nodded and quickly cleared her mind using the Tree in the Wind.

"Very good," said the GrandOak nodding. "Now I want you to try and communicate with two spirits at the same time."

"Did you have any spirits in mind?" asked Adessa.

With her mind, safely within the island of the Tree in the Wind it was easy for Adessa to focus on her training and forget her worries.

"Now that you ask," said the GrandOak. "You see those chrysanthemums." Adessa followed the GrandOak's eyes and sitting a few yards away were a group of brightly coloured chrysanthemums. "I want you to communicate with them and..." The GrandOak was silent for a moment as he searched his island for another spirit. "Aha," said the

GrandOak after a moment. "Twenty yards to your left is a young hare." Adessa turned to her left and sure enough there the hare was. The young buck was running through a patch of tall grass.

Adessa felt a wave of apprehension wash over her at the thought of trying to communicate with these two very different spirits, the erratic nature of the hare's spirit flowed through the Voice like a torrent while the soft peaceful spirits of the chrysanthemums trickled through.

With a deep breath Adessa touched the spirit of the hare first, it was pure wildness, she immediately focused her will onto the hare and asked it to stop and it did.

Alright now for the hard part.

Taking another breath Adessa focused half of her will over to the chrysanthemums, the peaceful aura of the flowers spirits washed over Adessa, but then the hare's spirit and those of the flowers met in the middle of her will and Adessa immediately felt herself splitting in two.

The part of her will that was in contact with the hare wanted to devour the calmer half and Adessa felt her head begin to hurt.

"You can do this," said OathKeeper as his voice filled Adessa's mind.

Adessa steeled herself and for a split second the two spirits and both sides of her will were in balance which is when Adessa caught a glimpse of the real power of the Voice.

Thousands of spirits beat in unison, casting every colour and emotion imaginable. Adessa was completely awestruck, if a Speaker were able to use the entirety of the Voice the world would bend to their will making them capable of anything. Adessa tried to imagine having that sort of power but as quickly as the sight came it disappeared and she once again found herself back in the physical world.

Adessa looked around, the world felt small and quiet compared to what she had just witnessed.

"What did you see?" asked the GrandOak.

Adessa wasn't sure what she had seen but it was something important she knew that, "I saw thousands of spirits beating in unison."

"What you saw was part of the Lifestream."

"Lifestream?" said Adessa slightly confused.

"Yes, every being that resides in Alfheim and even the world is linked to the Lifestream."

"Does every Speaker see this when they split their will?"

"No, for most they don't see anything beyond the two souls they are splitting their will between."

"So why split our will?"

"The obvious reason a Speaker is taught to split their will is that it allows you to communicate with numerous spirits at once but the other reason is that will-splitting shows you just how wild and dangerous the Voice is, you had a hard time talking with two spirits can you imagine trying to talk with ten or even a hundred."

Adessa tried to imagine it and it didn't look pretty, how could anyone balance so many spirits at once and still keep themselves centred or sane for that matter, but a darker part of her wanted to see that scene again and control it.

Adessa shook the thought away, no that wasn't the way of a Speaker, she wouldn't forcibly control the spirits of Alfheim, that was the way of a Speaker who had lost their way.

"Anyone could lose themselves in that many spirits," said Adessa finally.

"Exactly, no matter what happens in your life remember that, otherwise one day you may never come back to us."

"Don't worry I will never forget who I am," said Adessa and she meant it, finding out who her father was and how he had been killed was a hard thing to accept but now Adessa was completely sure of who she was and no matter what it cost, she was going to protect her home and more importantly her mother.

Chapter 15

"You no move," said a voice in thickly accented common tongue.

An acrid smell filled the air, Caleb slowly opened his eyes and tried to move, as he did pain streaked through his side and his head felt like it was going to split. Letting out a cry of pain Caleb closed his eyes and dropped back down onto whatever surface he was lying on.

"I tell you no move," repeated the foreign voice.

The last thing Caleb remembered was the world spinning as he fell, the sky filled his vision one second and the next the white coloured land came up to meet him. He had no idea where he was or where the *Zephyrus* and its crew had gone, these thoughts didn't last for long however as another wave of pain shot through him, clenching his teeth Caleb just managed to endure the pain, but he was sure he couldn't hold out for long, the pain was unlike anything he had felt before.

C'mon you gotta see how hurt you are.

With that Caleb shifted slightly, from the amount of pain that streaked through his body he guessed that at least three of the ribs on either side of his body were broken. Next he tried lifting his arms but strong hands stopped him. Caleb opened his eyes again and standing before him was a masked man, the mask was that of a smiling Daemon, great jagged teeth filled the masks mouth and long curving horns like that of a ram grew out the top, the man wore nothing apart from the mask and a loincloth, his dark body was covered in symbols, they looked familiar, then it hit Caleb this man had carved Hexes into his entire body.

"Stay still," said the masked man.

"Where am I?" Caleb's voice was hoarse and weak

"You in Akachi's tent." The man walked over to a cauldron, Caleb though the man wasn't going to say anything else but after he had stirred the cauldron a few times the man began to speak, "Akachi taking care of you, Akachi see battle of two ships, sees you fall from sky."

"You saved me?"

Akachi nodded in reply as he scooped the contents of the cauldron into a bowl.

"How long have I been here?"

Akachi held up two long fingers.

"Two days?"

Akachi shook his head.

"Two months?" said Caleb in despair.

Again, Akachi shook his head.

"Two weeks then."

Akachi nodded, "Two weeks," repeated the Shaman, tasting the words.

"I really need to get out of here."

The Shaman ignored Caleb's words and shoved the bowl into his face, "You drink."

Caleb gagged, whatever was in the bowl smelled foul.

"What is it?"

"Ooagi make you strong."

"I don't think a drinks gonna help me, my bones feel broken."

Akachi shook his head at Caleb, "Akachi heal bones, but Daemon still in mind, must be expelled, drink Ooagi."

Caleb looked down at the Ooagi, it was an unnaturally vibrant yellow.

He's helped me so far.

Caleb pressed his lips to the bowl and drank. The Ooagi tasted even worse than it smelt and Caleb had to fight the urge not to throw it back up.

As soon as he had finished the last of the Ooagi, Caleb felt his vision begin to sway from side to side and in the next moment it seemed as if he was floating.

What the hells happening.

The sensation of weightlessness continued and before long Caleb found himself looking down at his body and he was shocked with what he saw. Nearly every inch of him was bandaged, he could tell from his time spent being patched up by Luci that this man knew what he was doing, but as he drifted over to where Akachi stood Caleb was shocked to find that the Shaman held a bone carved knife in his left hand.

"What the hell are you doing!" cried Caleb, but his voice didn't seem to reach the Shamans ears.

Powerless Caleb was forced to watch as Akachi drew the knife across his other palm and began to chant loudly, one by one the Hexes on Akachi's head began to glow a deep red and in the next moment Caleb saw that his own bandaged head began to glow in the same manner.

What the...

Before he could finish his thought, Caleb found himself being thrown back into his body.

After a few moments Caleb opened his eyes and was welcomed with more pain than he had felt the first time he had awoken.

"What the hell was that?" said Caleb once he had gathered himself.

"Daemon banished, you safe now."

"What in the seven hells are you talking about?"

Akachi shook his head again, "You rest, Akachi prepare Pikra."

Caleb awoke some hours later to the smell of roasting meat, he lifted himself out of bed, surprisingly his body didn't hurt as much as he thought it should and the ache in his head had become a dull throb. Looking down at himself he saw the bandages that had been lining his body were gone and in their place, was a long white robe.

Following the aroma of the roasting meat Caleb made his way through the hut. Various dried herbs hung from the ceiling in thick bunches. Bones of different shapes and sizes lined all the shelves that ran around the edges of the hut whilst jars of pickled organs lay on the floor, Caleb knew he should have been questioning these troubling sights but his mind was preoccupied with the idea of eating a good meal. Pulling back the flap of the hut Caleb saw a goat roasting over an open fire, his mouthed watered at the sight.

As he sat down by the fire Caleb looked around. In every direction for miles all around all he could see was more of the strange white land he had seen up on the *Zephyrus*, at the thought of his ship Caleb looked up into the night sky, thousands maybe even millions of stars filled the black void.

"Stars tell much."

Caleb looked up to find Akachi standing over him, a set of black robes covered the shamans body now but more surprising was that his face lay bare. Caleb found himself shocked at how youthful Akachi's face looked beneath the Hexes.

Without another word Akachi made his way to the opposite side of the fire and sat down.

As silence once again filled the air Caleb found his thoughts return to the well-being of the crew and his friends.

The first person his thoughts turned to were Luci, she had been down in the medical bay helping the wounded during the battle with the enemy, which meant that even if something had happened to her she was surrounded by dozens of other medical officers as well as her mother.

Yeah Luci will be fine.

Once he had convinced himself of Luci's safety Caleb's thoughts turned to that of Vaeliria and the Captain, they had both been on the deck.

What if they went overboard like me?

Caleb shook the thought away, there was no way that either Vaeliria or the Captain would go overboard and even if they had surely Akachi would have seen them falling as well,

Moments later Caleb was awoken from his reverie by an intense fiery smell. Akachi was throwing a bright red powder over the goat which seemingly made the flames from the fire grow until they danced across the goat searing its flesh.

Once the powder had been burnt away the flames quickly died and Akachi began to carve the goat before placing the meat into two clay bowls, which were filled with rice.

With both bowels filled with a generous portion of goat Akachi picked up a small clay jug and poured the contents over the bowls before he held one out for Caleb.

"Thank you," said Caleb accepting the bowl.

Akachi nodded and Caleb went to tackle his meal when he realised he had nothing to eat it with.

Looking back over towards Akachi, Caleb saw that the shaman was eating with his hands. Caleb felt a wave of annoyance pass through him at the sight, a few weeks ago he wouldn't have thought anything of eating with his hands, but clearly his time on the *Zephyrus* and in the company of civilized people had begun to change him.

"Eat," said Akachi around a mouthful of food.

Caleb devoured the food with the animal like intensity he thought he had lost, the goat had a rich fatty taste which combined perfectly with the fragrant and aromatic sauce and the rice provide a wonderful base as it only had a slight flavour of its own.

After wolfing down the last of his food Caleb didn't feel sated at all and he eyed the remainder of the goat intently.

As if reading his mind Akachi took the bowl from Caleb and once again began carving the goat. One bowl turned into two and then three until all that was left off the goat was bone and sinew.

With his last helping cleared and finally feeling full Caleb looked up from his bowl. The fire which had been burning steadily was now little more than embers and overhead the sky seemed to be filled with even more stars.

A few moments later Akachi lifted the goat carcass off the fire and began to chant, the hexes on his arms began pulsing a deep blue as he did. Continuing his chant Akachi lay the carcass down on the ground before he ran his hands across every inch of the skeleton. As he watched Akachi work Caleb noticed that the hexes that lined the shaman's arms were growing brighter.

Eventually Akachi's arms burnt with the light of a hundred lanterns and Caleb had to look away least he be blinded. The intense light lasted for only a moment however and when Caleb turned back towards the shaman he found that the remains of the goat were now completely clean and shined a brilliant white.

What in the world?

In the next moment Akachi gathered the bones up and walked off into his hut, Caleb was still completely dumbfounded by what he had just seen and so remained where he was.

Caleb must have been sitting alone for at least half a candlemark, after all the fire had completely died and the moon was now high in the night's sky, but just as he was about to stand Akachi returned.

"What was that?" said Caleb.

Akachi looked at Caleb confused, this was the first-time communication had been a problem between the two men, both just looked at each other until Caleb broke the silence, "What did you do to the goat?"

"Akachi send spirit..." Akachi went silent, from what Caleb could tell he was trying to find the right word, finally he pointed up into the sky and said, "Sowana."

Caleb understood, Sowana must be the Onmori's afterlife, "You sent the spirit to the afterlife." On the last part Caleb pointed up into the sky to show that he understood.

Akachi nodded his head vigorously.

"You rest now," said Akachi changing the subject. "Azar be here tomorrow, take you to ship."

At the mention of ship Caleb shot up from his seat, "You know where the *Zephyrus* is?"

Akachi shook his head, "No, Azar know."

Caleb wanted to ask more but thought better of it, "Okay, I'll rest."

Caleb was awoken the following morning by a strange groaning sound, jumping up Caleb stretched and was happy to find that all his aches and pains had faded to dull undertones.

Whatever Akachi did to me seems to have worked.

Out in the main part of the hut there was no sign of the shaman but the strange sound continued to echo from outside. Caleb followed the sound, as he pulled back the flap to the outside, sunlight came streaming in blinding him, it was all he could do to blink the spots away let alone stop the tears from rushing down his face.

Once he had adjusted to the late morning sun Caleb looked around, again all he could see in every direction was the white land that shifted under his feet, suddenly a loud roar broke out from around the side of the hut, was Akachi in trouble. Caleb picked up a nearby knife and darted around the corner of the hut, the sight that meet him was nearly indescribable. Two beasts the size of wagons stood gnawing and growling at each other, as their large snouts opened Caleb could see rows of razor sharp teeth that looked capable of easily tearing a man apart, nostrils flaring the two beasts turned to face Caleb, blood red eyes pierced through a black abyss of fur, one of the beasts swiped at Caleb with its colossal paw, Caleb jumped away from the attack, the beast tried to lunge again but the chain around its neck became taught pulling the beast short. Caleb stood there his eyes transfixed on the beast that had attacked, it began pacing back and forth watching him in return.

"Balsa."

The massive beast stopped in its tracks and Caleb turned to see a robed woman standing by Akachi. The woman was about the same height as Akachi, her face was heart shaped and she had thick black hair tied back into an elaborate braid that hung around her neck much like the one Wraith had, but the robes concealed just about everything else but as the woman walked towards him Caleb could tell that she was a fighter, her feet practically glided across the ground, turning back towards the beast Caleb saw that it had laid down next to its companion.

Once they had reached Caleb, the woman looked Caleb up and down then turned to Akachi and began talking in the sharp language of the Onmori, Caleb didn't understand a word but he could guess they were talking about him, every so often the woman would turn back to look at him before continuing her discussion, which continued until Caleb couldn't take it anymore.

"Look if you've got something to say how bout you just say it," said Caleb in the common tongue.

The woman turned to Caleb, "You were on a Skyship known as the *Zephyrus*?" the woman's common tongue was nowhere near as accented as Akachi's.

"Yeah and...?"

"Your ship is docked at Teuengea."

Caleb stood dumbfounded for a few seconds, he could barely believe that it had been so easy to find out the location of the *Zephyrus*, "I need to get back to my ship as quickly as possible. How far is this Teuengea?"

"Five days ride maybe a week if the winds are bad."

"I'm ready to go as soon as you are."

"Good, because we're leaving now," replied the woman.

Out of nowhere Akachi produced a pack and Caleb's dirks and belt, Caleb put on his belt, it felt good to have his dirks at his hip again, inside the pack were his clothes, a half dozen strips of jerky, a skin of water, a mix of dried fruit and nuts and a sealed jar of Ooagi.

"Keep robe on, desert too hot for them." Akachi pointed at Caleb's uniform.

"Thank you for everything," said Caleb bowing.

"I heal," said Akachi bowing in reply. "Azar keep you safe, get you to Teuengea."

"Come along," said Azar mounting the beast that had attacked Caleb, "unless you want it to take another day, the winds are already starting to change."

"You don't expect me to ride that thing?"

151

"No Balsa is wild, you'll ride Quella she is more," the woman paused as if trying to find the right word, "understanding."

I seriously doubt that.

Caleb approached the other beast tentatively, it stood waiting, its blood red eyes stared at him questioningly.

"How am I supposed to get up on this things back?" said Caleb looking over at Azar.

Azar let out a loud clicking sound and immediately the beast knelt, "Better?"

Caleb still had to drag himself up the side of the beast and as he sat in the giant saddle he felt awkward and could tell that by the end of this journey he was going to ache, but that didn't matter, all that did, was that he make it back to the *Zephyrus* and find out if everyone was okay.

Chapter 16

The midday sun beat down on Darrius as he rowed. It had taken him two weeks to get back to his boat, when it should have only taken him one, but he had run into problems as soon as he had left the Speaker's home.

Firstly, the number of Enshyi that walked throughout the forest seemed to have quadrupled from when he had snuck in, and each seemed to be on high alert. Then Darrius had to loop around a large company of Enshyi who had camped out in the clearing that his escape route crossed, which lead to him getting lost in a dark part of the forest where nearly no light came through and he ended up walking in circles for another three nights until finally he had made it out of Alfheim and out onto the wide plains of the Sea of Grass, which is where Darrius had met another problem.

Rather than being on the south-western side of Alfheim, where it was an easy trek back into the Cerberus Mountains, Darrius had ended up on the eastern side. The subsequent trek around the plains had cost him another five days as he had to set aside a day to hunt and replenish his water-skin.

Fortune seemed to smile on Darrius as the hike through the mountains was straight forward and only took two days, but that's where Darrius's good luck ended.

As he had come down the other side into the Trynyrst tundra Darrius was met with a band of thugs, who had decided that they owned the road and wanted a payment of five gold pieces to let him or any other traveller pass. Darrius had told them to move along otherwise it wouldn't end well, but the leader, an ugly man with the nose the size of a beak, had laughed at Darrius before telling his two men to stick their knives into him.

The fight that ensued had lasted for less than a minute as Darrius easily disarmed either man and proceeded to jam their respective blades into each other's throat.

The leader having seen his two henchmen be so easily killed had immediately started to beg for Darrius to spare his life. His pleads had included money, women and even an estate, but Darrius just walked silently to the leader's side grasped his neck and twisted, a blood chilling crunch echoed out as the man fell lifelessly to the dusty ground and with that Darrius had continued on his way.

After a three-day walk Darrius, had made it back to the small fishing village of Twilli, he had allowed himself a day to recover, then he went to his boat and thankfully it had still been laying under the small pier that sat just off the Raultarnese Sea.

"By the Lady, its hot out on the sea today," said Darrius to himself as he took a break from rowing.

He reached inside his pack and grabbed a small apple and a bread roll, the apple had gone bad in a few places and the roll was as hard as stone but he ate them anyway he was going to need the energy. Finishing the last of his dreadful meal Darrius took a swig from his water-skin, the warm water did little to refresh him but it was better than nothing, stretching he took hold of the oars and once again began rowing.

After another two candlemarks of rowing, Darrius caught sight of his destination on the horizon, Seers Isle was an emerald gem in the middle of the sapphire sea and was the only place Darrius considered home, even from this far out he could see the Oracles tower, it was a masterful sight, the sun gleamed of the white marble stone that made up the tower and the gilded dome at the top shone like a beacon calling to him.

Half a candlemark later Darrius rowed into the isle's tiny bay and docked his boat on the beach, much to his surprise no one was around, there were no signs of the native islanders or his brothers and sisters from the Order, sighing Darrius slung his pack over his shoulder and began the long walk to the tower.

It had been four years since Darrius had walked this path last, in that time the forest had become more dense, thick shrubs marked either side of the trail and from the looks of it Myriana had grown more trees, deep within the thicket came the squawking of parrots, Darrius smiled at the sound, it reminded him of his first years here on the isle when things had been simpler.

Darrius shook himself free of the memories, those times were long gone, now he was a Sentinel of the Watchful Eye and as such he had no time to think about such trivial matters. Continuing down the trail Darrius came to a fork in the path, the left path would take him down into town while the right would snake up through the forest towards the tower, Darrius knew he needed to report back to the Oracle, but first he had a parcel to deliver in town and he could grab a good meal and a few hours of rest, there was no harm in that after all he knew he wouldn't get to stay here for long, the Oracle always had tasks for him but then again he wasn't called the *traveller* for nothing.

As the sun dropped below the tree-line, Darrius came walking into the town of Seers Isle, hundreds of the dark skinned natives rushed about their business, paying him no mind, Darrius walked through the crowd expertly dodging one person after the other until he came to the gates of Swansworth, the old wooden building was still just as grand as ever, it was the second tallest building on the isle after the Oracles tower standing five storeys, when he had first come to the isle the Swan had only three levels that were complete with the fourth in the process of being built. A seven-foot wall topped with iron spikes surrounded the property, Darrius had always wondered why Cosmo had built that wall, it wasn't like anyone was going to try and break into the manor what with the Sentinels being so close by, but then again he had always been a paranoid man right up until his death. Twelve marble swans stood in front of the building around a large fountain, which spouted a constant spray of clear water, creating a small rainbow in the evening sun.

Coming to the heavy iron gates Darrius was met by the hired guards, both men were natives, their dark skin was a stark contrast against the bright suits they wore.

"May I help you?" said one of the guards in the islanders' native tongue.

"Yes, I wish to speak with Lady Whitehall," replied Darrius in the same tongue, the islanders' language was the first he had learnt and it felt good to hear the language again after such a long time.

"I'm afraid Lady Whitehall isn't available this evening, what with the preparations for tonight."

"Tonight?" said Darrius confused.

The guard's face took on a look of bewilderment, "It's the Mid-year festival tonight."

Of course, how could Darrius have forgotten, Mid-year was one of the biggest events of the year here on the isle, that explained why everyone was so busy and paid him no mind.

"Could you send her a message then?"

"Of course."

"Tell her that Darrius wishes to speak with her at her earliest convenience."

"Why don't you tell her yourself?"

Darrius turned around to find Leon Whitehall walking straight towards him, Darrius couldn't help but smile at the sight of the young noble. The last few years had changed the boy, he was a good few inches taller now and the first signs of stubble marked his jaw, but Darrius noticed that not everything about the boy had changed, his hair was still the same white blonde of the Whitehall's and obviously, he still liked lavishly coloured suits, today he wore a bright turquoise piece with a pair of leather loafers.

Whitehall embraced Darrius in a tight hug. "Grandmother will be so pleased that your back, she's been asking about you for the past few months."

"Well I'd hate to keep her waiting any longer."

"Of course, of course," said Whitehall breaking the embrace. "Manu open the gate." Within seconds the two guards had unlocked the gates and Darrius was walking up the path towards Swansworth.

Darrius was led through the large wooden doors of the Swan and into the foyer, the room was exactly as Darrius remembered it, dozens of benches and chairs sat to either side of the room whilst a row of tables lined the centre of the room, the exotic plants of the isle sat atop the tables in ornate vases. Large paintings lined the walls, many depicted the scenes available here on the isle, but other were of far off lands, many of which Darrius had visited, like the Evallian Waterfalls or Mount Kakarus, clearly Lady Whitehall was ready for Mid-year, looking up at the balcony Darrius spotted more guards, a couple of them he recognised but most were new to him.

What did you expect?

"Are you coming, or are you going to admire the art all day Grandmother's waiting."

Snapping out of his daydream Darrius realised he had stopped walking, with a few quick steps he caught back up to the young Whitehall, the two men came to a short corridor lined with even more paintings, "Grandmother's in her study, you don't need me to show you in do you," said Leon with a smile. "I need to get ready for the celebration."

"No I'll be alright, thank you, Leon." Darrius bowed to the young lord.

"Anything for the traveller," replied Leon walking off.

Darrius closed the distance to the study door quietly, he didn't want a repeat of last time, he pressed himself up against the door and listened. Nothing. Darrius took a silent breath and focused his hearing, again there was nothing but he continued to listen and sure enough he began to hear a small clicking sound, Darrius took a moment to be sure. Yes. It was faint and on the periphery of his hearing but it was there, Darrius reached into one of the many pockets that lined his grey Sentinel garb and pulled out his set of lock-picks, the lock looked common enough but Darrius knew to expect the unexpected when it came to Lady Whitehall. Darrius placed his picks into the lock and began feeling. After a minute or so he felt the familiar feeling of security pins, letting out a silent curse he began the arduous task of reverse picking the lock. After about five minutes of fingering with the lock Darrius felt the last tumbler give way and he opened the door slowly, weary of what might await him on the other side.

Lady Whitehall's study was far homelier than the rest of Swansworth, there were no paintings lining the walls, no exotic plants sat on tables and there was no lavish furniture, in their place sat sturdy chairs and giant bookcases that ran from floor to ceiling filled the walls, hundreds of books lined the shelves and at the back of the study sat a wooden monster of a desk and behind this desk sat in a high-backed chair was Lady Katherine Whitehall. Lady Whitehall hadn't changed, despite her having seen her sixtieth summer this year, no grey marked her blonde hair and her emerald eyes still shone mischievously like that of a young girl who was doing things she knew she shouldn't be.

"What took you so long?" said Lady Whitehall in a disapproving tone.

Darrius bowed to the Lady of Swansworth, "I haven't had to reverse pick a lock in a long time, you must have had Aldric hard at work to come up with that combination."

"That lock was child's play, even Leon could have got through that and he doesn't know his elbow from his arse."

Darrius smiled, "May I sit?"

"Yes, yes," said Lady Whitehall waving a hand at Darrius, "by the Lady I thought Sentinels were above the noble niceties."

Darrius took up the seat opposite Lady Whitehall, as he did he noticed that she was wearing the traditional silk dress of Mid-year.

"You look lovely this evening," said Darrius cheekily, knowing how much she hated wearing dresses.

Lady Whitehall, let out a bark of laughter, "Ha, this thing feels like it's going to fall apart at any second, give me your Greys and a battle-harness any day."

Darrius smiled, "I'm sure you could teach me a thing or two."

"Damn right," said Lady Whitehall, taking a sip from her saucer.

Darrius took that as his cue, "I managed to track down one of the books you were after."

Lady Whitehall continued to sip her tea but Darrius knew she was interested, after all her eyes were screaming for him to hurry up.

Taking the opportunity to tease his old friend, Darrius slowly pulled the large leather bound book from his pack. "A black-market Bookkeeper in Pharc, managed to locate the book for me, his services cost a fair amount of gold but then again you said money wasn't an issue."

Lady Whitehall, put down her saucer and practically snatched the large tome from Darrius, she fingered the spine and ran her hand over the cover before opening it and flicking through a couple of pages. Darrius sat there silently watching, knowledge was Lady Whitehall's vice, she wanted to know everything, from farming techniques to war tactics. After a few minutes a smile crept across the old woman's face, "This is quite fascinating, thank you, what do I owe you."

"How about a good meal, then we call it even?"

"Done," said Lady Whitehall picking up a small bell, she rang it and within moments Clyde, the head butler appeared through a side door.

"You rang, milady," said the elderly servant.

"Could you get Stephen to whip something up for Darrius?"

"Very well milady, it shall be done." With that Clyde was gone and once again Darrius was left alone with Lady Whitehall.

"Are you coming to the celebrations?" said Lady Whitehall after a moment.

"No, I'm afraid I have to check in with my superiors and report back to the Oracle."

"That's a shame but I understand, the travellers work is never done."

"Quite right milady."

A few minutes later Clyde reentered the study, his hands filled with a silver tray that was laden with food. The butler set the tray down in front of Darrius without a word.

Darrius felt himself smile as he eyed the aromatic curry, it's accompanying flatbread, which smelt of garlic and coriander and the platter of fruit that sat before him.

Nowhere in the Five Kingdoms can match this.

"Will there be anything else milady?" said Clyde.

"No that's all for the moment," replied Lady Whitehall waving the butler off.

Once Clyde had left Lady Whitehall turned back to Darrius, "Well don't let me keep you, the food will do you some good."

"Thank you, milady." Darrius immediately began scooping the curry into his mouth with the flatbread, the spices of the curry and herbs of the flatbread filled his mouth with a warm sensation, which eventually spread down to his stomach, once both were gone Darrius tucked into the fruit, the sweet crisp tastes provided a wonderful relief from the heat that clung to his mouth.

Popping the last segment of orange into his mouth Darrius let out a sigh of satisfaction, it was good to eat a proper meal rather than the rations he carried on him when he travelled.

"That was wonderful, thank you."

"Is there anything else I can get you before you leave, perhaps a nice cold ale."

Darrius shook his head, "As tempting as that is I'll have to decline, I must be getting back to the tower."

Lady Whitehall nodded.

Darrius stood and bowed, "It was good seeing you again."

Lady Whitehall waved the comment away, as he left Darrius could hear her talking to herself as she began reading the tome aloud.

Later that night when the moon was high in the sky Darrius made it back through the forest to the clearing of the Oracle's tower, the giant stone structure stood proudly, clouds had formed in the night sky blocking the view of the upper section of the tower, but Darrius recalled from memory how the moonlight was reflected off the gilded dome. Laying before the tower were dozens of smaller stone building, most of which homed the members of the Order, other were used as storage houses for grain and produce. The building that sat next to the tower was used as the mess hall and where all meetings were held, even with the waning light Darrius could see the Sentinels on guard duty, the white masks they wore gave them away as Initiates, Darrius walked along the ridge and down into the clearing, once he was near the first line of buildings, Darrius heard the pulling of bow strings and he immediately stopped in his tracks and a young woman's voice rang out, "Who goes there?"

Darrius didn't reply, looking up he saw that five Initiates were aiming at him, two were on the buildings to his left and right, the last Initiate and the one who hailed him, was on the store house building straight in front of him.

"I said who goes there?" repeated the woman.

"Might I ask who you are?" replied Darrius.

In response to his question the woman fired her bow but Darrius didn't move, he knew this trick, Locklear had shown it to him several times, the arrow flew through the air and landed a few inches in front of his feet, "I'll ask the questions, now who are you and what is your business here?"

"Can't you recognise a Sentinel's clothing when you see it," said Darrius annoyed, he knew not to expect a grand homecoming but to be held at arrow-point was infuriating.

"You don't look like a Sentinel to me," said the woman, "now surrender quietly and come with us otherwise the next arrow goes straight through your eye."

"Are you being serious!" shouted Darrius his annoyance becoming full blown anger.

"One way or another you're coming with us."

The rational part of Darrius's mind called out to him, "*They don't know who you are and they're scared, I mean she does make a good point you do look more like a Brigand than a Sentinel, cut them some slack.*"

"Okay I'll come with you," said Darrius throwing his hands up in surrender.

Darrius was stripped of his weapons and led to the tower by the five Initiates in a pair of shackles, as they made it to the tower doors Darrius and his escort party were met with another two Initiates on guard, the two guards said nothing as they passed and their masks gave nothing away.

Where is everyone?

Walking into the tower Darrius was meet with the first recognisable face he had seen since making it back to the tower, sat behind the large wooden desk that sat in the towers base was Quinton the head scribe, Darrius sighed with relief, looks like he wouldn't be spending a night in the cells after all, the initiate who had shot at Darrius walked over to the desk, the other four stood with Darrius keeping an eye on him, not that they would have been able to hold him if he wanted to get free. The woman began talking with Quinton, Darrius started whistling it was only a matter of time, the woman pointed over at Darrius, Quinton stood up from his chair and looked over at Darrius, his face instantly dropped, the scribe said something to the woman that made her reel and within moments Darrius was being unshackled and his weapons and pack were given back to him and the five Initiates left all without a single word. Darrius walked over to where Quinton stood waiting, the Scribe hadn't changed a bit, his white hair was still as wild as ever and his face was just as gaunt as it had been when Darrius first met the man.

"My deepest apologies, Darrius," said Quinton whilst offering his hand.

Darrius grasped the old man's bony hand and shook it softly, "No need for you to apologise, old friend. Where is everyone, the only members of the order I've seen so far are Initiates?"

"The High Sentinel and the others have gone to pay their respects to the fallen and lay offerings to the Lady."

Darrius cursed himself, all he had done since coming back to the isle was forget, firstly he had forgotten that it was Mid-year today, which was bad enough but how could he have forgotten about the memorial service, it was one of the most important duties of a Sentinel and for the fourth year in a row Darrius wasn't going to be there.

"I should have remembered."

"Don't beat yourself up, Lady knows you've had enough on your plate."

"If I leave n"

Before Darrius could finish Quinton cut him off, "No it wouldn't do for you to turn up during the ceremony you know that, go speak with the Oracle, then pay your respects tomorrow your fallen brothers and sisters will understand."

Darrius sighed, he knew the old man was right but that didn't stop him from feeling like he was committing a great sin, the last three years he had been away on tasks for the Oracle, so he felt he could justify them but this time he was back so surely he should go, even if that meant pissing off the other Sentinels.

As if reading his mind Quinton spoke, "Don't go doing anything foolish now, Darrius, you have a hard enough time as it is around here."

"Fine," replied Darrius defeated. "Is the Oracle up in her chambers?"

"Yes, but her Holiness is still in prayer. Would you care to wait?"

"Don't worry," said Darrius making his way to the stairs. "I'm sure she's expecting me."

Before Quinton could reply, Darrius ran up the stairs.

Reaching the top floor of the tower Darrius felt good despite being covered in sweat and breathing heavily, the climb had allowed him to clear his mind of the distractions the night had brought. Stretching he began walking down the corridor towards the large stone door that marked the Oracle's chambers. Sconces lined the corridor, their flames burnt an eerie white, white flames meant the Oracle was in prayer and shouldn't be disturbed, as Darrius continued towards the stone door a gust of wind blew through the corridor extinguishing the flames, the darkness lasted for a few seconds then one by one the sconces began to burn their natural orange and the stone door opened, allowing Darrius entrance to the Oracle's chambers.

The Oracle's chambers were as large as any Queen's. A large four-poster bed surrounded by silk shrouds of every colour sat in the middle of the room. The finest gowns in all the Five Kingdoms hung in opulent wardrobes behind the massive bed whilst a series of exquisite paintings and tapestries hung around the room and hand woven carpets lined the cold stone floor. A long decoratively carved table stood on one such carpet, at least thirty people could be seated around it at one time, although only about four people in all of the isle were allowed in here, but none of these masterpieces could hold a candle to the shrine of the Lady that sat at the far end of the room. The statue of the Lady was made from marble, gold had been inlaid around the wrist and ankle on the left side while obsidian had been inlaid into the right side and two of the finest rubies money could buy sat in the statues eyes, in front of the statue stood a large basin filled to the brim with perfectly clear water. Darrius walked up to the shrine making the sign of the Lady as he did and found the Oracle sitting cross-legged on a pillow just off to the right of the shrine. The Oracle was around the same age as Darrius, but where the years had scarred him, she remained as beautiful as she had been when Darrius had first met her, her alabaster skin was still as flawless as a diamond and the river of flame red hair that cascaded down her shoulder's didn't have an ounce of grey in it and her pale blue eyes still shone as they had all those years ago, much to Darrius's surprise the Oracle wasn't wearing the traditional dress of Mid-year, but instead she wore a simple silk dress that barely covered her nakedness that lay underneath.

"Your Holiness," said Darrius bowing.

The Oracle inclined her and smiled, "Darrius, please sit."

Darrius did as he was told taking the pillow next to the Oracle, for a few moments the two sat in silence, before Darrius couldn't take it anymore and spoke.

"I gave the Speaker your message."

"Do you think they will act?" asked the Oracle turning to face Darrius.

"I was going to ask you the same thing, the Enshyi have spent the last century locked away in their forest, trying to protect themselves from the rest of the world."

"And?"

"And, I believe most want to keep it that way, but the fact that they have made a pact with the Angardians seems a move in the right direction."

"I hope so," said the Oracle, the unmistakable note of worry in her voice.

Darrius didn't know what to say, comforting people had never been one of his strong points, so he decided to ask the only question he could think of, "Has the Lady shown you anything else?"

The Oracle sighed, "No I'm afraid not."

"And the dark visions?"

The Oracle sighed even deeper this time, "The same as I detailed when I sent you your orders to go to Alfheim."

Darrius shivered despite the warmth of the night. In her letter the Oracle had gone into great detail about the horrors she had seen. The world had been on fire whilst women and children sat weeping in the streets as thousands of men stood in fields killing one another in battles only fit for nightmares.

"I've prayed to the Lady to show me the way through this darkness but so far she has remained quiet."

Darrius was stunned into silence he had never seen the Oracle so uneasy before, he turned to the statue of the lady and looked into the ruby eyes, he thought he saw a red mist begin to swirl inside the eyes but before he could be sure the Oracle's entire body shook in a fit of movement before becoming still, if this was Darrius's first time seeing this he would have been worried but after all the years he had spent in the Order he had seen the Oracle have a number of visions, he stood and scooped some water from the basin into a cup, the Oracle was always drained after a vision, seconds passed and then minutes until finally the Oracle's body was released from the iron hold of the vision, Darrius didn't ask her any questions he just pressed the cup of water into her hands and helped her take a sip.

"Thank you," said the Oracle giving the cup back to Darrius

Darrius sat down and put the cup to one side and awaited the Oracle's words.

"The darkness will come from the palace of Actalia," said the Oracle tiredly.

"Are you sure?"

"Yes, I saw an ocean of darkness begin to seep from the palace's grey walls like a sickness, covering the entirety of Angard in a blanket of evil, but it didn't stop there the darkness continued on until all of the Five Kingdoms were consumed."

Darrius's initial thought was that of the Enshyi and whether they had already sealed their demise by signing a pact with Angard, and from the look on the Oracle's face Darrius knew she was asking herself the same.

"What am I to do?" said Darrius casting his thoughts aside.

"You are to travel to Actalia and find the source of this darkness before it has a chance to assert itself."

It wasn't much to go on but Darrius wasn't the young man he had been when he first started going about the Five Kingdoms doing the Oracle's work and he was more than capable of finding the culprit.

"I'll leave as soon as possible," said Darrius heading for the door

The Oracle nodded, "You'd best rest, it's going to be a long and hard journey."

"Yes, your Holiness."

Chapter 17

Caleb had been travelling with Azar for four days now and still there was no sign of civilisation, just sand, sand and more sand for as far as the eye could see.

Despite his relatively short time here in the desert of Onmoria, Caleb already felt a deep hatred for the place.

During the day, the sun beat down on him with so much intensity that he felt he was going to dry out then and at night it became as cold as any winter Caleb had ever felt, but worse than the extreme temperatures was the sand, the grainy substance attacked Caleb at every opportunity, it scratched at his eyes and somehow the damned stuff had found a way into the folds of his robe where it rubbed at his skin with every step that Quella took.

"How much longer til we reach Teuengea," said Caleb tiredly.

"Are all Northerners as whiny as you?" replied Azar above the hiss of sand.

"They are when it's this damn hot, I mean it's like be" Caleb was about to continue his rant but the heat and sand had dried his throat out, he pulled out his waterskin. It felt uncomfortably light in his hand. Unstopping the skin, he peered inside, he had about a days' worth of water left if he was careful but it would have to do, it wasn't in his plans to die out here in this God forsaken desert and become food for the Vultures, he had to get back to the *Zephyrus* and his friends. Caleb lifted the skin to his dried lips and took a small sip, he swirled the warm water around his mouth before swallowing, the water made him feel better for all of five seconds and then he was back to feeling like a dried-out piece of leather.

The next few hours passed with Caleb silently cursing the Onmorians for living in such a hot and barren land, when finally, he caught sight of an Oasis on the horizon.

That can't be.

Azar had told him about the Oasis's and how they were used as waypoint for travellers.

Knowing my luck, it's a mirage.

Caleb blinked a dozen or more times but still the Oasis stood there on the horizon as a beacon of lush vegetation and bright colours, Caleb turned to Azar and was just about to ask if she saw it as well, but before he could Azar nodded.

"It's not a mirage, this Oasis is one that I use all the time on my route across the desert."

"Seriously?" replied Caleb in disbelief.

"Come, you'll see for yourself when we reach it," said Azar riding off.

When it became apparent that the Oasis wasn't a figment of his imagination Caleb kicked Quella into a run. He wanted to reach the Oasis as quickly as possible and from the speed at which Quella was running, the beast shared his desire,

As soon as the jackal's feet touched the Oasis, Caleb jumped off the beast's back and cast of his sword-belt before he ran straight towards the clear water, where he dove in head first heedless of the fact that he was still fully robed.

The water of the Oasis encased Caleb and for one glorious moment he felt as if he was in paradise, his dried skin felt rejuvenated, and his aches seemed to dull, but then his breath left him and he pushed back towards the surface.

As he broke the surface of the water Caleb sucked down a massive lungful of air and let out a shout of pure joy, but when he turned over to look where Azar was he saw she was staring at him with a disapproving look and he felt his joy fade.

"Time to head back to reality," said Caleb to himself as he began kicking his way back over to the edge of the Oasis.

Pulling himself out of the water as quickly as he could Caleb realised just what a fool he must have looked like what with running like a wild beast towards the water, even the two Razor Jackals had more restraint than him.

"Sorry about that just couldn't help myself," said Caleb picking up his dirks.

"I hope you show more restraint when we make it to Teuengea, otherwise you'll find yourself in some trouble."

"What kind of trouble?" replied Caleb ringing out his robe.

"The kind that finds you in the dungeon or dead."

"Don't worry I don't plan on causing any trouble."

Azar gave Caleb a look that said she was sceptical of his sincerity but she didn't say anything on the matter.

"I'll set up camp and refill the skins, you go and find us something to eat."

"Wouldn't you be better off finding the food what if I grab us something that's poisonous?"

"Don't worry everything here is perfectly edible, like I said I've used this Oasis many times before."

"Fine be back in a bit." With that Caleb walked off into the surrounding shrubbery.

The Oasis was like a small paradise, everywhere Caleb looked there were exotic plants and various fruit trees, the colours creating a living rainbow. Giant peaches, colourful apricots and vibrant plums hung from low branches all around, Caleb quickly grabbed an armful of the fruits before he continued on through the trees and plants. Caleb spent another candlemark looking for anything else he could gather and his persistence paid off, deep in the Oasis surrounded by dense bushes were a group of fig trees, two of the trees were easily twenty feet in height but the third was much smaller maybe only half the size. Caleb put the fruit he had already collected down safely and began circling the smaller tree looking for a way to get to the delicious fruit, but he couldn't see a way up, there was no way he could scale the tree, then an idea came to him, rushing back into the shrubbery he found what he was looking for. A long branch lay on the ground covered in vines, tearing the branch free he ran back to the fig tree and began swinging his makeshift tool up into the tree's branches. Within minutes he had managed to knock several figs to the ground, happy with his success Caleb decided it was time to head back to camp.

When Caleb finally emerged from the trees and shrubbery with all the fruit he had collected, he found Azar and the two Razor Jackals camped under a group of large palm trees, the two beasts were sprawled out on their sides, their enormous tongues stuck out as they enjoyed the rest whilst Azar was busy nursing a fire. Caleb made his way over to Azar and put the fruit down on a bunch of large palm leaves that lay just in front of the jackal rider.

"You were gone a long time," said Azar not taking her eyes of the fire.

"Thought I'd grab as much as I could."

Caleb dropped onto his back, it felt good to lie down, it gave his tired limbs a chance to relax and the view of the evening sky was pleasant enough to look at, what with its bold colours.

Maybe not everything in the desert is bad.

As the sky darkened Azar threw a handful of wood onto the infant fire, the fresh wood and foliage quickly caught alight and within minutes the fire was burning brightly. Caleb pushed himself up and went over to where the fruit lay, he grabbed an armful of fruit for himself before making his way back over to his side of the fire, as soon as he sat down he took a massive bite out of one of the peaches, the fruit was lovely and sweet and more refreshing than Caleb would have imagined, he would have devoured his small helping in seconds but he controlled himself, it wouldn't do him any good to look more like an animal what with his fiasco earlier. Azar sat on the opposite side of the fire eating silently.

It's going to be a long night.

Finishing the last of his meal Caleb took a deep gulp from his water-skin, the water from the Oasis was unlike anything he had experienced it was cool and clear, whereas the water in the lower city of Actalia was murky at best and always sat heavy in his stomach, Caleb shook the memory away and lay down near the fire, best to get some rest while he could heavens knows when he'd get the chance again.

The following morning came all too early for Caleb. Having spent another night laying on the ground had caused his already aching muscles to cramp and his eyes felt dry and painful.

Oh, the joys of sleeping on sand.

Still half asleep Caleb made his way towards the bushes to relieve himself, each step was hard as the muscles in his thighs protested with the movement, but nevertheless he carried on.

The sounds of insects filled the quiet morning air as Caleb made his water. In the distance the sun was just cresting the landscape, the giant fiery orb cast everything it touched in a deep orange light. A moment later a light breeze passed through the trees and shrubbery of the Oasis and Caleb felt the last of his sleep induced stupor fade away.

The walk back to camp was far easier for Caleb as his muscles had begun to loosen.

As he emerged from the bushes Caleb found that Azar had already packed up the camp and was sitting astride Balsa whilst Quella sat nearby waiting for him.

"We're leaving already," said Caleb putting on his belt.

"Is that a problem?" replied Azar.

"I was hoping to spend a little more time here."

"We can't stay here any longer."

"Just let me have a wash first."

"No time, the winds are building and Teuengea is another three days' ride from here."

"What! You told me that Teuengea was a five-day ride from Akachi's. Now you're telling me that it's another three from here."

"If you remember I said that it could take a week depending upon the winds; now, are you going to continue to whine or are we going to get a move on."

"Fine," said Caleb pulling himself up into his saddle.

Azar clicked her tongue loudly and the two Razor Jackal's began walking out of the Oasis.

The day went slowly, again there was no way for Caleb to tell how far they had travelled and what time it was, to him everything looked the same, more white sand as far as the eye could see, he wanted to ask Azar how she knew where to go but he decided against it, she probably wouldn't answer him anyway, he had learnt that about his guide, she wasn't a talkative women, that reminded Caleb of Wraith, maybe it was something to do with the Onmori culture, Caleb pondered on that as he followed Azar silently.

The sun was low in the sky now. Caleb sighed, he and Azar had been riding all day long and still there was nothing to show for it, Teuengea wasn't sat on the horizon, buzzing insects flitted around Caleb just waiting for their chance to steal the blood from his veins and a group of vultures circled overhead as if they knew he wouldn't make it to the city.

Maybe you won't.

Caleb took a sip from his waterskin and his stomach cramped.

See bodies giving out on you already.

Caleb tried to ignore the voice in his head but already he could feel other cramps, which at best meant he would spend another twenty minutes tonight walking around camp working the stiffness out of his limbs. Trying to get his mind off the aches Caleb began practicing his Skelwori, he regretted the decision immediately, his mind instantly jumped to the welfare of Vaeliria, which led to him thinking about Luci and then the rest of the crew, a million different possibilities went through his mind some were good but his mind seemed set to focus on the worst possible outcomes, he knew first hand that the world was cruel and it didn't matter whether you were good or bad, you could still be killed as easily as the next man, actually in the lower city anyone who didn't look out for themselves and tried to help others died a hell of a lot sooner than those whose only priority was their own welfare.

Caleb was awoken from his reverie by the sharp clicking sound Azar made to tell the jackals to stop. Looking down from the dune they stood on Caleb could see a company of Onmori soldier's setting up camp, most of the soldiers were putting up tents and tending to their own jackals, while others were walking the perimeter of the camp. Obviously, these men weren't expecting to meet anyone else out here in the depths of the desert because in the centre of the camp sat around a large fire were a group of men talking and jesting with one another. Caleb knew from his lesson's with Vaeliria that a fire was a luxury you never got unless you were absolutely sure no one was around as the light blinded you from seeing in the dark and made you completely visible to your enemies who could be watching from the darkness. Just off from the fire stood a giant iron-barred wagon, inside sat men, women and children who wore nothing but loincloths, each of the men sported an identically large tattoo across the left side of their face, whilst the children shivered uncontrollably. A moment later a soldier walked past the cage and made a series of obscene gestures towards the women and laughed. With another sharp click of her tongue Azar wheeled Balsa back down the dune, Quella followed suit lurching Caleb in his saddled as she did.

"What the hell was that all about?" said Caleb as Quella pulled up next to Balsa.

"This is bad, those are the Ghaul."

"And who in the seven hells are the Ghaul?"

"Their slavers," at the word Azar spat into the sand.

"They look like military, to me."

"I had heard rumours that a military patrol had gone missing in the desert but to think the Ghaul would be responsible."

"So maybe they really are military."

"Did you see the markings on the men?"

"Yeah."

"That's a slave brand, those men are going straight to Chinycur to work in the ruby mines, the women and children won't be branded until they've been sold off, most of the women will end up in whore-houses and the children, well only Haji knows what will happen to them."

"So what are we gonna do?" said Caleb feeling useless.

"We'll have to go around them, from the looks of it they're not moving tonight so we stick to this dune, loop around them for a mile or so and then we head straight for Teuengea."

"You can't be serious, what about the slaves they need our help."

"And how do you suppose we do that hmm? It's just the two of us and are you a Hexer cause I sure as hell ain't."

Caleb regretted his words, it was clear from the look on Azar's face that she wanted to help but she was right what could they do, there had to be at least thirty men down there each armed and even if they managed to get the slaves free would they be able to get them safely to Teuengea, maybe it was better for everyone if they just snuck around the slaver's.

"Fine, but what are we gonna do if they spot us?" asked Caleb feeling defeated.

"If that happens we run like Death herself is at our heels."

Caleb felt his heart race as he pressed himself against Quella's back, this was a terrible situation, one wrong move or too much noise and they would be spotted by the slaver sentries who now walked on top of the dune he and Azar had been on moments ago, but again Caleb was grateful for the idiocy of the slavers, it would take the sentries a while to become accustomed to the darkness, which gave him and Azar an extra few minutes to make their escape.

As they crept further along the dunes face Caleb noticed that Azar didn't have her hands on Balsa's reins, instead the jackal rider's hands were gripped tightly around a long blowgun.

How is she controlling him?

Caleb looked down and was stunned, from the looks of it Azar was controlling the Jackals pace with nothing but her legs.

Surely not.

But Caleb's suspicion was quickly confirmed as a moment later Azar clutched her legs against Balsa's flanks and the Jackal instantly stopped in his tracks.

Following Azar's gaze Caleb felt his stomach tense, two of the sentries stood directly above them, their voices ringing out through the quiet. Caleb felt utterly useless he didn't know what the sentries were saying and he had no way to take them out if they spotted him or Azar.

"Caleb."

Caleb turned his attention away from the sentries to find Azar staring at him, the jackal rider pointed at herself then up to the sentries followed by a gesture for him to stay where he was. As she dismounted Azar whispered in Balsa's ear, the giant beast gave a low snort and Azar gave his snot a rub before she began making her way up the dune.

Caleb watched Azar slowly creep up the dune, the jackal rider kept as low as she could and was moving with great care. The closer she got to the two sentries the more Caleb felt his heart pound and he instinctively made a sign to Yyja the Skelwori Goddess of luck.

When she stood a couple of feet away from the men, Azar redrew her blowgun and within seconds both men fell to the ground. Azar continued up onto the dune and pushed the two men's bodies down the sand to where Caleb and the two Razor Jackal's stood. Azar descended a moment later and without a word she remounted Balsa and pulled the beast away from the dune, Quella immediately followed suit.

As they drew further away from the safety of the dunes ridge Caleb felt as if his heart was in his throat. It would be easy for another sentry to spot them and raise the alarm, but no such event took place and once they were a couple of hundred yards away from the dune Azar kicked Balsa into a run.

The wind whipped around Caleb as he clung to Quella and sand showered his face, it felt like a thousand tiny knives were cutting into his face. Half a candlemark must have passed but still Azar showed no sign of slowing down, if anything she was riding Balsa harder than before.

"Surely we've put enough distance between ourselves and the slavers," called Caleb from Quella, but Azar made no sign that she had heard him, either the wind was drowning out his voice or she was choosing not to listen.

Caleb kicked his feet into Quella's flanks, instantly the jackal sped up and Caleb came level with Azar.

"Haven't we put enough distance between us and the slavers."

Azar turned to face him, "We have, but now we need to get out of this wind, there should be a cave up ahead."

"How far?" shouted Caleb above a gust of wind.

"We should be there any minute," replied Azar.

Caleb nodded and the two kicked their mounts into a full sprint, the wind replied tenfold, throwing great waves of sand at them tearing clothes and flesh alike, the onslaught also made it nearly impossible to see but they continued on through the painful storm of sand and they were rewarded, a black hole appeared within the barrage of sand, Azar and Caleb kicked the jackal's into a last ditch effort, the beasts weren't happy about it but they responded maintaining their sprint just long enough to reach the cave's mouth, flying into the cave Balsa and Quella collapsed, Azar skilfully dismounted but Caleb, who didn't have her mastery of jackal riding was thrown from his saddle, he rolled across the ground in a mass of tangled limbs. When he finally came to a stop, just about every part of his body ached but he knew from experience that it was nothing serious just a few cuts and scrapes and he pulled himself up. Azar was bent next to her jackal's stroking both of their snouts, she was saying something to them but Caleb couldn't hear it over the ringing in his own ears, slowly he made his way over to her and sat down. Quella and Balsa looked absolutely spent, both were breathing heavily, Balsa's face was covered with dozens of cuts and Quella had a deep gash across her left shoulder, Azar went to one of the packs that hung off Balsa and pulled out a cracked jar, a thick green goo oozed out of the crack, Azar dipped her hand into the jar and began smearing the goo over Balsa's wounds, the big Razor Jackal huffed in protest but eventually he quietened down.

"What's that?" said Caleb from the floor.

"It's a poultice, it will help with Balsa and Quella's injuries."

"Can I help?"

Azar looked at Caleb for a moment as if she was deciding whether he could be trusted to help heal her jackal. "Smear a large portion over every cut she has then do the same for yourself."

Caleb picked himself back up off the floor and made his way over to the jar, he could already smell the poultice, it smelt terrible, why was it that everything that healed smelt like dung. Caleb put his hand into the jar and scooped out a large handful of the goo, the smell was worse up close, it got into Caleb's eyes making them water and it hung at the back of his throat.

"What the hell is in this?" said Caleb fighting the urge to gag.

"No idea Akachi made it."

"Then how do you know it will help?"

"Because I've known Akachi for twenty years and not once has he steered me wrong, if he says it will help, it will help, he fixed you after all."

That shut Caleb up and he made his way over to Quella. The powerful beast was still breathing heavily and her eyes were unfocused.

"It'll be alright," said Caleb to Quella as he dipped his hand into the poultice.

With a gentle hand Caleb smeared the poultice over the large cut on the jackal's shoulder, he expected her to protest like Balsa but Quella barely moved.

Once the large cut was dealt with Caleb began smearing the poultice over the rest of the cuts that ran over Quella's body, the wind and sand had inflicted a great deal of punishment on the jackal, there were cuts just about everywhere, nevertheless Caleb took his time applying the poultice to each one, least he miss one and it turn septic.

It took a full candlemark for all the cuts to be attended to but once Caleb was finished Quella's breathing had become more steady and her eyes held some understanding, that was good it meant she wasn't in as much pain, he looked over to Balsa and found that the bigger jackal was breathing better as well, Azar however wasn't anywhere to be seen. Caleb walked around the jackals and found Azar sitting on the ground, the day had taken its toll on her, dark rings encircled her eyes and dozens of cuts lined her face and hands, but she managed a wan smile, which shocked Caleb he hadn't thought her capable of smiling but it was obvious that she cared for her jackals.

"Thank you," said Azar.

"Don't worry about it, it's the least I could do," said Caleb sitting down.

"We'd best get some rest." A heavy yawn escaped from Azar.

Moments later Azar along with the two jackals were asleep and Caleb was left alone with nothing save his thoughts for company and what poor company they were.

One moment he was thinking about the *Zephyrus* and whether he would ever make it back to his friends, the next he was thinking of the slaves in the wagon. He knew he couldn't have helped them but that only made it worse, he was supposed to be able to help people now that he was Caleb, not run away like a coward, as Asher had.

Guess you haven't changed as much as you thought.

Caleb awoke the next morning to find Balsa and Quella tearing into slices of dried meat that Azar kept for them, Caleb smiled it was good to see that they weren't too seriously hurt from the sandstorm, Azar was sat by the two jackal's eating some of the fruit they had taken from the Oasis, Caleb pulled himself to his feet.

"Seems your faith in Akachi was well placed," said Caleb stretching

Azar spun around in shock, obviously, she hadn't heard Caleb get up, "You move quietly."

"Force of habit," replied Caleb walking over to Quella, he stroked the jackal's long snout as he passed to her side and reached into the large pack that hung there pulling out his waterskin, the water was still cool despite them having travelled for an entire day, perhaps the Oasis was enchanted, that would explain how something so beautiful and luscious could exist in such a barren land.

"How long til we leave?"

"The winds have died so we can leave shortly."

"You think we'll reach Teuengea today?" asked Caleb searching the pack for something to eat.

"Yes and we'll have daylight to spare, once we get through Ormea's gate you'll be able to see Teuengea."

In the bottom of the pack Caleb found a couple of peaches, three figs and a plum, the peaches were overripe, the figs dried and the plum hard but that didn't deter him, he ate the small breakfast quickly, the prospect of getting to Teuengea filled him with new life, not to mention he could finally get back to his friends.

Before they left Azar did some final checks, she asked Caleb to check how much water he had left and food if any, she looked over Quella and Balsa's wounds, whispering to them in Onmori as she did and finally she made sure the harnesses and saddles were secured.

"Everything seems to be in order."

"Then let's get going." Caleb couldn't keep the excitement from his voice.

"Fine, let's ride." Azar leaped up into Balsa's saddle and kicked him into a walk.

Caleb followed suit mounting Quella with slightly more ease than he had at the start of his journey.

As they emerged from the cave Caleb was blinded by the light, once his eyes adjusted he saw the same sea of sand he had seen throughout the journey and his spirits dropped.

"I thought you said we were close, all I see is more desert."

"Look behind you."

Caleb spun around and the sight took his breath away, standing in front of him was a massive cliff of red coloured stone, at the base of the cliff face stood the cave, it created a tiny black hole in the mass of red.

"So where do we go now, cause I don't think we can climb that."

"We follow the Red Cliffs for about three miles, then we pass through Ormea's gate."

"Then we'll be at Teuengea?"

"Once through the gate, we'll be in Ormea's valley from there it's an easy run to Teuengea."

"Let's get going then."

Caleb felt good, the journey towards Ormea's gate was going smoothly, there was no sign of the wind picking back up and Azar had assured him that the Ghaul wouldn't dare travel this far east, due to the Jackal Riders who patrolled the area, but after a while the Red Cliffs seemed to loom oppressively over their heads, Caleb could feel eyes watching him, but when he looked around he saw nothing but jagged and gnawed rocks.

You're getting paranoid.

Suddenly a great thunderclap filled the quiet, looking behind him Caleb saw several rocks falling down the cliff, the noise was like a hundred cannons firing at once, the rocks hit the sandy earth with a final crash, a fountain of sand shot up into the air, instinctively Caleb covered his face least he get more sand in his eyes and mouth. When the sand had finally settled, he looked at the damage, as it turned out the rocks weren't rocks at all but boulders the size of wagons, Caleb was speechless, if one of those monsters had fallen over him and Azar they would've be dead.

"Don't stop moving."

"What the hell was that?"

"That was a rockfall."

"Seriously!"

"The Red Cliffs are a dangerous place at the best of times," said Azar matter-of-factly. "The sandstorm must have loosened some of the older parts last night".

"Great," said Caleb sarcastically.

For the rest of the journey along the Red Cliffs, Caleb kept a watchful eye out for any sign that another rockfall was about to happen, but thankfully none did and within a candlemark Caleb found himself at Ormea's gate, the gate was a narrow gouge that cut straight through the Red Cliffs like a wound on a colossal beast.

"Are you sure this is the only way?"

"There are only three ways to Teuengea, the first is to come from the sea, the second is to scale the Red Cliffs and come down the other side into Ormea's valley and the last is through the gate, the closest port from here is Saranthini, which is about eighty miles away, we've got maybe enough food and water to last a day out in the desert and as you said there is no way we're scaling the cliffs, so that leaves the gate."

"What if there's a rockfall."

"Then we'll both see the afterlife sooner than expected," said Azar riding into the gate.

Caleb sighed and followed suit.

The press of rocks was suffocating, Caleb thought it was bad enough when the Red Cliffs had been looming over him on one side but now that he was in the gorge, he was effectively trapped, blood red rock encased him on either side and there was nowhere for him to go. Rounding a corner Caleb was meet with an even narrower passage. Azar had dismounted and was leading Balsa by his reins through the gap, Caleb climbed off Quella and was about to do the same when Azar held a hand up.

"I'll lead her through, one wrong move and you could send the entire cliff down upon us."

Caleb swallowed nervously.

Azar disappeared through the gap and out of sight. Caleb stood completely still least he cause his own death.

After what felt like an eternity Azar returned, the jackal rider quickly took a hold of Quella's reins and began leading the beast through the cramped space at a tentative pace. The passage continued to narrow until finally it pressed against either side of Quella's flanks, Caleb's immediate thought was that there was no way the beast would get through without causing some kind of disturbance, but somehow the jackal squeezed through the gap without any issues.

Once he was through the gap Caleb made another sign to Yyja before he carefully remounted.

"Are you okay?" said Azar remounting Balsa.

"I will be once we get outta here."

For the remainder of the journey, Caleb was on high alert, everywhere he looked he saw a potential disaster, high above rocks stood tentatively on ledges just waiting for an excuse to fall. Strange little creatures crept along the ground hissing and spitting at Caleb as he passed, the long eye teeth that filled their mouths gave him all the warning he needed. After rounding yet another corner, the gouge began to widen until finally it opened out onto a ledge to reveal Ormea's Valley.

The valley was beautiful, a wonderfully blue waterfall ran down the side of the red cliffs into the valley, creating an Oasis of its own before finally flowing out towards the sea, thousands of trees filled the valley creating a rich expanse of green and brown and at the far end of the valley Caleb could just make out a few of the buildings of Teuengea, they had to be at least six storeys and each was a brilliant white.

Caleb's heart soared at the sight, he was almost there.

Without him realising Azar had begun to walk down the trail towards the base of the valley, Caleb pulled himself away from the sight to catch up, about half way down the trail dozens of brightly coloured birds appeared from within the trees, their squawks filled the quiet air with energy, Caleb turned to Azar and for only the second time in their journey he saw a smile creep across the Onmori woman's face.

"It beautiful here," said Caleb.

Azar's stoic look quickly reasserted itself and when she spoke her voice was cold like Wraith's, "Yes, it is."

Caleb didn't know what to say, clearly he had done something wrong but how could he apologise if he didn't know what he had done wrong in the first place.

Azar set off again, feeling awkward Caleb remained silent while Quella followed behind and went back to looking at the surrounding beauty.

Touching the valley floor Caleb thought he had been transported to another world, the view from up high had made the valley seem peaceful and idyllic but in reality, it was chaotic. Large bees buzzed from flower to flower, butterflies of various patterns and colours sat lazily on other plants whilst brown and red centipedes crawled out of the way of the Razor Jackal's massive paws and overhead between the leaves of the palm trees were monstrous spider webs, in one of the webs was a dragonfly struggling for freedom, the insects struggling had caught the attention of the webs maker, the hairy tarantula slowly made its way from the outskirts of its creation towards the helpless dragonfly. Caleb was transfixed by the event, slowly step by step the tarantula closed the distance, the dragonfly squirmed and shook with all its might but it was a wasted effort and then the tarantula plunged its teeth into its pray, the poor dragonfly managed a few more squirms before it became still, the tarantula quickly spun its web around its meal and then left it for later, Caleb shivered despite the heat, he understood what it meant to be helpless and have the strong impose their will on you.

Drenched with sweat and aching the two travellers and their jackals made their way out of the last line of palm trees. Thirty feet in front of them stood the gates of Teuengea, the gates were made from thick planks of wood and stood twelve feet high, large iron rivets sat in the wood, Caleb remembered from his studies with Thom that rivets were used to reinforce gates making it that much harder for an enemy to breach through into the city beyond, a twenty foot wall ran around the city from the gate but unlike the gate it was poorly built, some parts of the wall were taller than others, causing the parapets to be built at different heights to compensate and the mortar holding the wall together looked about ready to crumble and at what appeared to be random intervals sat squat towers, a worn ballista stood on top of each, on the closest tower Caleb could clearly see the weapons rope mechanisms, which looked more likely to snap then actually do its job. Caleb couldn't believe that a city would have such poor defences, if he were in charge he would have the walls rebuilt and the towers built higher so that the men could see over the jungle that lay before them.

Balsa and Quella crossed the short distance towards the gates.

Almost there.

Just before they reached the gate Azar pulled Balsa to a stop and dismounted, Caleb wondered what was going on,

Azar began rooting around in one of the packs that hung off the jackal, finally she pulled a long horn that was adorned with scrollwork out of the pack and pressed it to her and blew. The horn let out a loud bellow in response, once she was done Azar put the horn back in its pack and remounted, seconds passed and Caleb thought nothing was going to happen when a shout came from within the city, Caleb couldn't understand what was said but shortly after the gates began to open. Azar kicked Balsa forward and Caleb did the same, as they drew closer a group of five guards came marching out of the gate, each wore loose fitting robes made from crimson silk and a black turban sat on top of their heads, four of the guards were holding glaives, the sun gleaming off the polished steel, the guard in the middle, however, had a long sabre at his hip, the scabbard was made from bronze, and rubies and sapphires were set into the scabbard at various points making it the most ostentatious weapon Caleb had ever seen someone with.

The guard in the middle of the procession said something in Onmori and Azar replied, as they were talking Caleb gave the man a closer look, he had an olive complexion which Caleb found strange but before he could think on the man's origins anymore the guard turned to face Caleb and the two locked eyes, his deep brown eyes held something, but what Caleb couldn't say. The man suddenly smiled and laughed.

He said something to Azar, making it plainly obvious that he was talking about Caleb by pointing at him.

"What's he saying?" asked Caleb annoyed.

"I asked who you are and why you would be travelling with a jackal rider," said the man in the common tongue, Caleb was caught off guard he was under the impression that the man couldn't speak anything but Onmori.

Shaking his surprise away Caleb straightened in his saddle and in a clear voice said, "I'm Caleb Wintergrave of the Angardian Skyknights, my ship was attacked and I was separated from my crew, Azar informed me that my ship was docked here."

The man bowed, "I welcome you to Teuengea, Caleb Wintergrave, my name is Amir Rouhani, and your ship is indeed docked here."

"And my crew?" said Caleb anxiously.

"Your Captain and those not seriously injured in your fight with Irashaad's pirates are guests at his Lord's palace, the rest of your crew, however, are in the House of Healing."

"Do you know if Vaeliria and Lucianna are okay?"

"Your Commander is fine but I cannot say the same for this Lucianna."

"Why not?" shouted Caleb as his heart skipped a beat.

Amir paid Caleb's outburst no mind, "Because unlike your Commander I haven't actually met her; thus, I can give no account of her health."

Caleb felt sick, if anything had happened to Luci he didn't know what he would do, she had been the only friend he had ever known.

"Where's this House of Healing?"

"The House is located in the Awarea District, I'd be happy to escort you there."

Caleb dismounted and bowed to Azar, "Thank you for getting me back to my crew."

Azar waved Caleb's words aside, "I will be at the palace when you are finished with your business at the House of Healing."

With that Azar and her two jackal's disappeared off into Teuengea, leaving Caleb surrounded by Amir and his men.

"Shall we," said Amir smiling.

Chapter 18

The city of Teuengea was a busier place than Caleb imagined it would have been, he thought the people would be sat around lazily enjoying the sun, but that wasn't the case at all, hundreds if not thousands of men and women filled the streets rushing from place to place like skittering insects, many of the women were dressed in brightly coloured robes and carried heavy looking basket on their heads, children clinging to their arms as they did, the men on the other hand wore darker colours and carried large barrels, the contents of which were unknown. Amongst the bustling crowd were hundreds of stalls of varying sizes, the men and women who operated the stalls shouted out to the crowd. Caleb looked around as he passed by, there were stalls selling rugs of the finest looking quality, some had symbols and patterns stitched into them others seemed more like tapestries than rugs, depicting the local stories and legends. Exquisite plates, bowls, jugs and vases sat on other stalls, the majority were painted with intricate patterns, others were decorated with brightly coloured beads and a few of the more outlandish vendors had even decorated their wares with gems. Caleb couldn't imagine why someone would have something like that on display out here in the open, he could easily steal it, all it would take was for him to distract the seller and use a little sleight of hand and poof just like that the seller would be out a fortune and he'd disappear back into the crowd. The next group of merchants Caleb came across as he was led through the market had necklaces, bracelets and rings lining their stalls, the jewellery was mostly made from bronze, silver and occasionally gold, studded with amber and garnet, but as he looked from stall to stall Caleb spotted a ring made entirely out of a white material, curiosity got the better of him and heedless of the fact that he could lose Amir in the crowd Caleb walked towards the stall to get a better look, as he got closer he realised the ring was made from bone, a shiver crept up his back, why in the seven hells would anyone want to drape themselves in bone. The owner who had been busy with another customer at the time of Caleb's arrival saw Caleb looking at the ring and began saying something to him in Onmori, Caleb looked up at the owner, he was a small man with a bulbous nose and little piggy eyes that seemed to sit a little too close together, the merchant seemed to realise that Caleb couldn't understand him, seamlessly switching to the common tongue the merchant restarted his sales pitch.

"You have a fine eye, my friend, this ring is carved from the horn of one of the desert's greatest animals, yes the three-horned rhinoceros is a wondrous sight but wearing this is even more so, the Sultan in all his glory has band the poaching of the three-horned rhinoceros so this is one of only a handful of rings made from the legendary beasts, what do you say it's yours for thirty gold pieces."

"Thirty gold pieces!" replied Caleb in shock, even if he had wanted to buy the ring, thirty gold pieces was an extortionate amount to pay for such a thing.

"Okay," said the merchant holding his hands up, "because I like you I'm willing to go down to twenty-seven gold pieces."

Caleb was about to tell the merchant he wasn't interested but before he could he heard Amir's voice came from behind him.

"That's a fine ring you have there but if I'm correct the Sultan, outlawed not only poaching but anyone who was in possession of rhinoceros' artifacts had to hand them over straight away otherwise they would be tried as a smuggler."

The merchant looked up from Caleb and his face instantly paled, "Captain Rouhani, I didn't see you there, th... thi... this isn't what you think this ring is actually made from camel bone, I thought that I could convince the young man here into buying it if I told him it was rare, most travellers that come through here are looking for expensive and rare things and as of late my business has been struggling, please don't throw me in the dungeon I have a family, please, Captain."

Amir's face was an unreadable mask, Caleb had no idea what he was going to do and from the look on the merchant's face neither did he, after about a minute, Amir spoke, "Your name's Nazem, correct?"

"Yes, Captain I'm Nazem Kashnavi."

"Okay, Nazem, you won't be sent to the dungeon but instead I will accept a donation of fifteen gold pieces."

Caleb was a little surprised at what he was hearing, he thought Captain Rouhani above such things as accepting bribes, but then should he be that surprised, the guard's back in the lower city accepted bribes all the time and Caleb had delivered several himself on the behalf of old One Eye.

The merchant bowed to Amir before reaching into the coin purse that sat at his hip and slowly pulled out the fifteen gold coins required of him, Amir swept the coins up in one quick motion.

"Thank you for your generosity."

As Caleb followed after Amir he was sure he heard the merchant curse something under his breath, but the activity of the bazaar quickly drowned it out.

Making it through the last few stalls of the bazaar and the offers of those who occupied them, Captain Rouhani took Caleb up a wide cobbled path, Caleb sighed in relief, after his time spent in the desert where the only other person he saw for miles around was Azar it had felt rather suffocating being back in the press of such a crowd not to mention his pale skin made him stick out like a sore thumb in the crowd of dark skinned Onmori, which made him feel even more like a target. On either side of the path stood a series of one storey homes, the white walls shone brightly in the daytime sun, suddenly a swarm of children ran from the houses, their voices and laughter creating a symphony of chaos, without realising Caleb balled his hands into fists, Rouhani put a hand on his shoulder.

"Just a group of kids, nothing to worry about."

Caleb knew just how capable kids were when it came time to pickpocket but he allowed himself to relax a little, after all he knew just about every trick in the book so it would be easy enough for him to defend himself also it helped that the only things of value that he carried on him were his dirks and there was no way anyone not even Uhldir himself was going to part him from his most prized possessions.

As he Followed Amir up the street Caleb kept his eyes on the children around him, from the look of it the younger ones were playing make believe, some pretended to be knights and wizards while others played the roles of monsters or the villains, the older boys and girls on the other hand were kicking a leather ball through the street and one boy no older than six summers old was walking down the street on his hands, it was one of the most incredible things Caleb had seen, there was no way he would be able to do that. As Amir passed by women called greetings to him from their homes which the Captain returned dutifully.

If only they knew you were taking bribes.

About halfway up the street Amir turned down into a tight alleyway, Caleb was instantly on edge, this was a perfect place for a gang to wait in hiding before jumping them.

"Shouldn't we stick to the main roads?" said Caleb from the entrance of the alley.

"Too many people," replied Amir over his shoulder.

Caleb didn't know what to do, this could be a trap, he knew he couldn't trust Amir not after seeing him take that bribe from the merchant back in the bazaar, but on the other hand he needed Amir to show him around the city and it provided him with a certain amount of protection.

Better the beast you know than the one you don't.

Steeling himself Caleb followed Amir into the alley, everywhere he looked he saw danger. The low roofs of the houses could easily have men up on them and the drop down into the alley was one that even an inexperienced mugger could do, or one of the kids could've be a spotter for a gang, as Caleb had done when he was younger, however none of the scenarios Caleb imagined came to fruition and he emerged from the alley and onto yet another cobbled street.

"Are you okay?" said Amir.

"I'm fine," replied Caleb taking a deep breath, realising only now that he had been holding his breathe in anticipation of one of his imagined conflicts, "So where are we now?".

"We're on the Warriors' Road, from here it a straight walk to the House of Healing."

"Okay," said Caleb standing straight, "lead the way."

It quickly became clear to Caleb why this was called the Warriors' Road as dozens of marble statues stood proudly in the middle of the street at regular intervals for as far as the eye could see.

The first such statue Caleb came across was that of an elegant looking woman who stood with a staff in hand. Caleb was speechless, the artist who had carved this must have been without rival, after all Caleb half expected the statue to start moving it looked that lifelike.

The next statue was that of a bearded man whose face was set in a permanent roar of deviance as he held his spear aloft.

The one after that depicted a wizardly looking man, his face was marked with the deep creases that only come from old age, how the artist had managed to carve such lines without making the statue look ridiculous Caleb didn't know but the thought quickly faded as more statues followed suit, each as fascinating as the one that came before.

Before Caleb knew it, the Warriors' Road had ended and he found himself staring at a large archway. Standing at the top of the arch stood a woman with her hands open, her smile looked warm like how Caleb imagined a mothers would.

As Amir made his way through the arch he whispered something and made a gesture skyward, Caleb followed the guard-captain through and standing at the end of the long courtyard was a tall tower that had an intricate scrollwork covering its entire face.

I'm guessing that's the House of Healing.

Standing just in front of the house was a giant Acacia tree, its bark was gnarled and a pale red in colour, the leaves that grew from its spindly branches resembled feathers. Beneath the tree sat a ring of marble benches, one of which was occupied by a group of three robed women, two of the women wore white robes and veils whilst the third wore black.

Amir quickly crossed the distance towards the women and dropped to a knee and Caleb not knowing what else to do followed suit.

"Blessed sisters," said Amir in greeting.

The three women turned to regard Amir, but only the one in black spoke and she did so in the common tongue, "Captain Rouhani please stand," the woman's voice was like honey. "What brings you and your companion to the House of Healing?"

"This boy's name is Caleb Wintergrave he is a member of the Angardian Skyknights, he was separated from his crew when they were attacked, as a result he has only just arrived in the city, I informed him that you are treating a number of his crewmates."

The woman in black turned to Caleb, "It's a pleasure to meet you, Caleb Wintergrave, my name is Sister Tahalia, Captain Rouhani is correct, the members of your crew who were seriously hurt were brought to us."

"Did you have a patient by the name of Lucianna Estrada?"

"Lucianna was a patient of ours, but she isn't any longer."

Caleb felt his chest tighten.

"Do not fear your friend is fine," said Sister Tahalia reading Caleb's thoughts. "Your Captain brought her here as a precaution, she had suffered a nasty knock to her head, those sort of injuries are best to keep an eye on least the Daemons get in."

"Could you take me to her?"

Sister Tahalia stood, "Please follow me, Captain Rouhani will you be joining us."

"I'm afraid not, I do not wish to sully the house with the day's dirt, but I have an offering here from a most generous merchant."

Amir pulled out the fifteen gold coins he had taken from the merchant and handed them to the Sister. Caleb was stunned, he thought Amir was a crooked man, but if this was what he did with the money that he took from those he punished then he was one of the best men Caleb had ever met.

Maybe you should take a page from your own book and not judge people until you know all the facts about them.

"Be sure to thank this man on behalf of the Sisterhood," said Sister Tahalia as she put the gold inside one of the pockets that lined her robes.

Amir bowed to the Sister of healing, before he turned to Caleb, "I'll be here to escort you to the palace once you are done."

Caleb fell in beside Sister Tahalia and together they crossed the last of the courtyard towards the House of Healing.

The inside of the House of Healing was unnaturally quiet, there were no cries of pain and no one was rushing about trying to save lives; instead, the massive hall was quiet to the point where Caleb was very aware of his own breathing and the beating of his heart. Caleb stopped in his tracks, there was something in the air he could feel it, Sister Tahalia stopped and turned back to regard him.

"Is there a problem?"

"Something doesn't seem right," replied Caleb looking around.

"What do you mean?"

"This place feels different somehow, there's something in the air."

"Ahh, that's the blessing of Firtia the mother."

"Say what?"

"You saw the markings that run across the body of the house."

Caleb nodded.

"Those markings form a hex grid that pulls life energy from the earth itself."

"So you're saying that's what I'm feeling?"

Sister Tahalia nodded, "To be honest I'm surprised that you noticed it, most don't."

Now that she had mentioned it Caleb realised that he did feel better, all his aches and pains felt less of a burden and he was moving better than he had in days.

"Now," said Sister Tahalia turning back around, "shall we continue?"

Caleb followed the Sister through the hall, passing another stream of veiled women as he did, many wore the same simple white robes Caleb had seen earlier, others wore thick brown robes that engulfed their frame but none wore black like Sister Tahalia. At the end of the hall was a spiral staircase which Sister Tahalia began climbing and Caleb followed.

Coming to the top of the stairs Caleb found himself met with a crowd of people, all of whom looked like they had seen better days. A dozen or so of the white robed Sisters stood amongst the crowd handing out pieces of bread and water.

Caleb scanned the crowd in hope that he would find Luci but all he was met with were the stares of strangers.

"Hey, that's my bread."

Caleb turned to see two sickly looking boys wrestling over a crust of bread no bigger than his palm, the sight immediately reminded Caleb of himself at that age and instinctively he found himself rubbing the bite-mark scar that lined his left ear.

I better split them up before they end up seriously hurting one another.

Before Caleb could act on his thought, one of the white robed Sisters appeared and tore the two boys apart.

"Are you alright?"

Caleb turned away from the sight of the two boys to find Sister Thalia looking at him with concerned eyes.

"Sorry, zoned out for a second."

Sister Thalia continued to eye Caleb.

"I'm fine, honestly."

"Very well."

With that Sister Thalia once again began leading Caleb through the second floor of the house.

As Caleb was led deeper into the crowd he noticed a group of hollow looking men and women that sat in the far corner of the room and were cordoned off from everyone else, the men's hair and beards were wild hiding most of their faces, but Caleb could see the desperation in their bloodshot eyes, the women who crowded around them weren't in much better shape, dark rings marked their eyes and most of their mouths were black pits, teeth rotted away a long time ago.

Junkies.

As Caleb cast the useless thought aside he found that his and Sister Tahalia's path was being blocked by a group of men and women.

"Please, you have to help?" cried one of the women.

"We've gone days without food," cried another.

"Why are we stuck in here with junkies?" shouted a man, from within the depths of the crowd.

Caleb couldn't believe that all of these people were speaking in the common tongue and that's when he realised that they weren't, each spoke in the harsh tongue of the Onmori and yet he could understand them.

Before Caleb could further ponder on the cause of his sudden ability to understand those around him, a bedraggled woman who was little more than bones pushed through the crowd and came to stand right in front of

Sister Thalia. "Please, my son is suffering, you have to help?"

Caleb looked to the woman's arm and wrapped in a dirtied bundle of linen was a small child who was crying, from the babe's squashed face Caleb guessed the child was no older than a couple of months.

How could anyone bring a child into this world?

"Pass me your son," said Sister Thalia reaching out her hands.

The woman was quick to comply, she handed over her child, Caleb couldn't believe how small the babe was and how weak he looked. Sister Tahalia held the boy gently in her arms and began chanting in a language Caleb had never heard before, the child instantly quietened, as the Sister continued chanting Caleb felt a shift in the energy of the room and faint wisps of light began to dance around the child, gasps of awe and bewilderment came from the crowd at the sight and then suddenly the babe was lost in a bright yellow light, there were shrieks of worry, most of which came from the boy's mother, but as quickly as it came the light faded and Tahalia gave the child back without so much as another word, it was obvious to everyone that the child felt better, he wasn't crying anymore and he even smiled when he saw his mother, the mother instantly broke into tears and shouted her thanks to Sister Tahalia as the crowd parted.

At the end of the hall stood another spiral staircase but this one was twice as wide as the one before. Caleb climbed the stairs alongside Sister Tahalia, he wanted to ask her what she had done with the babe but thought better of it.

Coming up the last few steps Caleb was meet with a sight that lifted his heart, sitting in one of the beds that filled the third levels hall was Thom, the old engineer had a bandage across his head and his ribs were bandaged up tight but Caleb could tell he was okay after all a heavy leather bound tome sat open in his hands, sat next to the bed on a worn looking chair was Gustav, the younger engineer looked worse than Thom, his eyes looked sunken and his right arm was bound in a sling, before he knew what he was doing Caleb left Sister Tahalia behind and walked towards the two engineers.

"Would you stop worrying about me and look after yourself," said Thom to Gustav.

"You heard the Captain. Anyone who suffered a head injury has to have someone with them at all times."

"For the love of the Firstborn," cursed Thom, "there's got to be fifteen Sisters here that could help me if something goes wrong, plus," Thom swept his hand in front of him, "just about every one of our medical officers is here as well, so stop worrying about me and focus on getting better yourself, it's gonna take a lot of work to get the *Zephyrus* back up and running."

"I'm sure I could help you," said Caleb.

Both engineers spun around at his voice, Thom immediately broke out into a wide smile, Gustav on the other hand looked like he had seen a ghost, all the colour had drained from his face.

"Don't worry Gus you're not speaking with a ghost," said Caleb smiling, before he knew it Gustav had stood and pulled him into a hug.

"It's good to see you lad," said Thom from his bed.

"Same," replied Caleb freeing himself from Gustav's hug. "Is Luci here?"

"She's over there," said Gus pointing over to the other end of the room.

Caleb looked over to where Gus was pointing and sure enough across the room tending to the wounds of one of the crew was Luci.

Thank Yyja.

The relief that Caleb felt at seeing his friend quickly turned to concern as he noticed the thick bandage that ran around her head as well as the blood and vomit that lined her apron.

"Luci."

"I'll be with you in one moment," said Luci as she finished wrapping a bandage around the woman's arm she was tending too.

Caleb smiled, it was good to see that Luci was her usual caring self.

"Try not to move your arm too much, okay?" said Luci to her patient once she had finished the bandage.

"Sure thing Doc." replied the woman with a tired smile.

Luci nodded, "Now what can I do for you."

Luci turned to face Caleb and for a moment her face showed no sign of recognition, but then her jaw dropped and Caleb smiled.

"You're alive!" cried Luci as she buried her head into Caleb's shoulder.

"Alive and kicking," said Caleb hugging Luci tightly.

When Caleb put Luci back down he saw tears streaming down her face, "Is it that bad to see me?"

That got a smile from Luci, "I'm just so happy to see you."

"Same here." Caleb wiped a tear from Luci's eye. "I'm glad you're okay."

The smile that Luci gave Caleb melted his heart and a strange feeling sat in his stomach, it felt warm like the one he got just after eating a good meal.

"So how did you manage to survive? Riktor told me and mother that he saw you fall from the *Zephyrus*."

"I'm not sure all I remember is falling, then the next thing I knew I woke up in the middle of the desert in a hut."

"From the height you fell you should have broken several bones."

"I think I did but a man called Akachi healed me whilst I was unconscious."

"He healed your broken bones?" said Luci sceptically.

"I don't know how he did it but I think it had something to do with the fact that he could use Hexes."

Caleb could see the doubt in Luci's eyes, "Well I don't know how he did it but I'm thankful none the less, did he bring you here, I would love to thank him."

"No a woman named Azar brought me here."

"Then I'd like to thank her."

"That can be arranged she said she'd be at the palace, now that I know you're safe I'm heading over there to find Vaeliria and the Captain and find out more about who attacked us and why."

"Okay give me a minute, I just need to change wouldn't do to show up in this."

Luci disappeared behind a curtain, a few minutes later she emerged in a forest green dress and had her hair down, Caleb was taken aback he had never seen Luci in anything but her medical robes and her hair was always tied up, now though she looked like a completely different person, like a noble lady from the upper city, then it hit Caleb she was a noble, of course she was how could he have been so stupid only highborns became Skyknights.

"Are you alright?"

"Yeah," said Caleb shaking away his thoughts. "Shall we get going?"

"Ah, I see you found Lucianna," said Sister Thalia as Caleb and Luci came to stand before her.

"I was hoping you could take us back down to Captain Rouhani."

Sister Tahalia nodded and with that she led Caleb and Luci back through the House of Healing. As they walked through the second floor a child ran over to Luci and gave her a bright orange flower, who accepted it gratefully.

"What was that for?" said Caleb as they got down to the ground level.

Luci slipped the flower into her hair before she replied, "When I was allowed to get up from bed I started to help the Sisters with their work, Shakiba was the first person I helped."

"What was wrong with her?"

"She had a fever."

"And you gave her a tea made from Willow, Tamarind and Linden to reduce the fever," said Caleb remembering what he had seen in one of Luci's books.

"Yes," said Luci smiling, "it seems you still remember some of what you learnt whilst learning to read, once the fever was dealt with it was just a matter of getting her to eat and drink."

"I imagine that wasn't very hard."

"You'd be surprised," said Luci before Sister Tahalia led them back out into the house's courtyard.

Amir was waiting for them outside, he stood from his seat under the Acacia tree. "I see you found your friend."

"Captain Rouhani, seeing as you're heading to the palace would you mind delivering something to Shwani."

"It would be my pleasure."

Sister Tahalia reached into her robes and produced a sealed piece of parchment, Amir handled it like it was the most precious thing in the entire world and safely tucked it inside his own robe.

Sister Tahalia turned her attention back towards Caleb and Luci, "I wish you safe travels, Caleb Wintergrave."

"And I you," replied Caleb bowing.

"Luci, remember what we discussed and may Firtia guide your hand."

Luci bowed, "Thank you, Sister, I have learnt so much from you, in such a short time and I hope I can learn more before it is time for us to leave."

"I should be on my way; I have several patients who need immediate attention." With that Sister Tahalia walked back towards the House of Healing, leaving Caleb and Luci in Amir's hands.

"On that note, I think we should be on our way."

As Amir led Caleb and Luci through the streets of Teuengea, Caleb recounted his journey through Onmoria's desert to Luci.

"You really saw an Oasis," said Luci, excitement clear in her voice.

"Yeah, I Spent the night in one with Azar and her jackals," replied Caleb smiling at the memory of the luscious refuge.

"So what happened after you left the Oasis?"

Caleb's smile immediately died as he was reminded of the Ghaul and those he had left to their fate, "We came across a band of slavers known as the Ghaul."

At the mention of the Ghaul, Amir spat onto the ground and cursed in his native tongue.

"What happened," said Luci gently.

"There was nothing we could do for them," said Caleb trying to convince himself more than Luci.

"It's alright, I understand." Luci laid a hand on Caleb's shoulder and gave a reassuring squeeze.

Caleb smiled weakly before changing the subject, "So what happened after I went overboard?"

Thankfully Luci went along with the change in subject, "Once we were free from the enemy's grasp the Cannoneers opened fire with everything that they had."

"Did they get the bastards that attacked us."

Luci nodded.

"Good," said Caleb venomously, the hatred that he felt for those that attacked him and his crew still burnt intensely, so much so that he wished they had managed to capture the bastards alive just so he could send them to Aludin's abyss himself.

"Caleb, are you alright?"

Caleb snapped out of his dark thoughts to find Luci staring at him with eyes filled with concern.

"I'm fine," replied Caleb taking a calming breath. "What happened once the enemy ship was down?"

Luci still looked concerned but nevertheless she let it go and answered Caleb's question, "With the amount of damage that the *Zephyrus* had taken, Thom and Gus were forced to overcharge the core by fifty percent."

"It was that bad?"

Luci nodded, "Thom told me it was the only way that they could provide the *Zephyrus* with enough lift to make it over the Red Cliffs and to Teuengea."

"I'm guessing the Captain had to put the *Zephyrus* down in the water."

Again, Luci nodded, "Yeah it was the only way to protect the people of Teuengea."

Before Caleb could reply Amir spoke, "I'm sorry to interrupt your conversation but we've arrived at the palace."

Turning his attention away from Luci, Caleb realised that they did in fact stand before Teuengea's palace.

A large domed building made up most the palace, its white marble walls shone brighter than anything Caleb had seen. Holding the domed roof aloft were dozens of twisted onyx pillars, the shining black made them stand out against the pure white of the marble. A mural was painted on top of the roof, it depicted a man being blessed by an angel, the man looked strong but still he bowed his head to the angelic creature, Caleb couldn't tell whether the angel was a man or a woman, many of the murals features pointed towards a woman but when Caleb looked at the body of the angel it was more masculine than feminine, wide shoulders led down to a flat chest. At the top of the dome stood a tall golden pole, flying lazily from the pole in the gentle breeze was a crimson banner, Caleb couldn't really see what was on the banner but from the look of it, it was a Razor Jackal with a rider sat on top, sword drawn and ready for battle.

Standing around the domed building were three marble towers, each was a different size, the tower to the left was the shortest by far, barely standing half that of the domed building, standing on top of the tower were several guards in yellow robes and tanned leather armour. The tower on the right was slightly taller than that of the one on the left, more men dressed in yellow manned this tower whilst the tallest tower stood directly behind the domed building, it was easily taller than both the other two towers put together, if there were men manning this tower Caleb couldn't see them and encircling the entire complex was a ten-foot fence of wrought iron, men and women in blue robes walked the grounds with viscous looking dogs in tow.

Amir led Caleb and Luci to the gates of the palace, four guards in dark green robes stood at the gates, as they approached Amir shouted greetings in Onmori, one of the guards, a young-looking man of maybe twenty-two summers returned the greeting and the gates quickly opened.

Amir quickly led Caleb and Luci through the gates, "It's good to see you, Sa'ed," said Amir switching to the common tongue so Caleb and Luci could follow his conversation.

The guard who greeted Amir seemed to understand this as he too began speaking in the common tongue, "It's good to see you as well, Amir."

The two men embraced each other in a tight hug, "How is it being the Captain of the city watch?" said Sa'ed breaking the embrace.

"It's not what I expected, I have a mountain of paperwork that never seems to end and I have the heads of every guild and district jumping down my throat with the smallest problem."

"It can't all be bad."

"No you're right, at the very least I get to order people around now, instead of being the one given the orders," replied Amir smiling.

"Too true," said Sa'ed a smile of his own cracking his lips. "I would love to stay and chat but right now I have to go and kick some new recruits into shape, seems they fell asleep at their posts last night." Sa'ed was about to walk off but then he stopped, "Hey I have a great idea I'll be down in The Falling Tear later tonight, you should stop by if you get the chance, it would be great to catch up."

"The Falling Tear you say, as it so happens I had planned on going to Leila's for a drink after my last patrol, but drinking by myself doesn't sound nearly as appealing as a drink and a game of dice with you, after all it's been a while since I took all your gold."

"We'll see who's laughing tonight," said Sa'ed walking off towards the shortest tower.

Without a word on what had just happened Amir led Caleb and Luci towards the doors of the palace, the two guards at the doors nodded to Amir as they passed.

The entrance hall of the palace was marvellous, the floor was tiled with thousands of different coloured pieces of marble, Luci openly marvelled at the rainbow of colour, Caleb on the other hand just kept thinking about how much it must have cost to make. On either side of the hall stood twelve pillars, carved into the face of each pillar was a different symbol, Caleb had spent enough time around Hexes to recognise them when they were in front of him, some of the Hexes looked like they shifted under his gaze, Caleb blinked and when he looked again all the Hexes were still and he turned his attention back to the hall itself. Ornately decorated baskets hung from the ceiling, vibrant leaves spilled over the edges of each, creating a garden in the air and at the end of the hall was a great door of oak, two men in dark blue robes and hard leather breastplates stood on either side of the door, a short sword sat at the hip of one and a deadly spiked mace at the others, walking towards the door Caleb whispered to Luci, "You know why all the guards wear different colour uniforms?"

"It's to show the division we work for," said Amir before Luci could reply. "Red is for the city guard, yellow the archers, green is for the rangers like Sa'ed and blue is the royal guard".

"That makes some sense, but what about the civilians, wouldn't it cause confusion if they wore the same colours as the guard."

"It would but only members of those divisions may carry weapons openly, plus," said Amir reaching into his robes. "We carry these with us." Amir pulled out a heavy looking medallion from around his neck, it was made entirely from silver, the light gleamed off the polished metal, in the middle of the medallion was an insignia of two swords, both overlapped each other and a series of what appeared to be more Hexes ran around the blades in a perfect circle, "You see the Hexes?" Caleb and Luci both nodded, "No normal blacksmith can do that, you need a smith skilled in both silver work and Hexing."

"Which means that someone would have to kill you if they wanted that medallion," said Luci.

"Yes, but for what purpose I cannot say, each division is no more than a hundred men, meaning we all know each other and the only reason we got through the gate so easily is because the men on guard all know me by my face alone, so it's not like someone could use it to sneak into the palace and even if they did, what would they do kill the Jackeal," Amir let out a chuckle, "now that's something I would pay to see."

"Jackeal?".

"The lord of Teuengea and the man you are about to talk with."

The two guards didn't so much as question Amir when he walked up to them, they just silently opened the doors and let him walk right through to the throne room beyond.

The throne room was even larger than the entrance hall had been, the high vaulted ceiling stretched higher than any Caleb had seen before, painted onto the ceiling was a beautiful picture of Ormea's valley, the detail was exquisite, the waterfall that ran from the depths of the Red Cliffs looked exactly like it had when Caleb saw it, the artist had even gone to the trouble of painting dozens of brightly coloured birds in flight. The floor of the throne room was covered in the same rainbow pattern as the entrance hall part of which was covered by a long carpet made from purple silk, the light made the fabric shimmer and at the end of the carpet on a raised dais stood a throne, it was a magnificently crafted thing, the high-back was imposing standing at least as tall as a man, the arms had been carved into two Razor Jackal heads, the eyes of which were fiery red rubies and the wooden teeth looked nearly as sharp as the real thing, but the most surprising thing about the throne was that it lay empty, which surprised Caleb hadn't they come here to speak with the lord of Teuengea and find the Captain and Vaeliria. Standing in front of the throne were six of the royal guard, their leather armour looked freshly tanned and the swords, axes and spears they held freshly forged, Caleb looked around the room and realised that they weren't the only guards here, dozens of other guards filled the room, archers were high up on the balconies that ran around the room, their crossbows already loaded and ready at a moment's notice, other members of the royal guard stood lining the walls of the room.

Seems Amir was right no one could sneak in here.

A door at the back of the room opened and out walked a slimly built man with wispy white hair, he wore robes of white with golden thread inlaid around the edges of his sleeves which formed a complex weave and black leather boots polished to a near mirror shine lined the man's feet.

"Who's this?" said Caleb to Amir.

"That man is Vahid Cyrusi, Seneschal to Jackeal Teymour Biyabani."

In a few graceful strides Seneschal Cyrusi made it up onto the dais and stood in front of the throne, as soon as he laid eyes on Amir he raised his brow questioningly.

"Your report isn't due til tomorrow, Captain," said the Seneschal in the common tongue, Caleb was surprised how well he spoke, there wasn't a trace of accent in his voice.

"Forgive me, my Lord," said Amir, "but I have someone here who wishes to speak with the Jackeal."

Before anyone could stop him, Caleb stepped forward and addressed the Seneschal directly. "My name is Caleb Wintergrave, I am a member of the *Zephyrus*'s crew, I am here to speak with my Captain and Commander and with the Lord of your city."

"So you're the young man Azar has been telling me so much about," said the Seneschal walking down from the dais and towards another door behind the throne. "Please follow me".

"If its alright with you my Lord I will take my leave," said Amir. "I have some business to attend to back in the city."

"Of course, the Jackeal will be waiting for your report tomorrow," replied the Seneschal.

"Thank you, my Lord." Amir bowed before leaving the room.

Caleb and Luci were led through the door at the back of the room and down a long winding corridor, torches lined the passages walls, their flames bathed the corridor in orange light.

"Please watch your step," said Seneschal Cyrusi as he led Caleb and Luci through the archway that stood at the other end of the corridor and out onto the landing of a tight spiral staircase.

Caleb looked down at the grey steps of the staircase and immediately knew why the Seneschal had warned him and Luci, the steps were cracked and chipped in over a dozen places.

It's like they want someone to break their neck.

Heading down the stone steps Caleb took slow measured steps, least he trip and go crashing into Luci and subsequently the Seneschal.

After what felt like an eternity Caleb eventually made it to the bottom of the hazardous staircase and found himself in a small courtyard. Large flowers of orange, purple and yellow lined a patch of grass that ran down the middle of the courtyard whilst short palm trees stood around the edges, their massive leaves providing shade and relief for anyone who wanted it.

I could use a bit of shade.

As if reading his mind, the Seneschal led Caleb and Luci through the courtyard and into a small grove, the shade instantly made Caleb feel better, however he quickly forgot his relief as the sounds of people fighting echoed throughout the grove. Walking out of the line of trees and into a small clearing Caleb was me with the sight of Vaeliria being circled by a muscular Onmorian man who had an elaborate tattoo running across the entire right side of his torso, however that was nothing when compared to the man's hair, the thick braids ran down to the small of his back and were adorned with small silver bells and ribbons of yellow, red, blue and green.

"Is that the Lord of Teuengea?" said Caleb.

"Yes," replied Cyrusi, "his Lordship has been practicing every day with your Commander, he's found it quite refreshing to spar with someone who's actually a challenge."

Before Caleb could reply, Jackeal Biyabani sprang into action and threw a sharp kick at Vaeliria's knee.

He's fast.

As impressive as the Jackeal's speed was Vaeliria easily stepped out of the strikes way and immediately retaliated with a kick of her own, which connected straight to the Jackeal's stomach but rather than crumble as Caleb would have if he had taken the blow the Jackeal let out a joyous laugh.

"Haha, that was a wonderful shot."

How can this guy laugh?

Before Caleb could contemplate the thought anymore, Vaeliria pressed the attack throwing a sharp right left combination, the Jackeal skillfully blocked either strike but Vaeliria wasn't finished, dropping down she swept her right leg out and knocked the Jackeal flat on his back. Before he had time to recover Vaeliria pounced onto the Jackeal's chest and locked his arm into the same submission hold she had performed on Caleb when she initiated him into the Shakan.

There's no way he's getting out of that.

But much to Caleb's amazement that's exactly what the Jackeal did and a moment later both he and Vaeliria were back to their feet and once again began circling one another. Caleb was utterly speechless he had never seen Vaeliria work this hard before, sweat was dripping off her nose and her breaths were heavy.

The Jackeal's good.

In the next moment, the Jackeal attacked, his punches were lightning quick and Vaeliria was forced to retreat.

Doesn't this guy tire.

Punch after punch came at Vaeliria and still she dodged, until finally one of the blows caught her in the ribs, Vaeliria didn't cry out but Caleb could tell from the way her face screwed that she was in a lot of pain, the Jackeal followed the blow with a rising knee strike, Vaeliria tried to block but her guard wasn't strong enough and the blow went straight into her sternum knocking her to the ground, where she lay still, Caleb was just about to run to his Commander's aid when the Jackeal bent down and offered her a hand.

"That makes it four wins a piece," said the Jackeal helping Vaeliria up.

"You really caught me with that," replied Vaeliria wincing.

Seneschal Cyrusi let out a polite cough and both Vaeliria and the Jackeal turned to face the Seneschal, instantly a smile broke across Vaeliria's face and before Caleb knew what was happening he was being crushed in an embrace from her, after a few moments Vaeliria let Caleb go and looked him up and down. "I knew you wouldn't die so easily." She gave him a slap on the back that practically knocked the wind out of him.

"It's good to see you too," said Caleb a smile on his own lips.

"So what happened? Thom told us about the charges and that you fell but how did you survive and how did you find us?"

Caleb was just about to reply when the Jackeal interrupted: "Vaeliria, is this boy a friend of yours?"

"Yes, may I introduce Caleb Wintergrave, an initiate of the Skyknight order and my student."

The Jackeal smiled at that, "Tell me, Caleb, do you fight as well as your Commander?"

"I'm afraid not."

"Pity," said the Jackeal putting on a loose shirt.

Caleb was just about to ask the Jackeal if he knew about who had attacked them but before he could Seneschal Cyrusi spoke, "My Lord, you're due to meet with the heads of the merchants' guild."

The Jackeal's face dropped a little and he sighed, "Wonderful, three hours of listening to a bunch of craven old men tell me how much money they're losing due to Irashaad and his traitorous followers, my apologies." The Jackeal bowed his head.

"But," began Caleb.

The Jackeal held up a hand, "Azar told me all about your journey and the reasons for you coming here, but I'm afraid my duties as Jackeal come first."

Caleb wasn't happy but he knew there was nothing he could do about it so he just nodded.

The Jackeal turned to face his Seneschal, "Cyrusi, see that Caleb has a room and tell Sahi to cook something special for our guests."

"As you say, my Lord."

The Jackeal turned back to Caleb, "I will answer all of your questions when we dine together later this evening." With that the Jackeal turned and was gone, leaving Caleb with Vaeliria, Luci and Seneschal Cyrusi.

Vaeliria and Luci left Caleb as he was taken to his room, both agreed that it was best that he rest after his long journey, Caleb had protested but Luci had gotten that look on her face that told him she wouldn't be swayed and Vaeliria said that there would be plenty of time for him to tell her about his journey and that the Captain would want to hear all about it, so it could wait until they were called for supper, so he begrudgingly agreed and let the Seneschal lead him to his room.

"Here is your room," said Cyrusi opening a large door.

Caleb followed the Seneschal in and was immediately speechless, the room was filled with dozens of precious looking items. Large brightly coloured vases filled with white, red and pink roses sat along a long marble table, Caleb imagined they cost a fair amount of gold to grow, but that wasn't the end of the room's opulence. Paintings in gold and silver frames lined the walls, one painting in particular caught Caleb's eye. An enormous sun was setting over an ocean, each brush stroke was a masterpiece, the oranges and yellows of the sun danced and mingled with the different shades of blue that made the ocean, to form an almost perfect reflection whilst the sky was a mixture of purples, blues, yellows and oranges, each swirling into the other. Three large wardrobes took up the entirety of the room's left hand wall, Caleb couldn't imagine ever having enough clothes to fill one of the massive wardrobes let alone three, sat next to the wardrobes was the largest bed Caleb had ever seen, it could easily have fit Captain Brightfellow twice over, dozens of pillows lined the bed at one end and the sheets shimmered letting Caleb know they were made from silk.

"A servant will come and escort you to the Jackeal's private solar when he has finished his business with the merchants."

"Okay but what am I supposed to do til then?"

"That's entirely up to you."

Before Caleb could say anything else the Seneschal was gone leaving him alone with nothing but his thoughts.

Guess I'll get some sleep.

Caleb threw himself onto the bed, it felt like he was lying on a cloud, even his bed back on the *Zephyrus* which he thought was lavish felt tough in comparison, Caleb managed a smile before falling off into sleep.

"Sir it's time to wake up."

Caleb let out a low groan, "Argh."

"His Lord, the Jackeal awaits you in his solar."

212

"Okay I'm getting up." Caleb pulled himself up from the wondrously soft bed and swung his feet over to the floor, waiting for him by the wardrobes was a small Onmori boy, the brown robes that hung off his fragile frame were well worn but not in disrepair, his face was drawn and haggard and the skin around his eyes was a much darker hue than the rest of him, but when Caleb looked into the boy's deep brown eyes he saw a spark in them, and then Caleb saw it, the boy may look worn and fatigued but he was happy.

"What's your name?"

"The other servants call me Flea, Sir"

Caleb knew then that the boy was an orphan, only an orphan would get a name like that, after all he had gotten the name Asher due to his uncommonly pale complexion.

"It's nice to meet you, Flea, I'm Caleb." Caleb held out his hand for the boy to shake.

Flea cautiously took hold of Caleb's hand and gave it a light shake, "Shall I take you to his Lord's solar?"

"In a minute I just need to get changed first." Caleb walked over to where his pack lay on the floor, and pulled out the uniform Vaeliria had given him, it always filled him with pride to wear it, it made him feel like a real Skyknight and helped him to forget his life before he was Caleb.

Putting the last of his uniform on Caleb tied his dirk belt on and slowly caressed the handles of both blades.

Now let's go get some answers.

"Ready when you are," said Caleb turning to Flea.

Flea bowed, "Please follow me."

The corridors of the palace passed by quickly, for a small boy Flea sure could move, he walked the corridors as if they were a part of himself, Caleb was hard pressed to keep up and at one point he thought he had lost the boy, it was like magic one minute he was there the next gone.

After a mad few minutes of searching Flea reappeared, with a lantern in hand, it turned out that the boy had just turned around one corner and then quickly ducked into another passageway unaware that Caleb wasn't managing to keep up.

"My apologies, Sir, I forget how hard it is to navigate the palace's halls."

"No problem," said Caleb with a smile. "I know how it is, after you walk a place every day you forget that it's foreign to others."

Flea nodded.

Caleb joined Flea in the small passageway and the two set off again. The passageway was old, no it wasn't just old it was ancient and barely saw any use from the look of it, the mortar holding the walls together was dry and cracked, in some places it was even crumbling to dust, the floor was just as bad, every part seemed to be uneven and deep cracks ran through other parts, the small light from Flea's lantern was all that Caleb had to protect himself from the unseen obstacles, as they turned a corner Caleb saw rotten scones lining the walls, thick orange rust clung to the fixtures like diseased rashes, overhead a series of thick spiders webs covered the ceiling in a canopy of death, flies and other small insects buzzed trying to escape from their sticky prisons, the hairs on the back of Caleb's neck stood up but Flea paid the sight no mind and carried on.

After another few minutes of walking through the darkened corridor Caleb stood before a tall narrow door that seemed to mould into the wall itself.

How the hell does this thing open?

Caleb's question was answered a moment later as Flea reached his hand into a small hole and pulled. A muffled click rang through the passage and the door opened a crack.

What the hell is up with this place.

Without saying a word Flea pushed the door open and ventured into the room beyond, Caleb squeezed through the gap after Flea and found himself in the Jackeal's private solar, where he was met with Vaeliria, Captain Brightfellow, the Jackeal and surprisingly Azar all sat around a long oak table. Captain Brightfellow and Vaeliria sat on one side of the table, both were wearing their Skyknight uniforms and Caleb was glad that he had taken the time to change into his own.

The Captain smiled at Caleb but said nothing whilst Vaeliria gave a small nod.

Caleb nodded to both before he turned his attention back towards Azar, instead of the dark robes she had worn whilst travelling with Caleb, the jackal rider now wore robes the colour of sea foam, and a delicate tiara kept her long hair out of her face.

Azar much like Vaeliria gave a small nod in greeting which Caleb quickly returned before he looked to where Jackeal Biyabani sat at the head of the table, black robes inlaid with gold covered his entire body and atop his head sat a circlet of fiery bronze, rich red rubies, sapphires of deep blue, gleaming emeralds and golden quartz lined the side of the circlet.

"Sorry to disturb you, my Lord, but I brought Sir Wintergrave as you requested," said Flea bowing to the Jackeal.

"Thank you, little one, now could you pour me and my guests some wine, we have much to discuss."

Flea bowed to the Jackeal again before making his way over to a table at the back of the room, where various bottles of wine stood waiting.

"Please sit," said Azar, motioning towards the seat next to Vaeliria.

Caleb was still surprised to see Azar here but as he looked from her to the Jackeal, he saw the family resemblance, the strong jaw, the little bump that ran across both of their nose and their eyes were the same deep brown.

His daughter or maybe his niece.

As soon as Caleb took his seat, the Jackeal began talking, "Now as I was saying, you should not begin talks with the Sultan until Irashaad has been dealt with."

"I understand," replied Captain Brightfellow, "but surely Irashaad is a matter best left to the Sultan, I mean I wouldn't want to cause any tension between our two Kingdoms by undermining his Excellency."

"The Sultan is a fool who hides in the comfort of his city where none would dare attack and we've sent countless messages asking for aid, but as of yet we have had no reply."

"How many ships does this Irashaad have?" asked Vaeliria changing the subject.

"Nine if we include the ship you defeated on your way into our Kingdom, the smaller ships have roughly a crew of forty to fifty men while his flagship and war galley have easily double that amount."

Why would so many men follow this guy?

Clearly Captain Brightfellow had the same thought as he asked, "Why do so many men follow him?"

"I'm not sure myself," replied Jackeal Biyabani as Flea reappeared and placed a glass of wine down in front of him. "Maybe it's because they can make a better living as outlaws, or maybe they're just people who like murdering and pillaging innocents, what does it matter?"

"To defeat your enemy you must first learn to think like your enemy," said Caleb quoting a line from one of the books Vaeliria had given him to study.

Jackeal Biyabani turned to face Caleb before looking to the Captain and Vaeliria with a quizzical gaze.

"It's a quote from General Augustus's memoir of war," said Vaeliria, "it means that the more we know about this Irashaad the more we can predict his movements and thus give ourselves the advantage."

A smile quickly broke across the Jackeal's face. "I'm beginning to see why the Skyknights are held in such high regard, you not only fight well but you also have a mind for tactics." The Jackeal took a sip from his glass, before letting out a satisfied gasp, "So far Irashaad has only attacked the smaller villages and towns of the coast, from the reports we've had he never sends out more than two or three of his ships at a time."

"So that explains why we ran into that ship on our way into your Kingdom," said Caleb.

"Exactly," said the Jackeal with a nod, "you must have run into them as they were returning from their latest raid."

The hot bubbling feeling of anger overcame Caleb and before he could stop himself he was talking, "Look, the way I see it innocent people are dying at the hands of this bastard and we're stuck here anyway so why don't we help."

Everyone was silent for a moment, then Captain Brightfellow spoke, "Caleb's right, we can't leave those who are in need. Jackeal Biyabani you have my word as a Captain of the Angardian Skyknights that we will help you bring Irashaad to justice."

"Then I would like to raise a toast to the newly founded alliance between the people of Teuengea and the crew of the *Zephyrus*." The Jackeal raised his glass and everyone else did the same.

As Caleb drank, his thoughts turned back to the battle with the other Skyship and the carnage he had witnessed.

I'm coming for you Irashaad, and not even Aludin himself can stop me.

Chapter 19

"Harder!" said High Speaker Roujin blocking a blow from OathKeeper.

Adessa couldn't believe it she had given it her all and the High Speaker still said it wasn't enough, how could she deliver a harder blow, her arms were on fire and her breathing was laboured, but still she swung, she could already tell the blow was far too weak. High Speaker Roujin swatted the blow away with the flick of his wrist and Adessa nearly dropped OathKeeper, the light wooden blade felt more like a great sword at the moment.

"C'mon, girl, you ain't leaving until you get through my guard," snarled the High Speaker.

Adessa wanted to scream but she held her tongue, after training with the High Speaker for a couple of weeks she knew that it was best to keep quiet and follow his instructions, least he get angry and decide he was going to make it even harder for her.

"Well are you going to use that sword or not?"

Adessa willed all of her anger into OathKeeper and swung, the High Speaker met the blow with his fiery blade, again Adessa was thrown back but she didn't give in, ignoring her exhaustion she focused her mind and swung again and again, the ring of steel on steel rang like a high-pitched symphony as the two blades met, Adessa continued her assault but the High Speaker blocked every blow.

Just a little more.

Adessa embraced her anger and dove deeper into her Voice, the world around her began to fade into the background and she whirled OathKeeper faster than she ever had, but before she could land a strike, the High Speaker retreated out of her reach. Pressing Adessa, dove at the High Speaker with a lighting quick thrust, all her anger and fear was unleashed in the blow and the very world seemed to shake around her before turning completely white.

"Wake up!"

Adessa was back in the world without colour, everything from the grass to the sky was a shade of grey, overhead flew a group of sparrows, Adessa stood watching, the sparrows danced and twirled in the air, she should have been able to hear their beautiful cries but only silence filled the world.

"Damn it, girl, I said wake up!"

A heavy blow hit Adessa across the face and within the blink of an eye she was back in the real world, the first sensation that greeted her was that of her burning cheek, Adessa opened her eyes wincing at the pain she felt as she did but she quickly forgot about it because standing over her was High Speaker Roujin, his eyes were hard as ever and Adessa swallowed in fear but then she caught sight of the small smirk that lay underneath his thick beard.

"You are a stupid girl," said Roujin holding out a hand.

As Adessa was helped to her feet she noticed a small nick on the High Speaker's armour where she had struck with OathKeeper.

"Yeah you got through my guard." The High Speaker fingered the chip, "Now get out of my sight."

Adessa threw her brown Speaker robe back on and grabbed OathKeeper before making her way into the forest of Alfheim.

Autumn was beginning to take a hold, the air had a slight chill to it and a light drizzle was falling through the trees. Adessa took a deep breath and drank everything in, the smells of the forest filled the air, the grass, flowers and leaves mixed together to form a wonderful bouquet that reminded Adessa she was in the real world. High up in the trees the birds screeched and chirped in disapproval of the weather, Adessa reached out onto the spirit plane, the spirits of the birds were beyond her as they were for all Forest Speakers, she found it strange that she and her fellow Forest Speakers couldn't communicate with the birds of the forest, after all they could speak with everything else from the grass to bears, but Adessa remembered the explanation her grandmother had given her when she had asked the same question when she was younger.

The birds are spirits of the sky my little flower.

Adessa smiled at the memory of the nickname her grandmother had given her.

Adessa was quickly awoke from her reminiscing by the spirit of an old fox that was stalking in the underbrush towards a hare, its spirit flickered and winked, instinctively Adessa made the sign of passing and blessed the fox's spirit, hopefully that would help the fox when its time came to journey to the undying lands. The fox continued towards the hare, slowly the stalker closed ground on its prey but then the fox stepped on a twig and the hare was immediately alerted, in a split second the hare was off running at breakneck speeds, the fox gave chase but it was no match for the young buck, which easily cleared the obstacles of the forest without slowing, Adessa felt bad for the fox, but it wasn't a Speaker's place to mess with the natural balance of life and death, with a final prayer for the fox's passage Adessa walked off towards the lake of life, after the lesson with High Speaker Roujin, Adessa wanted to talk to the GrandOak about learning to better control her own spirit.

Leaving the protection of the trees Adessa was met with the full force of the wind, it swept at her robe and whipped at her face, thankfully though the rain hadn't gotten any worse, walking to the water Adessa called forth the bridge of vines and began the walk across, the wind battered at her as she crossed, but not once did Adessa fear falling off the bridge, this was like second nature to her now, after all she had been going to the GrandOak's island every day since she first heard his Voice, the quiet and peacefulness of which allowed her to forget her worries and focus.

Touching solid ground Adessa dispelled the vines and walked towards the GrandOak.

"How was your lesson with Roujin?" said the GrandOak as his face formed.

"About as well as diving into a bees' nest," said Adessa dropping down onto the ground, "on the bright side I finally managed to hit him."

"But?" said the GrandOak knowingly.

Adessa sighed, she wasn't going to lie to the GrandOak after all it would be pointless what with the bond they shared, but that didn't make it any easier admitting her failure, "I ended up collapsing again," she said finally

The GrandOak's aura shifted in concern, "This is worrying."

"I know but there doesn't seem to be anyway for me to control it, every time I train with Roujin I can feel myself losing control, I try using the mental techniques you taught me, which help for a time but then he pushes me further and something else takes over and..." Adessa tried to think of how she could describe it but before she could the GrandOak spoke.

"You lose your centre."

Adessa nodded.

The GrandOak became silent and Adessa felt his aura shift even deeper with concern, this was worrying, normally the GrandOak provide her with encouragement, but now it seemed he had no words or advice to give.

No, the GrandOak is the most powerful spirit in the forest of Alfheim, he has trained countless High Speakers in the art of Forest Speaking, there is no way he won't be able to do the same for me.

After what felt like an eternity the GrandOak spoke, "For today's lesson I want you to use the mental techniques I have taught you to focus on keeping your mind and spirit anchored whilst you're under attack."

"But I just told you that they don't work."

"Adessa as you know the techniques I have taught you help you achieve a calm state of mind thus making it easier to channel your Voice into the word around you, but if you let a negative emotion take over like you did during your lesson with Roujin you will begin to lose your connection to the spirit world and even the smallest task will become a challenge putting a great deal of strain on your body and mind."

"So that's why I end up collapsing?"

"Exactly, now prepare yourself."

As soon as the GrandOak finished speaking a great rumble shook through his island and Adessa jumped to her feet.

Moments later the ground all around Adessa gave way and three wooden men emerged.

By Enelya.

As Adessa made a sign to the first of the Forest Speakers another rumble broke through the ground and six more holes appeared. An eight-foot monster emerged from the hole that sat behind the three wooden men. Adessa was instantly reminded of the giants that her grandmother used to tell her about in her stories but the thought didn't last long as a group of fat childlike creatures sprouted from the five other holes that sat off to her right.

How am I supposed to fight all these monstrosities?

"Calm yourself," said the GrandOak.

Adessa took a deep breath, cleared her mind of all distractions and drew OathKeeper.

"You ready?" said Adessa to her blade.

"Always," replied OathKeeper.

At those words the wooden men came to life, their dull hollow eyes lit up with an eerie green glow, joints groaned and cracked as they began to move towards Adessa.

The first woodmen to reach Adessa was one that looked like an old decrepit man, lichen hung on nearly every part of the creatures body like a thick green fur, with surprising speed the woodman lashed out with one of its wiry arms, instinctively Adessa brought OathKeeper up and blocked the attack, cutting clean through the attackers arm, Adessa then pivoted and in one clean motion tore the head from her assailant's body, as the woodman's head hit the ground the green light in its eyes died and the woodman withered into nothing.

"Behind you!" sounded OathKeeper.

Adessa spun around just in time, one of the fat little creatures lunged at her with its razor-sharp arms. Adessa managed to block one of the blows but the other ripped through her robes and drew blood. A wave of panic and fear shot through Adessa, not even High Speaker Roujin drew blood, and whenever he did land a hit against Adessa he always did so with the flat of his blade.

"Focus," said OathKeeper.

Ignoring the pain Adessa re-centred herself and channelled her will back into her sword and struck at the dwarf's head, the wooden blade of OathKeeper passed through the dwarf with ease and within a second the creature lay at her feet lifelessly, but Adessa didn't have a moment to breathe, all around her the woodmen were closing in, the four remaining dwarfs stood directly in front of her, whilst the two men were off to her right and the giant her left. Adessa took a step back and then another trying to put some distance between herself and the crowd of wooden enemies, but the woodmen matched her step for step and eventually she found herself on the edge of the GrandOak's island, all four of the dwarfs then began to press forward as one, knowing that she could never deal with all four of them at once Adessa dove onto the spirit plane and looked for an ally, as she looked around Adessa saw that all of the woodmen were extensions of the GrandOak himself.

"Our enemy is almost upon us."

Adessa started to panic then and felt her grip on the spirit world waver, she tried to clear her mind but she could feel the fear and panic settling into her.

C'mon focus.

The dwarfs were only a couple of yards away when Adessa found her centre again, without thinking she called on the only spirit she could think of, a vine as thick as a man's leg erupted out of the ground in front of Adessa and shot right through the dwarfs, lifting them up into the air, with a swipe of her hand Adessa aimed the vine at the two men, the thick tendril crashed into them with such force that they were flung straight off the island and into the lake, the giant having seen the destruction of its fellows began to run at Adessa at an alarming pace, pushing her hand forward Adessa threw the vine at the giant, the earthen coil snaked its way around the giant's arms and legs at an incredible speed but the giant barely slowed. Adessa poured her will into the vine and made them as harder as stone, the giant began to slow until finally it was held in place not five yards away, Adessa closed her hand slowly, in response the vine began to tighten around its prisoner until finally Adessa balled her hand into a fist and the vine crushed the giant into a dozen different pieces, Adessa thanked the spirit for its assistance before she released her Voice.

Coming back to the physical world Adessa instantly felt light-headed and dropped more than sat down onto the ground of the GrandOak's islands.

"Now do you see how focusing your mind can help with Speaking," said the GrandOak after a few minutes.

"Yes," replied Adessa breathlessly from where she lay on the ground, "but there's no way I could do that again, I'm completely spent."

"Well we'll just have to practice this again."

"I'm afraid it may be too late for that."

Adessa lifted her head to find High Speaker Caewyn's vessel standing over her.

"What do you mean it may be too late?" said Adessa.

"I've just received word from the other Councillors that an Angardian Skyship named the *Notus* was dispatched from Actalia this morning with instructions to come and collect the Speaker who will be joining the Skyknights."

"How long will it take for them to get here?" said Adessa, fear bubbling up inside her.

"No more than a fortnight."

"That's not enough time, I still haven't made my vessel nor have I lea..." Adessa was going to continue but the High Speaker held up a hand and she fell silent.

"Adessa, I'm afraid there's nothing I can do, the other Councillors purposely didn't tell me about the Skyship's departure until it had already left because they knew I would try and buy you more time."

"So that's it," said Adessa pulling herself up into a sitting position, "I have a fortnight at the most to continue my training and then I will have to leave Alfheim."

The High Speaker nodded.

"How long is my apprenticeship to the Angardian's Skyknights?"

The High Speaker let out a long sigh "Truthfully, you may never return to Alfheim."

Adessa's heart skipped a beat.

No, I can't stay in the Angardian's Kingdom for the rest of my life.

"I'm sorry but you know this needs to be done."

Adessa couldn't speak, she thought she had prepared herself for this but clearly that wasn't the case, it felt like a belt was wrapping its way around her chest, each breath became harder to take then the one before, until she couldn't catch a breath at all, the world began to shrink back like she was in a tunnel, the High Speaker was still talking but she couldn't hear him.

I've got to get out of here.

Adessa jumped to her feet and burst into a sprint, she could feel the High Speaker's gaze burning into her, the GrandOak tried to talk to her through their bond but she blocked him out and didn't turn to look back, she needed to get to the Blood Roses, there she could calm down. Adessa ran straight towards the edge of the island, the bridge of vines quickly formed in front of her despite the fact she didn't use her Voice, the GrandOak must have been the one

225

forming the bridge for her. The water of the lake ran wildly underfoot, buffeting the bridge with choppy waves that made the vines slick in places and the wind hadn't calmed in fact it seemed to be worse, but Adessa paid neither any mind the only thing she was focused on was reaching the Roses.

Old oaks, spiky willows and feathery pines passed Adessa as she ran through the forest, each seemed to stare down at her, their gazes thick with judgement. Passing under a fallen tree Adessa splashed through a trickling stream, the cold water soaked her feet but Adessa barely felt anything. Clinging stubbornly to the edge of the stream were a series of shrubs and weeds, wind howled through the underpass bringing with it a sheet of rain that buffeted Adessa's face and pushed her back, steeling herself against the onslaught Adessa continued onward.

The world began to come back into focus and Adessa slowed to a walk along the stream bed, the cold of the water crept into her feet and the smells of the forest filled her nose, the musty smell of wet bark was the most powerful, beneath that was the smell of the earthy ground and sitting below that almost unnoticed was the beautifully sweet smell of all the flowers of the forest, Adessa let the smells enveloped her for a few seconds before she broke away from the stream and headed towards a thicket of blackberry bushes, the Blood Roses weren't far away now, as she passed Adessa plucked a handful of juicy berry from the thorny bushes and popped them into her mouth, the juice that filled her mouth was a combination of sweet and sharp, this was what she was going to miss about Alfheim. You could walk in the forest for hours and never see another person, High Speaker Caewyn had told her about how the capital city of the Angardian Kingdom was like one massive Anthill, the streets were always full of people and everywhere you looked there were monstrously tall buildings that bottled you up on all sided.

How am I going to communicate with nature in a city made from iron and stone?

Adessa shook the thought away and found herself standing in front of the Blood Roses, opening herself up to the spirit world Adessa felt the warm cheerful spirits of the Roses brush against her, Adessa instantly felt taller and her fears were pushed to the back of her mind, she walked through the swarm of red roses, running her hand along the flowers as she did, before sitting down in the centre and taking a deep breath. The Roses reached out to her but she shook her head, she didn't want to talk she just wanted to sit and enjoy their company, for all she knew it could be the last time.

Chapter 20

Darrius sat opposite the High Sentinel feeling awkward, despite all his years of being in the Order of the Watchful Eye Darrius had never gotten used to the High Sentinel's gaze. Owun Emberfang was a living legend amongst the Order, twelve years ago he had single-handedly defended the Oracle's tower against Malak and his band of traitors despite having taken an arrow to his shoulder and even now he was still capable of besting anyone amongst the Order even though he had seen his sixty-ninth summer not two months ago.

"Are you going to spend the whole of this meeting looking at your boots?" said the old Sentinel jokingly.

Darrius was amazed how much power the High Sentinel's voice still held, it was like the steady beat of a war drum, "My apologies."

Looking up from his boots, Darrius came face to face with Owun Emberfang, the years were beginning to show, the High Sentinel's short hair was more salt than pepper now, as was his neatly trimmed moustache, a pair of silver optics framed his dark brown eyes and a jagged scar ran down from his left cheek to hide beneath the collar of his black doublet, Darrius still remembered the incident that had caused it, back when Darrius was still a Initiate, a ship of Banetian pirates came to Seers Isle looking for slaves, it had been a hard battle during which the Captain of the pirates cut down many a Initiates until the High Sentinel had meet him in the centre of the battle, Darrius still remembered the monstrous grin on the pirate's face as he struck the High Sentinel across the face with his jewelled scimitar but that had been his undoing, as he turned and gloated to his men the High Sentinel had picked himself up off of the floor and ran his longsword through the pirate's back before collapsing.

"I hear you're leaving again."

Darrius was caught off guard, he didn't think the Oracle would have told anyone about his latest mission, but then again why else would the High Sentinel have summoned him.

As if reading his mind, the High Sentinel spoke, "Don't worry her Holiness didn't tell me the specifics of your task, but what she did ask was for me to find you a suitable companion."

Darrius bolted upright, in all his years travelling the Five Kingdoms in the Oracle's name he had never had a companion to speak of, let alone for a task as important as the one he was about to go on.

What is she thinking?

A polite cough brought Darrius back to the room, the High Sentinel was looking at him quizzically.

"My apologies," said Darrius sitting back in his chair.

The old Sentinel waved the apology aside, "Look, Darrius, I'm not going to pretend that I know what's going on but the Oracle has asked for my assistance and like you I serve, without question."

If only you knew.

"So who will be accompanying me?"

"I have three candidates," said the High Sentinel slipping three pieces of paper across the desk towards Darrius, "I can personally vouch for all three of them, but I thought it best to allow you to decide, after all you're the one who'll be working with them."

Darrius didn't like this one bit, a companion was a complication he didn't need, but the Oracle had spoken and he would do his duty as he always did. Darrius picked up the pieces of paper and gave each one a quick look, at the top of each sheet was a name, Darrius didn't recognise any of the names, but that wasn't much of a surprise, the majority of the Sentinels that Darrius knew had already succumbed to deaths embrace. Darrius handed the files back to the High Sentinel.

"Not even going to give them a proper look," said the High Sentinel putting them back on a stack of other papers.

"Looking at a piece of paper isn't going to tell me what I need to know," said Darrius with a shrug. "How about you show me what these three can do in person."

The High Sentinel immediately took the files in hand and stood from his chair, "Well then let's be on our way."

All eyes were on Darrius as he followed the High Sentinel through the Oracles tower as he passed by a group of Initiates they all stopped in their tracks.

They see me as a stranger.

A few of them began to whisper, but with his keen senses it was like they were talking normally.

"That's the *Traveller*," said one.

"I heard that he's a walking disaster, wherever he goes something bad follows, that's why the Oracle doesn't let him stay here for long," said another.

Darrius turned to look at the initiates and gave them his hardest stare, despite the masks they wore all averted their gazes and the whispers died. Darrius laughed to himself and followed the High Sentinel down the giant spiral staircase of the tower.

The Order of the Watchful Eye was out in full force, Initiates passed by in a blur, quick to get to their respective posts or lessons, Scribes carried thick tomes with them as they made their way to their own classes, even a few of the Messengers were here, their heavy packs looked full to bursting with letters and other mail from across the isle, Darrius didn't envy them, it must be a great burden having to lumber that monstrous pack around all day.

At the base of the tower Darrius took what felt like his first breath in ages, it was good to be out of the stares.

"So who's first?" said the High Sentinel looking to Darrius.

"I'll follow your lead."

Emberfang drew out the pieces of paper, "Okay, first up is Mikel, right now he should be over with Edwington practising swordplay."

Darrius and High Sentinel Emberfang walked through to the back of the tower, passing the men and women of the Stewards who were busy at work keeping the Order running on a day-to-day basis, no one paid Darrius any mind which he was grateful for, he was going to have enough people looking at him today, he didn't need anymore. After making in through the maze of corridors that ran throughout the tower's base, Darrius and the High Sentinel came to a wide circular shaped door, standing in front of the door was a thickly built Sentinel who Darrius didn't recognise, hanging from his belt was a studded cudgel, as he saw them approach the man stood at attention and made the sign of the Lady, The High Sentinel returned the gesture before walking through the door, Darrius followed without a word and was meet with the light and warmth of the morning sun, it took only a moment for Darrius to adjust to the light and was met with a surprising sight.

The training field which Darrius had remembered as little more than a small field had now grown into something completely different, the tree line which had been so thick that it blocked out the sunrise had been culled and in its place, were three groups of targets and behind them a large wooden building.

The first group were simple straw targets, made from a large cotton sack for the body and a smaller one for the head, the only thing that held these targets up was a wooden stake in the ground, the Initiates that stood attacking these targets looked clumsy, they held their weapons awkwardly and Darrius could see the frustration on their trainer's faces from where he stood.

The second group were wooden carved and had arms, worn and rusted armour was strapped to their chests and dented helms lined the targets heads, Darrius observed the Initiates attacking these targets, there was a good gap of

231

ability between these men and women compared to their brethren before them, gone was the awkwardness in their attacks and once a command had been given from their trainer it was executed quickly.

The last set of targets were unlike anything Darrius had seen, they stood life size and moved, Darrius blinked to make sure he wasn't seeing things but when he opened his eyes and looked again the targets were still there. Looking closer Darrius saw that the targets only moved in specific ways, one arm attacked with either a dull sword or axe in an arching slash whilst the other blocked with a shield of wood.

"One of Lazarus's inventions," said Emberfang breaking Darrius from his reverie.

"How does it work?"

"There's a clockwork mechanism in each of the targets arms, they get winded and that provides them with movement, all be it simple."

"And the purpose of this?"

"To build confidence in our Initiates, it's one thing to attack something that doesn't strike back, this gives them a chance to better practice their blocks."

"Why not have them spar? After all that's what we did."

"And do you remember how many of us got injured from fighting when we weren't ready."

Darrius didn't like this one bit, fighting another man was nothing like fighting a dummy, you couldn't look into a dummy's eyes and see the fear, or smell its breath or sweat and a man never attacked the same way time and again, unless he was a complete simpleton of course.

"Don't look so worried, these are the newest members of our order, none of these Initiates will move on until they are approved by the trainers."

"And when they are?"

The High Sentinel smiled, "Then the real training begins."

Emberfang led the way across the training field, passing the Initiates, their trainers and the dummies and headed towards the wooden building. The building was a simple thing built from the trunks of trees that had been joint together, large iron nails lined the joints and as Darrius neared the pungent aroma of pitch assaulted his nose.

Once inside Darrius was surprised to see a group of twelve Initiates sparring, swords collided with shields and in the centre of it all barking orders was a short slender woman wearing the uniform of a Sentinel trainer.

That must be Edwington.

Emberfang directed Darrius to take a seat.

"You see the tall lad in the back that's Mikel."

Darrius looked over to inspect the first of his candidates, tall was a bit of an understatement the boy had to be at least six and half foot, which was a strike against him already, Darrius didn't need a bruiser as his companion, but nevertheless the High Sentinel had recommended the boy so Darrius stayed in his seat and watched. Darrius wished he could get a look at the young man's face, after all you could tell an awful lot about someone from their face alone, but much to Darrius's annoyance the only thing that greeted his stare was the Initiate's white mask.

Damned thing.

Darrius quickly turned his attention away from the mask and to the boy's movements.

Mikel circled his opponent slowly, Darrius noted that he moved well for someone so tall, normally a taller man relied more on strength and reach rather than good footwork, Mikel's opponent suddenly darted forward with an upward slash, Darrius knew than that Mikel had won, Mikel brought his shield down on the attackers blade and struck with a blow of his own, if the blade hadn't been dulled the blow would have cut clean into the other boy's chest but instead all it did was wind him and knocked him to the ground. Darrius was impressed, Mikel reacted quickly and without hesitation but still there was something niggling at the back of his mind.

"So what do you think?" whispered Emberfang.

"He's good but I'd like to test him myself if it's all the same to you."

"I thought you might say that."

The High Sentinel stood and made his way towards the Initiates, Edwington shouted for them to stop and stand at attention.

"High Sentinel," said Edwington saluting.

"Trainer," replied Emberfang, "I would like to test one of your students."

"By all means, who do you want?"

"Mikel."

"You heard the High Sentinel, Mikel step forward the rest of you take a seat."

Mikel stepped up to the High Sentinel and bowed, "It's an honour to spar with you," said the massive Initiate.

"Oh I'm afraid I won't be your opponent."

"Then who is testing me?"

Darrius stood from his seat and walked forward, the other Initiates whispered amongst themselves but Mikel just bowed, drew his sword and raised his shield, Darrius drew his own sword, the blade was scarred and beaten from its years of use but its edge was still as sharp as the day Darrius got it.

"We don't use live blades," said Edwington.

"Don't worry he won't use the blade's edge," said The High Sentinel.

Darrius nodded his agreement.

"Fine," said Edwington clearly not happy.

Emberfang went back to his seat, Trainer Edwington raised her hand and shouted for them to begin their duel. Mikel instantly went on the offensive, throwing quick thrusts from behind his shield, Darrius knocked the strikes away with ease.

Good, He's testing the waters.

As one of his thrusts was retreating Mikel swung his shield forward, Darrius was slightly taken off guard it was a risky move and to use it so early in a fight was even more so but he still moved out of the shield's way, again Mikel came straight at Darrius this time rushing forward with his shield drawn, a split second before Mikel came crashing into him, Darrius pivoted around the Initiate and landed a hard shot with his free hand, Mikel shouted in pain and fell to one knee, before he could pick himself up, Darrius laid the edge of his blade against the young man's neck.

"Yield," said Darrius coldly.

A twitch in Mikel's shoulder told Darrius all he needed to, the boy wasn't going to yield, Darrius sighed before he punched Mikel around the face, the big Initiate immediately dropped to the floor unconscious, his mask cracking as he did, there were gasps from the other Initiates and Trainer Edwington cursed Mikel's foolishness. Darrius apologised to Edwington, sheathed his sword and slipped off the brass knuckles he wore on his other hand.

"Who's next?" said Darrius walking back to the High Sentinel.

"A young scout by the name of Jeremiah, he'll be in the forest practicing his archery."

"Then let's go I've seen all I need to here."

High Sentinel Emberfang nodded and led the way back out into the morning light.

Leaving the training field behind Emberfang led Darrius towards the line of tall cedars that marked the forest edge, Darrius found the sight welcoming, with so much having changed in the last four years it was good to see that these old giants had survived the culling, as they entered the forest Darrius took a deep breath, the smell of the trees, grass and mud told him he was home.

The sounds of the training field slowly receded as the two Sentinels advanced further into the forest and the sound of arrows thudding against targets slowly began to take over. Breaking out into a clearing, Darrius was meet with a dozen bows drawn his way, instantly Darrius drew his throwing daggers and was about to loose, when a shout came up from behind the scouts and out stepped Sebastian Locklear, the head of the Scouts. Darrius smiled, his old friend still looked as he remembered, his long hair was tied back just like always and not a single white hair mark it, a neatly trimmed beard lined his chin and his deep blue eyes had yet to fade, the black leather tunic he wore was beaten and worn as were his breeches and his boots looked near ready to fall apart, but you'd be damned if you were going to get him out of them, as soon as he got them he swore by the Lady that he would keep them until he died.

"Well I'll be damned, what brings the traveller out into my neck of the woods?" said Locklear, his throaty voice piercing through the trees like one of his arrows.

"I brought him here," said Emberfang emerging from the trees.

Locklear and his scouts instinctively stood at attention and saluted, the High Sentinel told them to stand down before he spoke again.

"We're here to see the skills of Jeremiah."

Locklear did well to hide his surprise but Darrius could see it in the way his old friends left eyebrow arched.

"You heard the High Sentinel, Jeremiah, you're up show em what you can do."

From the mass of bodies came a small slightly built lad, Darrius was instantly sceptical, the boy couldn't have weighed more than a hundred and thirty pounds and he stood a head smaller than the smallest of his other brethren, he bowed to the High Sentinel then to Darrius before he drew his bow, unlike the other scouts who used longbows, Jeremiah used a short bow.

Makes sense he probably can't pull the string of a longbow back.

The slight archer walked into the centre of the clearing and stood ready, twenty paces away stood a target, dozens of arrows lined the outer rings but none lay in the centre.

Locklear raised his hand, "Nock!"

Jeremiah drew an arrow from his quiver and notched it.

"Draw!"

The small boy pulled his bowstring back and took aim, Darrius could see the muscles in his arms bulge with the effort.

"Loose!"

The arrow shot out with incredible force, Darrius could literally hear the power as the arrow flew through the air, before it landed with a thud in the target, even without his keen eyesight Darrius would have been able to spot the boy's arrow it sat dead in the centre of the target, some of the other scouts shouted words of praise whilst other clapped, but Jeremiah showed no sign of emotion, he just turned to the High Sentinel and bowed.

"What do you think?" whispered Emberfang to Darrius.

"Impressive," replied Darrius also whispering.

"But?"

"I could have made that shot, I mean it's only at twenty paces now something at fifty that's a shot worth praise."

"Is there anything else?" said Locklear breaking into the conversation.

"Do you have any targets that are more of a challenge?" said Darrius.

"Of course," said Locklear clearly insulted by the question. "This way, Jeremiah, you're coming with me, the rest of you continue with practice and when I get back I expect every one of you to have hit the bull's eye at least once, got that."

"Yes, Master," said the Scouts as one.

Locklear led the group through a line of gnarled trees and prickly shrubs, Jeremiah followed behind the Master Scout and Emberfang behind him leaving Darrius to take the rear, the chirping of young birds filled the forest, whilst older birds flew from perch to perch, off in the distance Darrius heard the pounding of hooves, the isles wild deer must have been spooked by something, most likely a rookie Scout had underestimated the hearing of the deer, as if to conform his thought Darrius heard the curses of a group of men in the distance as they went running after their prey.

"Well we're here," said Locklear bringing Darrius out of his reverie.

Without realising it Darrius had continued to follow his old friend right out into another opening, much like the one before it dozens of targets were strewn around the grounds, but upon further viewing Darrius realised that the target were further away, maybe sixty to seventy paces and dozens of other targets swung from the branches of various trees and were partially hidden behind barrels and crates.

"So what should I have Jeremiah shoot at first?"

"Your choice," whispered Emberfang to Darrius.

Darrius looked around the range, "Okay, see the three staggered targets."

Jeremiah nodded and took his position.

"You get one shot for each and no shot can take longer than five seconds," said Darrius moving to stand with Locklear and High Sentinel Emberfang.

The young scout looked over to his Master, Locklear shook his head indicating that there would be no signal for the first shot, as the boy turned back to the targets, Darrius noted the deep breath he took to steady his aim.

Good.

In a blur of motion Jeremiah drew an arrow from his quiver, nocked it and fired, Darrius didn't look to see where the arrow landed he was more interested in how the boy transitioned to his next shot, swiftly Jeremiah turned to the next target whilst drawing another arrow.

His footwork's good.

The arrow was loosed, from the look that crossed over Jeremiah's face Darrius knew the shot wasn't what he wanted, but the boy quickly moved on to the final shot, loaded his last arrow and took aim.

This'll test him.

The last target lay at eighty paces but Jeremiah didn't blink, he let the arrow loose, Darrius waited for the thud before he looked down the range to observe the shots. The first shot was a straight bull's eye, the arrow embedded three quarters of the way through the target, which impressed him. The second shot sat in the outermost ring of the target, it was a terrible shot from anyone but again the power was there even at sixty paces the boy had managed to stick a third of the arrow in. The last shot though had redeemed the boy, it wasn't a bull's eye but it was close, sitting on the line of the bull's eye and the middle ring, at eighty paces Darrius knew just how hard that sort of shot was.

"Well, what yah think?" said Locklear.

"Very good," said the High Sentinel.

"And what about you?" said Locklear turning to Darrius. "Have you seen all you need?".

"He's got a surprising amount of power in his shots but his accuracy is wildly inconsistent," said Darrius looking back over the targets. "If he can make a shot like that at eighty then at sixty I expect a bullseye eight out of ten times."

"By the Lady Darrius the lad's been training for six months and already he's my best apprentice."

"Okay," said Darrius looking at his old friend, "one final test."

The Master Scout nodded, Darrius turned back to the young boy.

"You see that target hanging from the tree about fifty paces' away."

Again, Jeremiah nodded.

"Hit that and we'll call it a da"

Before Darrius could finish the small archer drew an arrow and loosed it, Darrius watched the arrow fly through the air and land just inside the bull's eye, the target swung back and forth from the power of the shot.

Darrius looked down at Jeremiah and realised the boy was smiling.

"That's the way, lad!" hollered Locklear as he slapped Jeremiah hard on the back.

"Do we need to go and see the other candidate or have you already made your choice?" whispered Emberfang.

Darrius had to admit that he was impressed by Jeremiah, the lad had done everything he had asked without question and he seemed like he could handle some pressure but one thing that Darrius had learnt is that it was better to cover all your options.

"No, let's go see the last one, I'll make my decision then."

"Very well." Emberfang turned to Locklear. "Thank you for the demonstration."

"It was my pleasure," said Locklear with a bow, "do you need me to show you the way back?"

"That won't be necessary, our next destination is actually further in."

Darrius was instantly aware of where the High Sentinel was taking him next.

"Oh," said Locklear knowingly. "Well I'll leave you two to your business."

"May the Lady watch over you," said the High Sentinel in parting.

"And you," replied Locklear.

Darrius offered his hand to his old friend, Locklear grasped it firmly and whilst the two were close he whispered, "When you're finished with whatever it is you're doing come see me I have a bottle of whiskey with your name on it."

Darrius smiled, "Sounds good."

Delving further into the forest and towards their next destination brought Darrius back to his first year as an Initiate of the Order of the Watchful Eye. The grief and anger that he had felt from his family's death and the loss of his village had been the fuel to drive him forward and it hadn't taken long before the end of this first year that Darrius found himself in the top five of all of his classes, but he wasn't happy with that, he needed to get better and so during a sparring session against Dominic, the number one in his hand to hand class Darrius had unleashed all of his fury, nearly killing the other Initiate with a choke hold, it had taken the combined efforts of Trainer Fisk and two other Initiates to break his hold. Darrius could still feel the shame of that event even now, it churned his stomach into knots and made his mouth dry, it was one thing to kill your enemy on the field of battle or as you defended yourself against an attacker but Darrius had nearly killed a comrade and there was never any excuse for that.

After another candlemark of brooding and trekking through the forest, High Sentinel Emberfang led Darrius out into another clearing and standing before them were the Pillars of Judgement, a shiver passed down Darrius's spine at the sight of the seven pillars and the chasm in which they stood.

Looking to the tops of the pillars Darrius found that three of the seven pillars were occupied, a man of maybe thirty summers stood on the second pillar, from the ease of his breathing and lack of pain in his expression Darrius knew he was finding it easy, on the fourth pillar stood another man, his face was twisted in pain and his legs were unsteady on the narrow platform, Darrius knew he didn't have much strength left in him.

I hope for your sake your times almost up.

Above him on the fifth stood a young woman, Darrius felt for the woman, the fifth pillar was heavily eroded which made for an incredibly unstable platform, the woman's legs quivered under the strain but they still looked relatively strong, her arms were out to her sides for support, sweat covered her face and plastered her kinky hair to her forehead. Darrius could see a fire in her eyes, she wasn't going to die here.

Standing in front of the pillars were two Sentinels, one was short and thickly built whilst the other was roughly Darrius's build, their swords hung from their hips ready at a moment's notice should the sinners decide to try and escape their judgement.

"So who are we here for?" asked Darrius looking up at the pillars and their occupants.

"We're here for her," replied Emberfang pointing to the woman on the fifth pillar.

"Okay, so what did she do to deserve the fifth pillar?"

"Fia, put three of her fellow Initiates in the infirmary, two with broken arms and the third has two broken ribs a punctured lung and a broken eye socket".

"Do you know why she did it?"

"The reports from the trainers say they had mocked her during gradings."

"Well I don't think they'll make that mistake again," said Darrius smiling, already he liked this Fia she had fire in her, which was good, just as long as it was channelled in the right place. "So how longs she got left?"

"Let's find out," said Emberfang walking towards the two guards.

"Excuse me, lads."

"Finally," said the shorter of the guards spinning around, "what took you guys so..." the Sentinel stopped mid-sentence when he realised he was talking to the High Sentinel, despite his dark complexion Darrius could have sworn he saw the man's face pale.

The other Sentinel on guard turned around then and was just as dumbfounded as his counterpart, his jaw hanging wide open in disbelief, from the fuzz that lined his jaw Darrius guessed the guard wasn't any older than twenty-three summers.

"My apologies," said the shorter guard standing at attention. "I thought you were the next shift."

"No need to worry," replied Emberfang. "Please relax, I'm here to ask you about one of the sinners."

"What do yah what to know?" said the other guard finally finding the courage to speak.

The shorter guards face practically turned purple, "Watch your tongue! This is the High Sentinel."

"Please it's quite alright," said Emberfang smiling, "could you tell me how much time Fia has left before she's absolved."

"Hmm, I'd say she's got about a candlemark left," said the younger guard scratching his furry jaw. "Not that you'd guess that from looking at her, looks like she could go another day easy."

The shorter guard pulled out a small hourglass, "Sev's right these sinners have got just under a candlemark left before they are absolved."

"Thank you," said Emberfang returning to stand next to Darrius. "Shall we wait or would you prefer not to watch, just in case."

"I'm fine," replied Darrius sitting down on a nearby rock.

Time seemed to slow to a halt, the sun moved inch by painful inch across the sky like a fiery slug, in the distance a dozen black angry looking clouds began to creep towards the pillars, Darrius sighed.

The monstrous clouds waited until they sat directly above the pillars before they unleashed their fury in the form of a thunderous downpour that soaked everyone to the bones within minutes.

"Where the fuck are those bastards!" cursed the shorter guard.

The younger guard laughed at his counterpart in response, "Haha, calm down Tick."

"Calm down!" yelled the shorter guard. "No fuck those twats and their mothers for ever birthing them."

Darrius shook his head and returned his attention back towards the sinners.

The man on the second pillar looked up into the sky and began to laugh manically, as if the rain was cleansing him.

Let's hope he hasn't lost his mind.

Looking to the fourth pillar Darrius found that the other man was barely holding on, his feet kept slipping on the now slick stone, he managed to keep himself steady for a while but then he overbalanced and his left foot shot straight off the pillar taking him with it. Darrius felt his stomach tighten at the sight, but somehow the man managed to grab a hold of the pillar.

"Please forgive me!" screamed the man as he clung to the pillar for life.

Darrius's heart sank, there was no way that the man was going to be able to pull himself back, it was obvious from the way his arm's trembled, the poor lad had no more strength left in his arms, next to Darrius the High Sentinel made the sign of the Lady.

Prayer's not going to help.

To confirm his thought the man lost the last of his strength and began to fall, but again he didn't fall to his death, as if out of nowhere another arm grabbed hold of the man and held him in place, Darrius looked up and was shocked to find Fia hanging from the fifth pillar. Her sinewy arms bulged with the effort, the taller of the guards openly gasped at the sight and even the High Sentinel seemed shocked by her actions, but Darrius knew it was for naught there was no way she was going to be able to haul the boy back up and if she hung onto him for too long she wouldn't have the strength to pull herself back up.

A moment later rocks began to pelt the two, Darrius looked around and was horrified to find the shorter guard loading a sling with rocks, before he could stop himself Darrius was moving.

"What in the hell do you think you're doing!"

The guard turned around a smirk plastered across his fat face. "Sinners aren't to leave their pillar."

"You moron, she's still on the damn pillar."

A look of confusion passed over the guard's face as he looked from Darrius to Fia and back again, then the spark of recognition lit up, "But sh..."

"What!" yelled Darrius, his anger becoming a full-on blaze. "You're going to condemn her for trying to help another human being."

"Calm down, Darrius." The High Sentinel had walked up behind Darrius unnoticed. "Show us the hourglass again."

Shakily the guard produced the hourglass, there was hardly any sand left in the upper half, maybe another thirty seconds.

Darrius flicked between the falling sand and the two hanging Initiates, he could see Fia didn't have much left in her, the pain was etched across her face and Darrius could see her hand begin to slip from the pillar.

Finally, the last grains of sand fell through the hourglass and Darrius was off running towards the pillars.

"Get off the pillars!"

The man who had been standing on the second pillar just managed to get off and out of the way before Darrius leapt passed him and onto the first pillar, the stone was slick from the rain but that didn't slow Darrius, he sprang from one pillar to the next until he reached the fourth pillar, where he dropped down onto his stomach and reached out his hand, the young man's face was fear incarnate.

"Grab my hand!" shouted Darrius above a crack of thunder.

But the boy just looked at him, the fear taking hold.

"Damn it just grab hold of his hand otherwise I'm gonna let go!" shouted Fia.

That seemed to get through to the boy, he reached out his quivering hand and Darrius grabbed it and in one heaving pull Darrius brought the boy up onto the pillar with him, Darrius looked back to see if Fia needed any help but she had already pulled herself back up.

Darrius slowly helped the boy down from one pillar to the other until finally they touched solid ground, the boy dropped to his knees, tears streaming down his face and kissed the wet sodden earth, before making the sign of the

Lady and thanking her for saving him, Darrius couldn't comprehend it, the Lady hadn't done anything it was the will of Fia that had saved him. Leaving the boy to his prayers Darrius walked over to where Fia stood crouch over.

"You alright?"

"Yeah I'm good, thanks for the help," said Fia breathlessly.

"No problem."

"So," said Fia before taking a deep breath, "what brings the High Sentinel and the traveller out here to the Pillars of Judgement?"

Before Darrius could reply Emberfang spoke, "We're here for you, my dear."

"Me!" said Fia incredulously. "What could you possibly want with me?"

This time it was Darrius's turn to interrupt the High Sentinel, "I want you to accompany me on a journey."

Darrius didn't look but he could imagine the surprise on the High Sentinel's face, he himself was a little surprised at this, but seeing Fia save the boy's life let him know that she was someone he could trust to have his back, and what more could he ask for from a companion.

"But I'm not even a fully-fledged Sentinel," said Fia dumbfounded.

"Count yourself lucky, I haven't left this isle in over forty years and I'm the High Sentinel."

"But...?"

Darrius held up a hand cutting Fia off, "Look if you don't feel up to it then I can find someone else."

From the look that passed over the young woman's face Darrius knew he had won.

"Where are we heading?"

"The Angardian Kingdom and we leave tomorrow at first light," replied Darrius walking off before Fia had a chance to reply.

"Well that was a surprise," said the High Sentinel falling in beside Darrius.

"You told me I had the choice so I made it," replied Darrius feeling drained from the day's proceedings.

"That I did, I just didn't expect you to make the choice on the spot like that."

"I saw all I needed to."

"Fair enough, now let's get back to the tower so I can change out of these wet clothes, I feel like a drowned rat."

Darrius nodded and the two men made their way back through the forest without another word.

The following morning just before dawn, Darrius was out on the beach of Seers Isle making his final checks, his pack was filled with a spare set of his Sentinel greys and enough rations to last a week, both his old set of throwing knives and a new set lined his chest, the new set had been waiting for him in his room last night with a note from the Oracle reminding him just how important his latest journey was (not that she needed to) and that she wished him well, Darrius had never been good at goodbyes so he was more than happy to accept the gift and leave it at that.

Darrius looked towards his small rowing boat, a few cracks were beginning to form on the bow but none of them were serious.

As he walked around to the port side of his vessel, Darrius spotted several barnacles clinging to the sun-bleached wood.

Best get rid of them.

Drawing his short sword Darrius quickly pried the barnacles free, before he moved on to the stern. Nothing marked the back of the tiny boat apart from the scrapes and scratches that come with time and use. Proceeding to the starboard side Darrius was meet with another load of barnacles which he quickly cleared and he moved his inspection to the oars, both were in good condition, but Darrius still knew it was going to be a hard couple days of rowing before they reached the mainland of the Banetian Kingdom.

Out on the horizon the sun was beginning to rise, the orange giant turned the sky from a deep dark blue to a mixture of oranges, yellows and purples, the sea reflected the view like a colossal mirror.

As Darrius stood watching the scene he heard soft footfalls coming across the sand towards him, turning Darrius was met with a sight that left him feeling confident he had chosen the right person. Fia was clad in the grey garb of a Sentinel, a heavy looking pack sat strapped across her back, the feathered ends of arrows poked out of the top and a large waterskin sat in the side pouch, on one of her hips sat a single handed crossbow and on the other was a short sword, apart from the Sentinel grab everything looked worn and used, Darrius nodded to himself, he felt it was better to have equipment you were used to then to replaced it for something new when it got a few knocks.

"So you're a fully-fledged Sentinel now," said Darrius as Fia got closer.

"Last night the High Sentinel came to me and took me to the Grove of the Fallen, the Oracle was waiting for us there and she performed my induction herself, you have no idea how surprised I was."

"Oh I can imagine," said Darrius remembering his own induction into the Order.

"So we're actually leaving," said Fia looking at the small boat and out into the vast sea.

Darrius knew how hard this must be for the young woman after all, the Isle and Order were all this girl had known and now she was going out into the world with a man she knew nothing about.

"Yep, hope you had a good breakfast you're gonna need the energy it's a long way to the Banetian shore."

"You ain't got to worry about me," replied Fia walking passed Darrius towards the boat. "Before I joined the Order I was working in the town as a fisher."

Fia slung her pack into the boat.

"Well it's good to know you can catch us some supper," said Darrius throwing his own pack in.

"I'm sure you're capable of catching your own supper."

Darrius smiled, maybe travelling with somebody else wasn't going to be as bad as he thought. With a few good shoves the two pushed the boat off into the shallows before climbing in themselves, before Darrius could take hold of the oars Fia grabbed hold of them and began rowing.

"Don't worry I got this, you can take the second shift."

And so, began another journey for the traveller, but this time he wasn't alone.

Chapter 21

The great forest of Alfheim was in complete uproar, children were crying and screaming, their mothers tried to calm them with reassuring words but to no avail, whilst younger women called to the men to do something.

"Protect us," came a call from one woman.

"What's happening?" cried another.

The men of the Enshyi looked just as scared and confused as the rest, so they began to call for the High Speakers to come forth and explain what was going on, but the High Speakers were nowhere to be found and the great black dot that had been hovering high above the forest for the last day still marked the skyline through the treetops.

Adessa knew what it was, it was the Angardian Skyship come to take her away, but that knowledge didn't give her any comfort, it only filled her with dread, from today onward her life would be a series of unknowns and her trying to accustom herself with another Kingdom's culture. The last few weeks had passed far too quickly what with the GrandOak and High Speaker scrambling to help her make her vessel so that she could communicate with the GrandOak again once she left, the process hadn't been as hard as Adessa thought it would be, all she had needed to do was pour her will into an acorn causing it to grow, from there she added a strand of her own hair, the acorn had instantly absorbed the strand and within a few minutes of continuing to pour her will into the acorn Adessa had been stood staring at a wooden version of herself, the sight had unnerved her no end and the feeling that she was now missing a part of herself only added to the unpleasant feeling but both the GrandOak and Caewyn had reassured her that everything was fine.

The cries of fear and anger continued until they reached an agonising climax, a few of the rangers called for order and that everyone remain calm but these calls were quickly smothered by outraged shouts.

"How can we remain calm!" howled a young man.

"Pleas" began one of the rangers, but before he could finish what he was going to say another voice called out.

"This is ridiculous, where are the High Speakers? They're supposed to protect us."

The angry crowd shouted their agreement.

Adessa also wondered where the High Speakers had gotten to; after all, High Speaker Caewyn had said that by noon today she would be on the *Notus,* and noon was fast approaching.

A candlemark passed and the crowd began to disperse, the people leaving begrudgingly to go back to their everyday duties, but a small collection of young Enshyi didn't move, the brown robes they wore gave them away as Forest Speakers and when Adessa looked over at the group she recognised Kaylessa Willowthorne instantly, Kaylessa was the most promising Speaker of Adessa's generation and was responsible for the majority of the abuse Adessa had experience in her young life, since she had found the GrandOak's voice Adessa hadn't seen much of her former classmates and for that she was grateful.

One of the other Apprentices that was stood with Kaylessa pointed at Adessa and said something to the group that got them all laughing, despite her best efforts Adessa felt herself blush, she was just about to walk away when a strong arm wrapped its way around her shoulder, looking up Adessa was meet with the smirking face of Quynn Starstriker, the sight of the young Fire Speaker knotted Adessa's stomach, he was Kaylessa's obedient lapdog as well as her lover.

"You weren't going to leave were you, Adessa?"

Adessa tried to break free but Quynn was too strong for her.

"Shall we go say hello," said Quynn, an evil smile touching his lips. "Kaylessa will be so glad to see you, after all she was beginning to worry that something bad had happened to you."

Kaylessa and the other Speakers were already looking over at Adessa but Quynn shouted to them all the same, "Look who I found!"

"Well if it isn't little Dessy," said Kaylessa mockingly. "Where have you been, hmm?"

Despite her best efforts Adessa couldn't calm herself down, she was trapped, the taller Enshyi encircled her, their smirks and gazes mocking.

"She asked you a question," said another Speaker who Adessa didn't recognise.

"I've been training with the GrandOak."

The group fell silent at Adessa's words, their faces pure shock, Kaylessa was the first to recover.

"Lies!" the anger poured from the Speaker in a torrent. "Only an Enshyi with the potential to be High Speaker can find the GrandOak's voice and you're definitely not capable of that, you're not even Enshyi, you're just some abomination."

Something inside Adessa snapped at those words, after having found out who her father was and how he had died, that was the last thing she wanted to hear, they didn't know anything about her or her father.

"Shut up," said Adessa quietly.

"Sorry, what was that I didn't hear you from down there," replied Kaylessa, the group broke out into laughter again.

"I said shut up!"

In an instant, the laughter died and all eyes turned to Kaylessa to see what she would do against such insolence from an abomination like Adessa.

Adessa could feel the anger pouring from the older Speaker but still she squared her shoulder's and kept her head high.

Kaylessa smiled and before Adessa knew what was happening a sharp blow caught her across the face and she was knocked to the ground.

Adessa's cheek was on fire but she ignored the pain, if there was one benefit to training with High Speaker Roujin it was that she had become used to receiving punishment.

Kaylessa lashed out with a kick but Adessa rolled out of the blows path and quickly got back to her feet.

"C'mon, Kay, teach this half-breed her place."

As if out of nowhere Kaylessa produced a staff of deep mahogany, Adessa's heart sank, apprentices were only given a staff once they had passed their final test and became a fully-fledged Speaker.

Kaylessa closed her eyes and instantly Adessa knew that she was using her Voice. The staff began to morph before Adessa's eyes until finally the tip shot out towards her at lightning speed, without thinking Adessa drew OathKeeper, the blade and staff met in a thunderous clash, the look of bewilderment that passed across Kaylessa's face was priceless, but it only lasted a second as the older Speaker quickly mastered herself and fired another blow, this time the staffs head snaked through the air, Adessa tried to follow the incoming blow but the movements were too sporadic and she felt the familiar feelings of anger and panic began to creep into her mind.

"Calm yourself," sounded OathKeeper's voice.

Adessa quickly cleared her mind from the fog that had begun to settle and at the last moment brought OathKeeper up to knock away Kaylessa's attack for the second time.

"I am going to kill you!" screamed Kaylessa in fury.

Thanks to her training Adessa remained calm and instinctively dove into the spirit world.

The spirits of the forest were shining all around but none more so than OathKeeper who was shining bright and true and Kaylessa's staff which shone like a star dwarfing the magical blade, but rather than feel fear at the sight Adessa found there was only anticipation.

As Adessa came back to the physical world she heard Kaylessa let out a frustrated roar and in the next moment the older Speaker slammed her staff into the ground. Dozens of vines emerged from the ground and swarmed at

253

Adessa, twirling OathKeeper around like High Speaker Roujin had shown her Adessa knocked away most of the incoming blows until one vine slipped passed and collided with her shoulder in a sickening thud.

Before Adessa could be thrown off her feet another vine whipped around her stomach and began tightening like a wooden serpent.

As the air was forced from her lungs Adessa found her centre begin to slip away.

Am I going to die?

"Focus!"

The voice of OathKeeper cut through the pain and for a split second Adessa could think clearly again, pouring her will into OathKeeper she made the blade as hard and sharp as steel and in one fell swoop she freed herself from the bondage of the wooden snake. Adessa's chest burnt as she took what felt like her first breath, pain lanced through her shoulder and her legs and arms felt heavy but there wasn't any time for her to worry about that, as Kaylessa was already reading herself for another attack, picking herself up Adessa charged straight at Kaylessa, gasps came from the crowd that were watching, they couldn't believe the audacity of it. Kaylessa shot more vines out but Adessa cut them down with quick strikes from OathKeeper and made the distance towards the older Speaker, but before Adessa could strike out with her blade a powerful and familiar voice tore through the air stopping her in her tracks.

"By the Flame-mother, what's going on here?"

Adessa turned to see High Speaker Roujin standing in front of her, his crimson armour shone a fiery red despite the lack of clear sunlight and his golden eyes almost seemed to be aflame. Everyone apart from Adessa immediately dropped to their knees, Roujin looked at Adessa in a way that told her she should do the same.

"Now I'll say again what's going on here?"

"Adessa attacked Kaylessa for no reason," said one of the Speaker's Adessa didn't know.

Anger flashed through Adessa, she hadn't done anything but defend herself from Kaylessa's attacks.

"It's true!" shouted Quynn.

High Speaker Roujin turned away from Adessa and faced Kaylessa, "Is this true?"

Kaylessa looked up at the High Speaker and without blinking said, "Yes she attacked me," it was like even saying Adessa's name was below her. "I merely asked Adessa where she had been for the past few months as I was worried about her, but before I could say anything she attacked."

"See it's like we said," said Quynn adding to the lie.

Roujin quickly turned his attention on Quynn, Adessa had never seen such fear etched on the young man's face, but she thought it looked better than that stupid grin he usually had plastered across his face.

"I don't remember asking for your opinion apprentice," said Roujin in his booming voice.

If it hadn't been for his already pale complexion Adessa was sure she would have seen Quynn blanch.

"Mmmm... mm... my apologies."

High Speaker Roujin didn't even acknowledge the apology and began to address the entire group, "This is not what I expected from the Speakers of the Forest, do you believe that just because your High Speaker is away that you can act as you please." Silence was all the response Roujin needed. "I didn't think so, now everybody apart from Adessa will report to the Hall of Learning and await my arrival."

One of the more daring or stupid Speakers depending on which way you look at it spoke out, "Why does she get special treatment?"

"Special treatment, don't make me laugh, Adessa is going to join your High Speaker in the Angardian Kingdom to help further our relations with the people there."

A few gasps escaped from some of the Apprentice Speakers, other nodded agreeing like this was something they had seen coming all along. Quynn's face was once again twisted into a grin but Kaylessa was unreadable, her face a mask.

"I don't suppose you want to go instead?" said High Speaker Roujin now grinning himself.

Silence.

"That's what I thought now get outta my sight."

The crowd of young Enshyi quickly dispersed, but Kaylessa took her time in leaving, a defiant action but one that Roujin let slide for now, as she passed she whispered, "Good riddance," into Adessa's ear.

The anger inside of Adessa had taken hold again and she was a just about to throw a fist into Kaylessa's pretty face when OathKeeper's voice filled her head, "Remember yourself."

With all of her will Adessa held herself in place and allowed Kaylessa to leave.

Once everyone was gone Roujin looked at Adessa like he was trying to figure something out before he began walking off, after a few steps he turned and beckoned Adessa to follow.

All eyes were on Adessa as she followed High Speaker Roujin through the treetop walkways of Alfheim, clearly word had spread that she was leaving and not one Enshyi looked sad to see her go.

Eventually, the stares and whispers became nothing but scenery and sound in the background and Adessa began thinking of her mother, the GrandOak and the Blood Roses. It would be a whole fortnight before she got to the Angardian Kingdom and who knew how many more before she developed another vessel to link with the one here, which meant no more evenings sat in the comfort of the Roses company, Adessa's stomach knotted at the thought but then she thought about how she wouldn't see her mother's loving smile or hear her soft encouraging voice or enjoy a quiet meal with her or. Adessa choked back tears. Damn there was so much she was going to miss about her mother and not enough time to tell her how much she truly meant to her daughter. Adessa continued to follow High Speaker Roujin in a stupor of self-pity.

Through the few gaps that the tree line allowed it was easy to see that the Angardian Skyship had begun to descend and at an alarming rate.

Adessa couldn't help but think that the ship looked like one of the dragons from her grandmother's stories, what with its massive wooden body and masts and sails that looked like giant wings, but the ships colossal size paled in comparison to the beautiful winged man that sat at the front of the ship.

Sweet Eilauver, that's beautiful.

The colossal ship continued its descent until finally it rested just above the tops of the trees in the distance and came to a stop, from its position Adessa could tell that the ship sat just above the Hall of Elements, no that couldn't be right why would the High Speakers allow foreigners so close to one of the holiest places in Alfheim, it was a miracle that they had been allowed so close to the forest in the first place.

As if sensing her thoughts Roujin spoke, "Don't worry, they won't be setting foot on our land."

"So how am I supposed to reach their ship?"

Roujin barked in laughter, "Ha ha, seriously, you're a Speaker of the forest you can just call upon a spirit to help you."

Suddenly, Adessa knew why the High Speakers had chosen the Hall of Elements as the place of rendezvous with the Angardian ship, it would stop the other Enshyi from panicking any more than they already were and if anything went wrong the casualties would be minimal also the High Speakers would get to show the Angardians a brief display of their power through Adessa.

Walking across the walkway towards the Hall of Elements Adessa spotted High Speaker Zydar and Rasesso waiting for her with her mother, at the sight of her mother Adessa began to fill her eyes tear up.

257

No I have to be strong for mother.

"High Speaker," said the trio in unison as Roujin and Adessa neared.

Roujin gave a respectful nod to all three before taking up his position next to Zydar.

All eyes turned to Adessa, making her feel embarrassed and insecure but she swallowed the awkwardness and smiled to the three High Speakers and her mother.

"Are you ready?" said High Speaker Zydar nervously, clearly he was just as worried as the other Enshyi.

Adessa nodded not trusting her voice.

"Good," said High Speaker Rasesso smiling, "there's no going back now".

Again, Adessa nodded.

"Could I have a minute with my daughter, before she leaves," said Sakala sadly.

"Of course," replied Rasesso. "Come on, boys, let's give them some privacy."

Once they were alone Sakala pulled Adessa into a tight hug, Adessa returned the embrace with the same intensity, "I'm so proud of you."

This time Adessa couldn't hold the tears back, a she shuddered in her mother grasp as she spoke, "Thank you for everything you've done for me and don't worry, mother, I'll become strong and protect you and Alfheim."

"I have no doubt that you will, now," said Sakala releasing her daughter from her arms and wiping away her tears, "we best get you on that ship we don't want to leave our new friends waiting."

"But what about my stuff."

Sakala held up a hand, "We've already loaded them up onto the ship."

Adessa was just about to thank her mother when the High Speakers returned and Roujin said "Ready?"

"Yes," said Sakala.

The High Speaker's turned to Adessa, "I'm ready."

"Okay let's get you up there," said Rasesso with a cheeky grin.

Before Adessa could say anything a great cyclone of wind began to spin around her lifting her quickly up into the air and onto the deck of the Angardian Skyship, some of the men on the deck fell over in surprise others stood completely still with looks of bewilderment on their faces and a few had even drawn their swords and guns. Adessa's heart hammered in her chest but she kept her face impassive.

Don't let them know your scared.

A moment later a man who was roughly the same height as High Speaker Caewyn stepped forward. Adessa immediately looked the man up and down, his heavily tanned skin reminded Adessa of the bark of a walnut tree, but more surprisingly than that was that the man's head was free from any hair whilst his chin and cheeks were covered in a thick brown beard.

Adessa found the sight rather amusing, it looked like all the hair on his head had migrated to sit on his face but she didn't let her amusement show and kept her face impassive.

The man began to say something but Adessa didn't understand a word, which both annoyed and scared her.

He could be saying anything.

A moment later Adessa remembered the piece of parchment that High Speaker Caewyn had given her, which contained instructions for Daniel Goodwin the Captain of the *Notus.*

Reaching into the left-hand pocket of her robes Adessa produced the parchment and handed it to the man.

The man's smile faded while he read the note but once he was done his face lit back up and he pointed to a pin that sat on the collar of his jacket. Adessa looked at the pin and realised that it was the rank for a Captain like Caewyn had shown her.

Adessa bowed to the Captain, who returned the gesture before he said something to his men. At his words the crew relaxed and sheathed their weapons and went about their business.

Well at least he seems to be able to control his men.

Captain Goodwin pointed towards a door at the end of the deck then back to Adessa before mimicking sleeping, telling Adessa that was her room for the duration of her journey. Adessa turned back to look one last time at the Forest of Alfheim, at this height she could see just how big the forest truly was, it stretched out in every direction for miles like a sea of green, looking down she waved to her mother and the High Speakers. Her mother and High Speaker Rasesso returned the wave where as High Speaker Zydar just raised his hand and Roujin tilted his head ever so slightly in recognition, lastly she looked off into the distance and saw the GrandOak standing as tall and true as ever, delving into her Voice, Adessa opened the bond she shared with the GrandOak and said, "I shall be back once I've made my vessel in Actalia."

The GrandOak's reply was short but filled with love, "I shall await that time."

As Adessa came back out of the spirit world the floor beneath her shifted and the Ship quickly began to rise back up into the air, suddenly feeling drained Adessa let Captain Goodwin lead her to her room.

Once inside the Captain quickly took his leave and left Adessa alone in her new room, much to her surprise the room was lavishly decorated with all manner of opulent furnishings but the only one that Adessa cared for was the large bed that at the back of the room and her own belongings which sat atop it.

Making her way to the bed Adessa sat down and opened the pack from her mother, inside were three pouches filled with all Adessa's favourite foods that would keep over the entirety of her journey, Adessa smiled, her mother had thought of everything, there were dried apricots, figs, prunes and dates in one pouch, dried berries in another and an assortment of nuts lined the last one. Adessa took a couple of dates and a handful of nuts and popped them into her mouth before closing the pack back up and dropping onto the bed beside her stuff, the mattress beneath her was softer than anything she had imagined possible, it felt like it was enveloping her, suddenly a yawn broke forth from her mouth.

I'll just rest my eyes for a bit.

Adessa fell into a deep sleep filled with dreams of her mother, the GrandOak and everything else she was leaving behind.

Chapter 22

Sweat poured off Caleb matting his hair to his brow and even made the loose fitting practice breeches stick to him in various places, he just counted himself lucky he was shirtless, the heat of Teuengea was far worse than that which he had experienced out in the desert, must be something to do with all the people and buildings, if it wasn't for the robes that he usually wore he swore he would have passed out a dozen times by now in the streets, but he couldn't fight in a robe and he was having a hard enough time as it was against his sparring partners, for weeks now he had been training in the palace's grove with Jackeal Biyabani and Vaeliria as the *Zephyrus* was being repaired and he had yet to get a clean hit on either of them whilst he left each day with a new set of bruises and cuts.

"Don't let your mind wonder," said Vaeliria throwing a roundhouse kick at Caleb's face.

Caleb dodged the attack more on instinct than anything else, the wind that passed by his face from the blow quickly brought him back to his senses. Vaeliria stood in front of him in a low fighting stance, the wiry muscles in her shoulders and arms were tight, telling him that he should be wary. Caleb shifted his weight on to his back foot and hunkered down into one of the defensive postures he had seen the Jackeal use against this very stance. Vaeliria smiled at her pupil before launching into an attack with the power and speed of a pouncing lioness, one fist followed the other in a barrage of lightning quick punches, Caleb just managed to dodge the blows by weaving his body from side to side whilst he retreated.

The Jackeal makes this look easy.

The onslaught continued and Caleb could feel himself beginning to slow, so he threw up blocks and slowed his retreat to try and catch his breath but Vaeliria wasn't having any of it, she pressed even harder mixing in kicks to Caleb's thighs and calves, each kick felt like being hit with an iron pole, knowing that he couldn't withstand this sort of punishment for long Caleb quickly dropped down and swept his left leg at Vaeliria, she easily dodged the attack but it gave Caleb all the opening he needed from his crouched position he rolled forward before launching into a handstand kick, it connected but he knew it wasn't clean and within seconds he found himself looking up at the sky in a heap of tangled limbs.

Overbalanced you idiot.

Before he could pick himself up a heavy boot landed on his chest knocking what air he had left in his lungs out in a hot painful burst.

"Do you yield?"

With what little strength Caleb had left he latched his arms around Vaeliria's foot and twisted, Vaeliria had to go with the twist otherwise she risked her ankle being sprained if not broken, as she hit the ground Caleb wrapped his legs around the top of her right thigh and keeping hold of her foot swiftly put pressure on the joint, knowing she was beat Vaeliria instantly tapped in submission. Caleb unravelled himself and lay on the ground breathless, pain shot through his tired arms and legs followed shortly by a sharp burning sensation in his chest as he caught his breath but despite all of that he found himself smiling, in all his months training this was his first ever victory and it felt good, looking up again he was meet with Vaeliria's outstretched hand.

"You're really coming along," said Vaeliria as Caleb accepted her hand.

"I'd hope so," replied Caleb smiling.

"That was quite the performance," said Jackeal Biyabani raising from his seat, the Onmori's barrel chest and thick arms gleamed with sweat.

"Thanks," Caleb took a deep drag from his waterskin, "think I got lucky."

"Luck has a part to play in any battle," said Vaeliria.

The Jackeal nodded in agreement, "I've seen skilled men cut down by lesser foes all because of bad luck, and speaking of being cut down, do you want a scimitar or sibat for our spar?"

Caleb hated both, scimitars felt heavy and clumsy in his hand whilst the sibat spear was slow and he couldn't use it fluidly, if he had his way he would always use his dirks, but Vaeliria had pointed it out to him that in the heat of battle he could lose his dirks and that the difference between him living or dying would be his ability to adapt and find another weapon to use.

"Well," said Jackeal Biyabani, "I don't have all day."

"Scimitar," replied Caleb quickly.

The Jackeal smiled before going to the masterfully built weapons rack that had been brought down from the palace armoury for Caleb's training, he quickly donned his leather practice jersey and selected a sibat with a wicked looking blade, although Caleb knew the blade had been dulled he still felt a pang of fear rush through him, after all he had the cuts and bruises to show just what a 'dull' blade could do.

With the help of Vaeliria, Caleb strapped on his own jersey and promptly selected his weapon, the long curved blade was a fine piece of work and Caleb knew that all it would take to make it battle ready was a few strokes of a whetstone.

Taking up his position opposite the Jackeal, Caleb bowed low in the crossed legged style that was custom in Onmori spars, the Jackeal returned the gesture if not as low and then they were off. Caleb knew that standing still against the Jackeal's incoming attacks would mean his loss so he rushed forward, sword and spear connected in a flurry of blows, Caleb hacked and hacked but each blow was easily blocked by the long metallic shaft of the Jackeal's spear, shifting his weight Caleb spun hoping to deliver a sweeping blow but his blade meet nothing but thin air, without anything to stop his momentum he spun in a circle, sensing that a blow was coming he pivoted and rolled away, clearly his intuition had been right as the tip of the Jackeal's sibat came slicing through the air where he had stood moments ago, jumping back to his feet Caleb swirled the scimitar in a series of crescent strikes.

Maybe I'm getting better at this.

As soon as he had the thought Caleb felt the strength begin to fade from his sword arm.

Not yet.

Caleb kept up his assault, but the strikes were completely wasted as the Jackeal didn't engage him and instead gracefully dodged around Caleb's strikes.

Faster.

Caleb whipped his sword around as fast as he could and yet he still couldn't find his mark and then in the next moment he felt his arm tire and his movements slowed.

Shit.

The Jackeal having seen Caleb's obvious fatigue quickly went on the offensive with a series of sharp jabs. Caleb tried to block the strikes but with his arm now tired he couldn't defend himself well enough and the Jackeal easily slipped the tip of his sibat passed his guard and delivered three jabs to Caleb's sword-arm. The first strike dug into Caleb's shoulder, the second his bicep and then his forearm, each blow stung like hell and Caleb knew his arm was now useless.

With as much grace as he could muster Caleb took a step back and switched the scimitar to his left hand, the heavy blade felt even clumsier than it had in his right but nevertheless he drew the sword up into a guard and waited.

Caleb didn't have to wait long as the Jackeal quickly leapt forward and once again began to pepper his guard with short sharp jabs and hard lunges. Caleb did the best he could but it was getting harder to block each subsequent blow from the sibat and he had no time whatsoever to produce any attack of his own and then in one quick blur his hand was empty, and the tip of the sibat was levelled coolly at his throat.

"I believe this is my win," said the Jackeal smiling.

Caleb held up his hands in surrender, even that was an effort.

Jackeal Biyabani picked up the scimitar and put both back in their respective places in the weapons rack before unstrapping his jersey and grabbing a drink from his own waterskin. Vaeliria helped Caleb with his jersey and gave him a stare that demanded more from him.

Was it that bad?

Of course, it was you got your ass handed to you yet again.

Caleb wanted to ask for a rematch but he knew the Jackeal had duties to attend to and he himself had his other lessons of the day, there would be his learning of the Skelwori language and history, which he thought was going well, he could now have a full conversation with Vaeliria in her native tongue all be it that he still used the wrong word from time to time and then he would spend the rest of his day roaming the city of Teuengea setting himself task, like seeing how long he could tail someone before they caught on or how fast he could get from one side of the city to the other without attracting attention before he finally did his evening practice of the Shakan.

"Now, if you'll excuse me I have a meeting with the head of the Armourers guild," said Jackeal Biyabani throwing on his robes.

"Good day," said Vaeliria bowing.

"Thanks for the spar," said Caleb.

The Jackeal smiled, "It was my pleasure."

Once the Jackeal had left Caleb couldn't look Vaeliria in the eye, he could already feel her gaze on him and it made him feel awkward.

"I'm sorry," said Caleb quietly.

"What was that?" replied Vaeliria.

"I'm sorry," repeated Caleb again.

"Speak up, cadet!"

"I said I'm sorry!"

"Eyes up." From her tone Caleb, could tell Vaeliria was all Commander at this point.

Caleb looked up at Vaeliria and was meet with an iron stare, there was no friendliness in his mentor's eyes.

"Don't apologise, do better."

Caleb was speechless, he had given his all and Vaeliria still didn't think it was enough, how was that fair.

No, she's right if you don't do better you'll find yourself dead in no time.

Caleb saluted, "Yes, Commander."

"Good, now get over to the docks, from Thom's latest report the *Zephyrus* is nearly flight ready."

Within a candlemark Caleb had made it to the dockyard and was stood on the deck of the *Zephyrus* with Thom and Gustav, the two engineers were talking about the final preparations that needed to be made before the *Zephyrus* could take back to the skies but Caleb's mind was elsewhere, the stare Vaeliria had given him was still on his mind, it was just like the way she had looked at him when they had first met when he was still Asher, the very thought of his old name brought back all kinds of painful and sad memories which he never wanted to relive.

"I think we should give it another couple of days," said Gustav even more reserved than usual.

"Nonsense!" barked Thom, Caleb smiled it was good to see the old engineer back on his feet.

"But we don't know how stable the Skycore is."

"The core will be fine," said Thom in a tone that made it clear this wasn't up for discussion.

From the look that passed over Gustav's face he wasn't happy but Caleb knew that he respected Thom enough to differ to his decision.

After a quick ride down the lift, Caleb followed Thom and Gustav out into the Skycore bay and was amazed, if he hadn't been there when the enemies javelins came crashing through the *Zephyrus*'s hull, he wouldn't have believed that it had ever happened, the hull was completely restored, but then he caught sight of the other members of the engineers and the scribes and realised there were fewer than before, looking around Caleb saw that a number of benches lay empty, the projects and tomes that lined them a memorial of who was lost. Over at the forges working away were Allie and Riktor, Allie was at her anvil hammering away, her giant arms rippling with the force of each blow and Riktor was stood at the grinding wheel sharpening a monstrous double headed axe. Caleb couldn't help but smile, he hadn't had many chances to come and see the other members of the crew what with his training and their own tasks, he hadn't seen Luci in at least a week and she was his best friend.

Caleb looked up at the Skycore, it was shining its usual light blue but here and there Caleb saw hints of deeper blues and purples, maybe Gustav was right to have concerns the core shouldn't be fluctuating like that when they were grounded.

"Don't worry, lad," said Thom following Caleb's gaze, "the cores fine, once we take to the air those energy pockets will burn off in no time."

Caleb nodded, of course he was right, that was one of the first things that had been addressed in the Fundaments of Skycore Technology, the authors had explained how Skycores built up excess energy if they weren't in use for an extended period of time and that it was quite safe because it would take decades for a core to reach a critical level and if it came down to it you could use some Hellstone to drain the crystal of all of its energy before it reached that point but then the authors went on to say that if not handled correctly or if the unstable core was suddenly damaged then you could have a catastrophe on your hands the like that hadn't been seen in decades since people first started using Skycore technology.

Caleb followed Thom through the throng and into his office, surprisingly Gustav didn't join them. Thom quickly made his way to his desk and Caleb joined him, the place was still as chaotic as it had been. No. It was worse, dozens of books sat atop one another on the floor, the two bookshelves were filled to bursting and Caleb spotted a couple of tomes lining their tops, a couple of new designs hung with Thom's older ones, Caleb still couldn't comprehend what they were, the new designs were labelled as a compression engine and the other Skyhook.

Sitting down in the chair opposite Thom, Caleb waited until it became clear the master engineer wasn't going to stop rooting through the many draws of his desk before he spoke.

"So the Commander says that the *Zephyrus* is nearly sky worthy."

"Ain't no nearly about it, she's ready whenever the Captain is," replied Thom not even looking up from his rummaging.

"Really!" Caleb wanted nothing more than to get back in the air, that way he could start tracking down Irashaad and bring him to justice, in the weeks that had passed since that meeting between Captain Brightfellow and Jackeal Biyabani, Caleb hadn't heard anything in regards to Irashaad and when he asked Vaeliria she said that he should be focusing on his training rather than worrying about something that was under control.

"Let's get her in the air then," said Caleb unable to hide his enthusiasm.

Thom stopped rooting through his drawers and looked up, "I want to hunt down the bastard who did this to our ship and crew as much as you but we wait for the Captain to make the decision."

"But."

Thom held up a hand, cutting Caleb off, "Have faith, the Captain knows what he's doing."

"Fine," said Caleb huffing, "you got any new books for me to read?"

"As a matter of fact I was just looking for Janus Magnussen's, Mastering the Art of Skysailing," said Thom going back to hunting for the tome.

"Why would I need to learn that anyway?" asked Caleb, "The other members of the crew deal with that, hell

I'm not even allowed on deck cause the Commander says I'll just be in the way."

"Ah ha here it is." Thom reappeared from below his desk with a large leather bound tome. "This book will teach you how to manipulate the sails using the rigging, rudder and sometimes you may even have to manipulate the keel to get the right results, also it will teach you to be aware of your surroundings, the sooner you can spot changes in the weather the sooner you can react and sometimes that means the difference between life and death."

"That doesn't really answer my question."

"Doesn't it," replied Thom arching an eyebrow, he always did that when he was looking for Caleb to find the answer himself.

And like that it came to Caleb, "If I learn how to do all of that then I can be of use out on deck."

"Exactly," said Thom nodding, "so if I was you I'd make a start as soon as possible," Thom slid the tome across the desk and into Caleb's hands. "Then when the Captain gives the order for us to go after those pirates, you can help out on deck."

"Right."

Caleb had just finished reading the twelfth chapter of Mastering the art of Skysailing when a light knock came at his door, jumping up from his bed, Caleb was hit with a wave of tiredness, hunger and the need to relieve himself.

The knock repeated.

Before he could make it to the door it opened and in stepped Luci, her green medical robes and apron were stained with blood and dirt and she looked tired but she smiled none the less.

"What brings you here, at what I'm guessing is a late hour," said Caleb picking up the pitcher of water that sat on his table.

"Haven't you heard?" from the way she said it Caleb knew something major had happened.

"I've been sat here in my room for the entire day reading." Caleb poured himself and Luci a glass of water, his hands were shaking in anticipation of the news.

"The Captain's issued the order."

Caleb's heart skipped a beat, "Do you mean?"

Luci nodded, "The *Zephyrus* is taking back to the skies."

Caleb dropped the pitcher and embraced Luci in a tight hug, this was great he could finally get back up into the skies and track down Irashaad, Caleb released Luci from his grip and smiled at her, Luci returned the smile.

"When are we departing?"

"First thing tomorrow."

Caleb couldn't contain his excitement, "And where are we going?"

"I don't know, the Captain and Vaeliria will be able to fill you in tomorrow."

Caleb was itching to find out the details of their plan, but he told himself that he would find out tomorrow.

"Well then I'll be off," said Luci heading for the door.

"What, you're leaving already."

"Like you said it's late and I think we both need to get some rest."

"Okay," said Caleb smiling again. "I'll see you tomorrow."

Luci nodded and left, leaving Caleb alone with his thoughts of vengeance, which didn't leave him even when sleep came and took hold for the night.

The chaotic choir of a hundred different voices woke Caleb the following morning, he immediately threw his robes back on and ran out into the corridor, almost colliding with a passing member of the crew who was carrying an arm full of supplies as he did.

"Watch where you're going!" cursed the man, but Caleb was already running off.

Dodging from side to side Caleb skilfully made it passed the stream of Skyknights that passed him, some cursed him like the man before, others offered a friendly smile and a select few didn't even acknowledge his passing, too busy with their own tasks, sometimes Caleb wished the *Zephyrus* wasn't as big as it was, at least then he could learn everyone's name and feel like he knew them at least a little but as it was they were just passing faces.

Making it to the lift Caleb turned the counterweight system dials that sat embedded into the wall to the correct points and waited, although he knew it only took a few minutes for the lift to rise from the lower levels to his own, Caleb still stood there itching to go, he needed to get up to the deck so he could speak with the Captain and Vaeliria.

Finally, the lift arrived on his floor, the ever present hissing and grinding accompanying it, dozens of people were inside, Caleb pulled open the grate that separated him from the lift and five of the passengers got off and passed by without so much as a word, Caleb stepped on and standing by the counterweight system inside was the woman who had been surprised at his arrival aboard the *Zephyrus*, Caleb wanted to question the woman about that meeting and why she and some of the other members of the crew were so shocked to find another Skelwori aboard the *Zephyrus*, but with the lift being filled with a dozen bodies he knew now wasn't the time and he silently closed the grate.

"Going up," said the woman as she turned the dials and sent the lift into motion.

Caleb tried not to fidget but the urge to just send the lift flying up towards the deck was growing with each floor they stopped at to let people off and on.

Arriving at the deck, Caleb opened the door and stepped out into the morning sun. The heat hit him like a wave, sucking the air form his lungs. Doing his best to ignore the heat Caleb walked forward, the deck was alive with even more activity than usual, the men and women of the crew were buzzing about with their tasks as usual but helping bring supplies on board were a whole host of Onmorian men, each carried a load that would easily have floored Caleb and up at the helm stood Captain Brightfellow and Vaeliria, both were wearing their Skyknight uniforms despite the heat, Caleb walked along the deck purposefully but took care not to get in anyone's way and quickly climbed the stairs to join them.

"So we're heading out?" said Caleb reaching the helm.

Both the Captain and Vaeliria turned to regard Caleb, Captain Brightfellow smiled broadly like a happy child whereas Vaeliria gave a curt nod but her eyes were soft letting Caleb know that yesterday wasn't held against him.

"We're just waiting on the last of the supplies," said the Captain.

At the Captain's words Taylor appeared, Caleb knew instantly that they were ready to depart, after all the lanky clerk oversaw the *Zephyrus*'s supplies.

"Excuse me, Captain." said Taylor. "The men have just finished loading the last of the supplies."

The Captain's face broke out into an even wider grin then it had just a moment ago, "That's great news, see that the Onmori who helped us are compensated for their time and tell the men to be ready."

"Yes, sir."

After Taylor left Caleb asked, "Where we off to then?"

The Captain looked to Vaeliria quizzically, clearly he thought she would have already informed Caleb of their next move.

"He needed to focus on his training," said Vaeliria answering the gaze.

Captain Brightfellow didn't say anything in reply and began addressing Caleb, "Jackeal Biyabani's scouts have sent word that three of Irashaad's ships have been spotted near a place called the Shards of Cradure to the north-west."

"We're not doing this alone are we?"

"No Biyabani sent messenger birds to the Jackeals of Saranthini, Myturir and Xanesul explaining our plan and asked for their assistance."

"And?"

"Saranthini has dispatched two ships, Myturir and Xanesul one each."

"What about Jackeal Biyabani's scouts?".

"The Jackeal's two scout ships will be waiting for us a few miles from the shards."

So, it'll be seven against three.

Captain Brightfellow didn't say anything else and turned to face the deck, grasping hold of the helm he shouted, "Release the anchor!"

"Aye," replied one of the crew.

Caleb steeled himself against the shock that rippled through the *Zephyrus* as it took back to the skies, in what felt like forever.

Once they were in the air Vaeliria turned to Caleb and said, "Let's see if that tome Thom gave you taught you anything."

Caleb couldn't believe what he had just heard he was sure she was going to tell him to go back below deck but this left him dumbstruck.

"Well don't just stand there."

Caleb saluted before running down to the deck below where he began helping other members of the crew with their tasks and for the first time in a long while he began to feel like a true Skyknight.

Chapter 23

"Speaker."

Adessa rolled over in her bed still half asleep, she was sure she had just heard a voice, but there was no one in her room, maybe it was Charles or one of the other cabin boys waiting outside come to deliver her breakfast, over the past couple of days Adessa had come to realise that nearly everything here on the *Notus* was run by a strict schedule, she ate at a set time once in the morning at sun up and then again in the evening when the sun began to descend and the sky darkened. After breaking her fast, she would then receive a basin of water and a washcloth as her plates were cleared and then she was basically left alone for the rest of the day and told that it was best if she stayed in her room, not that she had any desire to leave. She would spend the remainder of her day reading the book High Speaker Caewyn had given her on the Angardian language, which proved to be easier than Adessa had expected and throughout the day Captain Goodwin would make sure she was okay and ask her if there was anything he could do to make her journey more comfortable which provided Adessa with plenty of opportunities to practice what she had read, but every time they spoke it quickly became clear that she had only just scratched the surface of the language.

"Speaker."

Again, the voice, Adessa pulled herself up from the soft mattress and looked around, the room was still empty apart from Adessa's packs and OathKeeper.

Of course.

Adessa opened herself to the spirit world and the voice of OathKeeper immediately filled her head.

"Speaker, something within one of your packs is emitting a lot of spiritual energy."

That freed Adessa's mind from the last confines of sleep, "Which one?"

"The one by the wardrobe."

Adessa quickly jumped out of bed and grabbed OathKeeper before making her way towards the pack, using her Voice, Adessa could see what OathKeeper was talking about, deep within the pack that held all her clothes, was a light that was quickly growing brighter and larger.

"Be ready," said OathKeeper.

Adessa slowly opened the pack, as soon as she did dozens of clothes burst forth, Adessa jumped back with OathKeeper drawn in defence, after a few seconds of nothing happening Adessa lowered her blade.

"Adessa are you there?" that was the voice of High Speaker Caewyn but why was it coming from her pack, "I think there may be something wrong with the Vessel, I can't see anything."

"I'm here, High Speaker." Adessa rushed to the pack, she quickly dug through the robes that were in there and was swiftly met with the wooden face of the High Speaker, and the sight brought a smile to Adessa's own face.

"Could you get me out of here?" said High Speaker Caewyn.

"Of course I'm sorry, I'm just a bit shocked to see you that's all, I thought I wouldn't be seeing you til I got to Actalia."

Adessa reached into the pack and grasped the High Speaker's vessel, pulling him out slowly she was shocked to find that he was just a head, seeing her shock Caewyn spoke.

"I didn't have time to make a full vessel so I opted for this."

"But why make one at all?" said Adessa confused.

"You didn't really think I would leave you alone on your journey, did you?"

Adessa hadn't thought about it, everything had happened so quickly one minute she was fighting with

Kaylessa the next she was saying her goodbyes as the *Notus* set sail.

"I didn't know what to think, everything's happening so quickly," said Adessa putting the High Speaker on the table.

"I know, I'm sorry that it took me so long to awaken this thing but my duties as a Councillor have increased here in Actalia, I seem to be in meetings all day at the moment, this is the first time that I've had to myself in weeks."

Adessa didn't know what to say, whenever she felt like she had a reason to be mad at the High Speaker he came along and said just the right thing that seemed to justify his actions and somehow made her feel like she had been unreasonable for being mad in the first place.

"So," said the High Speaker bringing Adessa back into the room, "how are the Angardians treating you?".

"They're treating me well for the most part, as you can see they've given me this luxurious room to stay in." The High Speaker's glowing eyes shifted as he looked around the room. "And I'm fed quite well but I can feel the uneasiness in the men who bring me my food, the only person who seems calm around me is the Captain."

"Captain Goodwin, yes I did quite a bit of research on the man once I found out that the *Notus* would be the ship to bring you here and I have to say that the other Councillors picked the right man for this task, he's respected by his men and he won't shy away from dealing with anyone who causes trouble, but remember men fear what they don't understand and we Enshyi are a complete mystery to the Angardians."

Adessa nodded, she could tell from how cold the High Speaker's voice had gotten that he was trying to drive the point home.

"How is your Angardian coming along?" said The High Speaker purposely switching to the harsh foreign tongue.

"Well enough for a simple reply," said Adessa somewhat slower than she would have liked but she wanted each word to sound perfect.

"Good," said Caewyn smiling, "but let's try something a little harder and with a bit of purpose, introduce yourself to me as you would to any Angardian noble."

Adessa nodded before she straightened her back and dipped into a curtsy, "My name is Adessa Shinepacer of clan Shinepacer, Speaker of the Forest and child of Alfheim, it is a pleasure to be speaking with you today, My Lord."

It took the High Speaker a few moments to reply, "That was acceptable but barely."

Adessa was surprised she thought she had done everything right, what could she have done wrong, as if reading her thoughts the High Speaker began elaborating.

"Firstly, you repeated your clan name, the correct way to introduce yourself would be to introduce yourself as Adessa of clan Shinepacer."

Adessa cursed herself she shouldn't have made that mistake.

No there would be time to berate herself later she needed to listen now.

"And it would have been better to say that you were honoured to be speaking with me, not that it was a pleasure."

"Are you serious?"

"Adessa, don't underestimate just how much the Angardians put in etiquette, it's everything to them."

"I don't understand, what does it matter how long your name is or how many names you have."

"The Angardians believe it shows how civilised they are."

"But it just seems ridiculous, how does having a hundred different ways to greet and speak with one another make you more civilised than someone who speaks directly."

The High Speaker raised his eyebrows and huffed, "It doesn't matter what you think or how you feel, this is how they conduct themselves here in Actalia and that's the end of it."

"But," began Adessa, but before she could get another word out Caewyn cut her off.

"No buts, now continue your studies and I'll speak with you again shortly."

Before she could reply the High Speaker's vessel became lifeless and Adessa was once again left alone save for OathKeeper and her own thoughts.

Chapter 24

The sun began to dip in the sky and so far, only *Amber* and *Mother's Embrace* from Saranthini and *Sandfly* from Myturir had met up with the *Zephyrus*.

Caleb looked out at the other Skyships and felt a wave of disappointment wash through him.

These ships look like merchant vessels that have just had a few cannons thrown on-board.

Looking at Jackeal Biyabani's scout ships, *Firebird* and *Salamander* made Caleb feel slightly better.

The slim black Xebec's weren't outfitted with many cannons but Caleb could see that was by design.

They're all about speed.

Turning his attention towards the men who walked the decks of either ship, Caleb found that every man had the look of a veteran about him, whereas the crews of *Amber, Mother's Embrace* and *Sandfly* looked more like farmers and fisherman than soldiers.

Are you really one to talk, the first battle you were in resulted in you plummeting to the earth.

Caleb shivered at the memory but he quickly shook himself free and turned to the helm.

Captain Brightfellow and Vaeliria were stood with the Captains of the other ships. Captain Kodia of *Amber* was as stereotypical as any Onmori could be, all thick limbs and squat like a cannon ball. Captain Roshni of *Mother's Embrace* was far leaner than his counterpart but Caleb couldn't help but think he resembled a rat, what with his pinched features and tiny eyes. Captain Kavar of *Sandfly* was a young man of maybe twenty-eight summers and from his lighter olive skin and bright green eyes Caleb guessed he was mixed in his heritage. Standing next to the Captain and Vaeliria were Captain Tousi and Captain Ban of *Firebird* and *Salamander*, both stood tall and looked on with cool gazes at their fellows.

"Don't just stand their gawking, we gotta job to do," said Runa appearing beside Caleb.

Caleb looked to the scout confused.

"Captain wants us on watch," said the scout explaining.

Caleb followed Runa across the deck towards the main mast of the *Zephyrus* and up the rope ladder towards the crow's nest.

I can't believe he hasn't recognised me.

Well it's probably for the best, the fewer people who know who you really are the better your new identity will hold.

Caleb pulled himself up into the lookout and marvelled at how quickly he had made the climb, never in all his life would he have imagined he could do something like that so easily, maybe all the gruelling hours of training with Vaeliria were starting to show.

"Right I've got the south side you take the north," said Runa walking away.

"What exactly am I looking for?"

"Anything that strikes you as odd, the ship from Xanesul has yet to turn up and it's got everyone on edge."

"Got it," said Caleb looking out over the land.

The sun had continued its descent now dipping below the horizon, washing the sky with colour, before he had joined the *Zephyrus*, Caleb never realised just how beautiful the sunrise and sunset could be, dozens of silhouettes marked the sky as a group of birds flew past, taking refuge for the night and far in the distance the sea shimmered mirroring all, Caleb took a deep breath before settling down for the nights watch.

Hours passed without so much as a sighting of any other ships, Caleb slumped down in the lookout and let out a sigh.

"Lookout's not a pretty job," said Runa from his side of the crow's nest.

"You can say that again, feels like I'm going to freeze up here."

"Thought you'd be used to the cold?"

Caleb was just about to reply when he remembered who he was supposed to be, a Skelwori nomad should have seen far worse what with travelling in the frozen wastes of Skelwor and only having a tent to protect himself from the elements during the nights.

"True but at least in Skelwor it's always cold, I mean here in the desert it's hotter than a forge during the day and freezing during the night, I don't think I'll ever get used to."

Runa let out a chuckle at that, "Ha ha, you know you sound just like Vida, he won't stop complaining about this place, says it's worse than our home."

"Oh, where are you two from?"

"Storm's Eye," replied Runa his voice filled with longing, "it's a small town that sits on the coast of Angard, it always raining and at its worst the wind can sweep you clean off your feet."

"Sounds fun," said Caleb sarcastically.

"It's a terrible place for two boys full of energy to grow up but hey it's still home."

Silence fell and Caleb left Runa to his reminiscing.

Looking up into the now dark sky Caleb found the constellation's of Uzutas and Kuris, the Skelwori Gods of Valour and Duty stood close together but whilst Uzutas stood proud with his battle-axe raised high above his head, Kuris was down on a knee and used his sword solely for support.

"The price of duty," said Caleb to himself as he remembered what Vaeliria had taught him.

Caleb shook himself free of his thoughts and was about to look for the other Skelworian Gods when something caught his eye, far off in the distance sailing through the sky was a small Skyship.

Caleb's heart did a somersault at the sight.

"Runa, I've got something!"

Runa was instantly beside Caleb, "Where?"

Caleb pointed in the direction he had seen the Skyship.

"Well I'll be damned."

"Should I get the Captain?" said Caleb not sure what to do.

"No need," replied Runa ringing the bell that sat tied to the mast, a high-pitched clang rang throughout the quiet of the night.

Caleb could hear the rush of movement from below.

Once the ringing had stopped, Captain Brightfellow's booming voice cut through the air, "What have we got?"

"Ship off to the north-west, coming our way and fast," replied Runa leaning over the lookout.

"How far?"

Runa quickly looked out over towards the incoming ship before replying, "Four leagues and closing."

"Everyone to your stations, but wait for my signal."

The tension that followed was unbearable, Caleb kept looking out over at the incoming ship with his heart in his throat, this would be a close call, if it was an enemy everyone would have to be ready but if it was one of their allies and someone from the deck was even a bit jumpy they could have a serious case of friendly fire on their hands.

"Two leagues!" shouted Runa.

"Hold!" ordered Captain Brightfellow.

Caleb drew his dirks and stood ready although from this height there wasn't much he could do, but he'd be damned if he just stood there empty handed.

"Five hundred metres."

"Hold!"

"Captain are you sure if this is the enemy we should..." said one of the crew.

"I said hold!" growled the Captain.

"That's *The Horn of Xanesul*!" shouted Captain Roshni from *Mother's Embrace* as the little ship grew closer.

The Horn of Xanesul, slowed as it closed the last of the distance between itself and the other ships, even through the darkness it was obvious that this ship had seen battle and recently, deep scars and gaping holes lined the ships starboard side, chasms of torn wood lined the deck and everywhere were the bodies of men some whole others not so much. The sails of the forward mast were burnt to cinders and the main mast was torn to shreds, it was a wonder this ship had even managed to sail let alone at the speed it had but then up at the helm of the ship Caleb spotted what looked to be a group of maybe twenty individuals, immediately a call came up for the occupants of the ship to identify themselves but there was no reply, *The Horn of Xanesul* just continued its now slow approach until finally it came to a stop in-between the *Zephyrus* and *Amber. Mother's Embrace* and *Sandfly* quickly moved to surround the ship and again the call went up for the crew to identify themselves but again no reply came.

"I don't like this," said Runa next to Caleb. "Let's get down there."

The atmosphere on the *Zephyrus*, was dark and the tension had grown so intense it could've been cut with a knife, everyone on deck stood with a rifle, pistol or sword in hand ready for whatever was to come, even Captain Brightfellow had his gigantic battle-axe in hand.

Caleb quickly made his way across the deck with Runa towards the Captain, standing beside the Captain was Vaeliria, her long curved blade glimmered in the moonlight and Vida, Runa's twin stood with pistols drawn.

"What's the plan?" said Vaeliria to the Captain as Caleb drew close.

Captain Brightfellow was quiet for a moment the lines in his face creasing with thought.

"Okay," said the Captain finally. "Vaeliria take Vida, Runa and a few of our other men and go check the situation but be cautious."

"Got it," replied Vaeliria before turning to Vida. "Find your brother."

"Already here."

The Captain, Vaeliria and Vida all turned to look at Runa and that's when they noticed Caleb following behind.

"I'm guessing you heard that," said Vaeliria to Caleb.

"Yeah."

"And let me guess you want to come?"

"Of course," said Caleb adamantly.

Vaeliria let out a sigh, "Get ready."

Shortly afterwards Caleb along with Vaeliria, Vida, Runa and a small group of other crewmen made their way onto the 'Ghost' ship, as soon as they were on board the stench of decaying flesh washed over them, Caleb struggled not to gag and his eyes began to water, everywhere he looked was another body, beside him one of the other crew members openly threw up over the already soiled deck, mixing with the smell of death was the distinct scent of gunpowder. Vaeliria turned to Vida and Runa and motioned for them to take some of the men and go below deck, the rest including Caleb were to stay with her and make their way towards the helm, Vida and Runa nodded in unison, before leading their men off towards the hatch leading below deck. Vaeliria continued towards the helm at a cautious pace, every creak of the deck seemed amplified due to the deathly quiet that sat aboard this ship like a dark passenger, slowly they began ascending the steps towards the helm when a bloodcurdling howl broke through the quiet from below deck, Caleb's heart skipped a beat, what the hell was going on down there.

"What the hell was that?" said one of the men.

"Maybe it was a banshee, you know like the ones from the stories," said another the fear clear in his voice.

"What if they're in trouble?"

Vaeliria held up a hand telling the men to shut up which they were all too happy to obey, silence again filled the deck.

"They'll be fine," she said finally.

Nobody challenged Vaeliria and she motioned them forward, taking the last few steps Caleb was met with the most sickening sight he had ever seen.

Tied to a series of wooden spikes were the mutilated bodies of thirty or so men, every man was missing his eyes, ears and nose, a few of the more unfortunate souls were also missing their tongues as well as their teeth.

Caleb couldn't stop himself from gagging this time, and a moment later he doubled over and vomited all over the deck.

"You alright?" said Vaeliria, once Caleb was finished spewing his guts up.

"Yeah," said Caleb spitting.

"What the hell happened here?" said one of the Crew.

"Looks like a slaughter to me," said another giving his thoughts.

"This is a message," came a dry hoarse voice.

Caleb whipped his head around to where the voice had come from to find a man tied to the helm of the ship, the man's dark face was haggard and drawn, the skin stretched over his features like paper, his left eye was missing and the white of his right was completely bloodshot, ringing his rich brown iris in a sea of crimson, an Onmori Captain's uniform hung loosely off the man's torso, the white robes were covered in grime and blood and deep tears lined his sleeves showing scarred arms.

Vaeliria took a step towards the man when he let out a sharp bark.

"Stay back!" ordered the man.

"We're here to help," said Vaeliria.

"You can't help me I'm bound to the helm by Hexes." A few of the men cursed at those words.

"We have a Hex practitioner on our ship," offered Vaeliria.

The man shook his head, "There isn't any time."

"I don't see any Hexes," said Caleb.

"They're carved into my flesh," replied the man straining to look at Caleb.

"Sam, go get Wraith," said Vaeliria.

"Aye, Commander."

"What's this message you spoke of?" said Vaeliria returning her attention to the bound Captain.

"That you Angardians are to leave this land immediately and the men of Teuengea, Saranthini and Myturir are to return to their cities at once, otherwise Irashaad and his man will not only continue to rob from the people of the coast but they will burn the villages and towns to ruin and then they will come for you."

Vaeliria's face twisted in revulsion, Caleb knew from spending so much time with her that there was no way she would just walk away and neither would the Captain.

"Me and my Captain aren't just going to leave," spat Vaeliria.

The man smiled, "Then you need to hurry, Irashaad and all of his Captain's will be present at the Shards."

"The entire fleet?" said one of the men in surprise.

"Are you sure?" said Caleb taking a step towards the Captain.

"Yes, whilst Irashaad's witch worked on me I overheard some of the other pirates talking about how Irashaad had called everyone in for a meeting."

"How many ships are we talking?"

"Eight."

Before anything else could be said, Wraith came walking up the stairs to the helm, the *Zephyrus*'s Hex practitioner was as stoic as ever viewing the horrendous scene of torture with her usual blank expression.

"You called for me?"

"I need you to have a look at this man," said Vaeliria pointing to the Captain bound to the helm, "and see if there is anything you can do for him."

Wraith nodded and took a step towards the Captain.

"Stay back!"

Wraith paid the warning no heed and just continued walking until she stood next to the bound Captain, where she then reached a hand out and ran it over the Captain's arms, torso and then finally his face, with her hands cupped around the Captain's face Wraith looked deeply into the man's eye and said something in Onmorian, her monotonic voice gave nothing away but the Captain nodded before saying something himself. Slowly Wraith began to retrace the Hexes and one by one the markings began to light up a dull blue, as she worked Wraith chanted to herself.

As he stood there watching Caleb was reminded of the times Wraith had worked Hexes on him and he was surprised to see that the Captain's face wasn't twisted in pain like his had been but he was calm.

The last of the Hexes lit up and Wraith stepped back from the Captain, she stopped her chanting and spoke again in the Onmori tongue, in response the Captain haltingly released his hands from the helm and turned cautiously towards Wraith as if he had just found his feet for the first time.

Wraith spoke again this time in a language Caleb had never heard before, each word sounded ancient but the Captain seemed to understand, he smiled before taking a step, where he fell to the deck, Caleb rushed to his side but there was nothing he could do the Captain was dead.

"What the hell just happened!"

Wraith looked at Caleb with her stoic gaze, which lit a fire in him but before he could say anything Vaeliria stepped forward and spoke directly to Wraith.

"What happened, Wraith?"

"The Hexes were bound to Salah's life-force, he would have been stuck there for weeks before he finally died, I did the only thing I could."

"You killed him," accused Caleb.

If Wraith felt the weight of his words she showed no sign and instead addressed Vaeliria, "There was no way for me to save his life."

Vaeliria nodded before turning back to the other members of the crew, "I want you to start getting those men down, I'm going to see what Vida and Runa have found."

"Aye," said the men in unison.

Vaeliria turned back to Caleb, "You're with me."

Inside the bowels of the ship the vile smell of death clung everywhere like a fog, Caleb had to put his hand to his mouth to stop himself from retching again and even Vaeliria who had managed to maintain her poise up on the helm looked to be effected by the smell. At the end of the corridor sat on the floor by a large wooden door were a couple of the men Vida and Runa had taken with them, Caleb recognised them, one of them was Edward and he looked to be in complete shock, his face ashen white, the other was Daniel who was whispering words of encouragement to his stricken friend.

"Is he hurt?"

Daniel looked up and smiled weakly, "No he's just had a bit of a shock that's all, actually I think we all have."

"Bodies?" said Caleb already knowing the answer.

"Yeah and it ain't a pretty sight."

"Get him up on deck," said Vaeliria walking towards the door, "but stay away from the helm".

Daniel nodded and got to his feet, "C'mon, mate, let's get some fresh air."

In the next room Caleb and Vaeliria were meet by Vida, Runa and the rest of the men that had accompanied them below deck, all of the men looked physically disturbed, at the back of the room covered under a great sheet were the unmistakable shapes of many bodies.

"What have you found?" said Vaeliria addressing Vida and Runa.

"It's a massacre," replied Vida

"Show me."

The scout led the way to the back of the room where they lifted the sheets that covered the bodies and Caleb saw more of what he had seen up on the helm, eyes missing, lips peeled, teeth pulled, tongues cut out, but sitting in the empty mouths were the men's genitals. Caleb gagged and Vaeliria lowered the sheet back over the bodies.

"Let's go back and report," said Vaeliria her voice as cold as ice.

After having reported back to Captain Brightfellow and the Onmori Captains, it was decided that the best course of action was to send the men of *The Horn of Xanesul* off into the afterlife by lighting the ship on fire and sending it off over the Dultasar Sea where it would eventually rest.

"The men of Xanesul shall be with the Creator," said Captain Kavar, being the neighbouring city to Xanesul he offered to lead the service and everyone agreed it was best.

"As was meant to be," responded the crews from *Mother's Embrace, Amber* and *Sandfly.*

Captain Brightfellow had said that it wouldn't be right for him and his men to be involved in this holy ceremony so Caleb stood watching from the deck of the *Zephyrus* with Vaeliria, the Captain and dozens of other members of the *Zephyrus*'s crew. As the anchor of *The Horn of Xanesul* was cut, Captain Kavar signalled to a group of his men who drew their bows, another man who was stood with a torch in hand began walking down the line lighting the arrows notched in the bows, as the man worked Captain Kavar spoke.

"We light the fire to bestow their souls with the energy to take the journey."

"May Haji welcome them with open arms," finished the other men.

The archers raised their bows and Captain Kavar gave the signal for them to fire, the flurry of blazing arrows shot up into the sky where they sailed for a few moments before falling back to the earth and landed on the deck of *The Horn of Xanesul,* the pitch that had been spread throughout the ship caught and within seconds a great orange fire roared forth, from his position on the *Zephyrus*'s deck Caleb stood watching the fire and swore by Dymera the Skelwori Goddess of vengeance that he would make Irashaad and his men feel the same pain that their victims had even if it meant his life.

Chapter 25

The heavy birch trees groaned overhead as Darrius sat in the mud of a small thicket.

Winds howling.

Darrius shook the useless thought away. He needed to focus if he was going to catch his prey.

To distract himself from the turbulent howl of the wind Darrius turned his focus to the thick bushes of bramble that enclosed him on three sides. The plump berries that dotted the thorny thicket were the perfect lure for his target, but even then, a bit of luck would have to come in to play for this hunt of his to pay off.

A candlemark later the unmistakable footfalls of Darrius's mark echoed throughout the air as it approached from the west side of the thicket. Darrius felt a rush of adrenaline course through his body at the thought of what was to come.

Patience now Darrius.

The footfalls grew closer and closer still.

Darrius took one last deep lung full of air before readying himself.

Moments later the bush began to jostle as berries were picked from its prickly grasp.

Okay time to move.

With speed, more akin to a beast than a man Darrius leapt through the bush and came face to face with a large White-tailed deer. The buck immediately let out a cry of surprise before it kicked out with its front hooves.

Shit.

Darrius dove out of the path of the incoming blows by throwing himself straight onto his back, pain immediately rippled through his back but Darrius ignored it and drew two of his throwing knives.

Gotta be quick here.

Darrius rolled up onto his side and let both of his knives loose, one missed its mark by a hairsbreadth, the other blade however found purchase in the fleeing deer's flank. The buck cried out in pain but barely slowed as it bounded off.

Jumping to his feet Darrius gave chase.

Trees, shrubs and flowers passed in a daze of colour as Darrius sprinted through the forest, the buck was lost from sight but droplets of scarlet blood dotted the path leading the way, the frequency of droplets let Darrius know that the deer wasn't going to get much further before it collapsed so he slowed to a jog.

After a few more minutes of tracking the bloody trail Darrius found the buck collapsed under a tree, the magnificent beast's breathing was slow and laboured, Darrius approached slowly, even a wounded animal could have one last bit of fight in it, pulling his scarred sword from its scabbard Darrius knelt down beside the buck, the beast acknowledged his presence with a shift of its antlered head and a huff.

"Shhh, it'll be over soon."

In one quick motion Darrius drew his blade across the buck's neck, the deer jerked for a few seconds as it's life's blood spilled from its neck, once it stilled Darrius held a hand to the crystal at his throat and recited the incantation of strength. Energy began to flow through every part of his body, the pain in his side and all his aches faded and then disappeared altogether, Darrius took his hand away from the choker and flex his muscles experimentally, everything felt good, he then quickly tied the buck's front legs together before doing the same to the back and with his magical strength easily lifted his kill onto his shoulders and began walking back through the forest towards his camp.

By the time Darrius made it back through the last of the trees towards his camp the sun had set and darkness had begun to fall throughout the forest, in the centre of the small camp was a small fire, the orange glow was a welcome sight as now Darrius was beginning to feel his strength waning, sitting by the fire wrapped in a thin blanket was Fia, the light from the fire silhouetted the young islander, as Darrius approached he instantly spotted the knife held in her hand beneath her covering and shook his hand.

"You should hide that better," said Darrius from behind Fia.

Fia jumped straight to her feet and span, the knife arched through the air towards Darrius, but he stepped effortlessly out of the blades path and walked over to the fire, where he lowered the buck.

"You scared me half to death," said Fia from where she stood.

"Maybe you should be more observant of your surroundings," replied Darrius as he drew his hunting knife and began skinning and gutting the buck.

"How is anyone supposed to ready themselves against something they can't hear."

Darrius turned to his companion and raised a questioning eyebrow.

"You're like a spectre."

Darrius laughed to himself, "I thought I was making quite a lot of noise what with this beast on my back."

"How'd you carry that thing anyway?" said Fia changing the subject. "The thing has got to weigh at least three hundred pounds."

Darrius moved his hand back to the choker in answer.

Fia slumped back down into her seat, "It seems there's a lot the Oracle didn't tell me about you."

Darrius had no reply, he wasn't used to having to talk about himself and even if he was would he really share, the only person who knew anything about him was a woman who could look into the future. Silence stretched out between the two Sentinels as Darrius focused on the task of gutting, skinning and cutting. Once he was finished he picked up the entrails and threw them throughout the forest away from the camp to keep predators away, next he strung several cuts up from a nearby tree and rubbed a large amount of the salt from his pack into them, then he skewered another few cuts over the fire, before sitting down across from his companion, the fire hissed as blood dripped from the meat. Darrius could see the uneasiness in Fia's face and again he was reminded of the fact that she had only known the isle and the Order.

"Go on offer her some kind words," said a voice inside Darrius head. *"Lady knows you could have used it when you first left the Isle."*

Darrius wanted to ignore the voice but he knew it was right, his first few nights away from the isle had been the worst of his life and even now he could still remember how miserable he had felt whilst he had been sheltering from a storm, soaked through to his bones.

"It's hard," said Darrius looking into the fire.

"What is?".

"Leaving everything you've ever known behind because someone tells you that you're needed elsewhere."

Fia didn't say anything but Darrius knew she was interested in what he had to say, taking a deep breath to steady himself Darrius began speaking, "When I was young I lost my family to raiders." The images flashed before Darrius as clear as day. "I thought I was going to die with them but the Oracle saved me and brought me to the isle, it took me years to finally feel comfortable there and then just as I had, her Holiness told me that she needed me to go out into the world and do the Lady's work." Darrius was surprised at how bitter he sounded. "But I did what was asked of me and still do."

"Does it get any easier?" said Fia, hope in her voice.

The voice in Darrius's head told him to lie and give the girl the hope she so desperately wanted but this time he ignored it, best for her to know right away, "No, it doesn't."

"That's what I thought." Fia's face sunk and Darrius turned his attention back towards the fire.

The silence that stretched between the two Sentinels only grew as they ate their supper and settled over the camp like an oppressive companion as they retired for the night. Darrius stared up into the darkness of the night's sky wishing he could fall into the embrace of deep sleep but he knew it would never come and the most he could hope for were a few hours of sitting just below consciousness, his thoughts then turned to his companion who he was sure wasn't going to have a good night either, faced with the harsh reality he had provided.

Darrius rose before dawn the following morning and relit the fire, it only took a few minutes before it was burning strong again, from there Darrius took a couple of the strips that were hanging down from their hooks, skewered them and placed them on the fire and sat down himself, Fia awoke a few minutes later, yawing loudly as she did and sat down opposite him, dark rings lined her already dark eyes.

"How far we got til we reach a town or city?" said Fia shivering.

"I'd say we're a day's trek from Appleton," replied Darrius as he turned the meat over the fire.

"Well let's get moving I feel like I'm about to freeze."

"We eat first." Darrius passed one of the skewers over to Fia, which she accepted gratefully.

"You been to this Appleton before?" said Fia around a mouthful of Venison.

"No, but I've been to the neighbouring village."

"So why aren't we going there?"

"I wouldn't be welcome," replied Darrius simply.

"Why not?"

"Had a disagreement with one of the locals there, let's leave it at that."

It was obvious that Fia had more questions but she reluctantly let the subject go and instead asked another question, "So what do you know about Appleton?"

"It's a little village that's famous for its cider, the people are supposedly friendly enough if not a little ignorant of the world outside of their town."

From the look on Fia's face Darrius knew she was sceptical, "Just remember we're a pair of travelling merchant-hunters, looking to sell some of our wares."

"And if anyone asks we're on our way to Seacrest and Bluewater Bay," said Fia. "I remember what you told me don't worry."

"Good now let's finish our meal."

After eating, Darrius and Fia quickly packed up their camp and set off deeper into the forest.

Hours passed as the two Sentinel's made their way through shrubs, over fallen trees, up slopes and through streams, until finally they came to a ravine. When Darrius was last here the bridge that crossed the ravine had been nothing more than a couple of thin wooden boards that looked like they wouldn't hold a child's weight let alone a fully-grown man and the rope that held the thing together and acted as the hand rails had been frayed and worn, but that decrepit bridge was nowhere in sight and standing in its place was a bridge of heavy timber, the supports of which had been embedded deep into either side of the valley's faces below.

"I thought you said this thing was dangerous."

"It was the last time I was here," replied Darrius pleasantly surprised at the sight before him.

Fia walked onto the bridge first and Darrius followed, the beams beneath their feet only gave the slightest groan of complaint and before Darrius knew it they were on the other side and back on the muddy path towards Appleton.

From the bridge the path slowly snaked back down a hill where it then flattened out but forked, thankfully though a sign had been erected at the fork, Darrius reached up and wiped at the moss covered sign, the right path would lead down to the village of Greybarrow whilst the left headed towards Appleton, the two quickly made their way down the left path when a light drizzle began to fall, not being used to the icy rain of Baneta, Fia immediately threw up her hood, Darrius made sure that the antlers that sat tied to the top of his pack were covered before doing the same. As they continued on down the increasingly wet trail a carriage being pulled by a large brown draft horse advanced towards them, as it grew closer Darrius spotted the driver, an elderly looking man of sixty summers, his thick beard was as white as snow and hung down to his chest.

"Hulloo!" shouted Darrius from the side of the road.

The driver pulled on his reigns and the horse slowed to a stop, "Wat can oi do for yeh."

Friendly, that's good.

"Would yeh be able to tell us how far til we reach Appleten?"

The old man looked off into the distance, Darrius had seen that look a thousand times on the faces of the old, it was like they had to consider everything in greater detail then everyone else.

"Jus came from there meself," said the old man more to himself, but Darrius didn't interrupt him. "Yeh got another few marks, just stick to thee path and you'll be there in no time."

"Thank yeh," replied Darrius with a nod.

The old man returned the nod before cracking the reins, the draft responded with a huff and began pulling the carriage off down the path.

When Darrius turned around he found Fia looking at him with a strange look on her face, "What?"

"You didn't even realise did you?"

"Realise what?"

"That you started speaking in another language."

Darrius thought about it for a few moments, he must have instinctively just fell into the local tongue when he caught sight of the old man, "When you're as well travelled as I am you learn that people feel more comfortable speaking in their own tongue."

"So how many languages do you know exactly?"

"I can speak the languages of each of the Five Kingdoms and the numerous dialects that go along with them, plus that of the isle, the common tongue and a few that are rarely used today."

Fia let out a sharp snort of a laugh, "Ha, no wonder everyone on the isle talks about you like you're some legend, you seem to be able to do things that others would have to spend entire lifetime's learning."

"I'm just a man," replied Darrius not liking where the conversation was going. "C'mon we've got another few candlemarks before we reach Appleton and the day ain't gonna wait for us."

The old man had been right, after another couple of candlemarks of trekking along the ever muddier path Darrius and Fia arrived at Appleton, to either side of the path stood one homely cottage after the other, a small garden accompanied each property housed within a small picket fence, some people had decided to grow their own vegetables, the heads of carrots and turnips beginning to show, others kept chicken coups and one even managed to have a couple of pigs, thin veils of smoke emerged out of the people's chimneys who were trying to stave off the wet and cold, as Darrius and Fia walked further into town, it became clear that people were watching them, men who were working up on one of the thatched roofs despite the rain eyed them suspiciously, a group of women looked on from one of the gardens their gossip dying as they did and a few elders looked on through murky windows.

"I thought you said they were friendly," said Fia tensely.

"Seems I was wrong."

Darrius continued on casually through the street towards what he believed was the inn. The large three storey building towered over the villagers' cottages and a thick plume of smoke billowed forth from the chimney like that of a dragon's nose.

As he made his way towards the entrance Darrius looked in through the inn's thick glass windows to the common room beyond. Dozens of people filled the room and from the laughter and noise that escaped from their mouths it appeared everyone was having a good time.

Let's hope things don't get out of hand.

Darrius opened the inn's door and a wave of sound immediately assaulted his ears, turning back Darrius gave Fia a nod and the two entered the inn. The smell of freshly poured cider, the musk of men and earthy smell of soil filled the inn's common room, Darrius walked confidently towards the bar and the young man who stood behind it. The bartender, was busy serving a group of four men, mercenaries from the look of them, instinctively Darrius assessed the men for threats, jagged knives and dented hammers sat tied to hips, crude metal plates were patched onto leather armour, two of the men appeared to be related, both sporting the same bulbous nose and small angry eyes, the man who Darrius identified as the leader of the group was a meaty man, he had to have at least a head on his companions and was twice as wide, mainly around the gut, the bartender gave the men their drinks and quickly retreated, Darrius couldn't blame the poor man he looked worn and tired and the last thing he would want is trouble.

"What can I get yah?" said the bartender tiredly.

"Two mugs of your finest cider, please," replied Darrius politely.

The bartender quickly obliged and went to his taps, where he quickly and deftly poured a rich amber liquid into two large mugs before returning. "That'll be six coppers."

Darrius reached into the folds of his cloak and pulled out the six coppers required. "Thank you."

"It's good to see some folk still have manners," said the barkeeper taking the coins.

"I don't suppose you have any rooms available for the night?"

"I'm afraid we only have the one."

"That's fine," replied Darrius. "How much?"

"A silver a night?"

Again, Darrius fished out the required coin and handed it to the bartender.

"Hey, barkeep where's that wife of yours, me and my lads fancy some after drinks fun."

The barkeeper froze, Darrius scanned the room and quickly found the owner's wife, her voluptuous figure looked like it was ready to burst forth from the dress she wore and her fiery hair only called more attention to her. Darrius sighed, clearly they played on the fact that she was pretty. As the woman walked back towards the bar, the leader of the mercenaries called out, "Why don't you join me and my friends here? We'll show you a good time."

"Sorry but I'm spoken for," replied the woman leaning across the bar to give her husband a kiss on the cheek.

The group burst into laughter, "That's hilarious," said one of the men with the bulbous nose.

"He's more man than all four of you," replied the woman with venom on her tongue.

"Let him prove it then," said the leader coldly, standing from his seat.

The barkeeper immediately began apologising but the mercenary paid him no mind and walked straight towards his wife, to her credit the woman didn't flinch, despite the bulk that stood before her.

"Maybe I should take you right here, then we'll see how much of a man he is."

The bartender's wife slapped the hefty man clean across the face and suddenly the room fell into silence.

"You shouldn't have done that," said the huge mercenary dabbing a finger to his bloody lip.

"Go to hell, pig!"

The mercenary threw a meaty fist straight at the woman but before it could land Darrius was there, he parried the blow before grabbing hold of the man's wrist.

"This don't concern you!" Darrius looked up at the large man, his craggy features were twisted in a mask of anger but the thing that got Darrius's attention the most was the spittle that hung in his patchy beard.

"You expect me just to sit by while you hit a woman?"

The man smiled viciously before throwing his other weighty limb at Darrius.

Here we go again.

Darrius quickly ducked out of the way of the mercenary's fist before he retaliated with a punch of his own to the man's bottom rib.

"I'm going to fucking kill you!" howled the man as he lashed out with another punch.

Darrius didn't have time to dodge so he quickly threw up a block, but it wasn't enough to stop the mercenary's mace like arm and a moment later the man's fist plowed straight into Darrius's the chest.

"Smash his fucking face in!" hollered one of the mercenary's companions.

Staggered from the blow to his chest Darrius had no time whatsoever to recover before the mercenary charged him and both went crashing to the floor.

Blow after blow came raining down amongst cheers and shouts but Darrius avoided most of the punishment by keeping his arms between himself and his opponent.

"Not even going to fight back," said the mercenary as he rained even more blows down upon Darrius.

"I'm merely waiting for an opening," replied Darrius.

"Wha" before the mercenary could finish his word Darrius grabbed a hold of his shoulders and brought his head up and smashed it straight into his opponent's nose, cartilage gave way beneath the blow and blood sprayed all over Darrius.

"Fuck!" screamed the man as he instinctively brought his hands up to his now ruined nose.

With the merc now distracted Darrius easily pushed himself free from the man's grasp and quickly rolled to his feet where he delivered a sharp kick to the man's already bloody face, teeth flew from the merc's mouth and landed on the inn's wooden floor with a clatter.

Darrius knew that the sight of their leader being beaten would affect the other mercenaries in one of two ways, they would either turn tail and run or they would jump into the fray swinging.

Apparently, it was the latter as the three remaining mercenaries came running at Darrius and he readied himself for the coming fight, but before they reached him Fia came flying out of nowhere and roundhoused one of the fat faced men in the face with her heel where he went down in a spray of blood and teeth just like his leader.

"You bitch!" screamed the other fat face as he charged Fia.

Darrius didn't have time to intervene as the last man of the group rushed him, Darrius hadn't seen it before but this man was young, the small tuft of hair that marked his chin giving it away.

"You are so dead!" screamed the young merc as he threw a wide arching punch.

Darrius easily parried the blow aside and retaliated with a quick strike to either side of the boy's head. As the boy instinctively went to grab his head Darrius delivered a powerful kick to the boy's solar plexus and sent him flying onto his back where he stayed.

Fia.

Darrius quickly turned his attention back towards Fia and was pleased to find his fellow Sentinel holding her attacker by his hair, his already fat face was now swollen and he could barely speak from the look of him, but Fia didn't show mercy and delivered one final blow to the man's face that knocked the last bit of consciousness from him.

Seems I was right in my choice.

Silence filled the inn as one by one Darrius dragged the men from the inn and out into the street.

"Guess you won't be coming back through here either," said Fia as she came to stand by Darrius.

"You're probably right," replied Darrius wiping his bloodied face.

Darrius and Fia made their way back to the bar, whispers following them. Darrius sat down and took a long pull from his mug and motioned for Fia to do the same.

"Are we really just going to sit here and drink?" whispered Fia over her mug.

"Wait for it."

After a few more hushed whispers and cautious looks the barkeeper approached Darrius and Fia with his wife.

"Sir, my wife and I just wanted to thank you for dealing with those men."

Darrius put down his mug and wiped away the froth that lined his lips, "I wouldn't thank me yet, they might be back."

"Really!" said the barkeeper worryingly.

"Ha those dogs won't be back," said the woman confidently, "not after what you did to them, hell I doubt they'll make it out of town in their state."

"Possibly, but then again they looked like the types to hold a grudge."

The barkeeper's wife just shrugged, "Well if they do, I guess we'll just have to deal with them ourselves."

"I guess you will," replied Darrius nonchalantly. Turning to the barkeeper Darrius asked, "Is that room still available?"

"Of course."

"Thank you," said Darrius standing. "Me and my companion shall retire for the night, which room is ours?"

"It's at the end of the corridor on the third floor."

Darrius and Fia picked up their packs and made their way to the third floor, as they ascended the creaky wooden stairs, life seemed to return to the common room below, again people started to joke and laugh with one another, Darrius sighed with relief.

"You alright?" asked Fia.

"Yeah I'm fine, just need to rest."

"Same," said Fia yawning.

Walking into their room, Darrius slung off his pack and threw it down by one of the beds, before he looked around the room in search of escape routes.

The only exit apart from the door was a small circular window that sat in the inn's slanted roof.

It'll be a tight fit.

Moving away from the window Darrius walked back towards the door and began inspecting it. An old rusted lock was the sole source of security.

One kick is all it would take to get someone through this lock.

Darrius pushed the lock into place and returned to his pack, rooting through it he found his whetstone and sat down on the bed and began sharpening his throwing knives, one by one. As he did Fia began tinkering with her crossbow and checking her arrows tips, once she was satisfied she nocked an arrow into the bows firing mechanism and laid it down on the table beside her before laying down herself.

Darrius waited until it was clear that his companion was fast asleep before he sheathed his now sharp blades and made his way back to the rooms window.

Easy now.

With great care Darrius opened the flimsy wooden frame and lifted himself up and out onto the inn's wooden roof.

The night's air brought a chill that ran its way down Darrius's spine like an icy hand.

Shaking the feeling away Darrius made his way along the inn's slanted roof and rounded onto the back of the inn, where he was met with a large patch of ivy that had webbed itself up the entire length of the inn's back wall like a thick green fur.

Seems someone's on my side.

Darrius grabbed a hold of the ivy ladder and made his way down to the small garden below.

As soon as his feet touched the soft ground Darrius quickly broke into a crouched run and made his way out of Appleton.

Bryson sat by the fire nursing his broken nose and bloodied mouth. Lester seemed to have suffered the same sort of punishment, his mouth a bloody mass of missing, crooked and chipped teeth, his brother Hester sat next to him, complaining through swollen lips about how much pain he was in and then there was Yulie, the newest member of Bryson's gang lay by the fire, his eyes covered with a rag, every breath he took brought a wheezing sound, Bryson fingered around his own beaten mouth with his tongue and found that he had lost three teeth and a fourth was hanging from nothing but a thin piece of gum, reaching his aching fingers inside his mouth, Bryson grabbed hold of the dangling tooth and wrenched it free, before throwing it into the fire.

"Twhat bwitch is gwonna pay," said Hester for the sixth time.

"Yeah, we'll make her scream," joined in Lester, with every word a whistling escaped from his gap filled mouth.

"Would you two shut the fuck up!" shouted Yulie sitting up. "You two are fucking useless, getting your asses beaten by some woman."

"What'd you say?"

"I said you and whistler over there are useless."

Hester jumped to his feet as did Yulie and the two men squared up, Bryson felt his already pounding head getting worse, the two men continued to eyeball one another. Bryson pushed himself to his feet but before he could split the men up, Hester fell to his knees then the ground with a dagger protruding from in between his shoulder blades.

"What the Fu" before Yulie could finish the curse another dagger came flying out of the surrounding darkness and lodged itself straight in his face, for a moment the young man just stood there as if nothing had happened but then blood began to seep from his face and he quickly collapsed.

Bryson threw himself on the ground and motioned for Lester to do the same but the other man didn't listen, he quickly rushed towards his brother's bloody body and was just a few feet away when he was hit in the same spot as his brother had been and he fell to the ground.

"Stupid fuck," whispered Bryson to himself.

A few moments later Lester picked himself up and began to crawl towards his brother when another dagger emerged from the darkness and embedded itself in the base of his skull.

Shit.

Sensing his impending death Bryson quickly crawled towards the fire and threw his blanket on it.

Seconds stretched out with Bryson wondering when a dagger would find him but none did and the fire finally gave up its last slither of light and the camp was plunged into darkness.

With the fire now dead Bryson slowly began to crawl back towards his pack. His heart thumped with each movement but inch by inch he slowly made it back to the bulging loot filled pack.

Taking a few deep breaths Bryson readied himself and with all the speed he could muster jumped to his feet, slung the pack straight onto his back and ran off into the surrounding forest.

Bryson felt as if he had been running for an eternity but he dared not stop, he could feel the eyes of his hunter on him, but when he looked over his shoulder he saw nothing save the same inky darkness that had been in front of him.

Maybe I'm safe now.

As soon as he had the thought a dagger came spinning out of the shadows and landed straight into his pack, where it tore through the rough canvas and sent all manner of loot flying, though now with death so close to him Bryson could care less for loot and ran even harder.

Continuing his desperate sprint for freedom Bryson tore through a thorny bush and immediately regretted the decision, as dozens of spiny blades ripped into his clothes and tore his flesh.

Emerging from the bush Bryson found himself on a cliff edge.

Shit.

Bryson looked around for an escape route but when it became apparent that there was nowhere for him to go save over the cliff's edge he drew his blade and turned back to the forest where he saw a silhouetted figure walking through the bushes.

"I'm going to fucking kill you!" screamed Bryson, doing his best to keep the fear from his voice.

The silhouette said nothing in response and emerged from the forest, Bryson instantly recognised his attacker, it was the guy from the inn, he was covered in the same grey clothes he had been wearing at the inn but his scarred face was now covered with a kerchief leaving only the top half exposed, his grey eyes were cold and in his hand sat a blade just as scarred as himself. Before the grey man took a step forward Bryson charged and lashed out with a vicious downward strike, but his blade found nothing but air and he went stumbling forward, a sharp searing pain suddenly shot through his side and Bryson knew he had been cut, spinning back around Bryson looped his sword forward, blades clashed and clashed again but the grey man managed to hold his ground despite being the smaller of the two and then before Bryson knew what was happening he was being pushed back and then suddenly the grey man pivoted to the side and slashed straight through Bryson's extended sword arm, blood fountained from the wound and Bryson dropped to his knees and let out a chilling scream, the grey man walked beside Bryson and without saying a word ran his blade along Bryson's neck, a warm sensation radiated across his neck and then

Bryson slumped onto the ground dying, the last thing he saw before the last of his life left him was the grey man sheathing his sword and walking back off into the forest.

Chapter 26

From his perch, up in the crow's nest Caleb kept a lookout for any sign of the enemy, which so far there hadn't been, all he could see was spire after jagged spire.

I hope the Captains plan works.

After having cremated the *Horn of Xanesul* and learning the news that Irashaad along with his entire fleet would be at the Shards of Cradure, the Captains had agreed that now was the best time for an offensive against the pirate and his men.

However, the Captains knowing that they were at a disadvantage in terms of numbers, had devised a plan where they would converge on the Shards from all possible angles and deliver a coordinated attack. *Amber* and *Mother's Embrace,* were to enter from the north-west. *Firebird* and *Salamander* being the two smallest and most manoeuvrable ships were to advance through the dreaded eastern side whilst the *Zephyrus* and *Sandfly* took the southern passes.

C'mon focus.

Caleb shook himself free of his thoughts, and returned his attention back to the jagged rocks that surrounded him. After all he couldn't afford to become lax in his role.

The first thing he had been taught was that up here he was the eyes of the entire ship and if he missed anything it could spell disaster for the entire crew.

As the *Zephyrus* followed *Sandfly* further into the Shards, Caleb noted how the air changed around him, it felt heavier and hotter and an acrid smell like rotten egg rode on the wind.

We must be nearing the sulphur pits Tousi warned us about.

Looking down at the fractured and barren earth Caleb saw dozens of thick yellowish clouds seeping forth to form a diseased mist, that quickly obscured the view below.

"Eyes up," said Runa curtly, from his side of the crow's nest.

Caleb immediately snapped his head back up.

The jagged spires from earlier were nowhere to be seen and standing in their place were monstrous walls of stone, that had deep cracks running across their faces.

Seems we're getting closer.

After another candlemark of traversing through the tight passages of the Shards the two Skyship's arrived at what appeared to be a junction.

Eight paths splintered off in a rough semicircle, three of the paths lay between nine and eleven o'clock, even from a glance it was clear that the *Zephyrus* wasn't going to be going down any of them. The first was far too narrow, it's width only half of that of the *Zephyrus*, the second looked to have had a cave in, jagged spikes jutted out at all angles, which made it look like a stone hedgehog had taken up residence and the third path was nothing more than a dead end.

Caleb turned his attention to the two paths that stood directly in front of him.

Both looked like good choices but Caleb would have chosen the right path because it looked to be slightly wider than the left which would mean that the Captain would have an easier time with keeping the ship true.

Sandfly entered the pass but much to his surprise the *Zephyrus* began to drift away to the right and towards the three passages that lay there, straight away it became clear that the only one of these paths that would fit the massive Galleon was the path at three o'clock, it stood lower than all the other paths in the very heart of the cliffs face and that's when Caleb realised it wasn't a passageway at all but a tunnel.

No, the Captain wouldn't do that, would he?

But sure enough Captain Brightfellow steered the *Zephyrus* off towards the tunnel.

The inside of the tunnel looked like the mouth of a monstrous stone serpent, hundreds of stalagmites and stalactites covered the floor and ceiling respectively, the smallest of which was still easily the size of a two-storey house, sunlight hit the volcanic rock revealing dull colours of grey and black.

Deeper in darkness took hold, blotting everything in a inky haze, from the deck below the Captain called for lanterns to be lit and almost immediately small pools of light dotted the blackness until finally the deck of the *Zephyrus* and the immediate surroundings were bathed in firelight, the orange of the flames was reflected in streams of water that ran down through cracks in the walls, the gurgles and splutters only added to the feeling that this was the inside of a giant snake. Before Caleb knew it the walls had begun to close in on him, where they continued to until they stopped not five feet from the *Zephyrus*'s hull, worried Caleb looked to Runa, the older watchmen's face was eerily white despite the glow from the lanterns, following his gaze Caleb looked up. Dozens of jaggedly sharp points reached down at the crows-nest like the bony fingers of death himself, both men were awakened from their reveries by the voice of Vaeliria.

"Watchmen, report."

"It's getting a little tight up here but we'll be fine," replied Runa weakly.

"You sure?"

"Yeah, we're good."

"Okay, but keep an eye out, there's no telling what could be waiting for us."

"Aye, Commander."

The *Zephyrus* continued through the hell like cavern at a tentative pace, passing one rocky citadel after another, several times Caleb and Runa had to shout warnings down to the deck below so that they didn't run into one of the giant spear like structures that seemed to be waiting around every corner for them, until finally the huge Skyship escaped the blackness and was once again bathed in sunlight. Caleb was blinded by the light for a few moments but then his eyes began to adjust to the natural light around him, bringing the view into focus. The *Zephyrus* sat in another passage that looked nearly identical to the one it had been in when it first entered the Shards, tall spires and broken towers of stone stood all around, but the sickly fog from early had now become thicker and the stench permeating the air was enough to make Caleb gag.

"We wait here until first light tomorrow!" shouted the Captain.

"Aye!" replied the crew.

"You should go and get something to eat," said Runa dejectedly.

Caleb was about to ask Runa what was wrong when the older scout held up a hand, "This place gives me a bad feeling is all, now go eat, Evelyn will be cooking up something special, she always does when she knows we're going to battle."

Caleb nodded and climbed down to the deck, where he purposely ignored the activity around him and made his way towards the lift. Once inside he quickly set the counterweight dials to their respective positions, the lift shuddered into motion and began its steady descent towards the canteen, two floors away the lift came to a halt and beyond the iron grated door of the lift stood, Lucianna and another member of the medical officers, Caleb recognised Weller, his bald scalp reflected the lights overhead and his thinly rimmed glasses pinched his nose so hard it shone red like that of a drunk. As she entered, Luci gave Caleb a weak smile, it was obvious that she was worried and Caleb couldn't blame her, tomorrow the *Zephyrus* would engage in a battle that could very well result in the death of everyone on board.

"Going down or up?"

"Down," replied Weller, his voice hoarse.

"Doctor Estrada said we should get ourselves something to eat and have a few hours' rest," said Luci elaborating, as the lift kicked back into life.

"Runa said the same thing to me."

"Only the Firstborn knows if we'll get another chance," said Weller to himself.

Caleb had no words to reassure the older medic, and an awkward silence filled the room until the lift locked into place on the canteen floor. Without a word Weller opened the lifts door and left, Caleb looked to Luci with a questioning gaze.

"He's just stressed."

"I think we all are."

A wave of smells assaulted Caleb as soon as he entered the *Zephyrus*'s massive mess hall, there was the rich fatty smell of roasting goat, mixed with the aromas of tomato, rosemary and garlic, beneath those was the warm smell of freshly baked bread and the neutral yet still appetising smell of boiled rice. Surprisingly though there wasn't much in the way of conversation, everywhere Caleb looked were faces filled with worry and dejection, even Evelyn wasn't herself, gone was her usual smile and heavy bags lined her normally cheerful eyes, was everyone really that worried about the upcoming battle against Irashaad and his pirates.

"Hello dearies," said Evelyn with a smile that didn't reach her eyes.

"Hi Evelyn," replied Caleb and Luci in near unison.

"Something smells really good... what is it?" said Luci.

"Oh today with have roasted goat in a tomato, rosemary and garlic sauce, with rice and freshly baked corn bread." Evelyn deftly scooped a bed full of rice onto two plates before dealing a large portion of the richly coloured curry onto the rice, followed by a large crust of the yellow cornbread.

At the sight of the food Caleb realised just how hungry he was, for the past four days he hadn't eaten anything other than biscuits and jerky. Funny only a few months ago biscuits and jerky would have been a luxury for Caleb, maybe he was becoming too civilised.

"Here you are," said Evelyn as she handed the plates to Caleb and Luci. "Now, I don't want to see any food left on those plates you hear me."

Luci nodded furiously whilst Caleb gave a small nod in reply.

The solemn faces followed the duo as they sat down at their spot at the back of the room, Caleb being his usual self began to devour the meal before him, if not more refined than he once did, Luci on the other hand hadn't touched her food, after his fourth mouthful of food, Caleb looked up.

"You alright?"

"Just worried."

"I know how you feel, but try to eat you're gonna need the strength."

Luci nodded, before heaping a spoonful of food into her mouth.

Caleb smiled at his friend and went back to his meal, but as he did he felt a seed of worry creep into his own gut.

Chapter 27

A heavy gust of wind swept across the deck of the *Notus.*
Adessa pulled her hood up and drew her robes in tighter,
the men around her on the other hand didn't seem to
notice, they just continued with their tasks, it probably
wasn't that bad but to Adessa it felt like she was exposed,
how did these men cope when there was a storm, back in
Alfheim the trees protect her and all the other Enshyi from
the majority of the rain, wind and cold, and the Wind
Speaker spoke with the wind asking for it to calm, but up
here high in the sky where only the birds should sore there
was no protection.

"Are you alright, milady?"

Adessa turned to find Captain Goodwin staring at her,
his brow creased in worry, Adessa found his concern both
pleasing and annoying at the same time, on the one hand it
was nice to have a friendly presence when she was
surrounded by stares and whispers but then how weak
must she seem to this man that he would coddle her at
every turn, swallowing the conflicting emotions, Adessa
replied, "I am fine, when will we reach your capital?"

"We should reach Actalia by the end of the day I'd
wager."

"How can you be so sure I see nothing but the sky and
sea?"

A smile broke out across Goodwin's face, "Milady, I've
been sailing these skies for over twenty years and seen a
great many things from the Sapphire falls of Majopana to
the Citadel of Bloacland, so please trust me when I say we
are close."

Adessa stood dumbfounded, what was Goodwin going
on about, all she had asked was how he knew they were so
close to Actalia and rather than answer her question the
good Captain had decided to talk about other far off lands

that were just as foreign and scary to Adessa as her current destination.

"You didn't answer my question."

"Hmm," replied Goodwin with a look of bewilderment.

"You didn't answer my question," repeated Adessa, "how do you know that we're close to Actalia?" Adessa hid the pleasure she felt at saying the name of the Angardian's capital, the pronunciation had alluded her for days and now finally saying it and tasting the word upon her lips, she wondered how it had ever caused her such trouble.

"My apologies," said Goodwin bowing slightly.

Adessa returned the bow with a polite nod as was customary to show there was no disrespect felt.

"Do you see that white line marking the horizon?"

Adessa turned to look out over the bow of the ship, at first she couldn't see anything but the chaotic activity around her, men climbed the rope ladders to the nest above, others pulled on ropes that adjusted the sails to catch more of the wind, if they had a Wind Speaker with them then there task would be so much easier, but Adessa knew that wasn't going to happen, her and High Speaker Caewyn were the first of her people to leave Alfheim in over a century and none of these men had the potential to be a Speaker, being a Speaker was all about living in harmony with the elements not trying to control or defy them.

"Can you see it?" Goodwin's voice broke Adessa from her reverie and she quickly began scanning the horizon for the white line that Goodwin had spoken of and sure enough there it was amongst the ocean of blue that was the sea and sky, the thin line of white marked three quarters of the horizon.

"I see it."

"Those are the White Cliffs of Angard's southern coast, Actalia is about eighty miles north north-west of them so considering our optimum speed, the weather and wind, I believe we'll reach Actalia by the end of the day."

Not knowing what to say, Adessa thanked Goodwin for answering her question and focused once again on the activity around her and before she knew it the thin line that had been the White Cliffs came into full view.

The cliffs had to be at least a hundred feet tall and maybe four or five miles wide,

By Enelya's grace.

Looking down to the base of the cliffs Adessa spotted a line of boats heading towards the beach at the base of the cliffs.

Those must be the fisherman that the High Speaker spoke of.

Revulsion, anger and sadness swept through Adessa at the thought of all those poor creatures that must have be down there gasping for their lives all so these men could eat.

Why can't they live off the bounty provided by the plants and trees.

The disturbing scene was quickly swept away and replaced with that of a small town, dozens of white stone buildings stood dotted around the town, their flat roofs shining bright in the midday sun, surprisingly the grey cobbled streets lay empty. Adessa was about to ask why no was around when a deafening toll rang out from the largest building in the town, the sound seemed to vibrate through every fibre of Adessa's body and she had to put her hands over her ears as another toll rang out and then another until finally after the seventh the world became silent again.

"What was that?" asked Adessa, her ears ringing.

"The church bell," replied Goodwin. "It's Sun Day, which means midday prayer."

"To the Firstborn?" High Speaker Caewyn had also told Adessa about the Angardian's religion, it centred on a man known as the Firstborn and his teachings along with those of his disciples.

"Yes, seems you've already learnt quite a lot about us."

"The High Speaker suggested that I learn about it, least I cause offence."

317

"Smart man."

The sound of people drew Adessa's attention back to the street below, children ran around the fountain that lay just outside the church, their mothers and fathers calling after them, other men and women stood looking up at the massive Skyship with awe filled gazes but one man didn't even register the Skyship's presence, he stood at the doors to the church dressed in a purple cassock, rimmed in gold. A smile was spread across his bearded face as he said goodbye to everyone as they left the church, but again the scene was quickly swept away, leaving Adessa feeling dizzy and sick, just how big was the world that she now inhabited.

A knock came at Adessa's door, reluctantly she stirred from her slumber, she had been having a wonderful dream, she was back in Alfheim sitting in the field of Blood Roses with her mother, they had been talking about something but the details were already being lost in the wake of conciseness. Again, the knock came at her door, followed shortly by Captain Goodwin's voice, "Milady we've almost arrived at Actalia."

That knocked the last tendrils of sleep from Adessa's mind, she bolted upright her heart skipping a beat in the process, she had almost arrived at her new 'home'. Scrambling over the cloud like covers of her bed Adessa jumped down onto the hard-wooden floor and snatched up OathKeeper from where he lay on the dining table before crossing the room and opening the door. Captain Goodwin stood just outside the door, his features cast in torchlight, he smiled as was his customary greeting, Adessa returned the smile before speaking. "Can you show me Actalia?"

"Of course milady, please follow me."

Adessa followed Goodwin across the deck towards the bow, she could feel the eyes of the crew on her, clearly they were happy to nearly be rid of her, if Goodwin noticed his men's stares he didn't show it, he just continued towards the front of the ship. Climbing the small stairs to the forecastle Adessa looked around but saw nothing, the world was covered in darkness. High up in the sky where the moon and stars should have been were thick clouds. The massive clouds shone brilliantly whilst denying the light from reaching the rest of the world.

Suddenly, the bow was plunged into the darkness, Adessa drew OathKeeper and looked around, but there was no danger, Goodwin still stood where he was, he had just extinguished the torch.

"Sorry if I startled you, but the flame would only make it harder for you to see."

Adessa suddenly felt very foolish, her nerves were getting the better of her.

C'mon you've got to be stronger than this, you're the representative of the Enshyi.

Sheathing OathKeeper Adessa apologised and looked back out into the night.

At first all she saw was the same shroud of darkness as before but then her eyes adjusted and that's when Adessa saw Actalia.

The Angardian Kingdoms capital stretched out for as far as Adessa could see.

It's colossal.

As she continued to stare down at the urban sprawl Adessa spotted a row of large white stoned buildings, each was identical to its neighbour, from their pointed roofs to the small gardens that lay at their feet.

They look rather plain.

Adessa's thought was confirmed a moment later as she laid eyes upon a much taller wooden building that was painted a bright yellow. The sight filled Adessa with disgust.

How can someone disgrace the bodies of trees like that?

Turning away from the sight and looking far into the distance Adessa was met with what could only be the royal palace, it was everything High Speaker Caewyn said it would be.

319

Five massive towers reached high into the air from a massive body of stone. Adessa stood transfixed by the magnificent sight and a few moments later the clouds parted and moonlight shone down onto the palace, making the already striking site ethereal, the grey walls shone and looked like they were built from smoke made solid. Adessa could have spent all night looking at the wondrous event but nature had other ideas and the clouds quickly asserted their control back over the skies and the palace was plunged back into darkness.

Freed from her trance Adessa looked back down to the other levels of the city and there encircling the city was an impenetrable looking wall that stood nearly as tall as the White Cliffs she had seen not twelve hours before. Standing atop the wall were hundreds of cannons, they were much like the cannons here on the Notus, a large cone of cast iron that sat atop a heavy wooden frame, although they were much larger then the cannons that surrounded Adessa.

As the *Notus* grew closer Adessa saw that numerous men stood amongst the cannons, the skins of a dozen different animals lined their bodies and Adessa felt another wave of revulsion wash over her.

What is wrong with these people.

Closing her eyes and focusing her mind, Adessa felt the hot burning feeling begin to cool where it continued until she locked the feeling away deep inside herself. It wasn't what the GrandOak had taught her to do, the correct use of the Tree in the Wind was to embrace what you were feeling, but Adessa wasn't ready to embrace these feelings, maybe in time she could but not now.

Adessa felt Goodwin's gaze upon her, she must have shown her disgust.

You can't let it show you're a Speaker.

Adessa looked back at the Captain, "Is there something wrong?"

For a split-second Goodwin's face showed confusion but he quickly mastered it and replied with a smile, "No, milady."

Passing over the giant wall, the *Notus* sailed over a sea of shadows, the grey tops of a few buildings managed to poke their way out of the gloom, their flat squat roofs a far cry from the majesty Adessa had just witnessed and if she looked really hard she could just make out the vague lines of a few other buildings but beyond that everything else lay concealed beneath the black cloak of night. The *Notus* then passed over another wall, this one much smaller than the one before but still easily the height of the GrandOak, again men walked the wall but Adessa ignored them focusing on what was ahead.

After another few minutes of gently sailing through the sky the *Notus* came to a stop and began to descend, Adessa tensed, this was it she had finally arrived in the city of Actalia, Capital of the Angardian Kingdom and home to the Skyknights.

Finally, the *Notus* stopped its descent and in a flash the crew burst into motion, sails were drawn in, lines tied and the anchor was dropped down to the ground below as were other lines, Adessa wondered what the point of the added lines were but then a shout came from below.

"Lines secure, you're safe to depart."

With that a gangplank came up to meet the side of the *Notus*.

"Shall we go?" said Goodwin.

Adessa nodded.

"Then follow me."

Goodwin led Adessa across the deck and onto the gangplank, Adessa couldn't believe how steep the thing was, it was almost like walking down the side of a tree, if she tripped it was going to be one long and painful fall, but none the less Adessa put one foot in front of the other and soon enough she touched solid ground, waiting for her surrounded by a group of well-dressed men was a carriage, it was exquisitely made and at the head were two beautiful stallions.

As Adessa followed Goodwin towards the carriage the group of men moved aside and stood at attention, Goodwin said nothing to them and opened the door for Adessa.

"Lady Shinepacer it has been a privilege to have you aboard my ship and I hope we have the chance to meet again."

"You're not accompanying me?"

"No, I have to report to my superiors."

Adessa curtsied, "Then I to hope to see you again."

Goodwin bowed before offering Adessa a hand into the carriage, Adessa accepted and quickly climbed aboard.

"Hello, Adessa."

Adessa looked up and was shocked to find herself face to face with High Speaker Caewyn, Adessa barely recognised him, pale clear skin replaced what was once brown gnarled wood and where thorns and leaves had crowned the vessels head, the High Speakers was covered in a thick black wave of hair, about the only thing that was the same were Caewyn's eyes, the gold shining bright like they had in the vessels.

"Hello, High Speaker," replied Adessa with a bow of her head.

Caewyn smiled and for the first time since her leaving Alfheim, Adessa felt truly safe but then the High Speaker spoke and Adessa was thrust back into the moment. "We have much to discuss and little time to do it in."

"Why, what's happening."

"Tomorrow you will be brought before the other Councillors, the heads of the Skyknights and a member of the royal family, where you will be questioned and asked to show your abilities as a Speaker."

"Okay," said Adessa, "but."

Caewyn held up a hand and Adessa fell silent, "We'll talk more when we reach my apartments."

From his tone Adessa knew there was no arguing.

What have I gotten myself into?

Chapter 28

The first rays of light touched the sky and the world was plunged into colour, Caleb felt the knot that had been in his stomach since last night tighten. It was time for the *Zephyrus* to go to battle.

Caleb looked to helm and saw Captain Brightfellow handing over control to Vaeliria, his deep blue uniform would have made him invisible in the low light if not for the gleam from the many pistols that lined his belt and the giant double headed war-axe that was strapped to his back. The Captain made his way to look out over the deck and began speaking. "At the other side of this gorge lies our enemy. I won't lie to you; this is going to be a tough fight but we've all seen what these animals are capable of and there is no way that we as Skyknights are going to let them continue to plague the innocents of this Kingdom."

A sombre shout came from a few of the crew whilst Caleb and others just stood silent looking at their Captain.

"And remember that we are all one, you fight for the men and women beside you, for your fellows below and you fight for your families far away though they may be, now let's move out."

With that the *Zephyrus* shot forward through the passage, as the craggy walls passed by, Caleb felt the knot within his stomach grow making him feel nauseous. Taking a couple of measured breaths Caleb buried the nervousness in the deepest recesses of himself where he locked it away, he didn't have time to be feeling like this, he had to have his head in the moment otherwise he was just going to get himself killed.

Slowly the passage began to widen until finally it opened out onto a massive crater, the barren land was scarred with dozens of deep fissures which shot massive walls of steam up into the air but all of that faded away when Caleb laid his eyes on the eight crimson ships that sat floating at the centre of the crater. The same black flags Caleb had seen on the ship that had attacked the *Zephyrus* when they first entered Onmoria flew from their flags, the giant skulls pierced Caleb with their blood red stares.

Suddenly a horn sounded and the eight ships broke away from one another, at the same time, *Amber, Mother's Embrace, Firebird* and *Salamander* emerged from passages surrounding the crater, and immediately headed to engage the enemy ships closest to them.

This is it.

With a cry Captain Brightfellow swung the *Zephyrus* towards a mid-sized Barque that was running off to their right.

The smaller three-masted ship immediately opened fire, the sound was deafening and Caleb braced himself for the impact of a dozen cannon balls but with unparalleled speed the *Zephyrus* quickly avoided the barrage and manoeuvred back alongside the enemy.

As soon as the *Zephyrus* was in position the riflemen opened fire at the men standing on the opposing deck, the howls of pain that Caleb was sure were erupting through the air were lost as the Cannoneers launched their own assault on the enemy. Dozens of massive cannonballs shoot through the air in an explosion of sound and smoke, before colliding in the same manor albeit in a hail of splintered wood and screams, but the crew of the *Zephyrus* weren't finished there. Both the Cannoneers and riflemen launched yet another volley, this time, however, the Cannoneers targeted the enemy's masts and rigging. The small chain shots were dead on target tearing through both the fore and mizzen masts as well as numerous parts of the rigging and Caleb thought the fight was over but the enemy clearly had some fight left in them as they unleashed a barrage of pistol fire from their deck.

Caleb dropped to the deck to avoid being hit by the enemy fire as did the other men of the *Zephyrus*, one of the riflemen however wasn't fast enough and got hit straight through the throat, blood spurted out of the wound coating his companions in crimson red and he hit the ground lifelessly.

Motherfuckers.

Caleb tore his eyes from the dead rifleman and looked back out to the enemy Barque.

The ruined ship had begun to spiral out of control and continued to until it crashed into the hard-unforgiving ground and erupted into an enormous ball of flame.

Good riddance.

Turning his attention upwards Caleb saw that *Amber* was locked in combat with a broad Brigantine named *Asuna's Wrath* and from the looks of it Kodia was having a hard time. The port side of *Amber's* hull was peppered with holes from the Brigantine's cannons and the main mast was barely standing, whilst the enemy scarcely had a scratch on its hull.

Captain Brightfellow had obviously seen the same thing and immediately steered the *Zephyrus* towards its ally but as he did the two ships once again opened fire on one another. The thundering impact of cannon balls echoed through the air. *Amber* managed to get a good few shots on target, ripping through the lower levels of the Brigantine's hull but the smaller ship sustained at least twice as many wounds for its effort. All around him Caleb could hear the curses of the crew.

We're not going to make it.

The knot in Caleb's stomach tightened again at the thought.

A moment later *Amber* straightened and faced its adversary head on.

No, surely not.

With what speed it still possessed *Amber* shot forward, the Captain of the enemy had already figured out what Kodia meant to do and was already beginning to manoeuvre out of the way but it wasn't enough. The giant amber figurehead that gave *Amber* its namesake went crashing into the back end of *Asuna's wrath*, for a moment it looked like *Amber* would pass straight through the enemy unscathed but that hope quickly evaporated in the hail of timber, rigging and bodies that erupted from the two ships colliding. Captain Brightfellow pulled the *Zephyrus* away and just in time as a blast unlike anything Caleb had ever seen ripped through the air and knocked him off his feet. Caleb tumbled through the air and thought he was going to have another experience of going over board when he came crashing back down onto the hard-wooden deck of the *Zephyrus*.

Once Caleb had pulled himself back to his feet, he caught sight of *Firebird* and *Salamander*. The two Xebecs were working in perfect tandem, swarming around another Barque like mosquitoes around a wildebeest. The enemy ship was on its last legs, a huge chunk of its hull was missing and Caleb could quite clearly see the fiery glow of the ships damaged Skycore, and from the look of it Tousi and Ban had spotted it as well.

The two Captains circled their ships back around to the gaping hole and prepared for an assault on the exposed core, but the pirates weren't about to go down without a fight, launching volleys of gunfire and cannons at *Firebird* and *Salamander*. At the same time Tousi and Ban's men fired their own cannons, and within seconds the sky above Caleb was lit up like Actalia on New Year's. The smaller Xebec's dodged and dived out of the barrage, whereas the already damaged Barque was hit with every cannonball that had been fired by the Teuengean ships and plummeted to the ground to join its brother.

"Caleb, get your ass over here!"

Caleb looked around for whoever had called him.

"Over here, cadet!"

Caleb turned to find Vaeliria staring at him, a long barrelled rifle was in her hand, the smoke coming from its barrel indicating that she had recently fired it, despite the situation Caleb was amazed, his Commander was an incredible woman he had never seen her wield a rifle before and yet it seemed as natural to her as breathing.

"What do you need, Commander."

"Take this and get to shooting," said Vaeliria producing another rifle.

Caleb hesitantly took the rifle in hand, he had never held a rifle before but already he could tell the weapon wasn't for him, it felt cumbersome in his hands and when he lifted it to take aim he noticed just how heavy it was.

"Enemy at four o'clock!" shouted Runa from above in the crow's nest.

Before Caleb could react, Vaeliria spun around and opened fire, and the other riflemen quickly followed suit. Fumbling with his weapon Caleb eventually joined his fellows and was met with the sight of an incoming Cog. The single masted ship was tiny in comparison to the *Zephyrus*. All it would take to destroy the enemy was a single round of cannon fire, they had to know that didn't they and yet the smaller ship didn't make any attempt to turn and continued its headlong path and that's when Caleb spotted the barrel's lining the cog's deck and his heart sank.

"Commander, that ship's lined with gunpowder barrels."

"I see em. Captain!"

But Vaeliria's voice couldn't reach the Captain amongst the sounds of battle.

"Shit," cursed Vaeliria. "Men aim for the barrels; we need that ship out of the sky."

"Aye," replied the riflemen.

"That means you as well."

"Aye, Commander."

Caleb took aim and fired at the fast-approaching ship, but rather than hitting the barrel he had been aiming for, Caleb's shot hit one of the enemy straight in the chest, dropping him like a fly. The riflemen on the other hand found their targets, one barrel after the other exploded, sending men and wood flying in all directions but still the Cog continued its path towards the *Zephyrus*. Captain Brightfellow must have caught onto what the enemy was planning from the explosions, because the *Zephyrus* jerked into life, which nearly sent Caleb back onto his arse.

"We're not going to make it," said one of the riflemen.

"Open fire!" commanded Vaeliria as she fired her own rifle.

Again, Caleb and the other riflemen opened fire at the enemy, but with no more barrels to take aim at the shots were largely useless and the Cog grew ever closer to the *Zephyrus*'s hull.

Shit.

Caleb braced himself for the impact of the two ships colliding when out of nowhere came *Sandfly*.

The merchant ship opened fire with everything it had, and almost instantly the enemy ship blew apart like a giant firecracker, the force of which kicked the *Zephyrus* into a spin which sent everyone flying. Caleb hit the deck in a heap of tangled limbs before sliding into the hard-unforgiving bulwark, pain shot through him like a dozen fiery needles and stars danced before his eyes, but there wasn't time to worry about the pain.

I'm not going overboard again.

Drawing both of his dirks Caleb plunged the razor-sharp blades into the *Zephyrus*'s deck and held on for dear life.

The *Zephyrus* continued to spin in its downward circle, throwing men clear overboard. Caleb looked up from the deck and saw one of his fellow Skyknights hit the main mast with such a sickening crunch that the life left him instantaneously.

Goddammit.

Looking away from the morbid scene Caleb caught sight of Vaeliria hanging from the rope ladder, the muscles in her sinewy arms bulging with the strain, Caleb wondered whether she would be able to hold on long enough but then as if hearing his thought the *Zephyrus* jerked to a halt.

Tentatively Caleb released his grasp from his dirks and flexed his now claw like hands before pulling his blades free and jumping back to his feet, at the same time Vaeliria released her grip of the roped ladder and dropped gracefully back down onto the deck.

"You okay?" said Vaeliria as Caleb came to stand beside her.

Caleb gave a curt nod in reply.

"Good, cause it looks like Roshni could use our help."

At Vaeliria's words Captain Brightfellow kicked the *Zephyrus* back into life and within seconds the class one Galleon was back up high in the air and Caleb saw what Vaeliria had meant.

Mother's Embrace was being hounded by a Galleon named *Avatar of Death*. The massive Skyship dwarfed *Mother's embrace* and even looked to rival the *Zephyrus* in terms of size and from what Caleb could tell the enemy had decked nearly every inch of their ship with cannons.

Roshni doesn't stand a chance.

Mother's Embrace again tried to get away from its opponent but *Avatar of Death* had the smaller merchant ship outmanoeuvred and quickly cut off any chance off escape, desperate Roshni's men opened fire with everything they had left.

One cannonball after the other catapulted through the air towards the enemy but to Caleb's utter amazement the enemy dodged the barrage by diving below *Mother's Embrace* before quickly rising on the opposite side and opening fire itself.

Mother's Embrace was completely consumed in the ensuing onslaught but rather than becoming a ball of flames like the other ships that had succumb to the battle, the merchant ship literally shrivelled until it became nothing but a husk that quickly fell away to the ground below, where it crashed into a hundred different pieces and spewed bodies in every direction.

"What the fuck was that?" swore one of the riflemen.

"That was the work of a Hex Practitioner."

The monotonic voice could only be one person, Caleb turned and sure enough there stood Wraith, her cold grey features were still as calm as ever despite the death and destruction going on around her.

"Are you sure?" said another rifleman, his voice shaky with fear.

"I can feel his energy."

"Is he still on board that ship?" said Vaeliria.

Wraith nodded.

"We're fucked!" said the rifleman, his fear now turned to complete hysteria

"What's it matter," said Caleb annoyed, "we have a Hex Practitioner with us and look at her she's not some monster, she's just a woman, which means theirs is just a man, all we've got to do is blow that ship outta the sky."

Now that he had finished speaking Caleb realised everyone was looking at him and it made him feel awkward, but he couldn't help himself once he had started the words had just kept coming.

"He's right," said Vaeliria finally breaking the silence, "now fire!"

Within seconds' hundreds of bullets and cannonballs were flying between the two Skyships, Caleb ducked and dodged the enemy fire before reloading his rifle for what felt like the thousandth time and took aim. Instantly Caleb found his target, standing at one of the swivel guns that lined the enemy's deck was a fat weasel of a man. Caleb took a deep breath levelled his rifle against his shoulder and slowly pulled the trigger, despite his best efforts the shot didn't hit the man in the head where he had been aiming but dipped and strayed to the right hitting the man in the shoulder, shockingly the pirate didn't even flinch.

Damn it.

Caleb started to reload his rifle but already he knew that he wasn't going to be able to finish in time, already he could see the pirate taking aim with his miniature cannon, but before he could fire another bullet hit the pirate in the face instantly killing him, Caleb looked for who had fired the shot but there was no way he could tell not with so many guns going off at the same time.

Captain Brightfellow's booming voice snapped Caleb out of his thought, "Brace for impact!"

The two Skyship's collided with an almighty crash that shook Caleb to his very core, all around him wooden splinters shot through the air like the quills from a giant porcupine and both friend and foe were thrown overboard and off into the vast expanse of sky.

A moment later a wave of pirates leaped aboard the *Zephyrus*, their scarred, bearded faces were twisted with evil grins and vicious sneers.

"We're going to ki" before the pirate could finish his threat, Caleb smashed the barrel of his rifle into the man's face. Blood and teeth sprayed through the air but Caleb wasn't finished there, as soon as the pirate hit the deck he slammed the butt of the rifle down so hard he practically severed the man's jaw from his face.

Dropping the now useless rifle Caleb drew his dirks and leapt into the raging battle, where he hamstrung a fat pirate who was hounding one of the riflemen, the man fell in a cry of pain as his leg buckled under him, and a moment later Caleb ran his blades straight through the man's chest.

"Gun ain't gonna do any good at this range," said Caleb to the riflemen as he pulled his dirks from the now dead pirate.

Before the gunner could reply Caleb was off looking for his next opponent and it didn't take him long to find one. Standing dead in front of him was a mountain of a man who carried a massive spiked club. With a blood fuelled roar the giant pirate lashed out with his colossal weapon.

Shit.

Caleb dove out of the swings way and not a moment too soon as the ground where he had just been standing erupted in a hail of splinters. Caleb knew he should be afraid but his blood was on fire and he felt unstoppable.

As he got back to his feet Caleb tightened his grip on his blades before he gave a cry of his own and lashed out at the giant as fast as he possibly could, and yet his blades found nothing but air as the giant dodged around his strikes.

Damn this guy's fast.

"Haha, is that all you've got," said the pirate smiling.

Caleb hadn't the breath to reply.

The pirate looked disappointed at Caleb's lack of a comeback but quickly shook it off and raised his club high overhead, but as he did Caleb dove forward and sunk his dirks straight into the wall like man's chest.

"That's what I've got," said Caleb with a sneer.

The giant dropped his spiked club and Caleb thought the fight was his, when suddenly a meaty fist hit him around the face and he was sent flying through the air.

As he hit the ground Caleb rolled which helped absorb most of the damage and quickly got back to his feet and it was a good thing he did as the massive pirate came charging forward with Caleb's dirks in his hands.

Instinctively Caleb dropped into a Shakan pose and awaited the charging beast.

As soon as his opponent was in range Caleb pirouetted and lashed out with a side kick to the man's knee. With a satisfying crunch, the giant like man fell to the deck and a moment later Caleb unleashed a roundhouse kick to the man's face and he dropped like a sack of manure to the deck.

"Okay that's what I've got," said Caleb as he picked up his dirks and wiped the blood from his lips.

Caleb was about to head back into the battle when he caught sight of a man who could only be Irashaad standing at the helm of the enemy ship and found himself surprised by the man's features, he looked more likely to fit in at court then to be leading a band of savage pirates, what with his clean-shaven face and black robes trimmed with gold. The illusion was quickly broken however as two of Caleb's fellow Skyknights swung over to the enemy ship. Caleb recognised the two men as Willard and Rupert.

As they landed the two knights drew their swords and charged the Pirate Captain. With inhuman speed Irashaad danced around the blades of either knight and then just as quickly he struck like a viper, and plunged a clawed fist into the throat of Willard. The knights body jerked for a moment before becoming limp.

Despite his distance from the battle Caleb could have sworn that he heard Rupert let out a cry of rage as he charged the now smiling Irashaad.

Why's he smiling?

Caleb's question was answered moments later as Irashaad grabbed a hold of Willard's lifeless body and threw him towards his comrade. Rupert dodged under his companion's body but the distraction was all Irashaad needed as he kicked Rupert full in the face and sent the young Skyknight's head snapping back instantly killing him.

Caleb's hot blood turned cold for a split second before white hot fury took over.

I'm going to kill this bastard.

As he ran across the deck Caleb hacked, slashed and stabbed at every pirate he could before finally he leaped up onto the *Zephyrus*'s port side bulwark and out across the empty expanse of air. Despite the fire raging inside of him Caleb still felt a wave of nausea sweep through him as he hurtled through the air, but a moment later the emptiness was gone and Caleb was aboard the enemy ship.

The fighting was just as thick aboard *Avatar of Death* as it had been on the *Zephyrus*. All around Skyknights and Pirates were locked in vicious combat, Vida and Runa amongst them.

The two scouts stood out with their unique fighting style that combined acrobatics with knife fighting, but more impressive than the handstands and flips that they performed was the way in which they worked together, the brothers seemed to know what one another was going to do. As one dodged the other attacked or both attacked or dodged together, thus the two became one and they easily cut down those that stood in their way, but then five pirates rushed the brothers at once.

Shit.

Caleb broke into a sprint towards his friends, but before he could reach the two a snarling pirate dove at him. Caleb rolled out of the way and quickly jumped back to his feet, the pirate did the same and drew a long jagged knife from his belt.

"C'mon," said the pirate snarling again.

Caleb said nothing in return and merely indicated that the pirate should come at him.

The pirate was only too happy to comply and leapt forward.

Caleb deflected and parried one blow after the other with his two dirks, which only seemed to enrage the pirate even more as his already feral gaze became that of a Daemons.

C'mon you bastard.

With his next lunge the pirate put his entire weight into the blow.

Got you.

With a twist of his hips Caleb spun around the pirate's outstretched arm and delivered a deadly elbow to the man's temple which immediately knocked the man unconscious and Caleb set off across the deck towards Vida and Runa.

The two scouts had managed to take one of their opponents out but in doing so both scouts had suffered injuries of their own.

Caleb ran as fast as he could towards the line of four pirates that stood before him, but before he could reach them the colossal form that was Captain Brightfellow flew onto the enemy's deck, and in one clean motion he swung his massive war-axe in a deadly arc and cleaved three of the pirates in half, blood and innards spewed across the deck painting it crimson, with another swing he separated the last pirate's head from his shoulder, then in four of his great strides the Captain was upon the men surrounding

Vida and Runa, they didn't last long and for a split second Caleb almost felt sorry for them but it quickly passed and once again he turned his attention back to the helm and Irashaad who stood waiting.

A sinister grin was spread across the pirate's face twisting his almost regal features into those more suiting of a monstrous pirate. A moment later a tall robed figure emerged as if from air to stand beside Irashaad, the thick robes looked identical to the ones that Wraith wore but hanging around the Hex practitioner's neck was a necklace of bone and feathers, the knot that Caleb had thought gone shot back into his stomach and in that moment, he knew something terrible was going to happen.

The Hex practitioner swept a bony claw of a hand through the air and suddenly all along the deck of *Avatar of Death,* Hexes flared to life. Within seconds Caleb felt the strength begin to leave his body as a crushing weight forced him to one knee and then the other, no one else seemed to be fairing any better, Vida and Runa were pinned to the deck as if an unforeseen hand held them there, but that wasn't even the start of it other knights lay thrashing on the ground, clawing at their own throats trying to catch a breath, even Irashaad's own men weren't spared torment, blood spewed from mouths, eyes and ears as they were crushed, even Captain Brightfellow had been forced to one of his knees. The invisible weight continued to grow and Caleb could feel his lungs being compressed forcing the air from him, next his vision began to tunnel and everything felt like it was far away, until finally it was like he was looking through a pinhole.

I think this may be the end.

But as soon as Caleb had the thought the force disappeared and he sucked down a wondrous lungful of air, and then another and in a few moments Caleb had the strength to pull himself to his knees.

Once he was back on his feet Caleb found that Wraith stood in front of him and had extinguished the Hexes that stood around the deck of *Avatar of Death.*

Caleb immediately turned his attention back towards the helm but found that Irashaad was already down on the deck, a look of annoyance plastered across his face.

"Finally," said Caleb as he pulled himself to his feet.

Before Caleb had even taken a step, Vida and a group of four Skyknights that he didn't recognise surrounded Irashaad. The pirate captain's already annoyed face twisted into one of pure rage and with the same inhuman speed he had demonstrated earlier lunged at one of the Skyknights and punched him straight in the throat. The knights face paled as he fell to the ground.

"You bastard!" screamed one of the other knights as he broke from the circle and attacked.

Irashaad easily dodged the knight's erratic swings.

"Stand and fight you coward!" screamed the knight.

"As you wish," said Irashaad as he grabbed a hold of the knight's sword-arm and viciously snapped it.

The knight began to cry out in pain but in the next moment he was silenced as Irashaad manipulated his now broken arm and ran him through with his own sword.

"Who's next?" said Irashaad as he pushed the knight to the floor.

Before anyone could react to his question, Irashaad went on the offensive and quickly killed the last two nameless Skyknights with heavy blows that caved their skulls, thus leaving Vida as the sole survivor of the group.

Shit.

Caleb began stumbling across the deck of *Avatar of Death*, but already he could tell he wasn't going to make it to his comrade.

With his near impossible speed Irashaad lashed out at Vida with a series of sharp punches. Vida dodged and danced around the attacks with equally impressive speed until finally he stepped into Irashaad's guard and retaliated with a backhanded knife blow.

That has to land.

As if to prove him wrong Irashaad quickly parried the blade away before he slammed his free fist straight into

Vida's face. Vida tried to get away then but Irashaad grasped a hold of him by the shoulders and cracked him around the face with another punch. Teeth and blood spewed from Vida's mouth and the scout's legs became limp.

Fuck.

Caleb willed his legs to move faster but they wouldn't listen.

Irashaad hoisted Vida overhead and Caleb felt his heart sink.

"This is what happens when you Angardians mess with me!" With that Irashaad slammed Vida down across his knee. A sickening snap echoed through the air and Vida fell to the ground unmoving.

No.

From across the deck Runa let out a grief-stricken cry and Caleb felt his hatred for Irashaad multiply tenfold.

Using his hatred as fuel Caleb broke out into a sprint but as he did a massive explosion ripped through the deck of *Avatar of Death,* and he was sent flying backwards.

When Caleb opened his eyes next he found himself face to face with a wall of fire.

What the?

Caleb pulled himself to his feet and then everything came rushing back to him as he laid eyes on Irashaad standing on the opposite side of the fiery wall.

Caleb knew he should evacuate to the safety of the *Zephyrus* but there was no way that he was going to let Irashaad get away not when he was so close.

Breaking out into a sprint Caleb leapt through the blaze. Even though he was only in the flames for a moment the heat sucked the air from his lungs.

As he landed on the other side of *Avatar of Death,* Caleb fell into a roll before springing gracefully back to his feet, where he realised his jacket was on fire.

Shrugging off his now ruined jacket Caleb caught sight of Irashaad making his way back up towards the helm.

You're not getting away.

As Caleb darted across the burning deck towards the helm, a bull-necked pirate came stumbling out of a plume of smoke and straight into his path. Before the man had a chance to recover from his smoke induced blindness Caleb gouged his dirks into the man's stomach, before quickly stabbing up into his jaw. Blood spattered across Caleb as he drew his blades free and the pirate fell to the ground with a heavy thump.

With his path now unimpeded Caleb bounded up the steps and onto the helm, where he was meet with the sight of Irashaad cutting down the last of another group of Skyknight's with his gilded scimitar.

As the last of his enemies fell beneath his blade Irashaad spun around, his face and robes were covered in streaks of blood not his own and once again a twisted grin spread across his face.

"You people don't know when to give up."

"No we really don't," snarled Caleb.

Irashaad ignored the snarl and began walking towards Caleb, "You should have listened to my warning, because now once I'm finished with you and your 'friends' here, I shall unleash the fires of Mamemohr upon this land, then once everything here has been burnt to ash I will head for your Kingdom where I will wipe it from the earth one village at a time until there is nothing left but ruin and death."

"Just try it," said Caleb spinning his dirks.

Irashaad let out a sharp laugh before lunging forward, purely on instinct Caleb dove out of the scimitar's path but before he could even make it back to his feet a sharp kick connected to his stomach. Rolling with the momentum Caleb managed to absorb most of the kicks force and bounced back up to his feet, but as he did he felt the familiar pain of cracked ribs lance through his side.

"Done already?" said Irashaad as he twirled his blade through the air.

"You wish," replied Caleb.

Accepting the pain that coursed down his side Caleb took a breath before he lunged forward and slashed at Irashaad, but his blades found nothing save air as Irashaad skilfully dodged his attack.

"I'm going to kill you!" screamed Caleb as he cut at Irashaad.

"I don't think so," replied Irashaad as he stopped Caleb's strike with his scimitar and smacked him across the face with his free hand.

Stars danced before Caleb's eyes and his teeth rattled inside his head but he wasn't about to lose so easily. Pivoting Caleb unleashed a side kick that connected squarely with Irashaad's stomach and drove him back a few paces.

Can't let him recover.

Caleb took a step forward and was about to deliver a thrust with his dirks when pain laced through his heel and he stumbled. It felt like he had just kicked a stone wall.

Shake it off.

Caleb embraced the pain and pulled himself back to his feet and not a moment too soon, as Irashaad came back in with a wide sweeping slash. Lifting his dirks Caleb deflected the deadly blow, however the force of the clashing blades ripped his dirks from his grasp and before he knew what was happening Irashaad delivered a slash across his chest, which tore through his shirt and the light chainmail he wore beneath.

For a moment Caleb just stood there looking his enemy dead in the eyes, then his legs gave way and he fell to his knees.

What happened?

Caleb looked down and saw only crimson.

Did I get stabbed?

Looking back up Caleb was met with the sight of Irashaad's evil sneer, the pirate Captain raised his scimitar high above his head.

I'm going to die.

Vaeliria had just finished cutting down the last of her enemies, when a great explosion erupted from the deck of *Avatar of Death*. Giant gouts of flame leapt forth consuming everything and everyone in their path, immediately Vaeliria worried for the safety of her Captain and fellow knights. Scanning the enemy deck as quickly as she could, Vaeliria spotted the massive bulk of Captain Brightfellow, he was down on one knee and Vaeliria feared the worse but then he picked himself up and was off moving across the deck towards a figure that lay prone.

A moment later she spotted Caleb sprinting towards the flame wall, instantly she knew what her student was going to do and sure enough he leapt through the flames where he landed on the other side with a haphazard roll, as soon as he was on his feet Caleb shrugged off his jacket which Vaeliria saw was on fire and again he was off.

"Commander, behind you."

Vaeliria spun around just in time to block a knife blow to her kidney, the pirate who attacked her was covered from head to toe in soot making him look like some shadow come to life. Vaeliria quickly ran the man through but already more of the enemy were scrambling onto the *Zephyrus* aware that their ship was doomed, amongst them were dozens of knights including Captain Brightfellow, who held Runa over one of his gigantic shoulders, the veteran scout was crying and the screams that escaped from him sent chills up Vaeliria's spine.

Crossing the deck Vaeliria cut down any who stood in her way, until finally she stood next to her Captain.

"You okay, Captain?"

"Yeah," replied Captain Brightfellow tiredly. "Have you seen Caleb?"

Shit.

Vaeliria looked back over at *Avatar of Death,* the fire had spread across nearly every inch of the enemy ship's deck sending up thick clouds of smoke, if Caleb was down there then he was as good as dead already, but then

Vaeliria spotted movement up on the enemy's helm and a cold hand grasped a hold of her.

Caleb was fighting one on one with Irashaad, her student was on the offensive attacking with the ferociousness of a beast but even from this distance Vaeliria could tell that the blows were hitting nothing but air. Before she knew what, she was doing Vaeliria was moving. Again, a pirate came at her, armed with a knife in one hand and a short sword in the other, with brutal efficiency Vaeliria parried the pirate's attacks and took him straight across the bridge of his nose with her own razor sharp sword, the top half of his head flew through the air in an arch of blood. Across on the enemy's helm, Vaeliria saw Caleb stumble even though it appeared he had just landed a blow, he recovered, however, and just in time, as Irashaad came in with a deadly sweep, Caleb managed to block the strike but in doing so he lost his dirks, and in the next moment Irashaad's blade cut straight across Caleb's chest, for a moment it looked like Caleb was fine but then he slumped to his knees.

No.

Climbing up the stairs to the *Zephyrus*'s helm two at a time Vaeliria jumped up onto the aft bulwark and swung herself across onto the enemy ship, where she landed just in time to see Irashaad raise his sword high above his head.

A part of Caleb wanted to fight, to deny what was about to happen to him but he knew it was futile there was nothing he could do, his body wouldn't respond to his demands and already he could feel the life leaving him.

Maybe it would be better to die quickly.

But as Irashaad's blade came arching down towards his head Caleb knew it was a lie, he didn't want to die here, not like this, pouring every ounce of will he had into his body Caleb begged it to move but still it refused and the razor-sharp blade came crashing down.

This is it.

But rather than tearing through his skull Irashaad's blade was repelled and Vaeliria appeared. Irashaad immediately went on the defensive, with each blow the clanging of steel rang out like a siren keeping Caleb afloat.

As she broke through Irashaad's guard Vaeliria side stepped and delivered a thrust to her enemies exposed ribs, but rather than her blade running all the way through like it should have, Vaeliria's sword barely dug in below the tip. With a twist of his hips Irashaad broke free and threw a hook with his free hand, rather than retreat Vaeliria dropped her sword and grabbed a hold of Irashaad's sword arm, within a second she had the limb locked in a crane hold. Caleb knew from experience just how effective the hold was. With a pull on Irashaad's wrist Vaeliria stripped him of his weapon and the gilded sword fell to the ground with a clang. With his free hand Irashaad began throwing short sharp hooks at Vaeliria, rather than try and hold the lock Vaeliria spun out and transitioned into an arm bar and with a sharp jab Vaeliria dislocated Irashaad's elbow. The pirate Captain let out a roar of pain as his arm fell uselessly to his side, but rather than cradle it like most men would Irashaad left the limb and unleashed a torrent of jabs from his good arm. Despite the fact he only had one arm now Vaeliria was pushed back by the onslaught and Caleb felt a trickle of fear creep through his sluggish mind.

As if on cue Irashaad switched his stance and lashed out with a kick to Vaeliria's ribs, the blow connected with a crack and this time it was Vaeliria's turn to roar in pain as she was sent crashing to the floor, before she could recover Irashaad followed up with another kick to Vaeliria's ribs which flipped her onto her back.

White hot pain coursed through Vaeliria's side as blow after blow came crashing into her and the coppery taste of blood filled her mouth.

I have to do something otherwise I'm dead. No, not only me but Caleb will die as well.

Another kick landed and Vaeliria felt her ribs snap, but she embraced the pain and just as another kick came crashing towards her she rolled out of the way before she kicked out at Irashaad's leg and brought him to the floor.

Before Irashaad had a chance to recover, Vaeliria jumped on top of him and began raining punches down.

With only one arm to protect himself Irashaad's guard was easy to break and one blow after the other connected with his face, but then Irashaad rolled and Vaeliria suddenly found herself on the bottom of their grapple. Vaeliria instantly went for a knee to his groin but Irashaad defended against the shot by pinning her leg. Vaeliria then threw a couple of sharp jabs to Irashaad's ribs and crushing pain shot through her knuckles, it was like she had just hit steel plate rather than silk.

Seizing the moment Irashaad hooked Vaeliria around the head, stars danced before her eyes but Vaeliria quickly shrugged it off, she had experienced the sensation dozens of times over the years, so much so that it was almost like an old companion.

As Irashaad went to launch another attack Vaeliria brought her head up like a whip and smashed it straight into the pirate captain's nose.

"You bitch!" yelled Irashaad as blood exploded from his nose.

Vaeliria felt she had an opening then but before she could react Irashaad hooked her around the face again and her head bounced off the hard-wooden deck and everything went dark.

With her thoughts scrambled Vaeliria barely felt the hand clasp around her throat, but as soon as it began to squeeze she was brought back to the moment. Irashaad sat atop her his face a bloody twisted sneer.

"Die!" screamed Irashaad.

Vaeliria tried to lash out with her hands but found that they were pinned beneath Irashaad's legs and already she could feel her consciousness begin to fade.

C'mon you've got to win otherwise Caleb's as good as dead.

Vaeliria summoned every ounce of strength she had and tried to buck and roll her way free, but it was no use Irashaad had the advantage in both weight and strength, desperate Vaeliria began delivering knees to Irashaad's back but it was useless she was far too weak now for them to do anything and the world went dark and Vaeliria knew this was the end.

I've failed.

But then as if by magic the pressure around her neck was gone and Vaeliria opened her eyes to see a knife protruding from Irashaad's neck. The pirate Captain's face was a mixture of surprise and pain as he reached up towards the blade, but before he could the knife was withdrawn, crimson blood fountained from the gash and Irashaad fell forward lifelessly onto Vaeliria bathing her in his blood. With what little strength she had Vaeliria cast the pirate's body off her and took what felt like her first breath in ages.

"You okay, Commander?"

Vaeliria looked up to find Caleb standing over her, bloody dirk in hand, "Yes. I'll be fine."

"That's good," said Caleb wearily, before falling to the ground.

Vaeliria scrambled over to her student and her heart sank, he was soaked in blood and was eerily pale, that's when Vaeliria spotted the massive wound that cut straight across Caleb's chest.

I've got to get him back to the Zephyrus and fast.

Ignoring the pain that coursed throughout her entire body Vaeliria slung Caleb over her shoulder and broke out into a run straight for the *Zephyrus*.

As she ran towards the *Zephyrus* Vaeliria felt the heat of the flames snap at her heels and the wood beneath her feet began to give way.

I've no choice.

Breaking out into a sprint Vaeliria leapt up on to the bulwark of *Avatar of Death* and threw herself and Caleb through the air towards the safety of the *Zephyrus*, but it quickly became clear that they weren't going to make it. Vaeliria desperately reached out and just managed to grasp a hold of the *Zephyrus*'s deck.

As her body went crashing into the *Zephyrus*'s hull Vaeliria screamed out for help but it appeared no one could hear her above the destruction of the enemy ship.

Shit.

Vaeliria tried to haul herself up towards the deck but it was useless, she didn't have the strength and her grip was rapidly weakening. With everything she had Vaeliria screamed out for help and that's when Captain Brightfellow appeared. Vaeliria had never been so happy to see her Captain before. With one massive arm he hauled her and Caleb up onto the deck and immediately called for them to be taken down to the medical bay.

"I'm fine," said Vaeliria in protest as two members of the crew tried to help her stand.

"Nonsense," replied Captain Brightfellow. "Look at you, you look worse than I did when we first met."

"But you need every able-bodied man here."

"That's where you're wrong, we've won Vaeliria, the battle's over."

Chapter 29

Rain pattered against the windows of the carriage Adessa rode in as it made its way along the wide paved streets of Actalia's upper city. The cold stone faces of the noble's homes and businesses loomed overhead like miserable sentinels, dozens of pigeons sat atop their heads ever watchful for signs of scraps, Adessa found the creature's gazes to be rather unsettling so she turned her attention back to the streets around her. Hundreds of finely dressed men and women stood along the edges of the road, their pristine suits and elegant dresses a sea of colour in the otherwise grey day, surprisingly though there was not one child amongst them, which made Adessa even more uncomfortably than she already was, back in Alfheim the walkways were filled with children, their laughs and playful screams a sweet symphony of innocence and joy that Adessa only just realised she missed even though she had never been involved in any of the games or fun. Just then the scared neighing of horses penetrated the quiet and the carriage pulled to an abrupt stop throwing Adessa forward onto the thick carpeted floor, Adessa's heart pounded in her chest, what was going on out there, again the distressed cry pierced through the air, pulling herself back up Adessa made her way to the other side of the carriage and opened the small hatch that lay there.

"What's going on?" said Adessa in her best Angardian.

"I'm sorry, milady, cat ran across the road spooked the horses something bad," replied the driver as he wrestled with the reins, "but don't worry. I'll have em under control in a minute."

I doubt that.

Opening herself up to the spirit world Adessa quickly found the two stallion's spirits.

"It's okay, it was just a cat," said Adessa through the Voice.

The stallions began to calm but then the driver pulled on their reins and the two horses broke back out into blind panic. Adessa was knocked back into her seat by the sudden wave of emotion, and a moment later she felt her chest tighten and her mind begin to race with panic, and that's when she realised she was feeling the horses panic as if it was her own.

With a deep breath Adessa calmed herself and severed her connection to the spirit world.

These people have no idea how to live in harmony with nature.

The whines of the horses quickly awoke Adessa from her thought and she jumped back to her feet.

I have to help them.

The carriages door opened with a groan and Adessa leapt to the wet ground. Icy pinpricks shot through her bare feet as they touched the cold cobbles of the street but Adessa ignored the sensation and made her way to the front of the carriage and the panicked beasts that stood thrashing in their bindings.

"Milady!" said the driver surprised. "You shouldn't be out here it's not safe."

Adessa ignored the driver's words and instead addressed the two stallions: "It's okay, no one is going to hurt you."

The horses neighed and stomped at her in reply but Adessa wasn't deterred, she understood the animals' pain, they weren't meant to be bound in chains and forced to slave away carting people to and fro across the hard-unforgiving city streets, no they should be out on the plains running free with nothing but grass and mud beneath their hooves and the wind in their manes.

Opening herself back up to the spirit world Adessa once again sent calming thoughts to the horses, immediately the two stallions stopped their stomping and quietened. Continuing forward Adessa reached out a hand to either horses faces and waited, Adessa could see that the animals were still spooked but then one of the horse's auras calmed completely and it nuzzled into Adessa's hand, seeing its brethren become trusting the other horse tentatively followed suit.

"Thank you," said Adessa as she closed her connection to the spirit world.

With the physical world coming back into focus Adessa found herself suddenly aware that hundreds of eyes were watching her including the driver of her carriage, his big brown eyes were wide with fearful amazement. Adessa bowed her head and quickly made her way back inside the wooden carriage, slamming the door as she went.

Heart thumping Adessa fell back into her seat and once again the carriage was pulled into life, streets and buildings passed by in a haze as Adessa sat trying to calm herself, she could still feel the eyes of the citizens on her, much like the driver their gazes had been filled with mixtures of fear and awe, what did they have to fear she was the one in a strange land surrounded by people she didn't know or trust, how could the High Speaker leave her to travel alone through this city. Oh that's right he had left a note, saying that his duties as a Councillor had pulled him away, anger penetrated the calm Adessa was trying to wrap around herself at the thought, for years she had idolised the High Speaker, he was the most powerful and gifted Forest Speaker of his generation and when she had found out that she was going to be taught by him she had thought that things were finally beginning to look up, but in reality it was the worst thing that could have happened, before Adessa had a chance to deal with these thoughts and emotions the carriage slowly pulled to a stop.

Looking out the window Adessa was met with the sight of the Angardian Skyknight's Headquarters. Eight-storeys of glass and stone stood tall in an efficient square. Through the massive windows Adessa could see hundreds of people walking to and fro, like workers in a colony of ants. Lining the top of the building were a series of beautifully sculpted statues, depicting men and women of a time long ago. Adessa couldn't help but wonder why these people had such an obsession with such things, was it vanity or was it so they remembered who had come before, Adessa thought it the former because back in the High Speaker's apartments there were dozens of statues of beautiful women scantily clad, that was as sure a sign as any of their vanity wasn't it. To either side of the square building stood two massive towers, these monsters of solid stone were even more imposing then their companion, the deep scars that ran along their faces spoke of numerous battles and the hard-looking men who walked along their tops with rifles in hand only reinforced the forbidding feeling. The door of the carriage opened startling Adessa from her thoughts.

"We've arrived, milady," said the driver holding out a hand.

"Thank you," replied Adessa as she took the offered hand. "Are you not accompanying me?".

"I'm afraid not." From the driver's tone Adessa knew he was lying, he was happy to be rid of her.

"Then who will be escorting me."

"That would be me."

Standing in front of Adessa, was a handsome man. Bright green eyes shone beneath a head of straw coloured hair that was tied back in a tight ponytail, a warm smile was spread across his wide jaw.

"My name is Reuben Kaur," said the man bowing. "Admiral Reinhold asked me to escort you to your meeting with him and the Councillors."

Adessa bowed in return like she had been taught, "Good day to you, Sir Kaur. My name is Adessa of clan Shinepacer, Speaker of the Forest and child of Alfheim."

"It's a pleasure to make your acquaintance, Lady Shinepacer," said Reuben offering his arm.

Adessa lightly took the offered arm and let herself be led away towards the imposing headquarters of the Skyknights.

As she walked across the yard Adessa caught the unmistakable sweet smell of roses, but when she looked around all she saw was the same hard grey pavement as before.

Maybe I'm imagining it.

But no there it was again and that's when Adessa realised that the smell was coming from Sir Kaur. Adessa looked at her escort with a curious gaze but said nothing, it was just another strange practice performed by the people of this Kingdom that Adessa would soon have to get used to.

The inside of the HQ looked more like the High Speakers' apartments than the home of the Angardian's premier military force. Masterful paintings and finely woven tapestries lined nearly every inch of wall, beneath the murals and drapery were rows of benches and chairs, the sight of the carved wood made Adessa cringe, to these people the benches were nothing more than a decoration, but to Adessa they were the sacred remains of beings long passed. high overhead strange lights shone like miniature suns covering everything in a bright white light. At the other side of the room stood a long desk that curved in a semicircle, a man and a woman stood behind the desk, the man was short and wide like a boar whilst the woman was slender like a swan, from their raised voices it was clear the two were having an argument.

"Jared! Katherine!" shouted Sir Kaur, his voice cutting through the air like a sword.

Instantly, the man and woman stopped their arguing and stood at attention.

"Sorry, sir," said the man saluting.

"My apologies," added the woman.

Kaur said nothing in reply, but his gaze was more than enough to make the other knights uncomfortable.

From the desk Adessa was led through a door of solid oak and up one flight of stairs after the other passing dozens if not hundreds of people in the process, none paid Adessa any heed and she was only too happy to return the favour, finally they arrived on the highest floor, legs burning from the climb Adessa wanted nothing more than to sit down and recover but she knew that would only show weakness, where she had to show strength, taking a deep breath she pushed the pain from her thoughts and willed her legs forward, from there Sir Kaur led Adessa down a long corridor, the already miserable day had turned even worse during Adessa's brief climb, the grey clouds had now become thick black monsters, which seemed to be intent on washing away the city beneath them in a torrent of rain and wind, thousands of heavy droplets battered the grand windows in a chaotic frenzy, Adessa imagined all those elegantly dressed men and women out in the streets with nothing to protect them from the downpour and smiled.

Serves them right for not living in harmony with nature.

Coming to the end of the corridor Adessa was led through another door that gave way to a small waiting room. Inside standing guard was a pale, red haired man, the skin of numerous animals covered his body in a lacquered shell and at his hip sat a long slender sword, its silver scabbard reflecting the light around it, but then Adessa spotted another person sat in the corner of the room, their face hidden by a massive book, but from the purple coloured doublet and breeches that were trimmed with gold, Adessa knew that this person was someone of high noble stature.

"Seneschal," said Sir Kaur saluting.

The guard opened his eyes, in an instant Adessa felt his eyes on her, his stare seemed to penetrate to the very core of her and it was all she could do to not look away from his sea blue eyes, then he smiled but rather than the warm smile Sir Kaur had given her, Adessa was reminded of a wolf baring its teeth, burying the fear that threatened to overcome her Adessa curtsied.

"Lieutenant," replied the guard before turning his full attention to Adessa. "Lady Shinepacer, my name is Delander Hoshinki, Seneschal to his Majesty King

William IV and this is Prince Alistair, second son to his Majesty."

The prince lowered his book and stood, Adessa was instantly surprised, he couldn't be any older than eighteen and from the awkward way he held himself Adessa found herself questioning whether he really was a prince of the Angardian Kingdom.

"Lady Shinepacer," said the prince in a weak voice, Adessa turned to the prince and he instantly reddened, "on behalf of my father, I would like to welcome you to Actalia."

"Thank you, your Highness," said Adessa curtsying.

The Prince looked nervously to Hoshinki and the Seneschal nodded politely before speaking. "Admiral Reinhold and the Councillor's are already inside." Hoshinki motioned to the door behind him. "If you'd follow me, I shall announce your arrival."

Adessa curtsied once again to the prince, who bowed awkwardly in return before taking his seat again.

As Adessa crossed the room her heart pounded inside her head, again she focused and rediscovered her centre and pushed the fear away.

"Come along Lieutenant," said the Seneschal to Sir Kaur.

"Sir?"

"The Admiral has asked that you be present for this meeting as well."

With that Sir Kaur became noticeably uncomfortable, which surprisingly made Adessa feel better at least she wouldn't be the only one who felt uncomfortable during this meeting.

Seneschal Hoshinki knocked on the door and a moment later a booming voice beckoned them to enter.

The next room Adessa entered was massive, it was easily the same size as the High Speakers' apartments but where Caewyn's rooms were filled with numerous pieces of furniture, sculptures and books this room lay almost bare, there were no signs of sculptures or books and the only furniture that filled the room was a giant circular table and twelve chairs that stood around the table like the markings of a clock. Sitting at the table were six figures, Adessa immediately spotted High Speaker Caewyn, he wore a black doublet and tied around one arm was a purple band with the crest of the Angardian Skyknights. The sword and wing-tipped shield looked strange on the High Speaker's arm. Next to the High Speaker sat an ancient looking woman, who could only be Lady Elizabeth Grey, her skin was a mass of wrinkles and age spots, despite this, however, her blue greying eyes still looked clear and full of life, stood behind her was a stoic faced guard, from his steely gaze Adessa could tell that this man was a killer.

On the opposite side of the table sat a younger woman, Caewyn had told Adessa about how beautiful Lady Sarah Thorne was and Adessa could see that his words weren't exaggerated, bright scarlet hair flowed down across her heavy chest, covering the pale flawless skin that lay beneath in a sea of red. Next to her sat Peter Silvermane, the owner of the Silvermane mining company was almost as beautiful as his fellow Councillor, sharp chiselled features gave way to a thick mane of brown, blonde hair that cascaded down over his shoulders in heavy waves, and his bright emerald eyes seemed to be smiling despite the fact his face was a mask of polite intrigue. Adessa could help but think that Lord Silvermane looked more like royalty than Prince Alistair, who was all dark hair, dark eyes and pale.

At the head of the table were two men, both were old but apart from that the two men couldn't be any more different, the man on the left was broad and tall, his hard features and cold blue eyes spoke of battles and blood shed where the man on the right was thin and looked to be barely taller than Adessa own miniature height, but then Adessa remembered what the High Speaker had told her: "He might not look like much but Thomas Abaro is by far the most cunning of the other Councillors, don't let your guard down around him."

"My Lords and Ladies, may I introduce to you Lady Adessa Shinepacer, of the Enshyi and Speaker of the Forest."

Adessa curtsied before the Admiral and Councillors, "It is an honour to be here before you."

For a few seconds no one said anything but then Admiral Reinhold spoke, his commanding voice echoed throughout the room. "Lady Shinepacer, do you know why you have been brought here?"

"I have been brought he before you today to see whether I am worthy to join the ranks of the Skyknights," replied Adessa evenly, even though she really wanted to run the thousands of miles back to Alfheim.

"And to test your abilities as a Speaker," said Caewyn from his seat.

Gone was his usually warm tone, replaced by the hard harsh one he used when teaching.

"Yes, I'm quite interested to see what you can do," said Lord Silvermane lacing his fingers together.

"You can't actually be serious!" said Lady Thorne her contempt as clear as day. "There's no such thing as magic."

"Isn't there?" replied Silvermane.

"Of course there isn't. Mister Lightfoot has been here for nearly nine months now and we've seen nothing of this so-called magic." Adessa felt the room tense, Lady Thorne had just openly insulted High Speaker Caewyn by not using either his Enshyi title or the Angardian alternative.

To his credit though the High Speaker didn't look the least bit insulted, he was just sat looking calmly at Lady Thorne.

After another few moments of tense silence, Lady Grey spoke, Adessa had thought her voice would be weak and quiet, but she couldn't have been more wrong, the old woman's voice was strong and cut through the air. "You dishonour yourself and this Council with your words, Sarah."

Lady Thorne looked ready to retort but before she could, Admiral Reinhold slammed one of his meaty fists down onto the thick table top, instantly everyone turned their attention to the grizzled Skyknight and when he spoke his voice was seething, "Enough of this."

"I was onl" began Lady Thorne.

The Admiral held up a hand cutting of the younger Lady once again, "Lady Thorne, if the next words out of your mouth aren't an apology to Lord Lightfoot, I shall be forced to inform his Majesty of your actions towards the High Speaker."

At the mention of the Angardian King, Lady Thorne paled, clearly she wasn't loved enough by her distant relative to escape punishment for her words.

Lady Thorne turned back to Caewyn, "My apologies, High Speaker. I meant no offence."

"No offence was taken, my Lady," replied Caewyn bowing his head slightly.

"Well now that we've got that out of the way how about we get back to the reason why we're here in the first place," said Lord Silvermane.

"I agree," said Lady Grey nodding.

Adessa couldn't help but notice that Lord Abaro had yet to say a single word since the meeting began he just sat their observing his fellows.

"Lady Shinepacer, would you mind showing us some of your abilities as a Speaker," said Admiral Reinhold finally.

Adessa's heart skipped a beat, this was it.

Time to show these people what the Enshyi and Speakers are capable of.

Adessa dropped smoothly into a curtsy, "It would be my honour."

Admiral Reinhold clicked his fingers and appearing out of the shadows was a young Skyknight holding a bouquet of coloured tulips, "Thank you," said Reinhold taking the flowers.

The young knight bowed before returning to her post in the shadows.

"Lord Lightfoot tells us that Speakers of the Forest, such as yourself have the ability to communicate with plants and animals."

"That's correct, my Lord," replied Adessa.

"How would we know whether she is actually talking to the flowers, for all we know she could just make words up as she goes," said Lady Thorne finding her voice again.

"I'm inclined to agree with Lady Thorne," said Silvermane.

Before anyone could say anything else Adessa delved onto the spirit plane. The array of flowers shone brightly with colour much like they did in the physical world.

Reaching out Adessa made contact with the tulips, their cheerful spirits washed over her and she felt herself forget about her worries.

"I know this is strange but would it be okay if I made you grow."

The tulips quickly agreed and Adessa poured her will into the flowers.

Within the blink of an eye the tulips grew to twice their original size and all around her Adessa heard open gasps.

"Thank you," said Adessa to the tulips before she closed her connection to the spirit world.

As Adessa came back to the physical world she was met with a host of priceless expressions plastered across the faces of the Councillors. Lady Throne sat with her mouth agape, Lord Silvermane was smiling from ear to ear, Lady Grey's eyes sparkled with interest and Admiral Reinhold looked ready to burst into laughter, the only two Councillor's who didn't look impressed were Caewyn and Lord Abaro. The High Speaker sat watching his colleagues and their reactions whilst Lord Abaro's face was as expressionless as a wall of stone. Adessa hadn't expected Caewyn to be impressed, after all, he knew what she was capable of but why wasn't Lord Abaro impressed surely he had never seen anything like this before.

"This is marvellous," said Reinhold running a hand over the bouquet.

"I agree," said Silvermane still smiling. "What about you, Sarah?"

"Huh?"

"Isn't this impressive."

Remembering herself Lady Thorne hid her open amazement and replaced it with a mask of contempt, "If you say so, Peter."

Rather than take offence to the way Lady Thorne spat out his name, Silvermane turned his attention back to the bouquet of blooming flowers.

Maybe this won't be so hard after all.

But then Lord Abaro spoke, "Lady Shinepacer, while this is an impressive feat, I'm afraid I must ask, what good would this skill do during a battle?"

All eyes turned back to Adessa, "There is more to the art of Speaking than just this, my Lord. If you wish I shall show you."

"Please."

Adessa nodded and drew OathKeeper from within her robes, again the Councillors looked on in open astonishment, Adessa knew what they must be thinking how someone could hide a sword inside their robes, but all she had done was make OathKeeper the size of a small knife.

"As you can see, my Lords and Ladies, this blade is made entirely from wood." Adessa spun OathKeeper in her hands to show what she said was true. "So naturally this wouldn't be used for anything but training."

Admiral Reinhold nodded.

"But for a Speaker this blade can be used even in battle."

Lady Thorne let out a scoff, "As if that's possible."

"It's true, my lady," said Caewyn. "Sir Kaur would you mind drawing your sword."

The Skyknight tensed, "My Lord?"

"It's alright Reuben," said Reinhold. "Do as the High Speaker asks."

Sir Kaur nodded and drew his sword from its scabbard, the gleaming steel rang out as it was freed from its leather prison.

Adessa attacked then, swinging OathKeeper through the air in a downward arc, Sir Kaur instinctively blocked the blow and a high pitched ring filled the room as the two blades met, shock passed over the handsome knight's face for a split second but then his training kicked in and he retaliated with a blow of his own, Adessa quickly blocked the attack before pivoting and lashing out with a thrust again Kaur parried and the two continued their dance of attacking and defending until finally, Admiral Reinhold's voice cut through the room, "That's enough!"

Adessa stepped back from Sir Kaur and curtsied, "Thank you for allowing me to show some of my skills, Sir Kaur."

"It was my pleasure, Lady Shinepacer," replied Kaur bowing.

Adessa turned back to face the Admiral, "My apologies, I got a little carried away."

"That's quite alright, Lady Shinepacer. I think we can forgive a bit of enthusiasm after all you've shown us some incredible things today, wouldn't you agree Thomas?"

"Yes, Edward. I believe she has." Adessa didn't like the look in Lord Abaro's beady eyes, but she suppressed the fear as she had been doing for the entirety of this meeting.

"Then I believe we can take a vote, all in favour of Lady Shinepacer joining the ranks of the Skyknight's."

Caewyn was the first to raise his hand, followed shortly by Lord Silvermane, "I'm quite interested to see what else she can do."

Next came Lady Grey, the older Councillor politely nodded her agreement.

"The Skyknights are the premier fighting force of our country and should only be reserved for people of this country," said Lady Thorne. "I vote against this."

Adessa couldn't say she was surprised, the contempt Lady Thorne felt for her and Caewyn was obvious, but then again Caewyn had said that she was the most stubborn of the Councillors and least acceptable of change.

"What say you, Thomas?"

"I believe Lady Shinepacer would be a great asset to our country," said Lord Abaro still eyeing Adessa.

"Then it's decided, from this day forth you are a member of the Skyknights of Angard."

Adessa curtsied as low as she possibly could, "Thank you for the honour."

Despite the fact she had succeeded Adessa felt hollow, she was now forever tied to this country and the last flickers of hope that she had for one day returning home felt like nothing more than a fleeting dream.

Chapter 30

"Look I told yeh already ain't no way I'm setting sail not with winter so close," said the old sailor, the cracks and wrinkles in his sun weathered face flexing with every word.

"Are you sure there's no way I can convince you," replied Darrius revealing a few gold coins.

The old man stood transfixed for a few moments stroking his wild beard, Darrius could see he was interested, who wouldn't be Darrius had enough gold, silver and copper in his purse to buy a small manse but then he shook his head, "Gold's only good if you're alive to spend it." From the way he said it Darrius thought he was talking more to himself than to Darrius.

Before the sailor could say another word Darrius was off back down the docks, the old sea sodden wood groaned beneath his feet and Darrius let out a sigh, that old man had been his last hope for passage to the Kingdom of Angard, but he had just echoed what every other sailor had told Darrius, winter was now too close to risk such a voyage and while it was true that autumn was losing its grip Darrius reckoned there was still a good few weeks until winter laid it's icy hand over the lands of the Five Kingdoms.

Before he stepped off the docks and back onto the heavily cobbled streets of Seacrest, Darrius gave one last look at the fleet of ships that sat in the waters of Bluewater Bay.

Dozens of fat bodied Cogs bobbed in the choppy water. Darrius knew that the reason the local sailors and merchants favoured the single masted vessels was due to the amount of weight they could carry at any one time.

Peppered amongst the Cogs were a few Junks. The long horseshoe shaped ships were the perfect vessel for Darrius's journey, but every one of them was either anchoring here for the winter or heading somewhere other than Angard, and there was no way Darrius was going to even think about boarding the lone Galley that sat docked in the bay.

Don't want a repeat of Hakadan.

Tied at the farthest reaches of the docks sat a group of ten Cutters that belonged to the towns navy. The small fore-and-aft rigged vessels were built for speed and were used for scouting and patrols along the coast rather than for long open sea voyages even though they were more than capable.

Best get back to Fia.

The smell of saltwater, fresh fish and malted grains filled the air as Darrius walked through the backstreets of Seacrest.

Darrius knew that if he was to head into the centre of town he would find the streets laden with people as they perused the stalls of the local fisherman and farmers but he had no intention of bringing more attention to himself than he already had and carried on down the backstreets.

A candlemark later Darrius arrived at the inn where he and Fia were staying whilst they looked for passage to the Kingdom of Angard. The small wooden building looked like it had seen better days, years of wind and rain had bowed and warped the wood in many places creating deep scars that ran the entirety of the buildings face leaving it looking haggard and drawn like the face of a sickly old man.

The smell of stale sweat and cheap ale assaulted Darrius as he stepped inside the inn's crowded common room, but he quickly shook the sensations off and instinctively scanned the room for threats.

A group of six young sailors sat around the largest table in the room playing a hand of Seven Kings, despite their beefy frames none had the look of a skilled fighter. To either side of the sailors sat dozens of smaller worn tables, the men who occupied these looked like locals who had finished with their day's work and were now rewarding themselves with a drink.

Not a fighter amongst them.

Behind the bar stood the inn's owner, his wife and their son, neither the owner nor his wife were good-looking, his eyes were too small and too close together and she had fat bulbous lips that looked like they belonged more on a fish and unfortunately for the son it looked like he had inherited the worst of both of his parents.

Relaxing ever so slightly Darrius made his way over to the back of the room and the lone booth that lay there tucked away in an alcove and sat down across from Fia.

The young islander looked up from her bowl of fish stew and Darrius knew what she was going to ask before she had even finished chewing.

"You find us a ride?"

"No," replied Darrius matter-of-factly.

"Why not just buy a boat, I mean we rowed from the isle to this land in that little dingy of yours."

"That we did but you're forgetting that the waters around the isle are the calmest in all the Five Kingdoms, not to mention the fact that from here to the Angardian coast is about ten times further."

"Then just find a boat with a sail, I mean you're the traveller and I was a fisher before the Order so between us I reckon we can make the journey no problems."

Darrius sighed, for all her talent Fia was still young and like any young person she thought she was invincible.

Was I any different though?

"I wish it was that simple," said Darrius finally.

"Why ain't it simple?"

"These people make their living off their boats if I can't tempt one of them to ferry us how am I going to convince them to sell me their livelihood."

Fia's brows furrowed as she thought over Darrius's words, "Then what are we going to do?"

"I guess we're stuck here for the winter."

"But what about our mission?"

"There's nothing we can do," said Darrius trying to convince himself more than Fia.

"Excuse me." Both Darrius and Fia looked up to find the owner's son standing over them, his massive frame practically blocked out the lamplight, "Can I get you anything to drink or eat?"

"Can I get an ale and some of the fish stew please," replied Darrius.

"And your companion?"

Darrius turned to Fia, since their departure from Appleton, Darrius had taken every available opportunity to teach Fia in the ways of the common tongue, not that she couldn't speak it already but like many of the natives of Seers Isle her words were sharp and her sentences didn't flow well.

"Another ale would be nice," said Fia with a smile.

"Okay two ales and another bowl of fish stew coming up."

"Your common tongue's coming along well," said Darrius as the mountain of a boy walked off back towards the bar.

"Ain't been much else for me to do but practice it." The disappointment was clear in Fia's voice and once again Darrius was reminded of just how young she was.

Silence filled the air between the two companions until finally the mountain of a boy reappeared this time carrying a tray, "Here you go," said the boy laying two tankards and a bowl down on the table.

"Thank you," replied Darrius. "How much do I owe?"

"Five coppers."

Darrius pulled out the five coppers from the purse he left on his hip and handed them to the young man but as he did Darrius got an idea, "I don't suppose you've heard any of the sailors talking about heading to Angard?"

The young man's wide face screwed up as he thought it over, "Actually there were a couple of guys in here last night."

"And?"

"You know I can't rightly remember."

Darrius immediately fished out another copper from his purse, "Does this help?"

With one meaty fist the boy snatch up the copper before quickly tucking it away in his breeches, "They said something about having to leave tonight."

"Did they say where they were heading?"

"Oh yeah, said they were heading to some town called Windbrook."

"And I don't suppose you know where they are anchored?"

"I do but that'll cost you another copper," said the lad smiling.

Again, Darrius fished out another copper.

"One of them let slip that they were docked outside the city about half a mile up the beach."

Smugglers.

With that the young man was off, sauntering back across the room like a man who had just had his first time with a woman.

"What was that about?" said Fia switching to her native tongue.

"I think I've just found us a ride, but I'd better make sure."

Digging into his pack that lay under the table Darrius produced a large piece of folded parchment and spread it out across the table, taking care not to spill his or Fia's food or drink.

"What's this?" said Fia studying the complex lines that marked the worn vellum.

"This is a map of Angard," replied Darrius scanning the map.

"Where did you get it?"

"Before I left the Order for the first time I asked Master Hougaard, who was the head scribe at the time for copies of the Five Kingdom's maps."

"So you have a map for each Kingdom?"

"Yes, although I've added to them over the years."

"So what are you looking for?"

"This," said Darrius stabbing a finger into the parchment.

Fia peered over her bowl of stew and looked at where Darrius's finger lay.

"Our young bartender said that he overheard two men talking about setting sail tonight for a town called Windbrook." Darrius tapped his finger on the map. "This is that town."

Fia's eyes lit up with the news, "Then we've gotta get a move on suns already setting."

"Let's finish our meal first."

Soft white sand sucked at Darrius's feet with each step he took across the sprawling beach, inky waves crept forwards up the shore only to retreat a moment later in a hypnotic rhythm, far off out over the sea sat the moon, the massive white orb glowed brilliantly in the dark night sky like a second sun, reminding Darrius of a tune he had heard from a Rhymer over a dozen years ago.

Oh high, Oh high.
Up in the dark night sky.
Sits Lady Yuna.
Second daughter of Alus the father.

Oh high, Oh high.
Up in the dark night sky.
Sits Lady Yuna.
Sister of Soxtix the sun.

Oh high, Oh high.
Up in the dark night sky.
Sits Lady Yuna.
The guide for all who travel in the night.

It wasn't much of a tune but Darrius like it all the same, after all he had spent many a night with only the moon for company and every now and then he liked to think there was someone looking down at him, no matter how foolish he knew it was.

After another candlemark of walking across the shifting sand Darrius caught sight of the ship the boy had been talking about. A lithe Xebec sat bobbing out at sea, the distinctive hull with its overhanging bow and stern was a peculiar sight here in Baneta, typically the Xebec was favoured in the Onmori seas by the local merchant's, but then again smugglers tended to go wherever there was money.

Docked on the beach and surrounded by a dozen armed men sat a Cutter, the sail-less boat had oars for at least fourteen men and room enough for extra supplies, as they grew closer Darrius looked to Fia and the younger Sentinel nodded.

"Hello!" shouted Darrius with a wave.

Instantly the men dropped what they were doing and drew their swords and axes, Darrius held his hands up to show he wasn't a threat and Fia did the same, "We mean you no harm."

"What do you want?" said a thick necked man with a deep scar running across the side of his bald head.

"I merely wish to speak to your Captain about the possibility of us catching a ride on your ship, I hear you make sail for Angard."

"How about you fuck off before we cave your head in," said another one of the men, the thick caterpillar of hair that marked his top lip shook with every word.

"Look I don't want any trouble I just want to talk to your Captain," replied Darrius.

"And I told you to fuck off," spat the moustached man.

"What's with all the commotion?"

Darrius turned his attention towards the boat and emerging from the shallow hull was a woman no older than thirty summers, who looked to be an amalgamation of various races from across the Five Kingdoms, her white hair was tied in the classic Skelwori braid and hanging from her left ear was the traditional feathered earrings of the Hawk clan of Skelwor, but her rich olive skin spoke of Onmori ancestry albeit watered down and the uniform she wore was reminiscent of the Angardian navies albeit slightly more revealing.

"Sorry, Cap'in, but we've got us some travellers who say that what to speak with you," said a lanky man who looked like a vulture

The Captain of these men opened her eyes and Darrius was amazed at the sight, her left eye was a beautiful sapphire whilst her right was a shining emerald. Hopping out of the boat the Captain stretched and Darrius was surprised to find that she stood nearly as tall as him.

"So what can I do for you..." the way the Captain paused told Darrius that he was supposed to say his name.

"My name is Darrius, me and my companion were wondering if we could catch a ride on your ship to Angard."

"Oh and how do you know that's where we're going?"

"I overheard two of your men talking in The Sea and Gull back in Seacrest last night."

"Did you now," said the Captain walking around Darrius. "Lads were any of you in such a place?"

For a moment nobody said anything but then one of the men spoke. "Me and Quinn were there, but we didn't see him."

"Well with the amount you two were drinking, I doubt you'd remember me even if I had sat next to you for the entire night," replied Darrius with a smirk.

That got a few laughs from some of the other men but the Captain just eyed Darrius suspiciously before walking over to Fia and studying her, then much to Darrius's and Fia's surprise the Captain began speaking in the language of the isle. "So who are you?"

Fia stood there for a moment transfixed by the use of her native language by someone so foreign, but eventually she found her voice, "My name's Fia."

"Fia," said the Captain as if tasting the name, "quite a strange name for someone from the isle."

Darrius was worried with where the conversation was going if this woman had managed to travel to the isle then surely she would have heard of the order that watches over it.

"Have you been to the isle then?"

"No," replied the Captain not elaborating, "so what brings you this far from home."

"Me and my friend are travelling hunter-merchants, back in the forests we caught a majestic deer and we've heard that Angardian alchemists pay a great deal for antlers, plus what girl can say no to a little adventure," replied Fia.

That got a smile from the Captain, "Well why didn't you say so, I'd be happy to give you and young Darrius here a ride." The Captain walked back to stand in front of Darrius. "For a price of course."

"Of course," replied Darrius. "How much."

"Seven gold pieces."

Darrius was taken off guard he had thought that the Captain would set a high price for ferrying them but seven gold pieces was beyond extortionate, "That seems fair," lied Darrius reaching into his cloak.

"Each," said the Captain with a massive grin.

Darrius hesitated that was practically the entirety of his gold, but then a voice in his head chastised him.

"Its only gold you fool."

Reaching into his cloak Darrius found the money pouch that carried his gold and quickly drew out the fourteen golden coins and handed them to the Captain.

"Thank you," said the Captain with the grin still on her face. "Right, lads, time to set sail."

"What about Fredrick," said a one of the men.

"What about him?"

"I thought we was waiting til he got here before we set off."

The Captain shrugged, "We've waited long enough for that lecherous drunk, now let's get back to the seas."

With the smugglers being one man down Darrius took up the empty oars and rowed with the rest of the men through the calm night waters towards the main ship.

Once they were alongside the Xebec's hull the Captain let out a high pitch whistle which was quickly mirrored from aboard the deck and a rope ladder was thrown down over the hull towards the water, the Captain was the first up the ladder, carrying a large sack that looked fit to burst with her, followed shortly by Fia and then Darrius.

Pulling himself up over the smooth rail Darrius was met with a whole host of smugglers, many of whom were women, their icy gazes bore into Darrius but he just shook it off and walked to stand beside Fia, the younger Sentinel looked a picture of serenity and Darrius was glad that his companion wasn't allowing herself to be intimidated, after all you had to show these types of people that you weren't about to let yourself become a victim.

"Welcome aboard *The Flying Maiden*," said the Captain with a sweep of her hand.

Darrius knew the name, he had heard a great many stories in the last few years about this ship and its Captain, Claiborne 'Gem-eyes' Stafford, Darrius cursed himself for not seeing it before but the stories he had heard only spoke of the Captain of *The Flying Maiden* as a master navigator and nothing else.

"So you're Claiborne Stafford," said Darrius.

"The one and only," replied the Captain with a theatrical bow.

"I've heard some impressive stories."

Before Claiborne could reply the bull-necked man with the scar came bounding over, "We're ready to set sail whenever you are, Cap."

Claiborne nodded to her underling, before turning back to face Darrius, "Duty calls I'm afraid, but don't worry there'll be plenty of time for me to tell you about my exploits first hand, oh and, Tulock."

"Yeah Cap," replied the scarred man.

"Show our guests to their room."

With that Claiborne left for the helm, leaving Darrius standing alone with Fia and Tulock, without saying anything the scarred smuggler began walking across the deck, Darrius quickly followed and Fia fell in behind him.

At the other side of the deck Tulock led Darrius and Fia down a hatch into *The Flying Maidens* hold, the tight corridor was barely wide enough for Tulock to fit down and yet he dodged and moved out of his fellow smugglers way with ease, the same look of mistrust marked each of their faces as they caught sight of Darrius and Fia. Suspended from the ceiling by short iron chains were a series of oil lamps, which moved with each wave that hit the ship creating the strange illusion that the light was dancing from side to side, off to either side of the corridor lay room after open room. Walking past one such room Darrius caught sight of a smuggler in the process of getting changed, her bare breasts lay exposed as she fumbled around the room looking for a tunic, Darrius was surprised at the woman's lack of undergarment and just then the woman sensing that someone was watching her turned her head and locked eyes with Darrius, but rather than getting embarrassed or annoyed as Darrius expected the woman smiled and winked, then surprisingly Darrius found himself feeling embarrassed and he quickly looked away.

"You're in here," said Tulock pointing into the second to last room.

Darrius and Fia entered the small room to find two canvas hammock's hanging from the walls, Darrius threw his pack down beside the hammock on the right and turned to thank Tulock, but the huge smuggler was already gone.

"So," said Fia as she threw her pack up onto the hammock opposite Darrius's, "how long you reckon it's gonna take for us to reach Angard?"

"Three weeks, maybe more depending upon the weather," replied Darrius as he dropped down next to his pack.

"That long?"

"Could take longer if we run into the navy or pirates."

"You don't think that'll happen, do you?"

"Who can say, it's a long way from here to Angard and we are aboard a smuggling ship after all, both the navy and local pirates will want a piece of whatever this ships carrying."

"I guess I should've known what I was getting into when I decided to join you on this mission," said Fia to herself.

Pretending he hadn't heard her Darrius lay back on his bed silently for a few minutes before speaking again, "Best we get some rest, Lady knows we're going to need it in the coming days."

Fia agreed and within minutes the young Sentinel was fast asleep, but Darrius wasn't so fortunate, since leaving the isle he had felt like something was wrong, at first he had put it down to having a companion and brushed the feeling aside but the closer he grew to Angard the more that feeling had grown.

"Has the darkness already come?" said Darrius holding onto the crystal at his throat hoping for an answer but the only thing that greeted him was the creaking of the ship and the crashing of waves. Darrius released his grasp from the crystal and once again was left with nothing but his thoughts for company as he had been on so many of his journeys over the years.

Chapter 31

Caleb awoke to burning agony. Pain unlike anything he had ever felt reverberated throughout his entire chest taking his breath away and making him blind to where he was or how he got there.

"Calm yourself," came a familiar voice.

Tentatively Caleb turned his head and looked in the direction of the voice, sitting in a nearby chair was Vaeliria, deep bruises of black and purple marked her face and a heavy bandage was wrapped around her ribs, the sight of the wounded Commander brought everything back to Caleb, he had gotten cut across the chest by Irashaad's sword, as if on cue the pain returned wrecking its way back through him, gritting his teeth Caleb did his best to ride the agonising wave out.

Once the wave passed he dropped back limply onto his bed.

"Here drink this," said Vaeliria appearing beside Caleb with a cup of water in hand.

With all his failing strength Caleb pushed himself up against the back of the bed and let Vaeliria guide the cup towards his lips, the water was cool and refreshing and for a moment it took away the burning pain but as soon as the relief had come it was gone.

"You look like shit," said Caleb to Vaeliria as she took the cup away.

"I'm doing better than you," replied Vaeliria with a tired smile.

"What are you talking about I'm as good as ev" a bout of coughing cut Caleb short. Pain lanced through his chest with each bark bringing tears to his eyes and the taste of blood filled his mouth.

Once the fit passed and his eyes cleared Caleb looked to find Vaeliria's face twisted with worry.

"Don't worry bout me," said Caleb through gritted teeth, "it's gonna take a lot more than this to kill me."

"You're lucky to be alive."

From the tone of Vaeliria's voice Caleb knew that his injuries must be serious and looking down he was met with the sight of a massive dressing that covered his entire chest, the first drops of blood were already beginning to seep through the bandage.

"So we won," said Caleb turning his attention away from his wound and the worry that he might not recover.

"Yeah," Vaeliria's voice was flat and full of mourning, but she quickly snapped herself out of it and when she spoke again her voice was filled with the command and presence that Caleb knew from his Commander. "Once the pirate's saw their flagship fall they quickly tried to escape."

"Did any manage to?"

"Just one."

Fuck!

"What are we going to do?"

"Nothing."

"What!" Again, pain shot through Caleb.

"The crew is in no shape to go after the enemy and *Firebird* and *Sandfly* are so heavily damaged that they are barely skyworthy.

"We lost *Salamander?*"

Vaeliria nodded, "During the final moments of the battle *Salamander* was hit by a barrage from one of the enemies falling ships."

Caleb stomach tied in knots at the news, they had lost so many good men and women during the battle and the thought that one of the enemy ships had escaped felt like a failure to Caleb, what was to stop them from wreaking havoc once again.

"So where are we heading?"

"To Indaea, we were sent here to open trade routes with the Sultan after all and that still needs to be accomplished."

"So we're just going to forget about the pirates?" Caleb tried to keep the disgust from his voice but in his weakened state he probably didn't do the best job he could have.

"No," replied Vaeliria, fire in her eyes, "we'll never forget about Irashaad or his men and what they've done but our mission now is to open trade routes between Angard and Onmoria."

"I still don't like it."

"It doesn't matter what you like, you're a Cadet in the Order of the Skyknights and duty commands that you obey the orders given to you by your Captain and our Captain has issued the order that we sail for Indaea."

Caleb would have pressed the point further but deep down he knew Vaeliria was right, if the battle had been as hard on the other members of the crew as it had been on him or Vaeliria there was no way they would be in any position to engage in another battle no matter how damaged or beaten the enemy was and if Captain Brightfellow thought it best they sail to Indaea then Caleb had to have faith it was the right decision.

"Okay, I understand."

"Good," said Vaeliria with a nod. "Now get some rest, we'll need you back up to full strength as soon as possible."

"You can count on me, Commander."

Epilogue

Thick branches tore and ripped at the robes of the men of *Arda's Hammer* as they walked through the dense jungle.

At the head of the train leading the way through the seemingly endless labyrinth was a hooded figure, his thick robes hung off him loosely and it wasn't any wonder, the man's bony hands looked more like that of the dead then the living.

Why did Captain Harroun agree to follow the witch here.

But that wasn't the only worry that plagued Aseel's mind. He was sure that the witch had been on board Irashaad's ship at the start of the battle and yet when *Avatar of Death* had fallen and Irashaad had perished the witch had somehow appeared on their ship as if out of thin air.

A man shouldn't be able to do such things.

Aseel didn't have time to ponder on his thought as the trees finally began to thin and he along with the rest of the tired and wounded group were led out into an opening.

What the.

Aseel couldn't believe what he was seeing. Standing in the opening atop a pyramidal staircase was a massive temple, Aseel was instantly reminded of the great pyramids of Isha but where those inspired him this sent a wave of fear through his body where it webbed its way around his stomach and began to squeeze, where it continued to grow as they approached. To either side of the path were dozens of statues, each a visage of grotesque horror but for some reason Aseel couldn't look away even though he wanted to and he was faced with sights he thought only possible in nightmares, like that of a small child whose jaw was twice the size of that of a normal man's and filled with razor sharp teeth than closer resembled needles than teeth or of a man whose face was

375

covered in multiple eyes each a different size and shape but the monstrous sights didn't end there, lining the steps towards the temple were the faces of gargoyles, their horned faces were twisted in sinister grins and Aseel was certain their eyes were following him.

Coming to the top of the long staircase the witch led the group towards a massive stone door, with a swipe of his bony claw the witch commanded the door to open, the grating of stone on stone set Aseel's teeth on edge.

The inside of the temple smelled of death and decay, Aseel knew he shouldn't be here and yet he couldn't stop from following the witch further into the temple with his fellows.

As they crossed the hard-stone floor braziers began to light revealing a massive hall that was filled with even more robed figures, their faces were completely shrouded but Aseel could feel their eyes on him. Once they were at the centre of the room the witch dropped to his hands and knees in prostration, as he did the remaining braziers that filled the room lit in a gush of flames revealing a robed figure sitting on a throne, unlike the other figures around the room or the witch this figure wore a robe the colour of blood and a heavy iron chain sat tied around his neck, hanging from the chain by their hair were seven shrivelled heads, the eyes and mouths of which had been sewn shut, at the sight Aseel felt his stomach clench and a line of cold sweat began to run down his spine.

"Forgive me, Master, I have failed you." It was the first time Aseel had heard the witch speak with any emotion in his voice and for it to be fear made Aseel even more fearful for his own safety.

"How have you failed me?" the figure on the throne replied, the voice was thick with power and Aseel suddenly had the overwhelming desire to fall into prostration beside the witch.

"Irashaad and his fleet were defeated by the Angardians and the men from Onmoria, these are the only survivors."

The robed figure looked out over the group of wounded pirates silently. "I told you before you left that the Angardians had one who can use the Hexes as well and yet you didn't prepare."

"Forgive me," the witch pressed his head hard against the stone floor, "my arrogance blinded me to your words of wisdom."

"It's not my forgiveness that you need to ask for but our Lord Mamemohr's."

"Praise his name," chimed the other figures coldly.

"How might I ask for the Almighty's forgiveness?"

Silence filled the hall and Aseel knew something bad was about to happen, "The Almighty asks for you to make a sacrifice of blood."

The tight knot that had been in Aseel's stomach shot out through his entire body, he had to get out of here but when he tried to move he found that his legs wouldn't respond and that's when he saw the Hexes, the symbols writhed along his body in tight lines, looking to his comrades Aseel saw a reflection of his own fear in their eyes. The witch stood and drew a long hooked knife from within his robes and then he approached Captain Harroun. With one quick swipe the Captain's neck was opened and blood arced through the air like a fountain covering the witch in crimson, Aseel tried to scream but no sound escaped his mouth, the witch then opened another man's throat and then another's until finally the witch came to stand before Aseel. Blood dripped from the witch's hands and robes. With all his will Aseel commanded his arms to move but again they failed him and the knife was placed against his neck.

Someone save me.

"Stop!"

The witch withdrew the knife and if he could Aseel would have collapsed with relief.

"The Almighty doesn't want this one killed." The robed figure stood from his throne and descended the stone steps to the floor below, where he came to stand before Aseel.

"What is your name?"

"Aseel," replied Aseel, shocked that he could speak.

"You should feel honoured, Aseel, for you have been chosen to do the work of The Almighty Lord Mamemohr."

A deeper fear than even that Aseel had felt just a moment ago took hold.

Maybe I should have just died quietly.

With a click of his fingers the robed figure summoned two of his underlings, "Take him away."

Aseel wanted to protest but once again his ability to talk was taken from him and the two underlings began dragging him off towards a black abyss.

Acknowledgements

After having spent the past three years sitting at my computer typing away, I can say with confidence that this book wouldn't be what it is without the love and support of my family.

Mum, you've supported me in everything I've wanted to do and that's no different here, when I'm pursuing a passion I didn't even know I had until a few years ago.

Dad, you've taught me some valuable lessons over the years but none more so then what it means to be a good man.

Michael, my Bruhah, what can I say you're my best-friend and the enthusiasm and confidence you show in every day inspires me to think less and do more.

Hannah, the adventures we had as kids will be some of the best memories I'll ever have and I still find it hilarious that we trekked through a field of corn for no apparent reason.

Matthew, from helping me to get my first job to sticking up for me when I need it, I know you've always got my back.

Elizabeth, your loving and cheerful personality lights up whichever room you're in, never lose that because the world would be a much sadder place without your light in it.

And finally, I would like to thank you the readers for giving me the chance to share this story with you, I hope you'll be back for the next chapter in Caleb, Adessa and Darrius's story.

Lightning Source UK Ltd.
Milton Keynes UK
UKOW03n1838161216
290190UK00004B/14/P